Celtic Knots

A Novel

By

Audrey Nicholson

Celtic Knots *The Ties That Bind*
AUDREY NICHOLSON

Published by Antrim Road Publishing
PO Box 20516
Worcester, Massachusetts 01602
CelticKnots2012@gmail.com

Author Services, Cover and Interior Design
by Pedernales Publishing, LLC
www.pedernalespublishing.com

Author photo by Rachel Brownstein

Cover Art by Audrey Nicholson

Library of Congress Control Number: 2012954831

ISBN Number:978-0-9883912-9-1 Paperback Edition

In loving memory of my parents,
William and Lucy Nicholson,
Aunt Meta Tolman,
and for Shannon, and Nicole...
gone too soon.

Acknowledgements

As it takes a village to raise a child so also does it take the effort and support of many to birth a book.

"Celtic Knots" would have remained on countless Post It Notes and yellow legal pads had it not been transformed into a readable manuscript by the editing skills of Christopher Gainty, Dr. Barbara Ardinger, and chief nit picker Shelly Finn, whose guidance and friendship were and are invaluable.

I have been forced to abandon my Cro Magnon attitude towards technology. In support of this effort, I have found myself lucky to have had the kind support and patient encouragement from Barbara Rainess at Pedernales Publishing.

I have also been force fed the intricacies of Email and Microsoft Word by my granddaughters Amanda and Kimberley, daughter Tara, and my long time friend Patricia Wyld. Still chewing on that meal!

My sincere thanks for the support and love of my family, at home and abroad, Sisters Marcella and Valerie and my children in descending order: Rhonda, Fiona, Barry (thanks for the laptop,) Deborah, and Tara. And my grandchildren and great grandchildren by virtue of just being them.

I am indebted to my "readers" friends and family who have been press-ganged into service. Hazel Fleming, Eleanor Shirley, Kerry Scotton, Della Stein, Barry Scotton, Glenda and Sean Mc Donald and future readers who will hopefully enjoy their time spent between the covers of "Celtic Knots."

Celtic Knots

Chapter One

Lucy sat propped and sandwiched between two of her three daughters. The violet gown chosen for this occasion hung loosely from her frail shoulders. Diamonds glittered on her fingers and her wrists. She loved her diamonds and wore them where she might see and enjoy the play of light and color. Others might admire the pearls she wore at her throat and in her ears, but the diamonds were for her own pleasure. They made her feel secure, someone of substance. Her silver hair was arranged pleasantly, if not perfectly. *The hairdressers never got it right*, she thought, *no matter how many times I told them how I wanted it styled.*

Sitting between her daughters, she wondered, *When did I begin to shrink?* She used to tower over them. Now it was the other way around. It seemed to her that such was the story of life. Everything ended up the other way around.

She smiled as a series of familiar notes caught her ear. Although her hearing had failed somewhat in the past five years, she still recognized the strains of Purcell's Trumpet Voluntary. *Sure,* she said to herself, *you'd have t' be bloody stone deaf t' miss it.*

This grand occasion was a far cry from her wedding. America had been good to her family, and those days in the thirties and forties were long past. She was the only one left who remembered how it had been in Ireland. Now she was the matriarch, and her entire family, including the contingent from Australia, had gathered in bed-and-breakfasts around the picturesque New England village. Gold and crimson splashed the autumn countryside, and the white church among the trees on the common created a picture postcard setting for the last wedding she would attend.

The congregation rose to greet the bride and her uncle as they made their entrance. Twin tears slid down the tissue-thin skin of Lucy's cheek.

As she scanned the unfamiliar church, her gaze came to rest on the minister who would marry her granddaughter. A woman! *The saints preserve us*, she thought. *What next? Gettin' married in a Protestant church by a woman. What is the world comin' to? Me mother'll be turnin' in her grave, so she will. Still…I can't be throwin' any stones, after what I did.*

Even though everyone was forever telling her that you can't live in the past, Lucy thought it was a grand place to visit. The past, when she'd been young, healthy, and pretty and her mother, husband, and the rest of her family were still alive, when her fingers had been straight, she hadn't needed glasses, and her teeth had been her own and didn't spend the night grinning in a glass. She'd still had both of her breasts back then, and her gall bladder was still busy doing its thing. She had long ago decided that the reason for diminishing sight was so you couldn't see what was happening to the rest of your body.

Moreover, when she was young, no one ever spoke to her as though she were two years old and dim-witted to boot.

Arranging her features now in an expression of rapt attention that would fool anyone who missed the glazed expression in her eyes, Lucy thought about the forbidden mink stole…and how things had changed. She had wanted to wear the mink to this wedding, but her daughters and the other girls had told her that wearing fur was now considered passé.

She remembered a time when, far from being frowned upon, a fur was a prized possession.

~

One fur she recalled in particular was a skinny, limp, little thing at the best of times, but it was also her sister Ophelia's pride and joy. Feelie had bought it on the "never never," at a shilling a week out of her pay and had forbidden anyone to touch it. Nevertheless, Lucy not only touched it, but she wore it one evening to impress a fella, and then hid it outside, under the hedge, until she could sneak it back into the house past her sister's watchful eyes. Unfortunately, Feelie came home early and discovered that her precious fur had been left out in the rain. It was a bit absurd, Lucy had thought, to raise such a fuss. Surely the wee thing was used to getting wet. It was an animal, wasn't it? Offering to shake the fur dry, she sat down in front of the peat fire, giving it a good poke that sent showers of brilliant, short-lived sparks everywhere. Some day, she had silently vowed, she would own a whole coat made of fur. Still, she had no regrets. She and the fella Da had brought home for supper were drawn to each other, and when he asked her to go to a show at the Hippodrome with him, she'd agreed, even though she'd been a little disconcerted when she learned that his name was Bill. Which was enough to tell her that he was a Prod, since no self-respecting Catholic family would ever name their son after the despised William of Orange.

Bill Nicholson was tall, mostly long legs, and he carried his body loosely, as though his joints were on springs. His thick dark hair was slicked down with Brylcreem in the mode of the day. A pair of green eyes that twinkled more often than not was the keystone feature in a face that just missed matinee idol regularity. And his smile was frequent but shy.

Although Bill was a handsome man, the scar that began on one side of his jaw and ran to the other, just under the bone, marred his good looks. The hastily averted eyes and sharp intakes of breath of those who saw it for the first time never let him forget that it was there. Lumps under Bill's jaw had been cut out when he was a very young boy, and the country doctor had subjected him to a horrifying hack job. The lumps were gone now, but the scar was to plague him emotionally and physically for the rest of his life. Despite his self-consciousness and wariness of crowds, he was naturally outgoing, so much so that the older ladies would smile and say, "That fella has a bit of an imp in him." His sense of humor allowed him to see the funny side of most situations, and he believed everyone to be as honest and guileless as he was himself.

Lucy's father, Tom O'Leary, and Bill worked together at the Harland and Wolff shipyard in Belfast. Tom was what some people would describe as "dapper." His dark brown hair was streaked with gray at the temples, and he sported a carefully tended mustache to match. In recent years, his face had begun to reveal the lines of his personality, with fan shaped folds of laughter radiating from his blue eyes and frown lines between his brows that hinted at a mercurial temper. Not a tall man, Tom never slouched and made the most of his height.

Since the Battle of the Boyne in 1690, religious tensions between Catholics and Protestants in Northern Ireland were never far from the surface. Catholics were in the minority at the shipyard and were often the target for intimidation, which often led to violence. One day Bill overheard a plan to "get the Papist bugger," meaning Tom. His conscience wouldn't allow him to keep silent, so he quietly warned Tom, and the situation was avoided without incident. From that day on, the two men became unlikely friends, a generation apart and from different religious traditions. Although both were more rational than most of their neighbors, they were still Catholic and Protestant and thus carried just as much cultural baggage from their upbringing as everyone else.

What they shared was a love of dog racing, and after a particularly lucky day at the track, Tom decided to invite his young friend home for supper. "Sure," he said, "an' you'll be enjoyin' the wife's steak an' onions, and a pint." Bill had been hungry, so he agreed that it would be nice to round off the day with a home-cooked dinner. It was to be the most important meal of his life.

Lucy was the youngest of the family, now four girls, the only boy having died of pneumonia at thirteen. Wee Richard, the victim of a polio epidemic, had been Lucy's constant companion. She'd carried him on her back to the picture house and brought him around the neighborhood in a wooden cart set on four pram wheels. She'd loved and protected her crippled brother with a passion that brooked no interference. During the Troubles of 1920-21, when Churchill's Black and Tans had terrorized Catholic neighborhoods, Lucy, then still a child herself, had hidden the boy underneath the table, fearing that he'd be ordered outside with the other men for questioning. Her brother's disability would have made him slow to comply, and Lucy had been afraid that the terrorists would mistake his hesitation as defiance and shoot him.

One particularly cold November day, she had helped Richard into the makeshift cart and set off to buy a pair of cufflinks for their da's Christmas box. They had been saving money for the gift, and they checked the shop window daily, hoping the cufflinks would not be sold. They were that grand, all gold with a ruby red stone winking in the middle. The links were still in the window. The children were thrilled with their purchase. Their father had never had such a fine gift.

Three days later, Wee Richard came down with pneumonia, and a week after that he was dead. Just before, he died; he took all his toys out and distributed them amongst his sisters Ophelia, Mary Alice, and Nellie. When Lucy came forward, however, he turned his back to her, faced the wall, and took his last breath. For the rest of her life, Lucy blamed herself for Wee Richard's death. She should have made him wear his coat on that cold November day.

Now, in 1930, as Lucy approached her twentieth birthday, she joined the rest of the world in bidding farewell to the Roaring Twenties. She had grown into a slender beauty. Her fair complexion contrasted with a mop of dark brown curls and heavily fringed eyes the color of warm brandy. But her nose was a source of constant worry to her. She would have liked to pare the slightly prominent bridge and lop a few centimeters off the length. Her generous and mobile mouth was her most expressive feature, and her flesh was arranged perfectly on her five-foot six-inch frame. She considered her legs to be her greatest physical attribute, for she had always been told that she had "a well-turned ankle." Shoes were a weakness. She could not pass a shoe store without gazing through the window, mentally matching the shoes on display to imaginary outfits.

The youngest of the girls, she had been pampered to the extent her parents' limited means would allow. Her personality presented a study in contradictions: generous, miserly, judgmental, and forgiving. When she felt the situation warranted it, for example, she could and did use language that would put a navvy to shame. She did not suffer fools gladly and did not hesitate to apprise them of their foolishness.

The first two decades of the twentieth century were a time when no one in their right mind would cross the religious battle lines drawn up by ignorance. The British government and the Catholic Church had their own agendas, the interests of which were best served by keeping the factions defined and as thoroughly separated as possible.

Despite this, Lucy was attracted to the Prod her da brought home. Although she really liked Bill, she had her reservations. Her dreams did not include living the lives of her mother and sisters. She was determined to make something of herself, though she didn't quite know how. She knew education was the answer, but she also knew a more pressing need to work to help pay her keep. She was lucky in that her job at the flower shop was better than working in a factory, which was the lot of most girls with limited schooling. The women at the shop said she had artistic talent, and Mother Superior at the convent had personally recommended her to the shop's owner.

The shop was just 'round the corner from Queens University. Lucy dreamed of studying there, but these were dreams her mother had a hard time understanding. To her mother, it would be preferable for Lucy to marry money rather than to make it on her own. She often told her daughters; "It's jest as easy t' fall in love with a rich man as it is t' fall fer a poor one."

The wisdom in this escaped Lucy. *In the first place,* she thought, *how do ya meet rich men? And how do ya talk to 'em when yer accent sets ya apart? And what do ya talk about?*

Her older sisters hadn't been lucky in finding the elusive rich men and had settled for hard-working lads and the life that went with them. Lucy had no intention of doing the same, or of following in her mother's lonely footsteps. True, she did meet the sons of rich men every day at the shop, rich young men buying flowers for the girls they took to the dances or sending bouquets of red roses to their girlfriends. Once in a while, one would try a little flirting with Lucy.

She'd had a date with a law student once. He took her to the university teashop. It was a disaster. He was from England and spoke as if his mouth were full of marbles. She hadn't understood a word he said. Looking around the teashop, she'd also realized how out of place she was. Her thin cotton frock, a hand-me-down from her sister Mary Alice, was no match for the elegantly dressed young matrons and stylishly turned out girls she saw around her, chatting with each other on topics far outside her frame of reference, saying things like "I have to toddle on, darling" and "The mater is expecting me for dinner."

She might as well have been listening to creatures from another planet. Meanwhile, her date was busy expounding on some point of jurisprudence. Lucy didn't know any jurisprudence, or any other prudence. She did, however, know that she was out of her league. The minute she finished her tea, she concocted a splitting headache as her passport back to a life she understood.

But Bill, now—she sighed as she thought back to her date with Bill. He was respectful and had asked her father for permission to escort her to the movies. When the time came for the actual date, though, neither of them knew quite what to do, not having much experience with the opposite sex. Bill felt shy around girls and feared the scar on his jaw would turn them off. For her part, Lucy's parents had always been very strict with their youngest daughter as far as the fellas went.

Lucy was also extremely careful to observe the rules set down by the Dominican nuns, who warned their charges of the perils that would befall the unwary girl and advising them how to foil carnal advances. Pearls were out, the nuns said; the boys could see down your dress in the reflection. Highly polished shoes were likewise to be avoided, as it was thought that a boy might be able to see up your skirt in the reflection. And a large, thick book should be carried by a modest girl at all times. Strategically placed, it would prevent direct contact if you had to sit on the fella's lap.

Lucy had decided everything made sense except the book. No way was she carrying an encyclopedia around with her. Besides, as she hardly knew Bill, she could think of no situation where she would be required to sit on his lap. It would be a long time, she vowed, before such intimacies would be allowed…if ever.

Ellen, her mother, had instructed her to make sure to sit where she could make a fast exit should Bill attempt to take advantage of her. Obediently, Lucy selected seats in the last row of the balcony, near the usherette. A flutter of excitement ran through the audience as the house lights dimmed. The first feature was a "Baby Burlesque," and the audience was enraptured by the tiny, dimpled Shirley Temple.

Soon Bill began to wonder if Lucy would be insulted if he put his arm around her shoulder. Lucy was already wondering why he hadn't. Each considered the issue in private anxiety, and finally, Bill casually draped his arm over the back of Lucy's seat. Meeting with no resistance, he slid his arm around her shoulder and was rewarded with a shy, sideways smile.

After the pictures, they went for fish and chips, and then Bill escorted Lucy home in plenty of time for her ten o'clock curfew. There was no goodnight kiss. He took his leave, respectfully, in the presence of her family.

They made no plans for a future date. While they had both enjoyed the evening and the other's company, they also realized that they needed to think things over. The difference in their religious beliefs would lead them into uncharted waters.

The only problem was that Bill couldn't get Lucy out of his thoughts. He decided he wanted to get to know her better, differences be damned.

Lucy was also confused. *He really seems t' be a decent fella*, she said to herself. *We had a grand time at the pictures, an' I'd like t' see him again. Nothin' serious, o' course—there's the religion thing, but there's no harm in a bit o' fun.*

~

Lucy had been very close to her mother, a gentle, frail woman. Almost every Saturday, Ellen and her youngest daughter had sat together in front of the fire as Ellen tried to preserve her dignity by pretending to believe her husband's story that he was off to play cards. She had never been invited to accompany him. In fact, she was never invited to accompany him anywhere.

Ellen's health, never robust, was a trial to her earthy, lusty husband. But it was her devotion to her religion that created a fatal rupture in the foundation of their marriage and had driven him to enjoy the company of a certain lady whose lively personality and obliging morals suited him to a T. Every week, Lucy watched her mother's eyes fill with tears as her husband disappeared from view, whistling softly to himself, his hat set at a jaunty angle, and his mustache newly trimmed. He always wore a freshly laundered white shirt and starched collar, and his blue suit sported a red carnation in the buttonhole.

Lucy's suspicions had been growing for years as she witnessed this weekly charade. One day she'd had enough. She felt ready to confront her father and his lady friend. On Saturday, therefore, she took stock of her appearance in the hall mirror, then called out to her mother, "I'm goin' out fer a wee while, Ma. Won't be too long. Anythin' ya want me t' bring back?"

Her mother's voice was stronger than she was used to hearing. "Maybe ya could stop at Josie's and see if she has any ham. I feel like a sandwich with me tea t'night."

The request was unusual. Ellen was a poor eater. "Skin and bones" was the phrase people used to describe her. Heartened by her mother's apparent appetite, Lucy promised to stop at the corner store.

"Where ya off to, love?" Ellen called to Lucy's back. They usually spent Saturday evenings together, but Ellen knew it was just a matter of time 'til Lucy left to get married. She wondered if it would be to Bill or someone else. She would miss her youngest, but it was the nature of things. As much as she liked Bill, however, she hoped that Lucy would find someone of her own religion. Marriage was hard enough without starting off with that problem. Her oldest two, Nellie and Mary Alice. were married, leaving Lucy and Feelie at home, but Feelie worked as a live-in house keeper for the parish priests and so was seldom actually at home.

Lucy heard Ellen's question, but she decided to play deaf so she wouldn't have to lie. Opening the front door, she stepped out into the windswept street. It was a raw day. Shivering slightly, she pulled the hood of her raincoat over her head. Walking past the pin-neat homes of her neighbors, she rehearsed the confrontation she was going to have with her father and his doxy. She had learned the word "doxy" while reading a story in *True Romance.* It suited Tom's other woman perfectly.

Drawing her hood further over her head, she shivered again. *Th' wind sounds like a banshee come t' warn us of a death, so it does,* she thought. *Sure it's a desperate sound, so it is.* She was tempted to turn to see if there was any sign of the wee creature that, it is said, often came keening with death at its heels.

Shaking off her strong feeling of foreboding, she hurried up Fallswater Street to the Falls Road, where she caught the tram to Grosvenor Road. The doxy, whose name was Maggie, had a semi-detached house there. She'd followed her father that far once before. *Very respectable, if ya didn't count the goin's on,* Lucy thought. Jumping off the back of the tram, she landed in an icy puddle, adding the discomfort of cold, wet feet to her black mood.

Ten minutes later she was at the house. The front door was painted green, and there was a bright brass kick plate and a knocker shaped like a lion's head. Facing the reality of her mission, she suddenly feared her courage would fail her. Gritting her teeth, and wiping an angry tear from her eye, she lifted the fancy knocker and gave the door three resounding raps.

After what seemed an eternity, the door opened, and she was face-to-face with the enemy. Maggie was fortyish, five feet tall, and slender. Marcelled waves marched across a wide brow, drawing attention to a pair of china blue eyes opened wide in surprise. Confusion chased away the smile of polite greeting as her features tried to rearrange themselves, resulting in an almost comic expression. Her Kewpie-doll mouth froze in a perfect O, and her red tipped fingers laced and unlaced themselves in agitation.

For a moment, Lucy was nonplussed. She had rehearsed and rehearsed again what she would say to this woman, but now that her flesh and blood adversary was before her, she was finding it hard to put her feelings into words.

"I'm Tom's daughter," she said, finally.

"I know who ya are. I've seen yer picture. "Maggie spoke softly, then fell quiet.

"I'm here t' get me da t' go home," she said after an uncomfortable silence, her voice getting louder as she went. "What youse two are doin' is cruel and wicked. He belongs with his wife, not with you."

"Maggie, who is it?" Lucy heard her father's voice coming from somewhere in the back of the house.

"It's jest the insurance man," Maggie lied.

Lucy could hear music, a popular tune that was one of her da's favorites. The smell of a Saturday fry-up lingered in the hallway.

Maggie pulled the door nearly closed. "Go home," she said. "Yer father'll be mad as a bull if he knows ya came here."

"I'm not goin' anywhere 'til me da comes home. Youse are killin' me ma. He belongs with her…with his wife…not here with his hoor of a fancy woman."

At these words, Maggie recoiled as though she had been physically attacked.

"Ya'll not talk t' her like that. Go home t' yer mother." Tom's voice was quiet and controlled as he appeared behind Maggie. Lucy stood rooted to the ground, anger and shame fighting for supremacy. He was defending his doxy and dismissing his daughter.

Humiliation scalded her face as she turned to face him. "I can't believe yer stickin' up fer this home wrecker against yer own flesh and blood. Neither o' youse have any shame. It's a filthy sin, so it is."

Tom's eyes narrowed as he fought to remain in control. He clenched his fists. It was time, he decided, to talk to his daughter. He would try to make her understand his side of the story. "Maggie," he said, "go on inta the kitchen. Lucy, come with me."

Lucy didn't want to step into the house. If she crossed the threshold, she thought, she would be betraying her mother. But she needed to know what her father had to say, how he expected to justify himself and his sin.

Tom was already walking towards a door on the right side of the central hall. Maggie passed him without a word and made her way to the kitchen. Lucy reluctantly followed her father.

Stepping into the parlor, she couldn't help noticing how bright and pretty the room was. The walls were papered in a rose and ivy design, and the formal chairs and a sofa were covered in rose brocade. Highly polished mahogany tables displayed photographs and mementos. The fireplace was carved wood, and over the mantle hung a romantic print framed in gold. The picture was flanked by two gaslights, their mantles covered by glass shades fringed with tiny glass beads. A lace-curtained bay window would have allowed the sun to filter through if it had not been such a miserable day.

The room was spotless, everything shone. The doxy was a good housekeeper.

Lucy was saddened at the contrast with her mother's house. Their "two up, two down" row house, although kept tidy and clean with Lucy's help, lacked the obvious attention and care this home received. Ellen's poor health robbed her of the stamina required to keep a home in this condition. It seemed to take all of her strength just to prepare the evening meal for Tom. That at least she never failed to do, no matter how ill she was feeling. A man, she always said, needed a good meal to come home to. Lucy remembered watching her fuss over her father every night.

"Sit yerself down," Tom said. "This'll take a while." His voice was softer now, though his expression was still hard. The usual sparkle was missing from his eyes.

"Lucy, ye're no longer a wee girl. It took courage for ya t' darken this door. But ya don't know the ins and outs o' this situation." He cleared his throat. "Yer ma's a very, ah, devout woman. After ya were born, they told us she could have no more wains. The priest told her since the act o' love was a gift from God fer the gettin' o' children, that part of our relationship was over."

He swallowed, and Lucy was surprised at the hitch in his voice when he went on.

"We could never share our bed in that way again," he finally said. "An' that was that. But I don't believe as she does, an' we've had many a bitter row over it. How the hell can some priest, a fella with no experience of love and marriage, decide t' put an end t' the physical expression of it?"

Lucy couldn't believe her ears. To avoid looking at her father, she studied the pattern on the Persian look-alike rug. Her sisters had told her of the terrible fights following her birth, and how they hid in the coal hole with their hands over their ears, trying to block their mother's screams as their father backhanded her in his fury. Ma's face would be black and blue the next day, but amazingly, she dealt with this as she dealt with everything…with passive acceptance and a firm belief that it was God's will. The one thing their mother was passionate about was her religion. Indeed, that may have been the only thing that kept her sane, trapped as she was by the demands of two men with very different views on what her duty was and to whom.

After a while, the Saturday card games began, and then the rows and beatings stopped.

Tom was still speaking. "Yer mother chose t' do the priest's biddin'," his voice was getting louder, "and I found…comfort with Maggie. She accepted the way things had t' be. She knows I have a family and a wife."

Lucy raised her eyes to look directly into her father's. "Ye'll not come away with me, Da? Ye'll be stickin' up fer yon painted hussy over yer wife an' family?"

There was no answer, and at that moment, Lucy began to hate her father. "Livin' a sin ya are, with yon filthy slut!" she hissed. "Yer both bound straight fer the fires o' hell. Yer no better than alley cats. Yer nothin' but a stinkin hoormaster!"

Tom's hand cracked against Lucy's face and sent her reeling against a whatnot filled with china and glass. The sounds of porcelain crashing and breaking, and Lucy's cry, brought Maggie running into the room.

"Tom, fer God's sake, stop it! Ye'll kill her!" She yanked at the back of Tom's gray cardigan, knocking him off balance and got between them.

A red welt was spreading across Lucy's face. Blood began to gush out of her nose and drip onto one of the brocaded chairs. Shards of glass and bone china littered the floor.

Tom's face was white with anger. "Get the HELL out o' this house! Go back t' yer mother!" He took a breath that did not calm him at all. "Yer jest like her, all piety and no heart. ya think t' be judge and jury. Ya pass judgment on a decent woman whose sin it is t' love me more than she loves plaster saints, a woman who suffers shame rather than break up a family."

Maggie was visibly agitated. "Tom, let the girl be. She's covered in blood. I'll get a flannel t' wipe her face." She reached for Lucy, who backed away.

"Ye'll not touch me, ya brazen hussy." Lucy spat the words at Maggie, and then turned to face her father again. "As God is my judge, ya'll never again lift yer hand t' me or me mother. Yer nothin but a cowardly woman beater." She lifted the iron fireplace poker and raised it over her head. "Come near me again and I'll bash yer brains out!"

For a moment, the only sound was her breathing. Then, as she backed away from her father, her foot caught in the fringe of the carpet. She fell backwards and everything went black.

Chapter Two

Ellen waited well past teatime that day, but Lucy never returned with the ham, so she made do with a bap and butter. That was hours ago, and now she was beginning to get nervous. The wind was picking up, and the rain was beating an urgent tattoo against the window.

This wasn't like Lucy at all. She had never before stayed out for this length of time without letting her mother know where she would be. Ellen rose from her chair by the fire again and went to the window. Just as she pulled back the curtain, she heard a knock. Hurrying to the hall, she opened the front door.

"Mrs. O'Leary?" It was Kevin, the butcher's boy. He doffed his cap respectfully, despite the rain, and waited for her to answer.

"Yes." Ellen knew he wasn't bringing good news. "What is it?"

"I'm sorry fer yer trouble, Missus, but yer daughter's in the hospital. She's been hurt, and they took her t' the Mater."

Ellen made the sign of the cross. "Jesus, Mary, and Joseph! What happened? Is she all right? Who sent ya?"

"It was the sister. She sent me, gave me sixpence t' cycle over here and tell ya. Sure, I don't know what happened, but they want ya t' come right away so they do".

Ellen went back into the kitchen and opened her purse. Did she have enough money to take the tram and give the young fella a tip, too? It would take two trams to get to Crumlin Road, where the hospital was. She would have to use the Sunday collection money. Given the circumstances, God would understand.

The boy coughed.

"Come in outa the rain," she said. "Ye'll be catchin' yer death o' cold."

"Thanks, Missus." He sounded grateful, but a little shy.

"'Tis a raw day, not fit fer man nor beast," Ellen said as she pressed a three-penny bit into the boy's hand. "Thanks fer comin' all this way on such a foul day." She was ashamed to give him less than the sister had, but it was all she could afford and still have enough for the tram fare.

As he coughed again, she said, "Ya look foundered. There's a pot o' tea by the hearth. Help yerself. I have t' get ready and be away."

Kevin was grateful for the warmth of the house, the offer of hot tea, and the money. The nine pence, added to the pay the butcher gave him for making the deliveries, was more than he'd had in a long time. His ma would think it was Christmas! There would be money for coal brick, soda farls, tea, and the wee bit of meat Mr. Finlay always gave him for doing a good job. He was glad the butcher let him use the bike to run the message for the sister.

Ellen's stomach was in a knot and her heart was pounding, but she remembered how her mother had always warned her never to visit anyone in the hospital dressed in anything but her Sunday best. Her mother had believed that the patient would get better treatment if the family looked respectable, and Ellen thought that made good sense. Sure, no one cared to put himself or herself out for a dirty "shawlee." Many facilities even had different waiting rooms for those who wore a shawl in place of a more expensive coat.

She went into the scullery, closed the door, took off her blouse, and washed her face, hands, and underarms before going upstairs and changing into her black skirt, white blouse, and good coat. Gathering up her gloves and hat, she paused for a moment to bow her head and offer a prayer to the Sacred Heart whose picture hung on the wall at the foot of her bed. She shuddered, then crossed herself and said, "Thy will be done."

But sometimes, she thought, it was hard to accept God's will. She shook her head to chase the sinful thought away. Stopping at the door for her umbrella, Ellen dipped her fingers into the holy water font, blessed herself and called to Kevin.

"I'm off now. Lock the door when ya leave. I'm much obliged t' ya fer comin'."

The wind was even stronger and the rain was gusting in sheets, blown almost sideways. Ellen's umbrella turned inside out as she struggled to control it. The rain felt like pinpricks piercing her exposed face, blinding her.

Groping her way toward the railings that enclosed the tiny gardens fronting the row houses, she held on tight and made it to the top of the street. At the corner, however, a gale force gust lifted her frail body and dashed her to the ground. Lightning erupted around her in fragmented shards of light punctuated by thunder.

She tried to regain her footing, but the wind was too strong, and the worn and wet cobblestones were slick and offered no purchase. Then there was another gust and a loud crack as a great limb from an ancient oak fell and struck her on the head. After a moment, her blood joined the rushing muddy water to gather and swirl at the catch basin.

~

The crackling of an ember woke Kevin, and he reluctantly rose from the seat by the fire. Picking up his mug, he walked into the scullery, rinsed out the remains of his tea, and set the mug on the draining board. He felt much better. His coat was drier and warmer for its time spent in front of the fire.

Leaving the house, he remembered to lock the door, bumping his backside against it to make sure. His bicycle had fallen and was lying on the ground. *There's no way I'm goin' t' ride me bike against this wind*, he said to himself, and lowering his head and pulling his cap as far down over his ears as he could, he picked up the bike and started up the street. The wind and rain had subsided for now, but it was still difficult to walk. Controlling his bike as he pushed it alongside him was proving to be a real problem.

At the top of the street, he noticed a bundle lying on the ground. It was lit by the wavering light from the street lamp. As he got closer, he saw something white beside the dark bundle. A hand. Kevin stopped dead in his tracks. He tried to control his shaking, and then he screamed. One door opened and, then another, yellow light slicing through the darkness. Kevin screamed again.

"What in the name o' Jaysus is all the noise about?" a voice called from one of the doorways.

"It's Mrs. O'Leary," Kevin answered, his voice breaking. "Come quick, Mister. Come quick, I think she's dead. There's blood…oh, Jaysus…oh, God."

The neighbor ran out in his bare feet, and he and Kevin gently turned the body over. Ellen's face was ashen; her last expression was one of surprise.

Other neighbors began to gather and whisper among themselves.

"My God, is she dead?"

"What happened?"

"Where's Tom?"

"Jaysus, Mary, and holy Saint Joseph, save us all"

The gusting wind added its mournful howl to their prayers, as though it had no part in the tragedy.

~

In the hospital across town, Lucy felt a soft, smooth hand grasp hers. A figure dressed all in white stood over her and spoke, but the words it said were sounds without meaning, and then the voice faded. Lucy lay still. Now she was warm and happy, bathed in a light that was every color and at the same time none. She was drifting, weightless and free of pain.

Tom and Maggie stood helplessly by her bedside. The sister told them she had sent a young fella to fetch Ellen, and she should be arriving anytime. To prevent what would be an uncomfortable situation, Tom decided to take Maggie to her house and then go to his own to await his wife's return.

He was heartsick at the day's events and fervently hoped his temper had not caused his daughter any permanent harm. She shouldn't have provoked him, though. Then he felt ashamed. He decided that if Lucy recovered, he would do a novena in thanksgiving. He was sorry for his outburst. He was also afraid it was God's retribution for flaunting his relationship with Maggie in the face of the priest's edict. His conscience was more of an itch than a hair shirt.

Seeing a side of Tommy she had never seen before, Maggie was silent. She abhorred violence and had little patience for those who resorted to it to solve problems.

Leaving the hospital, they realized the weather had taken a turn for the worse. Because neither of them was dressed for the deluge they encountered, Tom suggested they wait it out in the little café across from the hospital. The café was busy, but they managed to find a booth in a quiet spot by the window. They had not eaten anything since the meal interrupted by Lucy's arrival, and they were both hungry and in need of comfort.

Bridie McGuiness, the waitress, approached the table. Working so close to the hospital, she regularly witnessed human emotions in all their extremes: a new father celebrating the birth of his first child, another man bemoaning his tenth, families huddled together mourning the death of a mother or father, and the lonely girl, heavily pregnant and shunned by her boyfriend and family, pushing her food around her plate wondering what she was going to do when her meager savings ran out. These two newest customers were not in a happy place, she thought.

"What can I get fer ya?"

"We'll jest be havin' a bowl o' soup an' a roll, thanks," Tom said.

Bridie nodded. "The pea soup looks good, jest right fer a day the likes o' this. It's thick and hot."

As Tom nodded, the woman with him lifted her head and looked at Bridie and nodded also.

Bridie was moved by the sad expression in the woman's beautiful blue eyes. *Poor woman*, she thought, *somethin' is sorely eatin' at her.* "I'll be right back," she said aloud. "Ya'll both be feelin' better with a good bowl o' soup t' warm ya up."

"She's a cheerful one," Tom said as he studied Bridie's retreating back. "Jest the right kind fer this type o' work."

Maggie nodded but said nothing. What was there to say? Her world was coming apart. She had accepted all the restrictions of a clandestine relationship. She looked forward from week to week to the Saturdays she spent with Tom, but there would be no children, and for most of her life she would be alone and lonely. There would be no holidays, no Christmas Eves spent together, no weeks at the seaside. They seldom ventured out of the house for fear of gossip, although the righteous ladies of the neighborhood had long since shunned her, anyway.

At least she would never have to worry about money. Liam, her solid but unromantic husband, had seen to that. After his death, she had been looking for the romance she had missed in her marriage when she and Tom had met at her friend Claire's house. Tom was everything Liam had not been, and that, she had just found out, included violent. She was shocked and saddened by the day's events. Her relationship with Tom had been dealt a lethal blow today. Their time together had been fun without substance or a sound foundation, but she had never before seen his temper. She had managed to turn Tom's family into mere ghosts on the sepia photograph he had shown her. They weren't real people. Not until tonight.

She had always thought she loved Tom, but now she wasn't sure she knew who he was. His flowers, his thoughtful little gifts, his playful little games had satisfied her need for romance, but now Lucy's visit had forced her to face the reality of the situation. She was the "other woman." Her relationship with Tom was built on the hardship of others. For the first time, she could not escape seeing Tom's wife and children as flesh and blood people, with feelings. They were his family. She was just a pleasant diversion. It was not enough, not enough for them, not enough for her.

"A penny fer yer thoughts."

She was startled by his voice. She looked up. He was studying her anxiously.

"Ya look very serious," he murmured. "What're ya thinkin' about?"

She decided this was neither the time nor the place to discuss her feelings. "I've a lot on me mind," she merely said. "An' so do you...ah, here's our soup."

"Here ya go, enjoy." Bridie set the steaming bowls in front of them. She tore a page from her pad and set it down on the table. "If ye're needin' anythin' else, jest let me know."

They were silent as they ate. The soup was hot and comforting. For now, they were content to push weightier thoughts to the backs of their minds.

CHAPTER THREE

In the absence of family members, the neighborhood began preparing an Irish wake, part Catholic ritual, part Celtic mystery, and part superstition. Kevin had given the neighbors the reason for Ellen's being out in such vile weather, and the news that Lucy was in the hospital elicited both a fresh round of sympathy for the family's troubles and yet another round of whiskey.

Mrs. Duggan sent her daughter Kathleen to tell Nellie and Mary Alice to come at once, but not to say their mother was dead. That responsibility would be left to their father. They supposed Tom was still at the hospital with Lucy, and Kevin offered to cycle back there to fetch him. The storm had done its work by this time, and all that was left were a few shredded black clouds sulking in the hills.

When the priest arrived to administer the last rites, with a distraught and disbelieving Feelie at his heels, it was decided to lay the body out in the back room of the family home until the undertaker arrived with the coffin. Since Feelie was the only family member there, it fell to her to close her mother's eyes for the last time and wash her body for burial. She performed this duty, mercifully numbed by shock, but when it was done, she closed herself in the lavatory in the back yard. There, her body convulsed by sobs, she retched and fainted.

Meanwhile, the preparations for Ellen's wake continued. Blinds were drawn, mirrors were shrouded, clocks were stopped, and candles were lit. A black crepe ribbon was tied to the front door knocker as the sign of a house in mourning.

Then the undertaker arrived with the coffin, which he put on two sawhorse-like supports. "If ever a man was cut out fer a job," Mrs. Gilvery whispered to her friend Mrs. Duggan, "it's that McNulty. A long drink o' water he is, with a face like a death's head, rubbin' his hands together like one o' them prayin' mantis creatures I've heard tell of."

Mr. McNulty was never a welcome visitor, nor was he a happy man. He ignored the whispers, but was always aware of the jokes about his mentally measuring everyone that he met for a coffin. He loved color and had always wanted to be an artist, but instead found himself forced into his uncle's business and doomed to a life enveloped in black... black everything, right down to the looks he always got from passersby. The only relief came from the beautiful, bright colors of the flowers. He loved the flowers, even with those damned black ribbons on them.

Ellen's body was dressed in the habit of the third order of St. Francis and laid out, her hands folded across her chest in an attitude of prayer and clutching the rosary beads her mother had given her for her first communion.

"Sure, an' she looks like a saint," said Mrs. O'Connor, nodding her head and smiling with approval. "There never was a more saintly woman that walked the earth, an' that's God's truth. She'll be sorely missed."

When Feelie regained consciousness, she wished she had not. The realization that her mother was gone and that she would never again hear her voice hit her afresh. There had been no time to tell her mother how much she loved her, and no chance to say goodbye. *Life is a strange journey*, she thought. *You think you will get around to saying and doing all the things that should be said and done, and then, without warning, it's all over and it's too late. The end of the race comes too soon.* Now she was sitting on a straight-backed kitchen chair, feet together, hands resting on her lap. She had torn her stockings and skinned her knees when she fainted, but Mrs. Gilvery had bandaged her knees and helped her find black stockings to replace the torn pair.

The front door opened and closed as people came and went. Feelie strained to hear the voices of her family. *Where in God's name are they?* She wondered. *Where's me da? What's happened to our Lucy? Sweet Jaysus, protect us.*

She glanced from time to time at the silent, gray-faced effigy that had been her mother and wondered where she had gone.

Across town, Bill was just getting home from work. He was glad the storm had passed, but he was still drenched to the skin. After a warm bath in front of the fire and a change of clothes, he felt much better and decided to ride his motorbike over to Tom's house, hoping Lucy would be at home. He also hoped it wasn't too late to be calling without the benefit of an invitation, but he knew Lucy often spent Saturdays with her mother. He figured he would be there by nine-fifteen or so, not too late, he assured himself.

Nearing Falls Road, Bill realized that the weather was changing again. The dark clouds had regrouped, the wind was picking up. The motorbike, he soon decided, might not have been the best means of transportation. This storm was not giving in gracefully. As he came near Tommy's house, he noticed a lot of unusual activity. A group of people stood talking and shaking their heads, and one or two crossed themselves. Slowing down, he stopped at the curb and kicked the bike rest. The little knot of people parted to allow him through. No one said a word.

With his head bent against the wind, he reached for the knocker, but instead of the hard brass, he felt the soft folds of the black ribbon. Instantly realizing its significance, he pulled his hand away as though he had been burned. His whole body recoiled and he stood there staring at the closed door.

Behind him a soft voice said, "It's the Missus. Killed by a fallin' branch, she was. Sure, it's bad cess to this storm, so it is, it's an evil wind."

Bill tried to gather his wits about him. He hadn't known Ellen well, but he had known that she had treated him with generosity and hospitality when he visited. His heart went out to Tom and Lucy in their sudden grief. Knocking softly on the door, he wondered how he would handle the situation, not knowing the proper way to conduct himself at a Catholic wake. He knew there would be a lot of ritual that would be more than a little alien to him, but he did not want to be disrespectful in any way.

A woman he had never seen before opened the door. Assuming she was a family member, he greeted her respectfully. "Sorry fer yer troubles, Missus."

"Thank ya, son," she replied quietly, "but I'm jest helpin' out. Feelie's the only one here, in the back room she is. Ya kin go on in."

Bill ducked his head as he entered the hallway. The door to the front room was open, and he could hear the steady cadence of the rosary. He also saw the flickering candles casting shadows that danced demonically against the walls. His first instinct was to flee. He hesitated a long moment at the door, then he found himself being gently pushed into the room by the woman who had greeted him. He stepped aside to let her by, and with quiet thanks, she entered the room, knelt down, blessed herself, and began to pray with the others.

Bill decided the best thing to do was to watch everyone else and try to fit in as best he could. Considering the small size of the room and the fact that he was the only one standing, this was difficult. Feeling self-conscious, he reluctantly lowered himself to his knees. He would hate for any of the lads in the lodge to see him now.

They'd most likely make me turn in me sash, he thought wryly, and then he noticed a statue of the Child of Prague smiling sweetly down at him. *Between takin' a fancy to a Papist and kneelin' before an idol, I'm really kickin' over the traces.* Bowing his head, he decided to wait until the prayers were over before paying his respects. He wondered where the rest of the family was. It seemed strange that Tommy wasn't here. And where was Lucy?

The thought had no sooner crossed his mind than there was a commotion at the front door. The neighbors praying stopped abruptly, and there was a deadly silence as three young women entered. Two of them searched the room with wildly frightened eyes.

Mrs. Duggan stood up and went to the girls. One was her daughter, who stepped aside as she pulled the other two toward her, an arm around each one. They bent in, close and private, and she whispered the news she had hoped their father would be there to tell them.

Ellen's oldest daughter, her namesake, was the first to react. "Ah no…Ah no, not me ma, please God, please not me ma!" she cried frantically. Shaking her head, she made her way through the silent mourners to the back room and the reality of her loss. Her sister Mary Alice stood rooted to the spot with both hands over her face, excluding the solemn onlookers from her shock.

"Where's me da?" she asked at last.

"Sure," Mrs. Duggan said, no longer whispering, "there was an accident an' yer Lucy's in the hospital. Yer da must still be there."

"What in the name o' God happened t' our Lucy?" Mary Alice was trying to make some sense of it, trying to come to terms with the loss of her mother, her sister's accident, and her father's absence. All of them were missing, all at once, at a time when they should all be together.

"We don't know what happened," Mrs. Duggan said. "A wee fella brought a message from the sisters at the hospital. He's gone back t' fetch yer da. Yer ma was on her way there when she was killed."

Mrs. Duggan wished someone else would say something. Uncomfortable as she was being the bearer of bad news, she saw everyone else just standing and nodding confirming her words. They were uncomfortable, also, at the family's lack of privacy. There should have been a decent time for them to mourn before having to face the world. Tommy should have returned home in time to take over and make decisions.

In his absence, the neighbors had finally called the priest themselves, and from that point, everything had progressed almost of its own volition. Now that a little time had passed and the panic of the moment was over, it was disquieting to witness the raw anguish of the daughters as they learned of their loss.

This was on everyone's minds. For Bill, the news that Lucy was in the hospital was the biggest shock in a night of shocks. Thinking further on it, he decided that he would go to the hospital to be with her. Tom must be on his way home, he thought as he pulled on his jacket. The storm was still holding off, so he decided it would be okay to ride his bike.

The three sisters were now seated beside their mother's coffin, accepting condolences as friends and family members filed by. They all wore identical black wrap-around smocks. Bill wondered if women kept these garments on hand on the off chance they should have a death in the family, then dismissed the thought as irreverent. He paid his respects and wound his way to the front door.

It was getting late, and the small crowd of mourners was beginning to thin out. No one lingered on the pavement outside the house. Sorry as they were for the bereaved family, they were glad to be able to return to their own lives, to find comfort, to feel alive and forget for a time that sorrow would find them, too, sooner or later. Already only close friends and neighbors remained inside.

~

Outside on the street, Bill's motorbike sputtered but started on the second try. As he rode through the wet streets, he wondered what had happened to Lucy. Why was she in the hospital? The news had given him quite a start. He suddenly realized that he cared a great deal about her welfare. How serious was her condition? And how would she cope with the news of her mother's death?

He vowed to be there for her, at least as much as she would allow him to be. At the same time, he was afraid that Tom's delay in arriving home might mean Lucy had taken a turn for the worse.

~

Across town, Tom was blissfully unaware of the toll this day's events were taking on his life. While he sorely regretted the outburst that had resulted in his daughter's accident, he was sure everything would soon blow over. After all, this wasn't the first time he had lost his temper with his daughters. He was sure everyone would be mad at him for a while, Ellen most of all, but equally sure that she and they would eventually forgive him.

Ellen always knows what side her bread's buttered on, he said to himself. Not every man would put up with a woman who refused to perform her wifely duties. Of course, he took care of his part of the bargain. He worked hard to bring home a pay packet every week, to put the food in their mouths and a roof over their heads. All that, he did. All he expected was a meal on the table and the respect due him as the breadwinner and head of the house. *Not much atall, considerin'…no, no, not much atall.*

Tom and Maggie finished their meal in silence, both caught up in their own thoughts until Tom said, "We'd best be goin'. The storm's let up a bit."

He paid the bill and ushered Maggie out of the café. Neither of them had much to say as they made their way back to Maggie's house.

When they arrived, Maggie fumbled for the key for a second. Finding it, she opened the door and led Tom into the kitchen. He was uneasy, however, and felt a deepening sense of foreboding. There were evil forces at work this night. He put his arm around Maggie's shoulder and felt her shuddering.

"I'd best be goin' now," he said as he made to kiss her goodbye. She averted her face. He could see the tears sparkling on her lashes as she pushed away from him.

He did not understand. "Will ya not be givin' me a kiss? It might be a while afore I see ya again."

He tried to embrace her again, but still she was having none of it.

When she finally spoke, her voice was sad. "Ah, Tommy," she whispered, "don't ya know we'll not be seein' each other again? Ya need t' mend yer marriage and tend t' yer family. And I need…I need t' find a life." She was crying now, great tears pooling in her eyes and streaming down her cheeks.

Tom was speechless. He knew things were bad, but he was not prepared for this, not prepared to feel as though someone had knocked the wind out of him. His stomach contracted painfully and his brain refused to function. Then a knot of anger untied itself from someplace deep inside him. His life was out of control, he realized. Everything was getting away from him. He had hurt his daughter, and now he was losing the respect of the woman whose loving had made his life bearable.

He softened his tone in an effort to control the anger. "Maggie, luv, what is it ya're sayin' t' me? Ya can't be meanin' fer us never t' see each other again." She didn't respond, so he continued, a little louder. "Ya're just overwrought. It's been a hell of a day. Ya jest be needin' a wee rest. Things'll look better in the light o' the mornin'."

She would not be soothed. "I'm sorry, Tom. But there is no future fer us." Now she tried to wipe her eyes. "There never was," she said after a moment, "but we were too selfish t' see it. We were havin' fun at everyone's expense, and now there's been real harm done because of us."

Tom was stunned.

Maggie went on. "I pray t' God that Lucy will recover. I don't think I want t' live with me conscience if she doesn't get better. Ya'd best be off t' yer family. Take care o' yer responsibilities."

She let that sink in, and only after another minute did she say, "Yer wife'll be needin' ya by her side, not gallivantin' with the likes o' me. I'm ashamed of us, so I am. I'm not sure what t' think about anything, me feelin's are all so mixed up."

"Ya're jest overwrought, like I said," he finally sputtered. "Ya can't be sayin' goodbye. We need each other!"

"We need someone or somethin'," she said slowly, "an' we filled each other's needs fer a while. But we're no good fer each other. Accept it an' go home t' yer family. I'll sorely miss our times together," she added with increasing certainty, "but I need more than ya can give me. I need someone t' be beside me an' be there fer me. I don't want t' be stealin' moments from someone else's life. There's a side o' ya that I can't fathom or understand and it frightens me—"

"What the hell are ya talkin' about? What can't ya fathom?" Tom was not prepared for what he was hearing. "What frightens ya? I love ya! I've been good t' ya all these years, woman, have I not?"

His anger was getting the better of him, and he spoke faster and harder. "What the hell are ya blatherin' about, can ya tell me that? Are ya tryin' t' tell me that we were jest a passin' fancy? I'll not be acceptin' that, nor any other piece o' shite. I'm here fer ya. We made a bargain. It's worked fer all this time. What's different now?" His face was flushed and his breathing was becoming labored.

She decided to try reason. "Ah, Tom," she said, "don't ya see? We have no future. Yer daughter was right. I have no real place in yer life, an' ya don't belong in mine. I don't want t' be yer fancy woman. I want a life o' me own. I want a man who comes home t' me every night, not jest once a week."

He didn't want to hear this. This morning things had been fine, and now she wanted him to go, and go for good. He didn't understand, couldn't understand, how things could change so quickly.

She was standing with her back to him now, but he wanted her to look him in the eyes. When he put his hands on her shoulders and tried to turn her to face him, he felt her stiffen and pull away from his touch.

"Maggie…ah, Maggie, what ails ya? Will ya not tell me?" The anger had subsided now. In its place he felt confusion and hurt.

Her reply was slower in coming and soft when it came. "Today I heard the words 'slut' and 'hoor,'" she said, "an' I realized I deserved 'em both. Tom, I knew what we were doin' was wrong, but I fooled meself inta thinkin' only of the romance of it. I saw another side o' ya that I had never seen before, an'… an' I don't really know who ya are. I don't trust ya any more."

This caught Tom off guard. "Maggie, don't ya understand?" he cried in desperation. "I was provoked! Any man would ha' lost his temper."

"Losin' yer temper's one thing," she said. "Strikin' a defenseless girl is the act of a coward."

"A coward is it you'll be callin' me now?"

"Aye, Tom. Though it saddens me t' say it. Only a coward beats on women an' girls."

This was too much. "Woman," he thundered, "I've heard enough out o' ya fer one night. Ya'd do well t' guard yer tongue."

"Why should I guard me tongue" she asked defiantly. "Can ya not be bearin' the truth then?"

"Maybe ya can't bear the truth," he shot back. "Maybe ya ARE nothin' but a SLUT an' a HOOR."

The words were no sooner out of Tom's mouth than he wished he had swallowed them. Maggie turned at last to face him and what he saw in her face was pure hatred. He instinctively lifted his hand to defend himself. She mistook the gesture.

"Will ya be goin' t' hit ME now, Tom O'Leary?" Her voice was getting shrill. "Get the hell out o' me house now or I'll call the peelers. Ya'll not be puttin' me in the hospital like ya did yer daughter!"

But Tom was stunned. He did not move. Maggie took a step backward, then turned all at once and fled from the kitchen. She was halfway out the front door before he knew what was happening.

By the time he got to the door, she was gone. There was no sign of her, He searched the neighborhood, but she had disappeared. Eventually, he guessed she'd taken refuge in one of the wee shops at the top of the street, but of course, he wasn't about to take their row into a place like that, not and make the whole thing public in front of her neighbors.

Damn her to hell anyway, he thought furiously. *Women're all the same, take all you have t' give an' then knock the shite out o' ya.*

He'd had had enough of females for one day. Thinking he would do well to seek some male company instead, he decided to head to his local. Arriving at the pub, he scanned the crowd to see if there was anyone he knew, but it was strangely quiet for a Saturday night. Two fellas were sitting in a booth in the corner, but they stopped talking when he came in and were staring at him with their drinks halfway to their mouths.

What the hell are they lookin' at? Tom thought with irritation. Deciding to ignore their bad manners, he settled at the far end of the deserted bar and hit the bell for service.

Seamus, the owner's son, came out of the back room, which was where the ladies' salon was located. Everyone, including his father and mother, had gone to the O'Learys' for the wake, and so there was little for him to do but stand behind the bar, polish glasses, and make sure there was no one waiting in the ladies' snug. He approached Tom with his head bent over the glass he was polishing.

"What'll ya have?" he said automatically and without looking up.

"Bushmills," Tom answered. It was a night for whiskey, he had decided, and a lot of it.

Seamus stopped dead in his tracks as he realized who was ordering. The two fellas in the corner were now watching with interest to see how Seamus would react to Tom's presence. *'Twas a strange situation indeed, the man's wife layin' dead, and here he was drinkin' in a pub. Sure, he needs somethin' t' take the edge off his sorrow, but drinkin' in a pub at a time like this is indecent, so it is.*

"I'm sorry fer yer trouble, Tom," Seamus said, feeling that some attention needed to be paid to the situation.

"Thank ya," Tom answered after a minute. "It was an accident, ya know, but she's in good hands now. She'll be right as rain."

The men in the bar asked themselves if the shock had been too much for their neighbor Tommy. How in the name of God could he think his wife would be "as right as rain" when she was cold as yesterday's porridge?

At a loss for words, Seamus busied himself pouring Tom's drink and giving him good measure.

"It's been a rough day, sure enough," Tom said, not noticing the effect his words were having on those listening, "but there's nothin' like a good Irish whiskey t' chase away the worst of it." He downed the shot in one gulp, set the glass on the bar, thumped his chest, and coughed. "Another, if ya please, Seamus, an' then I'll need t' be gettin' home, or the missus'll be stringin' me up, so she will."

Seamus was now positive that Tom had taken leave of his senses.

Tom accepted the drink and downed it as quickly as the first one. It was getting late, he was thinking, and Ellen would most likely be home from the hospital. She'd wonder what was keeping him. He was still angry at Maggie's rejection, but the whiskey had raised his spirits and restored his belief that everything would turn out for the best. Indeed, he felt quite expansive as he paid and left the bar, unaware of Seamus' stare and the men in the corner shaking their heads. But his mood couldn't last, and as he came closer to home it changed again. *A gray day, so it is*, he thought glumly, *and a cloud over all our heads*. He turned the corner and headed down his street.

As soon as he saw his house, he realized something was wrong. All the blinds had been drawn. Something was fluttering from the doorknocker…a black ribbon. He felt a sudden jolt in his chest. *No…not Lucy…she's alive.* He tried to remember, but suddenly he couldn't, exactly. *She's alive*, he told himself again, less sure this time. *She's goin' t' be all right, she has t' be.* It had not been that long since he'd left her. How could this be? There wasn't time.

He stood rooted to the ground, refusing to believe that his youngest daughter could be dead. Fear gripped him tight and held him fast, and all of a sudden his legs could no longer support him. He fell against his front door, which gave way under his weight. He fell to his knees as the door opened. He heard voices rising in a surprised babble, but it was as if they were far away, down a tunnel. He could not hear what they were saying.

"It's the shock, get him some water," said one of the voices.

A minute later, he was being helped to his feet, cold water being forced against his teeth and dribbling down his chin and onto his collar. He scanned the room. Candles. Shrouded mirrors, the girls dressed in black. His neighbors avoiding eye contact with him. This made no sense at all. *She was alive when I left the hospital!*

"Where is she?" he finally managed, pushing away the cup of water. He had to see her for himself. His daughters led him to the back room.

There was a coffin. Again, the pain in his chest. He closed his eyes, opened them, and gripping the sides of the coffin for support. He found himself gazing into the face of his dead…*wife?*

He searched the faces of those around him for some explanation. But there was none, and all at once everything began to swim before his eyes, and the ground rushed up to meet him again for the second time in minutes.

He was having a terrible dream. Lucy was dead. No, Lucy was alive, but she hated him. 'Twas Ellen that was dead, who didn't hate him, even having a reason to. He wanted to wake up, but he was awake. It was a cruel joke, but it was all too real.

Lucy was alive, but Ellen was dead. His daughter was alive, and he hadn't killed her, but what had happened to his wife? The shock was giving way to a building wave of grief and remorse. *I should ha' known*, he thought. *I should ha' been at home.*

"What happened?" he asked aloud, letting them help him to a chair by the fireplace. The whiskey warmth was gone, all in a second, and he was weak and chilled, his teeth chattering. Knowing the shock he felt and hoping the warmth would help, Mary Alice stoked the fire. Nellie went to the kitchen to put the kettle to boil for tea, Ireland's universal remedy in the face of trauma, whether emotional or physical. Tea always helped.

Finally, the explanation. "Ma was on her way t' see our Lucy in the hospital when she was killed by a fallin' branch," said Mary Alice. "An' will ya fer God's sake tell us what happened t' our Lucy?"

Tom moaned quietly and covered his face with his hands. *This is all Lucy's fault*, he thought desperately, even as he knew he was wrong. *She should never have gone t' Maggie's t' meddle in somethin' that was none o' her business.*

Everyone was waiting for him to speak, to explain. If only Lucy had stayed home with her mother like she should have, he thought, he wouldn't be in this position. Everything would be fine. But now Ellen was dead, Lucy hurt, and Maggie lost to him. What was he going to say? The expectant faces of his girls and the neighbors who had stayed to help them surrounded him.

Feeling his tongue filling his mouth, he began to speak. "I was visitin' a friend when Lucy dropped by," he began slowly. "She caught her foot an' tripped an' hit her head against the grate.

Yes, that's what happened, he said to himself as they still stared. *All very innocent, not my fault at all, I have every right t' visit anyone I like, so I do.*

"But, Da, what kept ya so long? The wee fella went t' fetch ya hours ago. Did he not tell ya what had happened?"

"I musta missed him." Tom felt a trap closing on him, even if the trappers were still unaware of it. How was he to account for the time he had spent with Maggie? "I went t' the chapel t' pray fer our Lucy, an' then I was in need of a wee drop, so I…ah, ah, I called in at the pub." Aye, that was it.

Now that he was here, his daughters and neighbors were relieved. There were no more questions. There was still much to be arranged, but they believed he would take over now. It was easier to accept his explanation than wonder at its being out of character. What did it matter, anyway? Nothing was going to bring Ellen back.

The sorrow still came in waves. For a moment, everything would seem normal, and mourners forgot to speak in hushed tones. Once in a while someone even laughed out loud before remembering. For a minute or two, there was almost a festive atmosphere in the room.

For their part, Tom's daughters wondered how people could eat and drink like there was nothing wrong. Mary Alice, in particular, wanted everyone to go home so she could have time to mourn alone with her family.

Tom was now the center of attention. Nellie had laced his tea with whiskey and was coaxing him to drink it, but in truth, he didn't need much coaxing. His girls were fussing over him and the neighbors were treating him with awed respect.

"It's a terrible loss fer ya t' bear, Tommy."

"Aye, that it is."

"Sure, yer Missus was a saint."

"Aye, that she was." The whiskey was dulling the shock and flushing him with pride and memory together. "I'll sorely miss her."

The girls had often wondered about the Saturdays, but they said nothing. It wasn't their place and now wasn't the time.

It was getting late now, and the remaining mourners were leaving, some a little drunk, some crying. They all felt the weight of the day. At last they were gone, however, and the family was alone. Tom was still sitting by the kitchen fire, and Feelie and Mary Alice were in the back room, sitting by their mother. Each sister was lost in her own memories. Now there was the silence. The wake would continue the next day, and then there would be the funeral.

Chapter Four

Tom met with the priest and the undertaker to make the final arrangements for Ellen's grand send-off. She was to be borne to her final rest in a hearse pulled by black horses, their heads adorned by black plumes. The family would ride in a carriage, and everyone else would follow on foot in a solemn procession.

And no expense would be spared. No one would ever be able to say Tommy O'Leary had skimped on his wife's funeral. He'd even ordered a large spray of white roses with a ribbon that said *Beloved Wife and Mother* on it.

Keeney, the publican, was instructed to deliver whiskey and beer to the house to be on hand for the mourners as they returned from the cemetery. Large plates of sandwiches and cakes were sent over by the neighborhood women to be set out by the girls.

Meanwhile, Lucy still lay unconscious in the hospital. Mary Alice, dispatched there to see how she was, returned with the news that she was still sleeping and did not appear to be any worse. That settled for the time being, the family prepared to bury its dead.

Tuesday dawned, a fine sunny day. Brisk winds had swept the sky clean, allowing the morning sun to shine through the trees and dance and dapple the ground. There was a clatter of hooves as the hearse arrived to carry the coffin to the chapel for the funeral mass. Feelie resisted, with difficulty, a strong desire to block the doorway so as to prevent them from taking her mother away. To Mary Alice, the undertaker looked like a vulture circling for the kill. Nellie whispered a quiet "I love you, Ma," as Ellen left her home for the last time.

Tom was gratified by the turnout. Imelda Donnelley sang the Ave Maria, and the chapel bell tolled for a faithful daughter. There wasn't a dry eye in the chapel.

Later, as the funeral cortege proceeded up the Falls Road toward the cemetery, the shopkeepers stood in front of their shops, doffing their caps and making the sign of the cross as the procession passed. Blinds had also been drawn as a sign of respect. Ellen O'Leary had been well thought of, and her passing touched them all, if only for the moment.

Tom sat in the carriage, acknowledging the silent onlookers with a dignified nod of his head. He was proud that he was able to send Ellen off in such grand style. Although he would never have admitted it—not even to himself—he enjoyed the importance of his position as chief mourner, with everyone deferring to his wishes. It was a new experience to have everyone hanging on his every word. It was, "Yes, Mr. O'Leary" this and "Yes, Mr. O'Leary" that and "Will that be all, sir?" and nothing but respect from the flower shop, the undertaker, the publican. Even the priest held his tongue for a change. Doors were opened for him; chairs were vacated and offered to him.

He was the man of the hour, and if he didn't think too much about the reason for all this attention, he could get used to it. He was glad he'd had the foresight to take out life insurance on Ellen as well as himself. Otherwise, he would never have had the money for this grand a funeral.

Maggie stood unseen at the corner of her street and watched the procession pass. She had been shocked to read the obituary, and now her emotions confused her. Never in her life had she wished anyone dead, and that included Tom's wife, but at the same time she'd often fantasized about a life where she and Tom could live as a normal couple with a normal life, instead of having to settle for the few hours stolen every week from his real family. It was ironic, she thought. Now he was free, a widower, and she no longer wanted to be with him. Her tears were for her own loss, for the capricious nature of fate. She was sure Tom had not accepted as final her decision to end their relationship. That made her afraid. His behavior on Saturday had showed her that he could be violent when his wishes were thwarted. A cloud of depression settled around her, weighing her down.

In the passing carriage, Tom turned his head just in time to see Maggie avert her gaze. He was glad she was here to see how the community was respecting him. Perhaps, he thought, she would think better of her outburst and forgive his. After a decent period of mourning had been observed, he would call on her. By that time, she'd be missing him and be glad to have him back. He settled back against the plump upholstery with a sigh of contentment. Mistaking the sigh as one of grief, his daughters exchanged a compassionate look. They were unaware of their father's duplicity, and his sighs were breaking their hearts.

There was a tense moment at the gates to the cemetery when the horse pulling the hearse stopped, there being an old Irish superstition that a horse would not pull the hearse through the gates of a cemetery if the inhabitant of the coffin was still alive. Many times it had happened when funerals had been halted and coffins opened to make sure.

Today, alas, there was a more mundane explanation. McNulty the undertaker always liked to introduce a little drama into the proceedings, and so he had reined the beasts in for just long enough to start tongues wagging, but not long enough to warrant investigation.

Soon, as the mourners watched at the graveside, the coffin was lowered into the waiting earth. The gravedigger handed the spade to Tom, who shoveled the first, ritual soil onto the coffin. It landed with a hollow thud, and Ellen's daughters shuddered at the thought of leaving their beloved mother in the dank, cold earth.

"Ma...ah...Ma," Nellie cried softly as the rest of the mourners took their turn with the spade and the coffin slowly disappeared under the dirt. Mary Alice buried her face in her husband's shoulder. Feelie worried her handkerchief into a tight, wet ball.

At last the priest finished the prayers and on Tom's behalf invited everyone back to the house, where the mood would brighten as neighbors caught up on the gossip and relatives who only saw each other at wakes and weddings marveled at how no one had changed a bit in the last ten years. Some mourners stood self-consciously against the wall, looking for someone they knew, and children dressed in their Sunday best, sensing the change in the general mood, began to skip and play and argue. For almost everyone present at Ellen's funeral, life began to resume its normal tempo.

For Tom and his daughters, life would never be the same. The rhythm of their lives had changed forever.

~

Bill had followed the procession with the other mourners. After staying at the hospital as long as the rules would allow the evening before, he had finally gone home. The sisters had been very kind and had explained Lucy's condition to him, but they had no idea when, or indeed if, she would regain consciousness. He had thus found the hospital experience unnerving. He hated the smell, a mixture of disinfectant, cabbage, floor wax, and fear. The rows of iron beds with their white covers, the spectral figures of the nuns gliding between the beds, tending to their patients, the squeaks of wheels as beds were screened to protect privacy…everything had seemed to run like clockwork. Every bed had been made up to a formula that did not permit wrinkles or movement, or so it seemed. The occupants of those beds were washed and combed to receive their visitors, two at a time. Flowers were brought, along with counterfeit smiles intended to cheer the patients. Of course, as often as not, the smiles were replaced by worried frowns as family members gathered in the hallways hidden from their loved one's sight. Above every bed was a reminder of Christ crucified, and on the wall at the end of the ward was a painting of Jesus. There was no getting away from the aggrieved saintly eyes. They followed you everywhere. Outside in the hall, Bill saw a painting depicting a man tied to a tree trunk with arrows protruding from every part of his body.

As a professional painter himself, he had passed some of the time trying to calculate how many gallons of pea green paint it had taken to cover every wall in the place. Lots, he had decided. The monotony was relieved only by treacle colored woodwork, and of course everything was reflected in the hand-buffed floors.

Sitting beside Lucy, he had wondered at the reasoning behind all the macabre pictures. They made him feel uncomfortable. He decided he liked being a Protestant. There were no statues staring at you, no gory pictures, and no need to say the same prayer over and over again as if God were deaf as a post and didn't hear it the first time. Just you, your Bible, your God, and your conscience.

Nevertheless, Bill was determined to return to the uncomfortable Catholic hospital as soon as the funeral was over. He had to see how Lucy was faring.

~

Tom's first night alone was restless and dream-ridden. In his dreams, Maggie and Ellen lay beside each other in unmarked graves, and the picture of the Sacred Heart at the foot of his bed now held a likeness of Lucy, rivers of blood rushing from her crown of thorns. The afterimage of his dream never left him, awake or asleep, not for weeks. The bed was cold, and his feet sought warmth, but there was none to be found.

The next morning, he woke to a dark, cold, and empty house. There was no fire in the grate, no kettle on the stove. He looked for his clothes, but none were laid out, and he had no idea where to find them. He had never made as much as a cup of tea for himself. The chamber pot had to be emptied, and he needed hot water, so the stove had to be lit. But where were the matches? He opened the door to the grate and saw that no one had set the fire. It had always been set, ready to be lit it in the morning, and he realized now that Ellen had been in the habit of preparing it the night before.

After two or three attempts, he got the fire going, and put the kettle to boil for tea. He decided to make porridge. He found the oats and put them in a pot with water, but after half an hour, all he had was a lumpy, barely edible mess. He would never get to work at this rate. Well, what would he take for lunch? Ellen had always prepared a billy full of soup for him, along with a hunk of cheese and homemade bread. Now there was neither soup nor bread to be found, although he did find some cheese in the scullery.

Rummaging through the laundry basket, he found his work shirt and pants. While the girls had been there for a few days, they had taken care of the things Ellen had done. They had cooked and cleaned and had laid out his good suit, white shirt, and black tie for him to wear at the funeral. A black diamond-shaped patch had been sewn on his sleeve as a sign of mourning.

But now he was on his own, and reality was catching up with him at breakneck speed. No more dinner on the table, no more clothes washed, ironed, laid out, and ready to wear. No more socks knitted or mended, no more buttons sewn on. No one to cluck over wet feet and fetch warm slippers. No one there to lend a sympathetic ear to his telling of the day's trials. No one to join in the celebration of a triumph.

Tom had lost his wife. It was coming as a shock just how much that loss would mean. It was dawning on him how many ways there were to miss a wife.

CHAPTER FIVE

On the day after the funeral, having quietly offered the night before to look in on Lucy during evening visiting hours, Bill went to the hospital straight from work. The family, grateful to him for his concern, had agreed that he should go. He had decided that he wouldn't have time to go home for a meal and still make it for visiting hours.

Never mind, he thought as he arrived at the hospital and shook the rain from his hat. *I can jest drop in t' the café across from the hospital and get somethin' there afterwards.* He wasn't really all that hungry, anyway.

Entering the ward, he was shocked to see that Lucy had been moved. Her bed was now near the door, a spot normally reserved for patients who were thought to be near death. He went in search of the nun in charge and found her in the chapel, comforting a young girl. Not wanting to disturb them, and afraid to hear the worst, he waited in the hall, pacing back and forth and muttering to himself.

It seemed like an hour, but in fact it was only a few moments later when the nun emerged from the chapel and asked what she could do for him.

"I'm here about Lucy O'Leary, Sister. Her bed's been moved t' the door and I'm worried, fer I've been told that they put patients there who're about t' die."

The nun's kind smile was like a warm balm. "I'm sorry you got a fright, son," she said. "We were thinking of sending her to another hospital where they care for those with chronic conditions, but she made some progress today, and so we'll keep her here for a while longer."

"Did she come 'round?"

The nun could hear the excitement in his voice. "No," she said, "but she gripped the doctor's hand and seemed to be listening to him. And she moved her head towards him when he spoke to her. It's a good sign. She has been restless on and off throughout the day. The doctor thinks she might be coming out of the coma. Thanks be to God and His Holy Mother."

Here the nun made the sign of the cross quickly, and her smile faded slightly. "Though I'm sure I don't know what will happen when she finds out about her mother's death," she added. "It will be a sad awakening for her." She shook her head and fingered the shiny brown beads of her rosary.

Bill was still excited. "Thanks, Sister. I think I'd best be goin' t' tell her father. He should be here when she wakes up."

Touched by his enthusiasm, the nun gave her little smile again. "I don't think it would be a good idea to tell her about her mother, you know, right away," she said. "I think Mr. O'Leary would be wise to talk to the doctor before telling Lucy anything that might send her back into shock."

Bill could hardly wait to get back to the family with the news. "Yes, Sister. I'll tell him that. But he should be here now, anyway. I'm jest a friend. Her family should be here when she wakes up. It's their faces she needs t' see first."

The idea that he might be the only one at Lucy's side when she woke up made him nervous. Although he had strong feelings for her, he had no idea how she felt about him. He was afraid that she would be upset with him for being there without being invited, and he certainly didn't want to be here when they told her of her mother's death. After the nun went on to see to her next patient, he sat by Lucy's bedside for a minute or two, watching her sleep, but he soon began to feel uncomfortable again and decided he'd best make himself scarce. He'd done all he could for now and would return when she was feeling better. This was family business. He did not want to intrude any further.

An hour later he knocked on Tom's door.

"Come on in," Tom called from the back of the house.

"It's me," Bill called as he entered. "I've jest come from the hospital."

"Hold on, Bill. I'll be with ya in a sec." Tom came out of the scullery, wiping his hands on a tea towel. "Take a seat by the fire. Will ya have a wee drop?"

"Aye, I could use a drop o' the hard stuff," said the younger man. "I jest came away from the hospital. They say Lucy's showin' signs o' comin' 'round. I thought it best fer ya t' be goin' on over there. Ye'll want t' be with her when she wakes up. The Sister told me t' tell ya not t' tell Lucy about her mother until ye've talked t' the doctor. They're afraid she'll go into shock again."

Tom, silent, busied himself pouring whiskey from a bottle he kept in the cupboard for special occasions. The bottle had been replaced far more frequently than was customary during the past few weeks. He was having a hard time sorting out his feelings. He dreaded Lucy's reaction when she found out about her mother, but he was also anxious to know if she was going to be the same as she had been before the fall. His major worry right now was that she would remember everything and tell the rest of the family what she knew about his relationship with Maggie. They had accepted his version of events leading up to Ellen's death. Anything Lucy might say would cause him embarrassment, to say the least.

His daughters had been very solicitous since their mother's passing, but that would change, he was sure, if they knew the whole truth. He thought they would not understand, any more than Lucy had, his involvement with a woman other than their mother.

Tom handed Bill a glass and sat down opposite him by the fire. "*Slainte*," he said, raising his glass. "How was she lookin', then?"

Bill raised his glass, and then lowered it for a quick swallow. "Cheers," he said, wiping his mouth with the back of his hand. "Well, she's still pale, and there was no sign o' movement while I was there, but that's not sayin' much, for I didn't tarry long. I got a shock when I saw they'd moved her t' the door. But the Sister told me they were goin' t' take her t' another hospital, then changed their minds when she showed signs o' wakin' up." He paused and raised his glass again, but instead of taking another sip, just lowered it. "Because, ya see, the other hospital is fer them people who're goin' t' be sick fer a long time and maybe never get better."

Now he finished his drink in one gulp and stared at the reflection of the fire in the empty glass. He felt tired, useless, somewhat depressed, and emotionally worn out.

He didn't feel comfortable visiting Lucy, at least not until she was much better, and then really only if she asked to see him. Considering the news she would be hearing, seeing him might very well never cross her mind.

And so he felt at a loose end. He had set the rest of his life to one side and now he had no desire to return to it. Watching a game on Saturday, followed by the usual post mortem at the pub over a pint with the lads had somehow lost its appeal. Meetings at the Lodge no longer interested him, and in fact, in that area, he had begun to wonder what the whole fuss was about, anyway. In the end, he silently asked himself, did God really care whether you went to church or to chapel? Did the wearing of an orange sash make you more of a patriot? And if so, where was your allegiance? To what country? Was he an Irishman or an Englishman? Having been born in Northern Ireland to Protestant parents, his allegiance to the English crown was for the most part predetermined. But Lucy had been born to Catholic parents who wanted no part of the English occupation. Her allegiance was to the Pope and to a united Ireland, and that, of course, put them on opposite sides of the fence. Good people set at each other's throats to ensure the continuation of intolerance…

Lost in thought, he had forgotten where he was until Tom broke into his reverie.

"Will ya have another? ya look done in, lad."

"No thank ya, Tom. I'll be away home. All of a sudden I feel bone tired."

Tom nodded. "Well, I'd best be makin' me way over t' the hospital," he said. "I'll see ya at work in th' mornin' and let ya know what's happened. An' thank ya fer all yer help," he added. "It's been a sore tryin' time fer everybody."

"Aye, that it has." Bill stood up and pulled on his jacket. "An' it's not done yet. Lucy is goin' t' need careful handlin' when she wakes up and until she's on her feet again."

"Aye. That's right ya are." Tom said. *ya have no idea how careful*, he thought.

Then the door closed behind Bill, and Tom was alone with his memories of Ellen as a young bride full of laughter, her eyes dancing with delight as she set about creating their home. Lucy was the image of her, but the likeness was only on the outside. Inside, Ellen was soft and quiet, given to introspection and prayer, whereas Lucy was quick-tempered and volatile. You could never be quite sure how she would react in any situation. Tom never could quite figure out just who Lucy took after, where she got the obstinacy, the quick temper, and all her other ideas about life. No, sir. He had no idea.

What he did know was that there were dark times ahead. With that thought, he seemed to shrink into the chair, and his eyes glazed as he stared into the dying embers of the fire. He must go to the hospital soon, he told himself, but not tonight. Visiting hours were over.

~

Lucy was drifting both closer to and further from the reality around her. There were voices near her, and she strained to understand what they were saying, but they were too garbled to make any sense. She was drifting away from the light to a dark place. She wanted to stay in the light, but the voices kept calling. Some noise disturbed her, and she raised her hand in an effort to push it away, but then she felt someone grasp it, hold it, and squeeze it. Response took too much effort. Her hand went limp and she retreated back into her quiet place. But the voices did not stop. They were calling louder now, more persistently. She wished she could swat them away like flies.

She finally opened her eyes, but all she saw were white, wavy blobs. She blinked, but that was too much of an effort, too, and she let her heavy lids close again.

"Lucy, dear, can you hear me?" Sister Domingo had seen the faint movement of her hand and the flutter of her eyelids. Dr. Hughes had said he was of the opinion that it was only a matter of time.

The greatest concern now was not whether or not she would regain consciousness, but would she make a full recovery. Head trauma was always a hard one to call. The girl was so young. Everyone was praying that she would not spend the rest of her life as a vegetable.

It was a worry, though…what would the news of her mother's death do to her? How would she react to that? A shock of such magnitude could knock her right out again.

Sister Domingo lifted the crucifix that hung at the end of her rosary beads, kissed it, and said a heartfelt prayer for her pale and silent patient.

"Evenin', Sister."

Tom had been standing behind the nun for several minutes, waiting for her to finish whatever it was that she was doing, and finally had decided to let her know he was there. He needed some information and felt that he wasn't going to get it at this rate.

Sister Domingo turned and greeted him respectfully. "Good evening, Mr. O'Leary. I'm sorry…have you been here long?"

"No. Jest a few minutes. How's our Lucy comin' along? I hear she showed signs o' comin' 'round."

Recognizing her father's voice, Lucy came a little more awake and tried to say something. She was angry and frustrated, and though she was also thinking faster and more clearly by the moment, she was still unable to make a sound.

The nun glanced down at her, and then looked at Tom again. "She has indeed made some progress in the last few days," she said. "Some eye movements, as if she was sleeping normally. And we have seen her try to move her hand, and even to grasp the doctor's hand at one point."

"I'm…here." Lucy struggled to get the words out, but they sounded like a strangled gurgle. Her mouth felt dry, her tongue was sticking to her teeth. Both Tom and the Sister turned at the sound.

"Did ya hear that?" Tom whispered. "She's tryin' t' talk."

"I did," said the nun. "Thank God. I think she's trying to tell us something." She bent over the bed and raising her voice, said "Lucy, dear, if you can hear us, lift your hand."

Lucy tried to obey. She could hear them, but her hand wouldn't respond to her wishes. Then suddenly it got the message and rose, slowly at first, then with more vigor but without direction. Finally, she felt a hand around hers.

"I'm here, I'm here," she gurgled.

"What's that?" Tom bent closer to catch the meaning of the sounds his daughter was making.

"I'm here, I'm here, I'm here!" Lucy was becoming less coherent and more frustrated.

The nun spoke again. "Don't try too hard, dear. Just relax. We can wait." She didn't want too much pressure on her patient. What Lucy needed now was time to reenter life in as peaceful a way as possible, time to gather her strength. The girl seemed to be agitated about something.

She turned to the father. “Mr. O’Leary, can you come into the hall with me, please?”

“But Sister,” he looked from the nun to his daughter and back again, “oughtn’t I to stay by our Lucy in case she needs me?”

“No, just come with me. I’ll explain.” They left the ward, and the nun ushered Tom to one of the benches that lined the walls at regular intervals. Motioning for Tom to take a seat, she sat down beside him.

“Lucy is at a very serious crossroads, so to speak,” she began. “She needs time to recover. I think the best thing for her at the moment is quiet and, believe it or not, a good night’s sleep. I know she looks like she’s been asleep for a couple of weeks, but this is different. She needs the kind of rest that mends, heals, and restores. Natural sleep. That’s the best medicine.”

“Aye, Sister.” Tom was relieved to delay the inevitable. “That makes a lot o’ sense. Ya think it best fer me t’ let her be?”

“I do, Mr. O’Leary, for tonight at least.” Seeing the expression on Tom’s face, Sister Domingo wondered at it. “The rest of your family will be eager to see her, but I think it would be better if visitors were kept to a minimum for the rest of the week. Then we will re-evaluate, and if all is well we can begin to introduce Lucy to her family again.”

Introduce her, Tom thought.

Sister Mary Domingo continued. “You can tell her young man that he should also wait. The only person who should be seeing her is you. At least for the time being.”

Tom nodded his head in agreement, although in truth he wondered if he should really be the one person to be with Lucy. He had grave misgivings on that subject. She would most likely do better with one of her sisters or Bill. Although, he told himself, on second thought, if Lucy was going to remember what had happened and the reason she had been at Maggie's that fateful day, he did not want her sisters to hear it. If he were the one to hear first whatever Lucy had to say, he might be able to do something in the way of damage control. Yes. He nodded his head with more conviction, yes; it would be better the way the Sister suggested. For more than one reason.

They rose from the bench, and the nun escorted Tom to the front door of the hospital, saying, "Come back tomorrow night. I have no doubt she will be more alert by then, and the doctors will have more information for you. Go home and pray for her full recovery…God willing."

Sister Domingo watched as Tom walked away, his shoulders slumped, his head down. *Poor man*, she thought. *He has had a rough time. I hope I have the best of news for him tomorrow when he returns.*

Interns scurried by as Tom joined the procession of visitors leaving the hospital. But he was deep in thought and didn't notice them, nor the nurses who also passed him, their white caps bobbing up and down as they shared confidences and the latest gossip, leaning towards each other with their blue and red capes gathered around them to keep out the wind.

Tom was feeling very alone, and the busy pulse of the hospital was contributing to his feeling of separation. He missed Ellen, and he missed Maggie, too, God forgive him. Ellen was gone. Would he ever see Maggie again? She had made no attempt to contact him.

Before he knew it, he was outside Maggie's house, though he couldn't recall having made the decision to go there. There was no sign of life about the place. A note pinned to the front door instructed the milkman, the bread man, and the paperboy to discontinue delivery until further notice.

Where had she gone? Tom sat down heavily on the front step. *Why is she doin' this t' me when I need her most?* He had been good to both of them, both Ellen and Maggie, and yet now they had both left him. How could he go on alone? He began sobbing and sat on the step until the cold seeped into his bones and his shuddering sobs finally dried up.

Suddenly he sat up straighter. The blame for it all belonged at Lucy's feet! And now that she was recovering, she would bring him more sorrow. She would blame him, would set the rest of his girls against him, would get her sisters to blame him for Ellen's death.

He was helpless to stop this run of misfortune. Why was he being punished? He had looked after Ellen even after she would no longer be a wife to him. Of course, there could never have been a divorce. But he could have left her. Many a man would have.

And what had he done to Maggie for her to turn her back on him? He regretted the names he had called her, but all that was said in anger. He never meant it. Didn't she realize that? What the hell was wrong with women, anyway? They were a scourge sent to torment him. He felt the familiar flame of anger begin to rise within him, but it had nowhere to go, there was no one on whom he could vent it.

In that moment he understood what it was to be alone. Somewhere deep inside, he felt Ellen's sorrow, and an echo of her loneliness curled around his heart. But he refused to acknowledge its presence or give a name to the feeling.

~

Sister Domingo returned again to Lucy's bedside to make sure she was comfortable. Checking the girl's vital signs, she assured herself that everything was stable and decided not to call the doctor. It would be all right to wait until rounds in the morning. Although Lucy was still pale, the nun felt a hint of tension that had not been there before, the palpable aura of the soul returning from its wanderings to take up residence once more in its earthly home.

The nun was sure that she had often witnessed the final departure of a soul, sometimes before and sometimes after the body had been officially pronounced dead. The doctors may have been given the legal authority to determine the time of corporal death, she thought, but God decides when to call home the soul. She glanced down at the girl again. And God had decided it was not yet Lucy's time. He was sending her back. There would be children, grandchildren, great-grandchildren, and generations of souls waiting to be born. Lucy had a life to live.

The girl was feeling the pull of life more strongly now. She was awake, but her eyes were still closed, and she was confused. *Where am I?* She asked herself. She knew that she was in a bed that was not her own. There were those voices again, too, but none were those belonging to anyone in her family. Sensing somehow that she was in good hands, she said to herself, *I need not be afraid.*

There was one voice that seemed to be more familiar that the others. She recognized it from her dream.

"Lucy, can you hear me, dear?"

Who did this voice belong to? She wanted to open her eyes and find out.

"I can hear ya," the girl wanted to say, but the sound that came out of her mouth didn't resemble the thought in her mind. With great effort, she opened her eyes. Everything was still a blur. But it was enough to let them know she was responding.

"Lucy," said the voice, "this is Dr. Hughes. He has been your doctor since you came into the hospital. He would like to examine you."

Then a new voice, deeper and clipped. "Good morning, Lucy. How are you feeling? You have been asleep for quite a long time. I just want to make sure everything is in working order. Can you squeeze my hand?"

Lucy felt a pressure on her left palm and gripped it reflexively.

"Good," said the new voice. "Now let's try the other hand…excellent. Now let's see what's going on with the legs."

The doctor continued to poke, prod, and shine lights until he seemed satisfied with what he found. Lucy, however, was far from satisfied; she felt like hell. Her tongue refused to hook up with her brain. She had a hard time mustering the strength to comply with the doctor's requests, to push this and squeeze that, and no sooner had the doctor finished with her than the nurses began fussing again.

It was just too much. She had no idea what she was doing here, and she didn't have the strength to think it through. She wanted to close her eyes again and find a quiet place in which to gather her scattered wits.

"She's dropped off again Just leave her be, you can finish up later."

Lucy was grateful to the familiar voice and smiled her thanks.

Before walking away, Sister Domingo said a prayer of thanksgiving for Lucy's safe return. She knew now that the girl would walk again. She had responded appropriately to the doctor's prompts and made tiny motions. There did not appear to be any brain damage. She was having trouble with her speech, but the nun was sure that was due more to disuse than to trauma. Sister Domingo was sure it was just a matter of time and care, *thanks be to God.*

~

Tom caught the tram to Crumlin Road after work the next day and spent the trip trying to prepare himself for the difficult task ahead. He knew the doctor would not be at the hospital, but he felt sure the Sister would be able to advise him as to the right thing to do. He didn't know what to expect from her, nor from Lucy. Nor, for that matter, could he predict what to expect from himself. Running and hiding were not options. That much he did know for sure.

Mentally squaring his shoulders, he entered the hospital and went to the ward to just peek in before talking to the nun. He was not prepared to see Lucy sitting up, wide awake, looking the picture of health, and drinking through a straw. She was facing away from the door, and so did not see him.

Jest as well, he thought, bemused. *I don't know what I'd say.* Taking a second look, he realized that her glow was most likely due to the heat in the ward. She had lost a lot of weight, and the hand that held the glass shook slightly. Still, the difference since he had last seen her was, to his mind, a miracle.

He backed out of the ward before she could turn her head and went in search of Sister Domingo. He found her in the office, working on some papers. She looked up at the sound of his knock and motioned for him to come in.

"Evenin', Sister," He remained standing awkwardly in the doorway.

"Good evening, Mr. O'Leary," the nun replied politely. "Have you been by to see Lucy yet?"

"Yes. I jest looked in on her. T' begin with, I couldn't believe me eyes, she looked so well, but I noticed she's lost a bit o' weight, and she seems t' be weak."

"Yes," said the nun, "but she's made a remarkable recovery. It's almost as though she decided she had been asleep long enough and now it's time to get on with her life." She smiled and then, as if to reassure him, added, "But she is very weak, as you say. We will have to be very careful until she builds up a little strength."

Tom shifted his weight and cleared his throat. "What am I ta tell her about her mother? She's sure t' ask me where she is."

"Mr. O'Leary, I can't advise a lie," was the answer in a slightly firmer tone of voice, "but I think for the time being, you should try to be as evasive as you can. Try to give her a few days to get on her feet, as they say. You could tell her visitors are restricted. That would not be lying."

Tom thought it over. *No…that ain't goin' t' do it*, he concluded ruefully. Lucy and Ellen had been so close he didn't think any excuse was going to hold much water with Lucy. The girl would know that wild horses wouldn't keep Ellen away if one of her children was in trouble.

All he could do was thank the nun and return to the ward.

This isn't goin' t' be easy, he thought as he walked. He wondered how Lucy would react to him. Would she remember the fight? Would she blame him for her injury, for her mother's death? He stopped well short of the room and sat himself down on one of the benches to consider the question.

She'll never believe her mother didn't come, he said to himself. Now what would she believe? What if Ellen was too sick to visit? The girls would have to be willing to go along with the story, as would the staff in the hospital. *An' it'll be not easy t' get Sister Domingo t' go along with a lie.* Maybe he could convince the Sister that Lucy wasn't up to the truth just yet. *Yer mother is feelin' poorly jest now*, he rehearsed silently. Nothing too dramatic, of course, but it would have to be enough to keep Ellen away from the hospital.

Armed with this story, he rose from the bench and made his way back to the ward. Lucy had finished her glass of water and was still sitting up, still looking out the window. Once again, she didn't see her father approaching.

"Lucy, luv," he said quietly from the doorway, "how are ya feelin'?"

She turned at the sound of his voice. "I've been better." The words came slowly but were clear, and she smiled a little, as though she were glad to see him.

He breathed a sigh of relief. The ice was broken. "Ya gave us all a scare," he said, his voice a degree cheerier, "but thank God, ye're over the worst of it."

She nodded as though agreeing with him then closed her eyes.

He could see that she was tired. Digging through his pockets, he said, "I brought ya some wee sweets. I'll leave them on the table beside ye." He laid the bag on the table.

Lucy opened her eyes again and nodded her thanks. "Where's me ma?" she asked then, her eyes scanning the room.

He'd known the question would come, but he was unprepared to deal with the tangle of emotions it evoked. He composed himself as best he could, but the lie stuck in his throat. He coughed to dislodge it. "Sure," he said, "sure, an' she's too sick t' come."

"What's the matter with her?" Lucy sounded alarmed.

"Flu," he said. "It's laid her low." Please, no more on the subject. The fewer lies he told, the less he would have to remember.

Lucy's eyes had fluttered closed again. She looked like she had gone back to sleep, but she hadn't. She was just too tired to talk anymore. And something else was troubling her, although just now she couldn't figure out what it was.

Tom sat beside her a few minutes, keeping a silent vigil. It was so quiet he almost fell asleep himself.

"What's the matter with me?" Lucy's voice shattered the quiet and startled her father. "What happened? Why am I here? How long have I been here?" She sounded panicked, as if she had just realized where she was.

"Now, now, luv, don't be gettin' yerself all wound up." Her father sounded a little wound up himself. "Ya had a fall, and hit yer head and got a concussion out of it." That was as much as he could manage right now. "We'll talk about it later. Ya need t' rest now, so ya do. Rising, putting on his cap and coat, he started for the door of the room, then turned as if he'd had a new thought. Rest'll do ya the world o' good. I'll be back tomorrow evenin'." He stepped back into the room and kissed her lightly on the forehead, then retreated again.

"Tell me ma I was askin' after her," Lucy called after him. "Tell her I hope she gets better soon."

Tom nodded as he made his way out of the ward. *That's one hurdle over*, he told himself. *I'll have t' tell the girls what t' say, but that can wait till they see her next week.*

He suddenly realized he was hungry and decided to eat before going home. The little café across the street was still open. It was as good a place as any.

The waitress who greeted him was the same one who'd waited on him that last time, when he had been here with Maggie. The memory of that night was still painful, but he was hungry, and tired of painful thoughts. Ignore it, he thought wearily, and enjoy the meal. It would be nice to be waited on.

Bridie, the waitress, set the menu down and left him to his selection, saying, "I'll be back in a jiffy." It didn't take him long to make a choice, and she was as good as her word, returning to take his order almost immediately.

"What'll ya have?" she asked, her pencil poised over her order book.

"Chips, peas, sausages, an' a cup o' tea, thanks."

"Right ya are. Won't be too long. Evenin' papers over by the door if ye'd like t' have a wee read while yer waitin'."

"Thanks. I'll do that."

Tom selected a paper and settled down for a quiet read and a pleasant meal. It would be nice to eat in the company of other folks, he thought, even if he didn't know them. The chatter of voices, the laughter, the clatter of dishes were a welcome change from the quiet of his home and the disquiet of his thoughts.

"Here we are then, pipin' hot." The food had arrived. Bridie set the plate down in front of him. "Can I be gettin' ya anythin' else?"

"No, thank ya." He laid *The Irish News* on the table. "Sure, this is grand."

The waitress smiled and moved on to the next table. Tom watched her as she went about her work. She was a study in graceful efficiency as she moved around the tiny café, greeting and seating customers, balancing multiple plates, clearing tables, all with a pleasant smile although she must have been on her feet for many hours.

Just watching her had a calming effect on him. He was glad for the respite from his troubles and for the tasty meal.

"Here ya are! I've been lookin' all over fer ya."

The familiar voice startled Tom. His mood popped like a bubble. He looked up. "Bill," he said, "what're ya doin' here?"

"I jest dropped by the hospital t' see what was goin' on with Lucy, but she was sleepin'," said the younger man. "But the Sister told me ye'd jest left, an' I should talk t' you. An' I guessed ya might be here." He seemed excited. "How're things with Lucy? The Sister said her condition had improved, an' that's the best o' news."

"Aye, that's right, so it is," Tom said after just a second. "She was sittin' up in the bed an' talkin'...shure, it's nothin' short o' miraculous, so it is. But she looked tired," he added, "an' I think she's lost a lot o' her strength." Indicating the empty seat, he motioned to Bill to sit down, asking, "Will ya have a wee bite with me?"

"Aye, I will that. Thanks fer askin'. I could do justice to a plate o' what yer havin'. I'm starvin', an' that's no word of a lie." He eased his lanky frame into the chair opposite Tom.

Bridie appeared at Bill's elbow to take his order. Tom noticed that she was still smiling.

"Same as me friend here," Bill said, "an' thank ya".

As Bridie took Bill's order to the kitchen, Tom gazed after her thoughtfully. After a moment, he said to Bill "She's a pleasant one, always seems t' be on an even keel, if ya know what I mean,"

Bill nodded in absent-minded agreement. His thoughts were elsewhere. "Tom," he suddenly said, leaning forward, "do ya think I should wait till Lucy asks t' see me?" He had to ask. "The trouble with that is she might never ask. Do ya think it'd be all right t' visit her in a few days, when she's a bit stronger?"

"Well," said her father, "I'm sure she'd be happy t' see ya when she's feelin' a bit more like talkin' t' people."

That said, silence took over, each man lost in his own thoughts. Tom studied his young friend. *Badly smitten, no mistake, and not the best at hiding his feelings.*

Reflecting, he realized he had no problem with Bill courting his youngest daughter. Of course, there was the difference in their churches, and that would be a big enough problem for some people to kill it right there. But as far as he was concerned, religion was a personal matter between you and your maker. He had no time for the bigots on either side. *Bloody fools*, he thought. Couldn't they understand the futility of fighting? There never would be a winner because the real problem was fear.

The Protestants, who were in the minority, feared for their homes and families without the protection of the English, and the majority Catholics had been given plenty of reason to fear brutal treatment by the English government. He doubted it would ever stop. Each generation was taught to hate at its mother's knee. Each side vilified the other, teaching and preaching suspicion and fear to the point where some Protestant children would run like hell at the very sight of a Catholic priest, for fear of being abducted and sacrificed at a papist altar. And Catholic children ran from any contact with a Prod for fear of being contaminated and consigned to the fires of hell.

Just then Bridie returned with Bill's meal, and her cheery voice brought him back to more immediate concerns.

"There ya go now," she said. "Is that all ye'll be needin'?"

"Sure, this is just what the doctor ordered, thank ya," was Bill's answer. "I'll be no empty skite when I wrap meself around this." And he immediately tucked into his meal with all the gusto of a young, hungry male.

Tom watched his friend with some amusement. Having lived among females for most of his life, it was almost funny to see a meal being enjoyed with such single-minded enthusiasm.

It was only when they had both finished eating that they continued their conversation.

Blowing the steam from a fresh cup of hot tea, Bill asked, "So, Tom, d'ye think Lucy'll make a full recovery? I've been sorely worried about that. I mean, I thought she might wake up, but the real question in me mind was would she be able t' walk, talk, do the things she liked t' do before the accident."

"Aye, that was a worry fer me, too," Tom answered. A worry, fer sure. Walk, talk. Remember. "But they say she should be fine jest as soon as she gets her strength back."

"Have ya told her about her mother yet?

Tom's answer was slow in coming. "No. They don't want me t' tell her yet. I had t' tell her a lie. I said her mother couldn't visit because she was sick. I don't know how she'll take it when she hears the truth of it, her mother dead and buried, an' she sleeps through the whole thing."

Tom and Bill finished their tea in silence and after bidding each other good night went their separate ways.

Chapter Six

Sister Domingo looked up from her work and smiled a greeting as Father Doyle entered her office.

"Good morning, Sister," said the priest. "How many do we have for communion today?"

"Fifteen, Father," she said after doing a quick mental tally. "I just finished the list. Lucy O'Leary has regained consciousness, and she'll need the Sacrament to help her through the next few days. They haven't told her of her mother's death yet."

"What have they been telling her? She would be looking for her mother to come to see her, would she not?" After a pause, he added, "She will indeed be needing all the strength the Holy Sacrament can give her. Well, I'll try to avoid a direct answer if she questions me. Short of a lie, that is."

"Of course, Father. Sometimes knowing too much can be a terrible burden." Sister Domingo hoped that Lucy's faith in God would see her through what promised to be a sore trial. The whole convent was praying for her. Prayer was a powerful force. Lucy's recovery was proof of that.

Father Doyle was frowning as he left the nun's office. He'd already decided to check on Lucy and take the measure of her physical and emotional strength, but now, making his way towards her room, he wondered how to best minister to the girl's spiritual needs while still respecting the family's wishes and without causing her any further distress. Or, for that matter, placing his own soul in jeopardy.

"Well now, how's the invalid doing?" he asked as he approached Lucy's bed.

She was awake and seemed to be alert. "Better. Thanks, Father." Her voice was still scratchy, but it sounded stronger now, more recognizably her own.

"Are you ready to take the Sacrament?" he asked. "I will hear your confession now."

"Yes, Father." Lucy made the sign of the cross and began. "Bless me, Father, for I have sinned...." Here she paused. She knew there was more to this, but couldn't for the life of her remember what sins she had committed.

Father Doyle sensed her confusion. "What sins do you want to confess, my child?"

"I don't know, Father. I can't remember."

"Don't be troubled. Just ask forgiveness for any sins you may have committed since your last confession."

Lucy closed her eyes and recited an act of contrition without hesitation. "Oh, my God, I am heartily sorry t' have offended thee and beg pardon for all my sins...."

The priest smiled and nodded as she finished the prayer. Some things thoroughly taught and learned were never forgotten, he mused. After imparting the sacraments of Absolution and Holy Communion, he also bestowed a blessing. Lucy's mouth was dry, and she had trouble swallowing the Host. Curling her tongue, she coaxed the wafer off her palette. The priest made the sign of the cross once more, patted her on the head, and by the time she had managed to swallow the Host, he was gone. He was pleased to be able to take care of Lucy's spiritual needs without having to answer any difficult questions regarding her mother's absence.

Because the doctors had decided to allow Lucy some limited time out of bed, Sister Domingo now instructed two of the orderlies to help her into the day room. It would be a welcome change of scenery for the girl, for the room was bright and sunny.

Lucy was grateful to sink into a shabby but comfortable chair by the window. Scanning the room, she thought wryly that the plants looked the way she felt. Limp and tired. Books, papers, and magazines were scattered on tables around the room. Lifting a well-worn newspaper from the table nearest her, she saw from the date that it was about two weeks old. *Still new t' me*, she thought. After a quick glance at the headlines, she decided she hadn't missed much. Robberies, fires, the usual political arguments filled the top of the folded front page.

Then she unfolded the paper and was confronted by the image of her mother's smiling face above the headline *Local Woman Killed by Falling Tree.*

Her scream was heard throughout the floor and brought everyone running to the day room. When Sister Domingo arrived, the anxious crowd that had gathered parted to let her through.

Lucy had hurled the crumpled newspaper at the wall and was bent over her knees, keening and rocking back and forth. "Please God," she wailed, "not me ma…don't take me ma…please God…."

Kneeling at her side, Sister Domingo gathered the grieving girl into her arms and rocked with her, murmuring, "There, there, hush, child. She's with God. It's God's will."

A bolt of white-hot anger shot through Lucy and her body arched away from the nun's embrace. "God's will, is it?" she shrieked. "God's will t' take me ma? God's will be damned!" There was a reflexive gasp in her audience at the blasphemy. "It's the work o' the devil!"

A collective intake of breath and a flurry of motion went around the room as those listening crossed themselves for protection.

"Me ma was a saint, so she was! She never hurt a soul, why would God let her be killed?"

As Lucy suddenly realized that she was speaking of her mother in the past tense, she curled into a ball as a fresh wave of grief and impotent anger washed through her. It was too much for her weakened body. The room began to spin.

Sister Domingo acted swiftly, tightening her arms around the girl to prevent her falling, then laying her gently back in the chair. She instructed the orderlies to move Lucy to a private room and designated another nun to sit with her until she regained consciousness. She was sure Lucy's body would recover, given a little rest and quiet. Fainting was often nature's way of providing respite from a situation too painful to bear. The girl's mental condition might take longer, however, for she had experienced both physical and psychological trauma.

But she wasn't shocked by Lucy's blasphemous outburst. She had heard worse. Grief often chooses God as the enemy.

~

Lucy woke in a dark, quiet room, feeling warm, cozy, and rested. She was groggy at first and only partly aware of the hushed voices in the room, though she had no real interest in what they were saying. She just wanted to stay where she was, to be left in peace.

Tom and the girls stood in a little knot in the darkened room, whispering. It had come as a shock to him the night before when he had come to visit Lucy and been told that she was in a private room. Then he learned she had suffered some kind of setback. After talking with Sister Domingo, he had decided that he should bring Lucy's sisters. Lucy had recovered from the fainting spell, the nun said, but was in such an agitated state that they had decided to sedate her.

She apparently had no memory of the events leading up to her mother's death, and he wasn't sure if she would ever remember. Well, he could worry about that later.

She was restless under the family's gaze, drifting in and out of consciousness, aware at times of familiar voices but unable to comprehend or respond. Her sisters exchanged worried glances, but they were at a loss as to how to help their ailing sister, so they contented themselves by holding her hand, applying cool compresses, and fussing with the pillows and bed linen. Tom stood quietly at the foot of his daughter's bed. Visiting hours were now coming to a close, and having kissed the unresponsive patient goodnight, the family filed out of the room.

Sometime later, Lucy regained consciousness and was overcome once more by a great wave of loss. Her mother was dead. She was in the hospital because her father had hit her. Had hurt her. Her mother was dead. Everything had happened on the same day. Her father had hurt her. Her mother had died. Her mother was dead.

~

Tom and the girls returned to the hospital the following night to find a No Visitors sign on Lucy's door, with instructions below it to report to Sister Domingo's office. The puzzled and nervous family made their way down the hall. The nun's door was open, and she gestured for them to come in.

Tom was the first to speak. "What's up with our Lucy? The sign says no visitors. What's happened? Is she worse?"

Sister Domingo shook her head. "Mr. O'Leary, may I see you alone for a moment?"

Tom nodded with a puzzled frown and signaled for the girls to leave the room.

"She does not want to see you, Mr. O'Leary. Apparently, she is holding you accountable for her mother's death."

Tom was dumbfounded. How was he going to explain this turn of events to the girls?

Sister Domingo rose awkwardly from her seat behind the desk.

"I have some things to attend to," she said. "I will leave you alone to talk. Please take as long as you like," she said, signaling to the girls to come back in. Then she left, closing the door behind her. The soft click of the latch was the only sound in the heavy silence.

As the girls exchanged confused glances, Tom remained silent. He had been dreading this moment. Now that it was here, he had no idea how he was going to make his daughters understand.

Nellie spoke first. "What's this all about, Da?" she asked, fearing she was about to hear something that would make her sorry she had asked.

Tom only shook his head and ran his fingers through his hair. Feelie and Mary Alice were silent and still. Only their eyes moved. He could feel three pairs of eyes fixed on his face. He searched for words.

"She's layin' the blame fer yer mother's death on me," he said finally, reluctantly.

"What happened? Will ya please tell us?"

He was cornered. There was no way out. What could he possibly say? He was having trouble formulating the words. What he was about to tell them might cause a rift that might never mend.

"I had a friend," he finally said, surprised at how thick his voice sounded. Like I've been drinkin', he thought.

There was a long pause. "Someone who loved me," he went on, and then suddenly the words came in a rush. "We had an understandin'. She knew I could never leave ya girls, or yer mother, but she was content t' be with me on those terms. I've been visitin' her every Saturday fer some time. We never meant t' hurt anyone."

The girls' eyes were wide, and their mouths dropped open, but when nothing was said, he continued, his voice slowing again.

"Lucy came round t' her house lookin' fer me. And there was a row. Lucy was disrespectful, both t' me and t' her, an' I lost me temper an' hit her. She fell an' hit her head." Another unbearable pause. "The rest ya know."

Feelie was the first to speak. "Disrespectful, is it? Yer sayin that's a good one." Her voice began low, but soon began to rise, cracking with contempt as it did. "Are ya tellin' us, Da, are ya tellin' us that ya were bein' serviced by some hoor, is that what yer sayin'? IS IT? And our Lucy was bein' disrespectful. To a hoor and her fancy man? Answer me!"

Tom shook his head as though he could not believe the words his daughter was using. He could not imagine where she had learned such coarse speech. "It...we...never...we never felt that way about each other. It wasn't like that. No, it was never like that." He sounded pathetic, even to himself.

Feelie stepped closer to him. "Oh, I see...ye loved this loose tart and broke yer marriage vows. ya sinned against God, disgraced yer family when it was convenient fer the pair o' youse?" Her color was high, and she was almost shrieking. She took one step closer to him. They were almost chest to chest now. "Yer hoormongerin' killed our mother! Our Lucy's right, isn't she? Ya have our ma's blood on yer hands, as sure as if ya took a knife and slit her throat. You and that filthy rotten bitch'll roast in hell fer the murder of a saint!"

Feelie's sisters were as shocked by her outburst as their father was. Didn't she know the way of the world? When men weren't satisfied at home, they went elsewhere. It happened all the time. It was a sin for a Catholic to have sex without the intention of conceiving a child. The church forbade birth control. Most women suffered in silence. But the men had other ideas, and their father apparently no different from any other.

Feelie had watched her mother try to put the best face on her husband's absences, and it had made her sick. She had vowed never to let any man put her in that position. She had watched her sisters walk down the aisle, decked out in their virginal white finery. *Like the proverbial lambs to the slaughter*, she thought. Nine months later, after hours of agonizing pain, the first baby would arrive and then year after year, another and another. The slim figures would disappear, never to return.

Meanwhile, the men would begin to cast their glances elsewhere. The girls spent their young lives buried under a mountain of dirty nappies, soothing colicky babies and trying to survive on two or three hours of sleep, while the men had a time in the pub or with some floozy. Not her. She would find another way to live her life. She felt Nellie touch her hand.

"Feelie, will ya not be makin' a show of us in front o' the whole hospital? Fer God's sake, keep yer voice down." Nellie, being the oldest, thought it was her place to keep the family in order since her mother's death, but Feelie would have none of it.

She decided to give full vent to her feelings. "I'll NOT keep me voice down! Too many women keep their voices down while the men keep 'em barefoot an' pregnant, an' then take off t' satisfy themselves!"

She thought of the priests for whom she cooked and cleaned. They had taken a vow of poverty. Some poverty, she thought. Four square meals a day served on china dishes. Well-appointed, comfortable rooms cleaned, and linen changed for them. Floors polished, dishes washed, clothes scrubbed, windows washed, and that was just in the rectory.

In the church the nuns did all the menial work: laying out vestments, polishing pews, cleaning silver, arranging flowers, filling the holy water fonts, and on and on, helped by an army of volunteer women who stretched a pay packet to its limits to feed and clothe the children mandated by the Church. There would be many a day when these women would subsist on a cup of tea and a piece of toast. If they were lucky. It was a man's world, all right, and women were the fools who gave them the power.

There were few options, Feelie knew, for a woman with her education outside marriage, but she had decided there had to be another way for her. She was determined to find it. She would not get caught in the marriage trap, and working for the priests was not the answer. She could see herself years from now, a dried-up old maid still dancing attendance on a crowd of demanding men of the cloth. No home of her own. In fact, nothing to show for years of service but a bent back and red, chapped hands. Yes, she would have to find another way to earn her living.

Nellie's voice broke into her thoughts and brought her down to earth. "Are ya all done with yer bad mouth?" she asked. "I've never heard the likes of it. Ya should be ashamed o' yerself."

"Oh? I should be ashamed? That's a good one." Feelie turned on her sister. "After me da tells us he's been lyin' to us an' committin' adultery. Where's yer loyalty to our ma? She's in the cold earth because o' him an' the woman."

Nellie did not back away. "Would ya be wantin' a bullhorn so the whole world'll know the way of it? Ma would never have wanted what happened in the family t' be common knowledge. Fer her sake, if fer nobody else's, can ya learn t' keep yer trap shut?"

Tom, who seemed to have been in a trance, blinked and stepped forward. "That's enough, girls," he said. "Ye'll both be behavin' like decent young women, the way yer mother brought ya up. Show some respect fer her memory."

But Feelie turned on him again. "Respect is it yer talkin' about? Ya should've thought about that when Ma was alive."

Mary Alice had been silent throughout the exchange. Her father's confession was a shock, and now she was suddenly learning a lesson in trust. She adored her father and had even married a man who resembled him. Was she, she was asking herself, was she following in her mother's footsteps? What could she do to rekindle the passion she and Brian had shared in the early days of their marriage? Nellie's marriage to Séan seemed to be a happy one. She would talk to her, get some advice. She missed her mother. But her father would be no help.

The room was silent.

Sister Domingo knocked lightly on the door, and when there was no response, she quietly came in. There would have to be some arrangements made with regard to Lucy's eventual discharge. They would also need to make new visiting rules for this family while Lucy was still in the hospital. Lucy refused to see her father, but had asked to see her sisters.

The nun touched Tom on the shoulder. "Lucy would like to see her sisters," she said as normally as she could manage. "Perhaps you would like to wait here while the girls visit?"

Tom nodded and sat down heavily in the chair by the door. He was surprised by the girls' reactions. Mary Alice had said nothing. Nellie had not condemned him. Most surprising had been Feelie's impassioned outburst. Her language had come as a shock to him. She had never spoken like that before. He'd expected a strong reaction from all of his daughters. Given Lucy's devotion to her mother, he had feared her denunciation would be the worst, but it seemed that the married girls, at least, had some understanding of his situation. Despite the emotional response from both Feely and Lucy, he hoped they would forgive him, in time.

It seemed to him that marriage had mellowed Nellie and Mary Alice, and he was surprised to realize that he wasn't so sure that was a good thing. Some of their fire had been dampened. He had obviously failed to notice the subtle changes that had taken place. Lucy had always been a firecracker, but Feelie used to be much quieter. Where had all her animosity towards men come from? Was it his fault? What else was going on in the lives of the other girls?

He had no idea. His daughters had always been something of a mystery to him, and he'd left it to his wife to mold them into women he could be proud of. She supervised their schoolwork and religious instruction, taught them cooking and sewing, and prepared them to be good wives and mothers.

But now his wife was gone, and he was at a loss as to how to deal with his daughters. It had never occurred to him to be involved with their upbringing, and after Lucy came along, he and his wife had drifted apart emotionally, with Maggie filling the void. Tom had convinced himself that his wife was content with the life he gave her. She had her girls, he observed, she had her home and most importantly to her, he was convinced, her religion. That had always seemed to be enough.

Now, hearing Feelie's bitter condemnation of him, he wasn't so sure, not at all. He wished he could go back in time, back to the days when he and Ellen were young and in love. Could things have been different for them? Or were they doomed from the start?

He realized that he would never know. A blanket of despair settled over and around him then. He felt broken, bereft of his daughters' respect as without a backward glance they filed out of the nun's office.

~

Lucy looked up as her sisters entered the room. She was feeling a little stronger and was happy to see them.

"How're ya feelin', luv?" Nellie asked by way of a greeting.

"I could be better," Lucy answered, "but I am better than I was. Thanks."

She motioned for her sisters to sit beside her. For a moment, they all looked at one another, and a mixture of tenderness and tension filled the room.

Then Lucy sat up a little straighter. "I want t' know what happened t' Ma." Her sisters recognized her tone. It was one they had heard many times before. "Nobody will talk t'me about it. I jest have the piece in the paper. Will ya please tell me?"

There was an awkward pause, and Lucy's three sisters lowered their eyes. It was Feelie who answered.

"Sure, ye're not well enough t' be talkin' about that yet," she whispered. "We'll tell ya everythin' when ye're a wee bit stronger."

But Lucy wanted answers now. She needed to know what had happened while she slept. "I think I have a right t' know now," she said.

Seeing her sister becoming agitated, Nellie decided it would be better to risk telling her the truth than for her to become hysterical and possibly to pass out again. They had been there for each other after hearing the news. Now Lucy deserved the same support. But Nellie knew she would have to be very careful in the telling. She knew Tom blamed Lucy and Lucy blamed Tom. *An' whatever the truth is*, she thought, *havin' someone t' blame won't bring Ma back*. She took a breath.

"I'll tell ya, luv," she said, "but ye'll have t' promise t' stay calm. Ye're still weak, an' ya don't want t' have t' stay here longer than ya have to."

She took another, deeper breath.

"Well, you know from the newspaper piece, Mammy was on her way t' see ya in the hospital."

The other girls, for whom this was not news, began to sob quietly. Lucy did not speak, although her eyes began to narrow slightly.

"It was a foul night and a fallin' tree limb hit her," Nellie continued. "It crushed her skull, an' she died instantly. Sure, she never saw it comin', an' she didn't suffer at all. She was buried beside our Richard. It was a grand funeral, an' well-attended."

Lucy closed her eyes. Yes, the weather had been miserable that day. "Did she know why I was in the hospital?" she asked, her eyes still closed.

"No, I don't think so. A wee lad came t' tell her ye'd been hurt, but he didn't know the whole story."

"Are ya sure she didn't suffer? Who found her? She could've been lyin' in the rain an' nobody there t' help her."

Nellie shook her head. "No, she was found by the same wee fella, an' she had just left the house a few minutes before he did. It was quick an' merciful, thanks be t' God."

"Do ya know how all this came about?"

"Yes. Da told us just now."

Lucy exploded. "Did he tell ya he was with a woman? Did he tell ya that he struck me an' put me in the hospital? They killed our ma, they did. Murdered her, so they did. She died little by little every time he went out t' see the woman an' left her sittin' by the fire. The branch jest finished her off."

And now Lucy began to cry, dry, racking sobs, as her sisters looked on, helpless to comfort her. After a minute, Nellie climbed onto the bed and held her youngest sister in her arms, but she knew her grief would have to run its course.

Lucy's voice was softer when she spoke again, without the same bite, but they could all still hear the steel in it. "I…I…I don't ever want t' set eyes on him again," she said. "I'll never be able t' do it without seein' Ma's face an' rememberin' what he did t' her."

Nellie found a hankie and wiped her eyes. "Hush, hush now, ya don't want t' be sayin' things ya don't mean." She knew it was too soon to try to talk Lucy into a forgiving state of mind, but felt she had to try.

"Ah, but I do mean it," Lucy hissed. "So help me, God, every last word of it."

Mary Alice hoped a prayer would help Lucy feel she was doing something to help their mother. "Ya need t' rest now," she said. "Let's say a prayer fer Mammy's soul." And so she led them in a decade of the rosary.

As usual, the quiet, repetitive drone of voices chanting in unison had a soporific effect, and Lucy, depleted by emotional stress, closed her eyes and succumbed to sleep. Her sisters slipped out of the room.

Chapter Seven

When Bill returned to the hospital eight weeks later, his intention was to find the nun and ask after Lucy's progress. The wait had been much longer than he had anticipated. Tom had not gotten in touch with him after their shared dinner in the café, and they were now working different shifts at the shipyard. Bill knew that this time in the life of that family was especially tricky, but he had gotten too impatient to hear the news. So here he was, pacing the hospital corridors without a clear idea of where to go. Rounding a corner, he all but sent Lucy's sisters flying.

Recovering from the surprise, Feelie was the first to speak. "Ah Bill, it's good t' see ye."

"An' I'm sorry I almost knocked ya down," said Bill, flustered. "I was in too much of a hurry and not minded t' look where I was headed. I feel like an' eejit, so I do."

"Don't be beatin' yerself up," said Mary Alice. "Sure it was jest an accident an' no harm done at all." She liked Bill and wanted to put him at ease as quickly as possible.

"Thank ya kindly," he said. "I jest came t' find out how Lucy is doin'. Have ya been seein' her?"

"Yes," said Feelie, "an' she is much improved, but still on the weak side. We jest left her t' sleep fer a while."

"I'd like t' see her," he said, as if there were any doubt, "but not until she feels like havin' visitors. Would ya be askin' her, please, if I could come by? An' when?"

"Well," said Nellie after only a brief pause, "she can't have any visitors except the family right now." Then, when Bill's expression changed, she hastened to add, "But I'll be sure t' tell her you were by. I'm sure she'll be glad t' see ya as soon as they'll let her."

Nellie was afraid that Bill would ask how Lucy had reacted to the news of her mother's death. She didn't know just how to tell him the story without going into the situation with the other woman, which she thought was best kept in the family. *Bad cess to the whole thing*, she told herself. It had brought nothing but trouble to her family. She also feared the story would be a juicy piece of gossip for the neighborhood battle-axes. After all, Ellen's funeral had been the main topic of conversation for weeks. Nellie knew that some of the old biddies had been jealous of the fine turnout, considering it an indication of Tom's regard for his wife. They would just love to sink their teeth into this morsel of news. But then, upon further reflection, she remembered that Bill had no more than a nodding relationship with any of their neighbors, coming as he did from the Protestant part of town. *An' he seems a decent lad*, she said to herself, *an' it'd be nice t' get the perspective of another man, one not involved in such a situation.* Perhaps she could confide in him and seek his discretion. She would discuss it with her sisters, she decided. But it could wait until later. She didn't have to tell him anything just yet, as he would still not be seeing Lucy for a while.

Bill's voice interrupted her train of thought. "I'll be goin' along then," he said. "Tell yer father I was askin' after him as well, will ya?"

"We will that," said Nellie, "an' we thank ya kindly fer all yer help. I'll leave word with Sister Domingo when our Lucy's fit t' see visitors. Ya can check with her on yer way home from work. It's closer than me da's house or ours.

Promising to check with the nun the following week, Bill agreed, and took his leave of the sisters.

Nellie breathed a sigh of relief. She would have a few days to discuss things with her sisters and her father before Bill spoke with Lucy. She wasn't sure how far her sister's relationship with the lad had progressed, but she was sure it would continue if Bill had anything to do with it.

And so, early the next week, Bill was glad to hear from Sister Domingo that Lucy was well enough to receive visitors and would welcome a visit from him. The nun cautioned him against staying too long, however, as Lucy still tired easily.

He was a little nervous as he approached the room. So much had happened since he had last seen her. Everything had changed for her. They had had so little time to really get to know one another, and she was unaware of the vigil he had kept at her bedside while she lay unconscious, time spent thinking how much he cared about a girl he hardly knew. He hoped she would allow him the chance to continue getting to know her when she was released from the hospital. Entering the room, he was surprised to see how well she looked. She was sitting in a chair by the window, her hair caught back with a bright blue ribbon. A blanket lay across her knees. As he approached, she laid aside the book she was reading and greeted him with a warm smile.

"Well now," he said, "don't ya look the picture o' health."

"Thanks, Bill. I'm feelin' much better." Her voice was strong and clear. "Me sisters tell me ya were here while I was unconscious. I'm indebted t' ya fer yer kindness."

"I was glad t' be of help while the family was goin' through such a sad time," he replied. "I'm sorry fer yer loss, Lucy. It must've been a terrible shock when they told ya."

"Aye.... But shock's not the word fer it." Her expression clouded over, and she seemed to withdraw.

Bill was sorry he had mentioned her mother's death, but he could hardly ignore it. In an effort to change the subject, he offered the flowers he had brought. "I brought ya these wee flowers. I hope the bright colors will cheer ya up. Do ya know when ye'll be gettin' out o' here? ya must be itchin' t' go home."

"I'm itchin' t' get out," she said in a quiet voice, "but not t' go home. I'll never go there again."

This was said with such vehemence that Bill wondered what other can o' worms he had opened. He was beginning to think the best course of action would be to keep his mouth shut, but he couldn't just sit here without saying something. He cast about for something safe, but all he could come up with was a rather lame. "How so?"

"I'll never set foot in that house as long as me da is there."

Now Bill had the feeling he had disturbed a wasp's nest. What on earth was going on with that family? He didn't think he wanted to know, but he had a feeling he was going to find out whether he wanted to or not.

"They killed me ma," said Lucy. "Those two...me da and his floozy."

"Lucy, what on earth are ya sayin'? Yer mother was killed by a fallin' tree limb."

"Aye, that was the end of her, but those two were the cause of it with their carryin' on…me da committin' adultery an' breakin' me ma's heart."

Now Bill was really alarmed. He had no idea that Tom was engaged in a relationship with anyone other than his wife. How could Lucy be laying the guilt at Tom's feet? There was more to this situation, he thought, but he didn't know if he wanted to hear the rest of the story. Tom was his friend. He decided to tread cautiously. At the same time, he needed to learn more in order to understand Lucy's anger. Now that she was out of the woods health-wise, he hoped that they could continue to get to know one another better. He had so far envisioned her return home as a joyful occasion, one that the family was sorely in need of in light of the events of the past few weeks.

But that now appeared to be out of the question. *I'm caught between th' devil an' th' deep blue sea*, he thought. How was he to juggle his friendship with Tom with his courtship of Lucy?

"Where are ya goin' t' go if not t' yer home?" he asked cautiously.

"Oh, I'll ask me sister Mary Alice. There's not enough room at our Nellie's, but Mary Alice has a spare room till the new baby comes."

"When is the baby due? And what will ya do after that?"

"The baby's due in about three months," she said. "I'm not sure what I'll do after, but I'll figure somethin' out before that, so I will. Bill, don't be worryin' yerself about me…fer where there's a will there's a way. That's what me ma used t' say, may she rest in peace."

Bill observed a moment of silence, as much to give himself time to think as to show respect for the dead. He decided it would be a good idea to try to get off this subject and on to a more pleasant one.

"I was wonderin' if, uh," he ventured, "if, when ye're feelin' up t' it ye'd be likin' t' go fer a spin in the country? The fresh air would do ya the world o' good."

Lucy's face lit up at the idea. "I would that! It'd be grand t' feel the wind in me face again. Maybe we could stop at the Cave Hill an' have a wee picnic?"

Now that they had plans, Bill decided this would be a good time to bring the visit to a close, before the subject of her father's dalliance—if that's what it was—came up again. He was surprised that Tom's daughter would think her father was having an affair, also surprised that she blamed it for her mother's death. But he thought it better to leave on a happier note. No doubt she would tell him more, but it would be safer to wait until she was stronger.

"I'd best be goin' before they throw me out," he said. "They said not t' tire ye, an' I don't want t' outstay me welcome. I'll be comin' back, if that's all right with ya." He stood up and made for the door, then turned. "Do ya need anythin' special?"

"Thanks fer comin'," Lucy said warmly, "an' sure, ya can come again. I'll be lookin' forward t' it. Oh, I know, since ya asked could ya bring me a wee poke o' brandy balls? Me throat gets that dry in here."

"Brandy balls it is," he said. "Try t' get some rest. I'll be back tomorrow."

Lucy's family situation was not something he knew how to handle. As he left the hospital, he began pondering the advisability of mentioning it to Tom the next time he saw him. He wondered if Tom was aware of Lucy's feelings and, if so, how he would respond to her accusations. If Lucy were right, then things would be very difficult indeed.

Bill did not approve of a married man carrying on with a mistress, but on the other hand, it was family business, and he was not family. The safest route to travel, he decided, would be one of silence. *Least said, soonest mended*, as his own dear mother had always said. She had drummed the words and their meaning into his head from the time he was a wee lad, and the advice had always stood him in good stead and kept him from uttering many a word better left unsaid.

He decided to stop by the café to have some supper.

~

As the door closed behind Bill, Lucy lay back against the pillow and thought about his visit. She felt a little guilty for involving him in her family's troubles, but he had a way of making her feel safe and protected, and somehow she had known he would understand.

He was a nice fella, to be sure, kind and considerate. Not the type she could fall head over heels for, though. And he was a Protestant, anyway, and that was trouble in the making. Still, she liked him and enjoyed his company, and it wasn't like she was marrying him, was it? They hadn't had time to really get to know each other. But they could have some good times together, she decided. *No harm in that, for sure.* She smiled at the thought of a pleasant ride in the country on the back of Bill's motorbike...another reason to look forward to the day when she could say goodbye to this place.

~

Bill crossed the street to the café, where he wove a path to the back of the room and settled himself into a booth by the window. Through it, he saw Lucy's sisters walking towards the hospital.

An' where's Tom? he asked himself.

The thought had no sooner crossed his mind than the man himself entered the café. The waitress, Bridie, Bill remembered her name, was the same one who had waited on them before. She crossed the floor and greeted Tom with a smile and a pat on the arm. The two of them began talking together in the manner of old friends. Or maybe…. And then, as Bill watched in shocked fascination, Bridie laid one hand on Tom's shoulder, went up on her toes, and whispered something in his ear, which elicited a knowing smile from him. This was far from the friendly but businesslike service they had received on their last visit.

Was this, Bill was wondering, the woman Lucy had told him about? No, it couldn't be the same one. Her attitude had been quite different the last time. The waitress looked happy as she settled Tom at a table in the corner of the little café. They were still talking, and when she slapped him playfully, Tom laughed, caught her hand, and brought it to his lips.

That did it. Now Bill felt like a voyeur. He didn't want to witness this scene. He wondered how he was going to get out of the café without having to acknowledge Tom's presence. He hadn't ordered yet, and the waitress was obviously too busy with Tom to notice, so he decided to make a run for it. He slipped quietly out of the booth and made for the door. Once outside, he headed back to the hospital. He had to think of some way to divert the girls. He hated to think what would happen if they happened upon the cozy little tryst in the café.

What the hell am I gettin' meself into? he asked himself. *I should jest go home an' wash me hands of the whole situation. It's none o' me business, anyway.*

But then he thought of the girls, so recently bereaved, and his conscience, as usual, got the better of him. They didn't need this. He was furious at Tom. What was the man thinking? Was he fooling around with two women? He needed a good kick in the arse, the selfish bastard. *How am I goin' t' get the girls out o' the hospital an' far enough away so they'd not run into their father?* He would have to be very creative.

He ran down the street to the confectionery and tobacconist at the corner and bought a quarter pound of brandy balls. This would be his excuse for returning to Lucy's room. Then he would invite the girls to have an ice with him at the Italian's place at the rear of the hospital. That way, if they accepted he could maneuver them out the back of the hospital and away from the café and any sight of their father.

He could hear the girls laughing in Lucy's room, and when he heard his name mentioned, he realized they had been teasing Lucy about his visit. He knocked and opened the door at their invitation to come in. The sisters looked a little sheepish as they lowered their eyes and giggled quietly, as girls will when caught in the act. Lucy was the first to recover her composure and her manners.

"Ah, Bill," she said, "we were jest talkin' about ye. What brought ya back? Did ya ferget somethin?"

"No. But I brought ya somethin'." He was amused at the very offhand way she had confessed to talking about him and wondered just what the interrupted conversation had been about. "So ya were jest talkin' about me, were ya? And what, might I ask, were ya sayin?"

Mary Alice smiled at him. "Oh, nothin' bad, t' be sure," she said. "We were jest sayin' how pretty the flowers were an' Lucy was sayin' how ya had brought 'em fer her." She hoped he had not heard them ribbing Lucy about stepping out with a Prod. He was such a nice fella. If the other Prods were like him, maybe she could be persuaded that Protestants weren't all that bad. Bill reminded her of her Brian when they were first married. That seemed like such a long time ago. She sighed to herself, and the laughter faded from her eyes.

"Well, an' I'm glad it was nothin' bad," Bill said. "Here, I brought Lucy some sweets she asked fer. She said she got dry in here. I didn't want t' leave it till tomorrow…."

Lucy was touched. "Oh, Bill, thank ya, but ya needn't have gone ta all that trouble. I'm much obliged, though, fer yer kindness."

They could hear the nurse coming down the hall to begin telling visitors that visiting hours were over. Bill decided he'd better act quickly.

"Well," he began, "I expect we'd better be gettin' along. I'm feelin' a bit on the dry side meself. Would you girls allow me ta treat ya to an ice cream? It's no fun eatin' on yer own."

Put like that, and in the light of his many kindnesses, the girls could do nothing but accept his offer.

"I wish I could go with ya," Lucy said wistfully.

Taking her hand, Bill promised her that on the day of her release from the hospital, he would buy her the biggest Peach Melba she'd ever seen. He was very proud of the way he had manipulated the situation, hopefully to avoid further trouble. He couldn't help thinking that there would be murder done if Lucy knew what was going on across the street.

So they all said their goodbyes and trooped out, promising to come back the following night. Sister Domingo watched from her office as they passed, chatting among themselves, and smiled at them, thinking how carefree they looked in spite of everything. The way young people should be, she thought, and she hoped the black cloud of misfortune was at last lifting away from them....

The black cloud had other ideas.

Chapter Eight

Tom sat at his table until Bridie was off-duty. They were going to the pictures, but Bridie had told him that first she would love an ice cream at the little place at the back of the hospital, the one she sometimes visited on her way home from work.

Tom wasn't one for ice cream, but if that's what Bridie wanted, he decided, that's what Bridie would get. He was feeling closer to her than to anyone in a while. They had been out together a few times over the past few weeks, as he needed someone to comfort him in his sorrow over the loss of his beloved wife. Bridie was tenderhearted and lonely. She could see no harm in comforting him.

As for Tom, well, Ellen was gone, and Maggie, too. He figured he was free to do as he liked, and he liked Bridie. He planned never to marry again, but he needed a woman in his life. This time on his terms, however—no responsibility, no promises, and no priests telling him what to do. For the first time in his life, he was a free man, and he was going to stay that way. That was his plan.

Although Bridie certainly didn't mind a little kiss and cuddle, she was no loose woman. Long hours on her feet left her with little enthusiasm for energetic nocturnal pursuits. A tub of hot water to soak her aching feet was her idea of nightlife. Past the first bloom of youth, and possibly the second, although she had determined that she was not yet an old woman, she was ready to settle down. She could still have a husband and home of her own. And she planned to have them. All she wanted was a little security, some pleasant company, and a warm body. Maybe even a child, though that was getting less likely with each passing year. Tom was a little older, but that didn't bother her. He was fun, and he treated her as a lady should be treated. That was enough for now.

As they were leaving the café, there was a crack of thunder followed immediately by a sudden downpour. Taking shelter in a small doorway directly across the street from the ice cream place, they huddled together against the driving rain. Bridie had her back to the road. Looking over her shoulder, Tom was horrified to see the door of the ice cream parlor open as a small group emerged. Jaysus Christ! It was the girls! And Bill was with them.

The rain let up as swiftly as it had begun, and Bridie was beginning to turn towards the street. Tom pulled her toward him and kissed her. It was a long kiss. Bridie could feel his heart pounding and responded to his excitement. Placing her hands against the sides of his face, closing her eyes she kissed him with more passion than she knew she possessed.

His eyes were wide open. He was still watching over her shoulder as his family turned the corner and vanished from sight. His mind was in a whirl as other parts of his body were having a hard time deciding where to send the adrenaline. The need for "flight or fight" was over, but something else was definitely going on.

He'd been a married man and had a mistress, but he had never been kissed like this before. His chaste Catholic wife had never taken the initiative; indeed, he'd often thought she was secretly happy that the church had forbidden them intercourse after Lucy's birth. So he'd turned to Maggie to fill the void, but she, too, was reserved in their lovemaking. Now this…this was something he hadn't even known existed. He wanted more. Drawing Bridie closer into the circle of his arms, he kissed her again, his heart and body reveling in this new sensation.

Bridie was breathless. When had the pounding of the thunder ended and the pounding of her heart begun? It was as though her years of lonely solitude had just now melted and lay in a puddle at her feet, and she was as boneless and light as a feather. She felt young again, and a long-forgotten giddiness overcame her. Was this what people meant when they spoke of happiness? She had long been resigned to, and sometimes content with, her lot, but now she felt cheated. So much time wasted, so much to make up.

They stood in silence for a while, collecting their thoughts. Tom was the first to speak, his voice shaking slightly.

"Oh, my God," was all he said. Taking her hand, he guided her across the street and bought her the promised ice cream.

Chapter Nine

A week later, Lucy was discharged from the hospital, and Mary Alice agreed to put her up until the baby arrived. Lucy thanked the doctors and nurses and gave special thanks to Sister Domingo for all her kindness. She was a little sad to say goodbye to the kindhearted nun, but thankful to see the end of her hospital stay.

When Bill offered to take the day off and see Lucy safely to her sister's house, she accepted gratefully. They gathered the assorted gifts and cards she'd received and packed her bag. Bill hoisted it and, cupping her elbow, ushered her into the outside world. It was a beautiful, brisk afternoon, the sun peeping out from the lambs' wool clouds as they scudded across the azure sky. Lucy stopped for a moment to lift her face to the warmth of the sun and take a deep breath of fresh air.

Suddenly, there was commotion as a raucous group of young men approached, shaking tin cans. One was dressed as a baby with a nappy fastened by huge safety pins, a large pacifier swinging from a ribbon and banging against his hairy chest. Another was wearing the robe and wig of a judge, and behind him came a grotesque, bearded ballet dancer, six foot two with the muscular legs of an athlete encased in bright pink tights that matched his tutu. On they came, seeming to compete with each other to look the most ridiculous. They were followed and accompanied by a long parade. At first the noisy crowd startled Lucy, but then she realized they were students from Queens University. It must be Rag Day, the day the students took over the city, raising hell as they collected money for charity. If you were foolish enough to refuse to make a contribution, you would find yourself taken prisoner and unceremoniously dumped in a portable cage on wheels and paraded around town.

Of course, most of the prisoners were young attractive girls who would eventually be ransomed by some gallant student who paid to have her released. The idea was that she would be forever grateful to her rescuer, who would demand a kiss to repay him for his chivalry. It was all intended to be good-natured fun, but sometimes the lads had a little too much to drink, and since the costumes made them anonymous, the play could unexpectedly turn a little rough.

Lucy panicked a little when she realized she had no money, but Bill fished the required contribution out of his pocket and placed a sheltering and proprietary arm around Lucy's shoulder. She was grateful for his protection, but a little wistful. She had always wondered what it would be like to go to the university. Dressing up in ball gowns for dances, being escorted by well-spoken young men in evening dress, studying in the great hall for exams, and dashing from building to building with your gown billowing out behind you—it all sounded so fabulous. Finally, graduating with cap and gown and a brightly colored silk hood. She loved to sit on a bench on the university grounds on graduation day and imagine it was her father and mother driving up in a fine, shiny, black car. The chauffeur would open the door and her mother would alight, dressed in a flowery dress and a big picture hat. Her father would follow, impeccably dressed from his top hat right down to his gray spats. They would be proud of her as she received the diploma and thanked the dean.

After the ceremony, her daydream went on, her whole family would go to the reception under the big tent and mingle with the other parents and families, and the faculty, too. Eating little pastries and drinking tea out of dainty china cups, her parents would introduce her for the first time as Doctor. Her father's chest would swell with pride. Being a self-made man, he had never gone to university. And having a doctor in the family was almost as good as having a priest. Well, she thought, since her brother was dead, there would be no priest, and so she could be the one to make her parents proud. This had always been her favorite daydream.

Returning to the real world, she sighed and remembered with a shudder that her mother was dead and her father was responsible. She would never again seek to please him. Her mother would never again be there to be proud of her. Some of her dream she would keep intact, but some she would have to change. She would still become a doctor, and she would develop a cure for a dreaded disease and she would endow a chair at the university in her mother's memory. In her maiden name of course, she thought.

And when her father and his woman contracted smallpox, she wouldn't lift a finger to save them. Sure, it was a grand dream.

Bill was propelling her across the road, away from the noisy crowd of students. It was comforting to be with him, to have him protecting her and keeping her from harm's way.

Bill and Lucy arrived at Mary Alice's house just as Brian returned from work. He was a handsome Celt, with glossy black hair and vivid sapphire eyes. His once-athletic body, however, was beginning to show the signs of too much time spent in the company of John Barleycorn. Mary Alice invited Bill to join the family for a special dinner to welcome Lucy home from the hospital. She had gone to great lengths to make sure her sister would feel welcome.

Indeed, her home was a reflection of her warm personality. Comfortable, overstuffed chairs sat around the hearth in which a peat fire glowed softly. The children had been fed and put to bed, the table was set with her best china, and a glass vase held a simple but happy bunch of yellow daisies. The house smelled of Sunday dinner, smoky peat, Brasso, and wax polish with a starch finish.

Bill agreed to stay, and they all settled down to enjoy the celebration dinner. He assured his hostess that he had never tasted roast pork to match hers, and Mary Alice flushed prettily as she accepted the compliment. She had worked hard to brighten Lucy's homecoming and hoped that the little family gathering would be of some comfort to her sister. Lucy, on the other hand, was trying to keep up a brave front. She missed her mother desperately. *Without Ma, no family gatherin' will ever be the same*, she thought.

For his part, Bill decided privately that Brian was a dour sort of bloke who offered little to the conversation. He wondered if Brian was uncomfortable having a Protestant at his table, or if perhaps there was something else on his mind. He noticed Brian's eyes wandering towards Lucy and thought he could make out a speculative expression in the gaze, a kind of assessment.

Will ya not be makin' mountains out o' molehills? Bill scolded himself for being fanciful and maybe a little jealous, too. *Sure, the bloke's her brother-in-law*, but he knew that Lucy had also felt the heat of Brian's gaze and averted her eyes. Mary Alice now sensed the charged atmosphere at the little table and chattered on nervously as she cast around to find the reason.

Suddenly, there was an ear-piercing scream. One of the babies, having found a piece of toffee in the other one's hair, had decided to remove it, hair and all. Now both appeared in the doorway, both wailing, one from pain and the other from frustration, as toffee didn't taste as good wrapped in hair. The adults went from shock to helpless laughter, and the mood changed and was forgotten…almost. At the end of the meal, Mary Alice served a golden syrup pudding, and everyone left the table with a sweet taste in his or her mouth.

Sitting by the fire, they regaled each other with family stories, traded snippets of gossip, and then played a game of Snakes and Ladders, lastly rounding out the evening with a final drink. It was the closest to normal they'd been since Ellen's death. Bill thanked everyone for a grand night, and everyone in turn thanked him for taking such good care of Lucy, and bringing her home safely. On the surface, 'twas a pleasant evening for all concerned.

As time passed, Lucy grew stronger and steadier. She'd been out of the hospital for six weeks, and having recovered most of her energy, her thoughts were turning to finding a job. The flower shop had not been able to hold her position open.

Meanwhile, she and Bill were spending a lot of time together. She enjoyed his company, but as she realized that he was becoming more and more attached to her, she was not at all sure how to handle the situation. She wished her mother were available for counsel. She knew she could talk to her sisters, but it was her mother's wisdom that she missed. Lucy had reservations beyond the obvious issue of their religious differences. She wanted a different kind of life. Bill was respectable, he had a good job and was kind and good to her. And, yes, there was a tiny spark. But she wanted romance, travel, fine clothes, and a breathless love affair that would last a lifetime. She had seen what happened with her sisters after their marriages, and she didn't want to be trapped in that kind of relationship. What Lucy didn't understand, of course, was the fleeting nature of the romantic love that she saw in the Hollywood pictures of which she was so fond. The films only showed the spark. Only with patient care, understanding, compromise, and commitment could the spark kindle the kind of slow-burning fire that would last a lifetime.

I like his company, she kept saying to herself. *But he's a Protestant…an' if it comes t' marriage, who'd marry us?*

Bill would have to become a Catholic. No priest would marry them otherwise. Or the unthinkable…he might expect her to turn her coat, to change her religion to his. *There's no way that's goin' t' happen*, she resolved.

Suddenly there was a hell of a row going on in the next room. Lucy had been sitting on the couch with her thoughts, her knees pulled up under her chin and her arms wrapped around them. She tried not to hear it what was being said, but the walls were thin, and she had no choice.

"I'm tellin' ya once more," it was her brother-in-law speaking, "don't be bringin' that Protestant bastard into me house again." Brian's voice was slurred and angry. He had just returned from the pub, where the lads had listened to his tale of the usurping Prod who was coming to his house, eating food bought with his hard-earned money, playing with his wee ones, and worst of all, "sniffin 'round" his sister-in-law. The lads had expressed their sympathy.

"Sure, an' it's not yer own home any more," one of the boys had said. "Ya should throw the bugger out by the scruff o' the neck."

"Bedad," another joined in. "I'd be cuttin' that one off at the knees."

A third spoke up. "Ya need t' tell yer women who holds the reins in yer house."

And a fourth lad: "Do they think yer a man or a mouse?"

And another: "What's the matter with yer sister-in-law?" he asked. "Can she not find a good Catholic lad? She's a good looker. Many a lad would be glad t' take her home t' meet his ma."

Now, back at the house, Brian was still confused and angry, and there were other feelings as well. His wife was in the last stages of her pregnancy and wouldn't let him near her...not that she was all that appealing in her present condition. But a man had needs, so he did. It was only natural. Mary Alice reminded him of a great cow. Every time he looked at her she grew more repulsive in his eyes. With her tree-trunk legs, swollen belly, and pendulous breasts, she was a sorry sight, she was. He wondered what had happened to the slim beauty he had married, how the soft brown eyes formerly so full of love had turned into muddy pools lurking behind puffy slits of flesh, how the luxurious mane of black hair had become twisted into a torturous bun impaled by two murderous spikes to keep it off her sweaty neck.

Mary Alice spoke up. "Oh, sure, our Lucy's steppin' out with the lad. How can we tell him not t' come callin' anymore? He's never done anythin' wrong."

"He's a bloody bastard Prod," Brian grunted. "An' they're all the same…murderin' swine." There was a rumbling in his throat, and he turned and spat in the sink, tasting as he did the cigarettes and whiskey, the bile and spite that had been his evening. "I'm tellin' ya," he said, "best keep him out o' me house, or it'll be the worse fer him." He felt it would be better if Mary Alice dealt with Bill, at least at first, one on one. Privately, he wasn't too sure how he would fare if he got into an altercation with the tall Protestant. Yes, best to let the women handle these things.

When the proper time came, though, he would have no worries. This was a Catholic neighborhood, and any Prod who chose to challenge one of the lads would come out of it the worse for wear.

"Brian," said Mary Alice, "will ya guard yer tongue? Our Lucy's tryin' t' sleep in the next room. What do ya think she'll be feelin' about all this? Bill's been nothin' but kind to all of us. He never comes but he's carryin' somethin'. There's sweets fer the wee ones. Flowers fer me and Lucy. An' he even stands ya to a pint at the pub."

Mary Alice's praise of the Prod enraged Brian. It was like waving a red flag at a drunken bull. He stepped closer to his wife, took her by the shoulders, and thrust his face as close to hers as he could. She smelled the whiskey on his breath, saw the spittle gathering at the corners of his mouth. She was nauseated.

"Mind yer mouth, woman," he hissed at her. "If ya know what's good fer ya, hold yer yap. Keep that bloody bastard out o' me house and away from me family. If I catch him around here again, I'll beat him to a pulp. The same'll go fer ya fer encouragin' him. De ya hear me? Well? Do ya? Answer me, woman."

Mary Alice felt the baby stir within her. She lowered her eyes and whispered, "Aye, I hear ya."

Brian released her, and she went into the scullery and closed the door.

"Aye," she whispered savagely, tears of rage running down her cheeks, "I hear ya, ya great drunken hulk o' pig's swill. If ya ever think t' lay a hand on me while I'm carryin' this baby, I swear before God an' His Blessed Mother I'll run ya through with a kitchen knife while ya sleep."

But Brian was satisfied with the outcome of his encounter with his wife. She would do as she was bid, he was sure of that. He'd put the fear of God in her. Feeling the need of male approval, he decided that a return trip to the pub to tell the lads of his victory would be just the ticket.

"I'm goin' out," he shouted as he left.

"Ya can go t' Hell," Mary Alice whispered behind the closed door. "The devil's expectin' ya."

Returning to the pub, Brian assured all there that he had put an end to the invasion of his little piece of Ireland. "No whoreson Protestant get is takin' over me home and hearth," he said. "An' he can keep his dirty paws off me sister-in-law as well."

Heads nodded in agreement, and Brian was hailed as man of the day and treated to a congratulatory drink. It was a fine thing indeed when one of their own got the better of a representative of the British Crown, even an insignificant Black Mouth Presbyterian like that Bill.

Soon it was closing time. When the bartender called out, "Time, gentlemen, please," there was the usual scramble to order the last drink of the night.

Not long afterwards, Brian staggered out of the pub arm in arm with three of his mates. Drunkenly vowing eternal brotherhood and after much backslapping and fraternal hugging, they reluctantly disentangled themselves and headed in the general direction of their homes.

Entering his house Brian called out, "Are ya there, luv? Come an' give us a wee kiss."

There was no answer. He thought that he spied some movement in the parlor.

"Come out, come out, wherever ya are," he called out in a voice that mocked the innocence of the children's game. Crashing through the parlor door, he almost fell down, before righting himself and regaining his balance. "There y'are, ya sleeked wee thing," he slobbered. "Tryin' t' hide from yer husband, are ya?"

The shadowy figure stood trembling in the corner, clutching her nightgown round herself.

"Go—go away. Ye're drunk! I'm not—"

"Ye're not what? Ye're not goin' t' get away that easy." He reached out menacingly with powerful arms. "Come on, give us a wee kiss an' maybe a wee fuck, too, it's been a while...."

The white figure wavered in front of him, her eyes no longer slits, but large and shining. He had to have her now before she changed back into the cow. This was his girl. His woman.

She tried to slide past him, but he caught her by the arm and twisted it behind her back. As she screamed, he smashed her against the wall. He was getting angry now. He'd waited long enough. She would do his bidding and like it.

"Come here, ya fuckin' wee tease...ye'll do as I say!"

Pinning her against the wall he thrust his knee between her legs and started to rip the nightgown away from her neck. She struggled to free herself, but he was too big, too strong.

Now he had his arm across her throat, cutting off her air supply. He reached down, caught the hem of her nightgown, and tried to pull it up over her head. She struggled fiercely to free herself, but he could tell she was losing the battle.

He was out of control now. Lust, frustration, and desire fed by alcohol yapped at his heels. Restraint long since gone, Brian was one with the beast. He moved his arm away from her throat to tear at her nightdress again.

She drew a shuddering lung full of air and tried to scream, but the sound that emerged was a mewling whine. It annoyed him. He slapped her hard. And then, quite unexpectedly, he slumped to the floor, unconscious.

Mary Alice stood over him, clutching a cast-iron frying pan in both hands. She was trembling from head to toe. "Oh, God, have I killed him?" She was staring at her husband's inert body. She couldn't bring herself to touch it.

Lucy was still in shock. Her jaw hurt from the slap, and her neck was swelling, making it difficult for her to speak. It took a few more minutes for her to compose herself, but when she did, she guided her trembling sister to a chair. Bending over Brian's body, she felt for a pulse.

"No, he's still alive," Her voice was raspy. *More's the pity*, she said to herself. The shock was wearing off, anger was taking its place.

"What in the name o' God got into him?" Mary Alice was wringing her hands. "I can't understand it."

Lucy shook her head, trying to clear it. "In his drunken state," she replied, "he somehow got us mixed up. He thought I was you."

Neither of them knew what to make of this. Either way, his actions were unforgivable. Whether he was trying to rape and beat his pregnant wife or his sister-in-law, a virgin living in his house and supposedly under his protection, things would never be right again. Mary Alice was sobbing. Her husband had attacked her sister. What would the rest of the family make of it?

Lucy tried to comfort her as best she could, but she was sore in need of comfort herself. What was she to do now? She couldn't stay under this roof. Whatever Brian had been thinking, whoever he had thought she was, there was no excuse for his actions. She had narrowly missed being raped or strangled or both. She had to get out of his house.

Mary Alice was still staring into space and wringing her hands. She had been ignoring the throbbing discomfort she felt, brought on by her exertion, but it was becoming more persistent. Suddenly, the rhythm changed and a pain caught her that forced the air out of her lungs.

"Oh, Oh, Mother of God," she cried. It was too early for the baby, six weeks too early, but everything seemed to be happening at once. Her water broke. The pain subsided and she called out to her sister. "Get the midwife, the babe's comin' early!"

Frightened by the panic in her sister's voice, Lucy pulled a shawl off the peg next to the door, wrapped herself as well as she could, and ran next door and asked Mrs. Noonan to mind the wee ones while she went for the midwife. As they came back into Mary Alice's house, she hastily explained Brian's prostrate body as the result of having "a wee drop too much," and Mrs. Noonan tutted and clucked, expounding on the useless nature of men.

After helping Mary Alice to bed, they began to make ready for the lying-in. The midwife would need the usual things, most of which, fortunately, Mary Alice had already prepared. Mrs. Noonan put the requisite kettle of water on to boil. Never having been blessed with children herself, she often wondered what the water was for. You couldn't wash your hands in boiling water, and neither could you wash the baby in it. She shrugged the question off. It was enough that it was the done thing.

Mary Alice was now in real distress. Collecting a flannel and a basin of cool water, Mrs. Noonan made for the bedroom. Mary Alice's screams would surely wake the children, she observed, and that bloody ne'er-do-well in the front room was less than useless.

The ne'er-do-well was in fact just about to re-enter the land of the living. His head felt as if someone was driving red-hot pokers through his eyeballs. When the pokers reached a certain place in his brain, it felt as though they had been laid on an anvil, hammered into arrows, and shot off in every direction. This was the mother of all headaches. To add insult to injury, someone was screaming, and he wanted to wring that person's neck. It was hard enough dealing with the pain in his head without having it made worse.

Lucy ran all the way to the midwife's house, only to find that the woman had left to attend to another patient. Not knowing what else to do, Lucy waited, pacing. When Claire, the midwife, returned, not long afterwards, Lucy lost no time in explaining the situation. Claire agreed that Mary Alice was in dire need of her services. Without another word, the midwife set off on her bicycle, with Lucy following on foot.

Claire's breath was coming hard as she pedaled up the Falls Road, and she scolded herself for having put on too much weight. She was worried about her diet…too many wee buns accompanying the gallons of tea she consumed while waiting for another soul to be assisted into the world. Upon her arrival, she lost no time in examining Mary Alice and her condition. She wasn't happy with what she found. It was a transverse breech, with the baby lying across the birth canal, having failed to turn. The baby couldn't be born while in this position, and Mary Alice was laboring in vain.

Lucy returned, out of breath, as Claire was finishing her examination of the patient, Mrs. Noonan still hovering nearby. The midwife explained the situation and asked Lucy to be prepared to go to the post office. "I've decided t' try some exercises to turn the infant meself," she said. "I don't think I can do it, so ye'd best be prepared t' be off t' the post office and telephone for an ambulance."

Lucy was horrified to see the condition her sister was in. Mary Alice's face was pale as death's head, her skin was stretched over her bones, and every part of her body was bathed in sweat as she moaned and arched her back in the effort to deliver her baby. She kept screaming and pleading for deliverance, but her screams were getting weaker as her body grew tired of the fruitless labor.

The midwife was unsuccessful in her attempts to change the baby's position, and so Lucy was dispatched to call for the ambulance. As she was leaving the house, she spied Brian sitting on the sofa with his head in his hands. Her anger boiled over.

"Yer wife's dyin' upstairs, ya good-fer-nothin', drunken lout. Get up off yer backside an' take care o' yer poor wee wains. They shouldn't be hearin' their ma's agony. Take 'em over to our Nellie's house." She wanted to shake him, but she didn't dare go near enough. "D'ye hear me? Get goin'. NOW."

Incredibly, this seemed not to register with Brian. "Ah, Lucy," he groaned, "don't be talkin' like that. Sure, me head's splittin' in half. I can't see straight, much less take care o' the wains."

It was not until Lucy slammed the door behind her that he reluctantly made an effort to rise from the chair. What was she talking about…saying Mary Alice was dying? Sure, she was just having another baby. He'd heard the sounds of labor before.

It was taking a long time, though. It seemed she'd been screaming for hours. He'd best go check and find out for himself. Reaching the top of the stairs, he saw the children huddled together outside their mother's door. They were all crying.

"What's wrong with our ma?" the oldest one asked.

"She'll be fine," said their da. "Jest go back t' yer room an' get the wee ones together, an' anythin' ya might need fer tomorrow. I'll be takin' ya over t' spend the night with yer Aunt Nellie."

Shannon, the eldest, knew better than to question her father any further. She had learned that too many questions were apt to get one's ears boxed. So she ushered the rest of the children into their room. Taking a battered suitcase down off the top of the wardrobe, she stuffed some clothes into it, grabbed their coats, and declared the children ready.

As they left the room, the door across the hall suddenly opened, and a minute later they could see their father leaving his wife's bedside. Mary Alice's body was drenched with sweat and her ashen face was contorted in another agonized scream.

A much-sobered Brian left with his children. Still at a loss to understand Lucy's anger, he held his pounding head and tried to figure out what was happening. He had no recollection of the evening's events. He had experienced this kind of confusion before, but this time, there seemed to be a sinister element lurking in his blacked-out memory.

Chapter Ten

Lucy was running as fast as she could, with her head down against the rain that had begun to fall. It was the darkest hour of the night, the hour when many souls took leave of their earthly bodies. The darkness had an eerie feel to it, and Lucy's lively imagination was working overtime. She hoped the postmistress would answer the door quickly.

Miss Gamble was a crotchety old biddy at the best of times, and she ruled her domain in a manner befitting an appointee in His Majesty's Service. Her hair was always tightly woven in a basket weave arranged in a coronet around her small skull, and the liveliest features in her face were her shoe-button eyes, which were shielded by the bony overhang of her brow. Her nostrils curled as if to suggest everything beneath her nose had a foul odor, and as her lips attempted to restrain her prominent teeth, they formed a thin scowl.

Lucy didn't fancy rousing Miss Gamble from her bed in the middle of the night. *Sure, but that's her job*, she told herself. *We can't be the only ones needin' the telephone in the at this late hour.* Arriving at the little post office, she knocked on the door. When there was no answer, banged longer and louder.

At last the door swung open, and Lucy squealed involuntarily at the sight of the apparition that presented itself. Gone were the braids. Instead, a backlit nimbus of white hair stood out from the postmistress' head as though electrified. The teeth were missing, too, and the lips seemed to have been swallowed. All that remained was a Punch and Judy face, the shoe-button eyes glittering fiercely.

"Well," said the postmistress, "don't stand there like ye've seen a ghost. What's up? What da ya want at this ungodly time o' the night?" Miss Gamble was used to being disturbed during the night for emergencies. Truth be told, she didn't altogether mind being roused for some crisis or other.

What WOULD they do without me? She asked herself, and felt a rush of affirmation. It was her policy, however, always to be as cranky as possible, lest she be taken for granted.

"It's me sister," Lucy managed to say. Her throat was still painful and swollen. "The midwife sent me t' ring up the ambulance. Our Mary Alice has been in labor far too long, and the baby won't come out. Somethin's fearful wrong. I'm afraid she's goin' t' die!"

It was clear to the postmistress that this was a bona fide emergency, one that would indeed merit her help. Admitting her petitioner, but then turning her back on her, Miss Gamble called the hospital and requested the immediate dispatch of the ambulance, stressing her official position so as to lend urgency to her request.

As anxious as Lucy was to get back to her sister, she allowed the postmistress to offer her a cup of tea.

"'Twill warm ya up before ye're beginnin' yer long walk back in the rain," Miss Gamble said.

Tea consumed with hardly a word exchanged between then, Lucy accepted an umbrella and raincoat from Miss Gamble and set off. Surprised at the sudden change in the postmistress' attitude, she remembered hearing someone say, "There's nowt as queer as folk." She agreed with that philosophy, but was still grateful for the unexpected kindness.

Half-way to Mary Alice's house, she realized that there was no point in her going back there, as the ambulance would have arrived and the children would already have gone to Nellie's. She decided to head for the hospital instead. As she walked through the rainy night, she thought bitterly of both her encounter with Brian and her father's betrayal of her mother. Were all men so violent and deceiving? Then she thought of Bill. He seemed to be so decent, and he treated her with such thoughtfulness. A new question came into her thoughts: did men become drunken oafs and philanders only after they got married?

~

Having left the children with his sister-in-law, Brian returned to his house in time to accompany Mary Alice in the ambulance. He sat beside her in the back, greatly shaken by the night's events and in mortal fear that his wife was dying. The ambulance bounced along the bumpy road at breakneck speed. *If ya weren't sick when ya got into this contraption*, Brian thought darkly, *ya sure as hell would be by the time ya got out of it.*

Sitting there, he considered his callous behavior toward his wife and his distaste for her condition, a condition for which he was, after all, responsible, as she had not wanted another baby so soon. If anything were to happen to her, what would he do? How would he cope with raising the children on his own? He didn't have the first idea of their needs.

Maybe Lucy would help. He brightened a little at the thought. Then he remembered. Lucy was mad as hell at him. Was it because he was drunk? Something, some act, some event, was darting in and out of his memory, but try as he might, he couldn't quite catch it. Whatever it was, it had an ominous feel to it.

There was a particularly jarring bump, and a low moan ended his musing and brought him back to the present situation. Mary Alice was unconscious. The midwife had given her something to ease the pain. The hours of labor had weakened her, and she looked close to death.

He was afraid to touch her, afraid to even look squarely at her. Instead, he looked at the midwife, who was sitting beside Mary Alice. He tried to read the expression on her face, but was none the wiser for the attempt. His wife was moaning quietly, the midwife was whispering reassurances, and Brian was wondering what the hell good he was to anyone.

Useless as tits on a bull, that's what I am, he said to himself. *Useless.*

~

The next day, as Bill was about to leave the shipyard, he heard someone call his name.

"Bill, hey, Bill! Wait fer me." Tom was breathless by the time he caught up. "I...I haven't seen ya in a donkey's age," he said. "Where've ya been hidin' yerself?"

Bill's emotions were having a championship fight, and he hadn't the foggiest notion how to handle this encounter. He had, in fact, been carefully avoiding Tom since observing him with the waitress. Lucy's bitterness and anger toward her father were apparently not without reason.

On the other hand, his friendship with Tom predated his relationship with Lucy. Truth be known, Bill had missed Tom's company. The dogs weren't as much fun on your own. Half the fun was the discussion over a pint after the races. The merits of one dog's form as opposed to another could keep them entertained for hours.

And there had been many a night when Tom had kept Bill enthralled with tales of the ships he had worked on, including the ill-fated *Titanic*. He told of sailing into the Irish Sea on the great vessel's trials and recounted the near collision between the *New York* and the *Titanic* before the latter had even left port.

Bill was thus confused as to where his loyalties lay these days. He had been avoiding the lads at the lodge and skipping the meetings, mentally folding his orange sash and hanging up his bowler hat until further notice. He felt his life and ideas about it changing, primarily due to Lucy's influence. Of course, he wasn't sure whether or not the relationship with Lucy was actually going anywhere. His religion posed a serious problem for Lucy, just as hers was an issue for him. Yes, he thought, should their relationship go a step further, religion would be a major issue for both them and their families.

But his beliefs had been shaken. He no longer thought of Catholics as the enemy. While some of their rituals were, to say the least, a little scary, Lucy's people were just the same as his. They hurt, cried, laughed, fought, loved, ate, drank, and danced. *Jest like us*, he thought.

Trying to put aside his thoughts of division and conflict, he stopped and greeted his friend. "Tom, how are ye?"

"As well as can be expected, considerin'," was the answer.

Considerin' what? Thought Bill. *His wife's death, his estrangement from his daughter, his clandestine associations with women, his loss of dignity and the respect of his family. That's a lot t' consider.*

"How about a pint t' wet yer whistle before ya set off fer home?" Tom asked. "It's been a while, an' I've missed yer company."

What the hell, Bill thought. He would enjoy a pint and a yarn with Tom, and maybe he'd be able to worm a little more information out of the man. As a friend, he was entitled to some explanation.

At the same time as he longed to share the older man's wisdom, he also doubted its value. He wanted his friend to be the man he had looked up to. In the back of his mind, he heard his mother's voice telling him to accept his friends, warts and all. Tom had fallen off his pedestal, but perhaps Bill shouldn't have put him up there in the first place.

"Aye, Tom," he said aloud. "It's been a while. A pint sounds good."

Bill fell into step with the older man and they headed for the pub. But as they walked, they were silent, each of them searching for a safe and comfortable topic to bridge the sudden gap in their friendship.

For his part, Bill was still wrestling with his right to have any opinion of his friend's relationships. Part of him thought it was none of his business, whereas the other part believed he deserved an explanation, having been a witness to the hurt Tom had caused his family. So far, he'd been only a silent observer, but his deepening feelings for Lucy were making it increasingly difficult to keep his own counsel. If he were going to renew his friendship with Tom, he might run the risk of losing Lucy. He had to come to terms with that possibility.

Tom, on the other hand, was dealing with a very disturbed conscience. He sensed Bill's uneasiness. He was unaware that Bill had seen him with Bridie, but he knew the family had told him of the situation with Maggie.

Now that his girls were giving him the cold shoulder, he suddenly missed the warmth and closeness of his family. Lucy would have nothing to do with him, and Feelie also avoided him as much as possible. Those two were the worst. Mary Alice and Nellie were a little softer, and, thank God, the children knew nothing.

The only bright light in his life was Bridie. When they were together, the world seemed a wonderful place. Giddy with their late blooming love, they delighted in sharing new experiences. Tom knew, though, that in order for things to go any further, he would have to marry her, for although she was free with her affection, she was firm in her morals. She believed in the best part of him, and he was somewhat surprised to find himself wanting to live up to her expectations.

If only the rest of his relationships weren't such a tangled web. Bridie knew about his daughters, but she thought Maggie, with whom she had seen him weeks earlier, had been his wife, who was now dead. Allowing Bridie to believe that had been a monumental mistake. The lie had taken on a life of its own, forcing him deeper and deeper into deceit.

'Oh, what a tangled web we weave, he recalled Ellen telling the girls, *when first we practice t' deceive." I should've paid more attention at the time*, he thought wryly.

Keeping his family life separate from his love life was becoming difficult. True, Bridie understood, at least to a point. She was giving the family time to mourn their mother, making no demands and agreeing to a somewhat clandestine relationship.

But that could not last forever. Sooner or later, he would have to introduce her to the girls. And she would learn the truth. He should have been truthful with her from the start. Now, he thought, he needed to talk with someone.

Can I trust Bill? He asked himself. His other friends would never understand the complicated situation and might even be jealous. But Bill would know how it felt to be in love, even a love that presented many problems to all concerned. On the other hand, he was afraid that Bill's feelings for Lucy might cloud his vision.

And so Bill and Tom continued to walk in silence, each mentally rehearsing the conversation he wanted to have with the other, each trying to decide how to present his point of view to its best advantage. Reaching the pub, they ordered and then sat quietly for a few minutes, drinking and smoking and trying to negotiate the emotional minefield they both faced.

Having decided to make a clean breast of it, Tom was the first to speak. Making no excuses for his behavior, he told Bill about his loveless marriage to Ellen. He confessed his affair with Maggie, both how it had started and how it had ended. Finally, he told Bill about Bridie and the strength of his feelings for her.

Bill listened without much visible reaction. While he understood the power of love, he knew he lacked the wisdom to advise the older man as, after all, he had little experience in matters of the heart upon which to draw. After hearing Tom's story, he felt less ready than before to discuss his own situation with Lucy, but he also felt more sympathy for the man than he had previously felt, and so he offered as much comfort as his conscience would allow.

An hour later, Tom set off for home, his step a little lighter. He was unaware that fate had dealt him yet another cruel blow.

Chapter Eleven

For the second time in six months, the chapel bell tolled for a faithful daughter, wife, and loving mother. The plain pine coffin rested on the shoulders of six men, her father, her husband, her brother-in-law, and three cousins. Followed by her three sisters and the oldest of her three living children, Mary Alice and her stillborn son left the chapel for the last time.

The midwife's husband, Angus, played a heart wrenching lament on the pipes as the little coffin was placed in the hearse. Watching in respectful silence, men doffed their caps and women wiped their eyes, and even McNulty the undertaker had shed a tear when he placed the stillborn babe in his dead mother's arms. The baby had been delivered by Caesarean section…too late. In the end, both the baby and his mother had just been too tired to breathe.

Bridie, who had sat in the last pew during the funeral mass, watched from across the street. She longed to comfort Tom, but knew she must keep her distance. He had seen her there, of course, and had acknowledged her with a ghost of a smile as he passed. Then he was gone with his family, following the hearse to the cemetery where Mary Alice and her baby were laid to rest in her husband's family plot not far from her mother's recent grave.

After the funeral, the family returned to the house of the widower, Brian, to receive the condolences of family and friends. Claire, the midwife, and Mrs. Noonan, Mary Alice's neighbor, had prepared refreshments and set the house in order. After learning of the deaths, Mrs. Noonan had sorrowfully removed the baby's cradle and clothes.

Claire was still wrestling with feelings of guilt, wondering if she had waited too long before going to the hospital. She had done her best, to be sure, but had her best been good enough? She had never before lost a mother, let alone a mother and baby together. Of course there had been no word of reproach from the husband or the rest of the family, but then they were all in a state of shock. Now she wondered if the blame would come later. She felt she owed it to the family to do anything she possibly could to help them cope with their loss. She could not imagine having to endure their pain—the losses of Ellen, Mary Alice, the newborn, on top of Lucy's time in the hospital must be overwhelming, she thought—and she was thankful for the support of her good husband, who understood her anguish. He was a man in a million, and the love of her life.

Later, after everyone had eaten and drunk and expressed their sympathies and left, the family sat around the fire. Nellie's sister-in-law had taken all the children for the day, and so as the adults sat with their heads bowed, not knowing what to say, the only sounds in the room were the soft hiss of the fire and the tick of the clock on the mantle.

Finally, Feelie stood up and asked if anyone would like a cup of tea. When everyone agreed that tea would be grand, she went to put the kettle on. Thankful to have something normal to do, she busied herself with the cups, saucers, milk, and sugar.

But there was also the business of the letter. Some time ago, she had applied to a hospital in England for acceptance to their school of nursing. The very day of her sister's death, she had received a letter informing her that her application had been accepted. She had been instructed to present herself to begin training on the twenty-fourth of the month.

She had not told her family of her plans, at first out of superstitious fear that telling would jinx her chances, and then out of her unwillingness to introduce what she was afraid might seem to be something entirely selfish into what had been of late a serious and somber mood. Nevertheless, she was determined that two weeks from now she would be leaving Ireland for at least three years.

She had to go now. At twenty-four, she had just made the age requirement, for the hospital's nursing school wanted no applicants older than twenty-five. She had saved up for her fare to England, and because she had chosen to train at a psychiatric hospital, she could expect to receive a small stipend while in training, enough to cover necessities. This was her chance to start a new life, the first step on her way to achieving her goal. Some day she would be the matron of a big hospital.

She returned with the tea tray and busied herself with the ritual of pouring. They drank in silence, each member of this sad family lost in his or her own thoughts. Lucy gazed at the fire and thought of the last night of her sister's life. She alone knew what had happened, as it was obvious that Brian had no memory of the attack. She had no doubt his actions had brought on the premature labor and caused her sister's death and that of the baby. First it was her mother, and now her sister, and her nephew. All of them gone, and all of their deaths a consequence of a man's lust. Lucy would never forget her sister's face as she lay in agony, laboring to deliver a baby that was not ready to be born. Yes, it was Brian's behavior that had brought about the premature labor,

Lucy had offered no explanation, and the family did not ask, but she had determined that she would stay no more under Brian's roof. But she was also still unwilling to return to her father's home. She and he had nothing to say to each other. Her friend Kathleen had agreed to put her up until she could make other arrangements.

Of course, she said to herself, of course there was Bill. Bill had been a tower of strength, comforting her as best he could. He ran errands for the family, cooked meals, and even took care of the children while they made arrangements for the funeral. Brian had wanted Bill the Prod out of his house, and now ironically it was Bill who was more accepted than ever. *He's almost part of the family*, she thought, and the thought scared her a little.

Seated slightly apart from the others, Brian felt as if he'd been gob-smacked. In the past three days, his life had been turned inside out. His wife and baby were gone, and he was tortured by remorse and guilt. The thing was, though, he wasn't exactly sure exactly what he'd done. His recollection of the events of the evening on the night Mary Alice died was hazy. He knew there had been a row. He remembered threatening her. He remembered going to the pub. The next thing he remembered was Lucy screaming at him to take care of the children.

But something else had taken place that night, something so bad that Lucy had not spoken to him since. What had happened? What had he done? Was it simply that Lucy was mad at him for his resentment of Bill? He didn't think she would react so strongly to that. She would be upset, to be sure, but she would have forgiven him in this time of sorrow. He also remembered his wife defending Bill, and now, sober, he had to grudgingly admit that she had been right. Bill had never done anything to incur Brian's hatred, other than being born a Protestant. And that was not enough, was it? No, there was something else.

Brian was compelled to admit the truth, even if only to himself. *I'm jealous because he's with Lucy*, he admitted. *I was lustin' after her meself, and, God fergive me, I still am. With me wife not yet cold, I'm jealous that me sister-in-law is with another man.* The thought brought on another fit of shameful remorse.

Lucy watched Brian crying again. *Crocodile tears*, she thought with contempt.

From the big chair in the corner, Tom rocked as he quietly studied the faces of those around him. Would they ever recover from these tragedies? He had lost his wife and then his daughter, yet his other children were offering him scant comfort. Lucy had not even spoken to him, and the other two girls were coldly polite. The only person who might comfort him was forbidden to him. He thought longingly of Bridie. Would he lose her, too?

He had also noticed that Lucy was keeping a distance from Brian and that the expression on her face when she looked at him was one of disgust. What was going on there? Brian appeared to be heartbroken. Why was Lucy acting so cold? She and Brian had been friends once. Was Lucy laying the blame for her sister's death at her husband's feet? *Jest like she blamed me*, thought Tom, *fer the death o' her mother.*

But women often died in childbirth. Why did Mary Alice die? Tom thought about his daughter and the grandson he would never know. Mary Alice had been the quietest of the four girls. A gentle soul, she'd put up with a great deal of provocation before she finally lost her temper, and she'd been ferocious only in the defense of her children and her family. She'd been a kind and competent wife, daughter, and mother. Now she was gone and they would all miss her cheerful ways.

For a moment, grief sucked the breath out of him, and he lowered his head to regain his composure. He was the head of this troubled family. He could not afford to lose control of his emotions. There was too much to be decided.

For starters, Nellie could not be expected to mother Mary Alice's children as well as her own, and it was obvious there was bad blood between Brian and Lucy. That left Feelie. She was single. He would talk to her in the morning. She would have to take care of the children until Brian found a new wife. He was a strong young man, and Tom was sure he would not stay single long.

The shadows lengthened as night approached, and eventually Brian sat alone by the dying fire. Everyone else had gone his or her separate way. He was glad of the solitude. He was tired, depressed, and confused, and his brain could not be quiet as it jumped from thought to thought like a flickering silent movie. One vignette after another appeared in his mind's eye. Mary Alice as a shy and radiant bride. Days at the seaside with the children splashing in the puddles left by the tide, laughing as they chased the gulls and each other. Mary Alice shooing their daughters off to bed on Christmas Eve, and their excited giggles as they tried to sleep, knowing Father Christmas would not come until they did. Sunday dinners with the whole family scrubbed and in their Sunday best, eager to tuck into a fine, plump, roasted chicken with Mary Alice's special stuffing. And then…Mary Alice's dead face, silent, sad, and reproachful. The stillborn son that would never inspire another memory.

What was he to do? How would he take care of his motherless children? They were so little, Deirdre still in nappies and not yet weaned from the bottle and Siobhan just a wee toddler. Shannon, just starting school, would try to help. She had always been her mother's little helper. The littlest ones didn't understand yet, but Shannon was devastated. She had clung to him all through the funeral, as if afraid that he, too, might leave her at any moment. She couldn't understand why her mammy had gone to heaven and taken their baby. Why, she'd asked her da, why did she leave us behind?

He had tried to explain that it was God's will, but Shannon didn't understand this God. The God she knew was a kind, bearded man who lived in heaven with his beautiful lady. The lady was his mother. Why did he need her mammy? He had one of his own. It wasn't fair, the little girl had protested to her bereft father. Nothing made sense to her. They had put her mother and baby brother in the ground. Heaven was in the sky. The devil lived in hell and hell was in the ground. Why did everyone say they were in heaven? She had seen them put them in the ground with her own eyes. Her mammy was good and only bad people went to hell. Visions of her mother and brother burning in the fires of hell haunted her dreams. It would, Brian knew, be a long time before the nightmares would stop.

~

Tom awoke from a troubled sleep, confused for a moment by the feeling that something was wrong. Then he remembered the reason for his sadness. First his wife, then his daughter. He forced the grief to retreat by making plans. He would go to the rectory to see Feelie. He knew taking over the care of her sister's children would present some hardship for her, but if he were to help her financially, he was sure she would agree. She would have to move back home with the children, of course. This would be a hardship for him, but there was no other way. And, he thought, Brian might have to be persuaded to give his consent. Feelie could not move into Brian's house. Her reputation would suffer, tongues would start wagging, and that would never do.

He wondered how Bridie would react to the changes in his family. He hoped she would understand. They would have to find a way to see each other quietly, at least for the time being, but he was determined to make a clean breast of things. Living a life of lies was beginning to wear on him. He hoped she would understand and forgive him, but either way it would have to be done, for sooner or later she would find out that he had allowed her to believe that Maggie had been his wife, Ellen. He knew that no relationship could thrive built as it was on a foundation of evasiveness. He wanted Bridie with him for the rest of his life. Having decided on this course of action, he arose and prepared to leave the house.

~

Feelie halted her dusting to pull up the shade in Father Doyle's bedroom. She was surprised to see her father walking toward the front door. *What's he doin' here?* She wondered, and felt an icy flutter of fear run through her. "Please God," she prayed aloud, "please, no more trouble."

Her father smiled at her when she answered the door and asked if there was somewhere they could talk in private. She showed him into the parlor and then excused herself to tell the priest that her father was visiting. Returning, she found Tom standing at the window. He turned at the sound of her footsteps and asked her to sit beside him on the parlor sofa.

"Some important decisions have t' be made," he said without preamble. He was feeling a little nervous and unsure of how Feelie would react to his plan. "The children are without a mother," he began. "I've decided that ye'd be the best one t' take care of 'em."

Feelie felt the bile rise in her throat. For a moment she was speechless, and then she repeated his words slowly. "Ye've decided," she said. "What d' ya mean, decided?"

She waited for her father to explain himself. She had opted a long time ago to forego marriage, as she was determined that no man would ever be allowed to map the course of her life for her. If that meant living the lonely and celibate life of a spinster, so be it. But now it seemed that her father was trying to force her into a life of servitude. This was something she was determined to avoid.

Seeing her stunned expression, Tom decided to continue before she could speak again. "Fer some reason," he said, almost stammering in his nervousness, "Lucy and Brian seem t' be at odds with each other. Nellie has her own wee brood t' take care of. That leaves you. Ye're single. An' the children need ya."

Feelie stood up. "Yer decidin' that I should take care o' the children without ever talkin' t' me about it?" she asked. "I have plans fer me own life. Plans that don't include marriage, or children."

Tom was thunderstruck. Everything had happened so fast, and now Feelie's reaction to his decision was much stronger than he had anticipated. Well, he thought, she could refuse. She was a grown woman. But why would she not obey her own da?

Feelie walked across the room. Since the age of sixteen, she had taken care of herself and contributed to the family household, giving her unopened pay packet to her mother every week. She had always taken only enough for tram fare and a few shillings for herself. She didn't really need any more, with no rent to pay and no food to buy. But now she was twenty-four, with still no sign of a man in her life, still no children of her own. She turned to glance at her father. He obviously thought that for her to take over care of her dead sister's children was the best and most logical solution.

But her logic ran along a different line. As she understood it, she had spent almost the first half of a normal life span always doing the right thing. But now she deserved to have a life of her own, even though the hand of fate appeared poised to force her along its predetermined path. But she didn't believe in fate. She believed that she was in control of her own destiny; she held the reins of her life in her own hands. That belief was at that very moment being challenged. She took a step toward her father and politely asked him to leave.

Tom could only blink and shake his head. What was he to make of this? It was not seemly for his daughter to terminate the conversation with his demand unanswered. But he stood after a moment, and with an awkward shrug backed out the rectory door, thinking, *She'll see how right it is.*

After the door had closed behind her father, Feelie went out by the other door, crossed the rose garden, and entered the side door of the chapel. Kneeling before the statue of the Blessed Virgin, she asked for guidance. *Heavenly Mother*, she prayed, *help me t' do the right thing, not only fer me nieces but also fer meself.* Why, she asked, should she have to give up her own dreams and aspirations? She did not want to end up an embittered old maid, which was what was likely to happen if she became nothing but a nursemaid. On the other hand, she told the Blessed Virgin, she could follow her dream and help a lot of needy human beings along the way. But then... what would become of the motherless children?

"I don't know what t' do," she said aloud, "an' this decision will change me life. One way or another, me life'll be changed ferever. Holy Mother, help me an' guide me."

She was startled by a soft touch on her shoulder and almost jumped out of her skin.

"Daughter, what ails you?"

Father Doyle had seen Tom's abrupt departure. He knew something was amiss in Feelie's family, and so he had followed her into the church and heard her whispering to the Holy Mother. He couldn't hear what she said, and that wasn't his business, anyway. But it was easy to see that she was wrestling with a dilemma. She was disturbed, and that was his business. She was a part of his flock and had been a member of his household for the past eight years. He felt a paternal fondness for the girl.

"Oh," she felt her heart pumping, "Father, ya scared the wits out o' me."

"I'm sorry," said the priest. "I just thought you might be in need of a friend to talk to."

"I am that," she said after a moment. "But I don't know where t' start."

He smiled and reached out to help her up. Leading her to the first pew, he gestured for her to sit. "The beginning is usually a grand place to start," he said as he sat down next to her. "Here now, let's chat. You can tell me all about it."

For the next half-hour, the priest listened quietly as Feelie told him of her dilemma. He nodded as she told him of the letter from the hospital in England and her dream of becoming a nurse and someday reaching the top of that profession. He also nodded as she explained her decision to stay single and devote her life to reaching her goal. He understood her anger and frustration when she explained how her father had made decisions about her life without so much as the courtesy of discussing it with her. If she stayed to take care of her nieces, she concluded, it would be too late for her to enter the training program.

They sat in silence for a minute or so before the priest spoke up.

"Well," this is indeed a big decision to make," he said finally, rubbing his jaw. "You're a good daughter and a good aunt. The tragedy of your sister's death has placed a great burden of conscience on your shoulders. Whatever path you choose to take, it looks like there's likely to be another death of sorts." Warming to his topic, Father Doyle began to gesture, sketching and pulling the air around him to bring his words to life. "The death of a dream can cause as much grief as any other," he said. "If you choose to leave now, another kind of death may be the result—the loss of your closeness with your family, who may see your leaving as a kind of desertion. If your goal is truly to take care of the sick, that's one thing."

Now he raised a stern eyebrow. "If, on the other hand, you are seeking to escape family responsibilities to achieve a selfish ambition, that's another thing altogether. The raising of another woman's children can be, and often is, a thankless undertaking. But done the right way, and for the right reasons, it can bring rewards the like of which you can find nowhere else."

He paused for breath, and when he spoke again his words came slower. "You must be careful as you make your decision," he said. "If you choose to stay, it must be for love. Staying with the sting of bitterness and regret in your heart will sour your life. It will bring misery to the lives of those three little ones." He laid one hand on her head. "Go with God, my child. Go commune with your mother and sister and our holy Mother. Ask for the grace to do the right thing and find happiness in the doing of it."

The priest stood up, took the stole out of his pocket and draped it around his neck, and gave the troubled girl his blessing. He hoped that God had granted him the wisdom to give good counsel.

"Thank ya, Father" were the only words Feelie could force through the lump in her throat.

There was no further need to pray for guidance. She thought she knew what God wanted her to do. The message had come through loud and clear. What she had to pray for now was the strength to put her dreams aside as she accepted God's will and subjected her will to her father's dictates.

~

Tom had mixed emotions after his meeting with Feelie. She was confused, he thought, as he walked into town. She was not happy at the prospect of taking care of her nieces. He wondered what she had meant by saying that she had plans for her own life. She had not told him just what her plans were, but he could not imagine a higher calling for a woman than the rearing of children. Especially since she was a single woman, a woman alone without any obvious prospects.

Right now, though, he had other problems to face. He was on his way to the café to see Bridie. She was working a half-day today and should be getting out soon. When he arrived, she greeted him with her usual cheerful smile.

"I'm all done," she said. "Jest have t' get me bag." She made her way to the back room. The café was empty, and the other waitress was busy setting the tables for the supper rush. She cast Tom a knowing look and giggled to herself.

But Tom felt like smacking her. Stupid girl. He was in no mood for frivolity.

Then Bridie reappeared with her handbag tucked under her arm. Tom held the door open, and the two proceeded through the doorway and down the street.

"It's good t' see ya, luv. How're ya doin'?" Bridie said after a moment. *He's quiet today*, she thought.

"I've been better," he said. "It's been a sad week."

"Aye," she said, pressing his arm in sympathy, "it's been that and then some. Ya must be done in. How're yer son-in-law an' the wee ones doin'?"

"Ah, sure, everyone's still in shock. The oldest girl is takin' it bad, an' the other two are confused and cryin' fer their mammy. It near breaks me heart t' see 'em."

"Poor wee things. What's goin' t' happen t' 'em now?"

"I had a talk with Feelie," he said. "I hope she'll agree t' take care of 'em fer a while. Brian's a young man. I'm sure he'll soon find himself another wife."

Bridie nodded in agreement. "But he'll be hard pressed t' find another the likes o' yer Mary Alice," she said, although she hadn't known Mary Alice personally. *But I've heard good things*, she told herself. *An' he needs cheerin'.*

"So he will," Tom said heavily. "I know it'll be a hardship fer Feelie, but I don't know what else t' think of."

"I'm sure no matter what the hardship, yer daughter'll do her duty," Bridie reassured him, giving his arm a gentle squeeze. "She'll be rewarded in heaven. God has a special place in his heart fer those who look after the wee ones."

Tom wasn't convinced that a reward in heaven in the far distant future would be of much if any comfort to Feelie. He nodded, but said nothing more on the subject.

They walked without speaking for a few minutes, and then Bridie broke the silence, saying, "Tom, I know yer heart is broken, but I have the sense there's somethin' else troublin' ya as well. De ya have somethin' ya want t' tell me about?"

Tom's response was quicker than she'd expected, as if he was glad not to have to speak uncued. "Aye," he said. "I'm thinkin' ya have the sixth sense. Somethin' has been weighin' heavy on me mind fer a long time. Somethin' I've been puttin' off tellin' ya fer fear o' losin' ya. I have t' make a clean breast o' things one way or t'other. I love ya, Bridie, but we can have no future built on lies."

A heavy sigh shuddered through his body as she said nothing and he gathered the courage to go on. "I haven't been honest with ya," he said in a low voice. "Ye mistakenly thought the woman ya met at the café that once was me wife, an' I let ya go on thinkin' that. She wasn't...she was a woman I had been seein'."

"I know," Bridie said in a gentle voice. "I've been wonderin' when ya were goin' t' tell me."

"Ya knew!" He was astonished. "How? When?"

"I saw the woman at mass a few weeks ago."

"She's back? Why didn't ya say somethin'?"

"I was waitin' fer ya t' tell me yerself, an' hopin' ya would."

"I don't understand."

"If ya didn't tell me yerself," she said, "I could never have been sure. I knew if ya ever meant t' marry me, I'd have t' meet yer family. It would all have come out. The only way it could remain a secret would be if ya never intended t' stay with me. Then there's the matter o' trust. Love an' trust go together. The way I see it, ya can't have one wi'out t'other. Bridie was weeping softly now. She had given him time. That had been the right decision after all.

But it had not been easy. She had wanted to confront him. She had been shocked to see the woman, Maggie, kneeling in front of her at mass. At first she had thought her eyes were playing tricks on her—Tom's wife was dead? How could she be here in the chapel?

But when the woman had risen to receive communion, Bridie had been forced to admit that she appeared to be the genuine article.

Her shock had been followed by confusion. Then who was this woman? Tom had told her his wife was dead. Had he lied to her? She had gone to confession and spoken of her involvement with Tom, and Father Doyle had assured her that Ellen O'Leary had indeed departed this life, God rest her soul. The question of the other woman still remained unsolved.

At that point, her anger and sorrow had known no bounds. First, she had blamed herself for being so gullible. She had never been lucky in love. Her first love had been snatched away, killed in the Great War fighting for the English. Now her innate common sense had almost deserted her. Still, something inside, some tiny voice of reason had bade her wait, told her to give Tom either the time to tell her the truth or the rope to hang himself with.

Now he had told the truth. Bridie was overjoyed. Nevertheless, she had one more question. "Tom, there's somethin' I need t' know. Do ya still have feelin's fer that woman?"

"No, luv, I don't. We had a good time together. But it's over, has been fer a while. Maggie's a good woman. She deserves t' find what I've found with you. I thought I was in love with her, but she knew somethin' was wrong. I had a hard time acceptin' it."

She could hear the sincerity in his words and was reassured.

"It's taken me a lifetime t' know what was missin'," he went on. "Ellen was a virtuous an' pious woman, a kind an' lovin' mother. But she took the wrong vows. She should have been a nun." He was silent for a moment. "I can't find fault with her. We were young an' misguided. When the doctor said no more children, and then the church said no more relations, well...well, I became bitter. I became selfish, unfaithful, an', God fergive me, even violent."

He paused again, and then the words came in a rush. "I deeply regret the hurt an' shame I brought on meself an' me family. I regret ill-treatin' Ellen. I was rejected, an' rejection fueled a fierce hurt an' anger in me. It grieves me t' admit it."

Bridie listened quietly, trying to sort out her own reactions. The Tom she knew was kind and considerate. He had accepted without argument the limits she had set in their relationship, foremost among them, her refusal to go to bed with any man unless he was her husband.

Now the man she loved was telling her that he had been unfaithful to his wife, that he had mistreated the mother of his children. What was she getting herself into? How much did she really know about this man? She had wanted the truth, but her joy had paled on hearing it. Now she didn't know what to do with it.

Tom stopped talking, and she realized that she had withdrawn her arm from his. Their silence now was not a comfortable, companionable one.

Her heart was at odds with her common sense. She didn't want the burden of this knowledge. She wanted things to be as they were. They had been happy with each other, and now she was angry with Tom for casting this shadow over their love. She was angry at being forced to make a decision.

Tom walked on beside her in silence, keeping the promise he made to himself. No matter what the outcome might be, he was not going to behave as he had with his wife or Maggie. If he did end up losing Bridie, it would be just punishment, but he was not going to bring it on himself. His temper had brought enough misery to him and those around him, and he was determined not to allow it to drive Bridie away. He hoped she would give him a chance to prove that he was a changed man. She must know that her love had changed him.

But Bridie needed time to think. She knew this would be a turning point in their lives. Although she thought she loved Tom, she knew that they did not yet really know one another. They had both been overtaken by emotions so strong that neither of them could think straight.

One thing was sure, she thought. She would not grant Tom absolution for his sins. It was not her place. She had not been hurt as Ellen and, to a lesser degree, Maggie had. And what of his family? Where did they stand in all of this? It would take time for her to sort her feelings out. She must try to do the right thing for herself, for Tom, and for everyone else.

They had reached the crossroad, both geographically and emotionally. Tom lived in one direction, Bridie, the other. Normally, from here they would take the tram into town or go for a walk in the park. This was not to be one of those normal nights.

Tom stopped at the curb. Bridie stopped slightly behind him. When she spoke, finally, her voice was strong but at a slightly lower than normal pitch. "Tom, I have t' go home. Me thoughts 're jumbled up, an' I don't know if I'm comin' or goin'. I have t' thank ya fer tellin' me the truth of it, though I am sorry t' hear it."

Tom was not prepared for the pain he felt at the thought of losing her. For a moment, he felt his old defenses stirring within him, and it was hard to keep his promise to himself, but he realized that lashing out would only invite more suffering. He would hold his temper this time…come what may.

"Ah, luv," his voice was thick with emotion, "I…I'm sorry ye're disappointed in me." He was silent for a moment, then, "All I can say now is I love ya. If ya can see yer way t' givin' me the chance t' prove it, I'll wait ferever 'til yer satisfied that things've changed. I'm no longer the man I was. Ye're the best thing that's ever happened t' me. I'm not sure I deserve t' be with ya, although it jest seems we belong together…."

Bridie made no attempt to answer. She was too confused by her own emotions. Overriding everything else was a leaden sadness. She had not felt this way since the news of her fiancé's death overseas. Now she needed to go somewhere quiet to think. "Tom, I've changed me mind. I won't be goin' home jest yet. I think I'll be goin' over t' the chapel. Give me some time t' think things over."

He nodded. "When can I see ya again?"

"I don't know…I can't seem t' get me mind t' settle on anythin', much less make plans fer the future."

"Bridie, don't leave me like this. At least let me know there's a chance fer us."

"Tom, I don't know if I'm comin' or goin'. How can I tell ya if we have a chance or not when I'm not sure how I feel about anythin'? Where do we go from here? I don't know atall, atall. Jest let me be fer now."

"Kin I see ya at the café?"

"It's a public place, sure it is. It's not up t' me t' tell ya t' come or not t' come." As confused as she was right now, she didn't want to burn any bridges. The café was probably the best place for them to see each other, for they would not be alone unless she wanted to be.

Her head was pounding. She badly needed to be alone. "I'll

be goin' along now." This was all she could manage through the knot that tied her tongue.

Tom nodded and kissed her on the forehead, then turned and walked away. She watched him until he rounded the corner and was out of sight. She wanted to run after him, to feel safe in his arms, she wanted him to comfort her, to be on her side, but of course he couldn't be on her side because he was the reason she was hurting.

He was the enemy; or rather, his past was...something she must guard herself against. She needed him, but he couldn't be there for her. Hot salty tears gathered in her eyes and spilled down her cheeks.

It took her thirty minutes to walk to the chapel, and she was thankful to sit down when she arrived. She chose the front pew facing the statue of the Blessed Virgin with the infant Jesus in her arms. The flickering candles had a calming and hypnotic effect on her and the familiar scents of incense and beeswax hung in the air.

Sitting there, Bridie thought about the petitions represented by the candles. She had recently added her own, and now she wondered if the Mother of God had time to intercede for all the poor souls who asked for help. How foolish she was to question the capabilities of the Blessed Virgin. She hoped it wasn't a sin. She then realized something else. She was allowing her mind to wander away from her problem. She was thinking about everything and anything but what she should be thinking about.

God helps them who help themselves, she told herself, *an' I have t' try t' find me way out o' me own dilemma.* She was thankful to have a quiet and sacred place to come to. She would find an answer here. She just had to be still and listen.

Tom walked home. He needed time to compose himself. He wasn't sure what reaction he had expected from Bridie, but he had hoped for more understanding than she had shown. On the other hand, he reminded himself, he had no right to even hope that Bridie could be sympathetic A man who beat his wife was not likely to be the recipient of much compassion. But still, she had not altogether banished him from her life. She had left a tiny door open. He would give her time. He would hope he could persuade her to give him a chance.

Then he remembered the promise he had made to do a novena if Lucy recovered. He had not yet made good on it, but he would do so right now. He would appeal to St. Jude, the patron saint of lost causes, to intercede for him, both to regain his daughter's affection and to convince Bridie to give him the opportunity to prove his love for her.

Tom wasn't much of a chapel man. He resented the Church's interference in the lives of its followers. *Priests are useless altogether*, he always said to himself, *a bunch o' leeches livin' off their parishioners, pokin' their noses in peoples' personal business.* The Protestants had the right idea, talking directly to God with no outside interference. Direct discourse with God suited Tom's way of thinking, although admiring it from a safe distance was as far as he could go. He was born a Catholic, after all, and he would die one. It wasn't about the religion so much as it was about loyalty to one's family and community. His people were Catholics, and that was all there was to it. He would go to the chapel and complete the ten weeks of the novena as promised.

Right now, though, he was heading for the pub. All this soul-searching had brought on a terrible mean thirst.

Chapter Twelve

Lucy and Bill walked hand in hand along a footpath beside the river. Bill stooped down slightly as he listened to Lucy tell him about the job she was after.

"I know I've never done anythin' like this before," she said, "but I'll have a room, meals, an' a pay packet t' call me own. I can't be stayin' with me friend much longer an' wear out me welcome." She paused. "Bangor's not that far away, an' it's a small hotel, so I should be able t' learn the ropes quickly enough. Livin' by the seaside will be a change, fer sure. I love the ocean, don't you?"

Bill nodded. "Aye, I do that, always have since I was a small lad. Me da used t' take us all to the seashore fer a few days in the summertime. We had a grand time. We each had our own bucket and spade. Me ma'd pack a picnic, an' for a special treat, our da would buy us a packet of dulce."

As Lucy made a face at the idea of eating seaweed, Bill caught her expression and grinned. "Sure, ya don't know if ye'd like it or not if ya haven't tried it."

Lucy decided it would be easier to agree with him than to argue. "Aye, ye're right." she said. "I'll try some when I go t' Bangor, that's a promise." But she had her fingers crossed behind her back. Bill smiled and nodded again. He knew she was humoring him to shut him up.

Their mood was the most lighthearted it had been for a long time, and he felt it was a good time to "test the waters," as they say, before Lucy went to her new job. He wanted to be sure that they could still be seeing each other, even if they were living in different places. Suggesting that they rest a while and enjoy the river, he found a soft spot under a sheltering tree and invited Lucy to sit with him. They sat quietly for a few minutes, surrounded by the scent of the hawthorn trees, the gentle lapping of the water, and the soft spring breeze. When Bill draped his arm around Lucy's shoulder and pulled her close, she nestled her head under his chin. Her hair smelled like lemons, which surprised and delighted him. He felt the softness and warmth of her breasts, and his body quickened and responded.

Tipping her chin, he raised her face to his and gently kissed her. He found her mouth and body yielding to his touch, and suddenly the tender kiss turned passionate and demanding. An overwhelming rush of desire coursed through their bodies, begging for release, yearning for a respite from months of heartache, illness, mourning, anger, loss, and sorrow. Their young bodies sought satisfaction, their souls longed for relief, conflicting with their deeply ingrained convictions of right and wrong. They were saved from themselves by the arrival of an unlikely intruder, a terrier puppy yelping as he tried to pull himself out of the river, hindered by the remains of a burlap bag that clung to his back legs.

Startled by the commotion, Bill and Lucy sprang apart. The depth of the emotions they felt had shaken both of them. Taking a few seconds to gather their wits, they went to rescue the puppy.

"There now, boy," Bill slid down the embankment dislodging a few stones along the way, "'tis a fine mess ye're in. I'll have ya out in a jiff." The puppy was losing its battle with the running water, but Bill reached him just in time and fished him out.

"Oh, Bill, the poor wee thing," Lucy cried, a bit more passionately than she might have in normal circumstances. "Someone was tryin' t' drown him! Can ya imagine doin' a thing like that to a defenseless wee creature? Thank God, ya were here t' rescue him."

Bill shook his head, wondering who had rescued whom. Another minute, and they would have passed the point of no return. The puppy would have drowned and he and Lucy would have been in a mountain of trouble. How could he have faced Lucy's family? He had never known temptation could feel so wonderful. It was little wonder people gave in to it. He thought of Tom with new sympathy and regretted judging him so hastily.

Reaching the bank, he set the pup down and turned to Lucy. "I'm sorry, luv. I never meant for things t' get so out o' hand. Can ya fergive me?"

Lucy raised her eyes and looked into his. "There is nothin' t' fergive. I wanted ya as much as ya wanted me. We were lucky yon wee dog stopped us from commitin' a sin."

"But it didn't feel like a sin," he said, "an' that's the worst of it. It felt like the most natural thing in the world. Sin is the devil's work…bein' with you felt like heaven. How can that be?"

"Aye, it's confusin' alright. It jest wasn't the right time or the right place." As Lucy gathered their belongings, Bill asked himself just when and where that time and place would be. He hoped he hadn't lost her respect, in spite of what she had said to the contrary.

Now she broke into his thoughts. "What are we goin' t' do about the wee dog? He looks half-starved, he does. I can't take him, though he's a dear wee thing, an' that's fer sure.

Bill picked the terrier up again. "I'll take him with me. He has the makin's of a fine dog. He is fer sure a handsome wee fella. And besides, I'll be glad o' the company."

Hearing the sad note in his voice, Lucy wondered if she was doing the right thing in taking the job in Bangor. She was feeling confused. Was she falling in love with him, she wondered, or was she just falling in love with falling in love? She missed her mother and her sister. Was she trying to use Bill to fill the void? If she weren't in love with Bill, she would just be using him. Was she taking the job in order to put distance between them?

Her head was spinning with unanswered questions. She had felt so safe, so protected, so desirable in his arms. His kisses had awakened sensations she had never felt before, powerful, urgent, and dangerous. She had almost been ready to give herself completely to him...but that would have branded her a loose woman. Which at the time had seemed not to matter at all. As ashamed as she felt of her wantonness, she could not lay the blame at Bill's feet. She had been just as eager as he was.

They walked silently along the riverbank quietly hand in hand, trying to make sense of their thoughts. The puppy was tucked under Bill's arm, his tail going a mile a minute. He was definitely the happiest of the trio. Bill smiled down at his new friend, whom he had decided to name Hero. He was feeling glad, he decided, that the wee dog had saved them from themselves. Bill wanted more for both of them. He wanted Lucy to marry him, but not because she had to. Because she wanted to.

These thoughts were interrupted by a rumbling in his belly and the realization that he'd had nothing since breakfast. "I'm starved," he said. "It's all this excitement, so it is. How about fish 'n' chips fer tea?"

"Aye, that'd be lovely," said Lucy. "But what about the wee dog? They'll not be lettin' him into the fish 'n' chip shop."

Bill smiled at her, then at the puppy. "I'll jest go by our house first an' leave him with me sister. She'll be chuffed with him."

Changing direction, they set off for Bill's house. Lucy had never been in this part of town before. Large paintings of King William of Orange, sword aloft, crossing the river Boyne, adorned brick walls. *No Pope Here* and *God Save The King* slogans were everywhere. The Union Jack flew proudly above many buildings, large and small.

She felt like she was visiting a foreign country, one in which she would not be welcome. Uncomfortable and increasingly nervous, she tightened her grip on Bill's hand. He understood, but said nothing. He had felt the same uneasiness in Lucy's neighborhood.

The door to Bill's house was open, and they could hear a radio playing somewhere in the back. "Come on in," he said, "an' meet me sister."

She hesitated, feeling unaccountably shy. "Oh, I don't know if I should," she said. "She doesn't know I'm comin'. She'll not be expectin' t' have company, especially…." "Catholic company" were the words left unsaid.

"Ah, don't be an eejit," was the answer. "She's dyin' t' meet ya I've been tellin' her all about ya. Come on, then, she's in the kitchen. She's a grand girl. I'll miss her when she goes."

Lucy took a deep breath and stepped forward. "Where's she goin', then?"

"She'll be off soon to Australia t' live with me brother an' sister-in-law," he replied. "They've been after me t' go, too, but I'm not sure." He paused and followed her through the doorway. "It's a long way from home, an' I don't think there are many shipbuildin' yards there. I'm not sure if I'd get a job."

There was, of course, another reason. Neither of them felt able to mention it.

"Yer a painter," she said. "Ye could work anywhere. Ya don't have t' be in a shipyard."

Bill had no answer to that.

She laughed a little. "An' ye're after teasin' me about a lack of adventure? Ye're worse than I am."

"Is that you, Billy? Who's that with ya?" It was Martha, his younger sister, walking down the hall toward them. She was in silhouette for a few moments as she squinted and came toward the door and the light. She was on the tall side for a woman, but, indeed, most in the family were tall and slim. Her dark hair was drawn to one side and secured by a silver colored slide, and the word "merry" would best describe her twinkling eyes and wide smile. After wiping her hand on her apron, she offered it in greeting.

"Ya must be Lucy. I'm very glad t' meet ya at last."

Lucy shook the proffered hand. "Many thanks, Martha. I hope I'm not puttin' ya out. Bill said ye'd not mind me comin' without bein' invited."

"Oh, fer goodness sake! We don't stand on ceremony. In our house, any friend o' Bill's is welcome any time." Martha noticed the puppy. "Bill, where did ya get the wee dog?"

Instead of answering her directly, Bill hoisted the dog, giving it a look at his sister. His eyes were twinkling. "Hero," he said formally, "this is my sister Martha. She loves animals. I'm sure you two will get along famously."

Martha smiled but said, "Bill, sure we can't keep him. He must belong t' someone. We should put an ad in the lost and found. He looks half starved. And none too clean."

"I'd not be worryin' too much about his family," said Bill. "I fished him out o' the Lagan, trailin' a burlap bag behind him. Somebody tried t' drown the poor wee fella."

Martha frowned and reached out to let the puppy sniff her hand. "There's no accountin' fer some folk," she said. "If they didn't want him, why didn't they take him t' the RSPCA? Drownin' is a cruel death, so it is."

Hearing her angry tone, the dog laid his ears back.

"There, there now, sure," Martha said, soothingly, "I'd not be hurtin' ya." She reached out again and gathered the little animal in her arms. "Sure, he's shiverin'. Let's go into the kitchen an' I'll get him somethin' t' eat. I think he's shakin' from fear as well as cold an' hunger. We can take care o' the cold and the hunger, but it'll take a wee while t' make him trust us."

Lucy was watching. She had been as nervous about meeting Martha as the dog was. *I should've known better*, she thought. *She's as kind an' decent as her brother is.* Lucy wasn't sure what she had been expecting. This was supposed to be enemy territory, and she had expected the enemy to be very different. Exactly how, she wasn't sure.

"Lucy," Martha broke into her thoughts, "I'm sorry. I'm fergettin' me manners, so I am. How about a nice cuppa? I'll just pop the kettle on. It'll be ready in no time at all."

"Thank ya," Lucy said, still feeling shy, "but we don't want t' be puttin' ya t' any trouble."

"Sure, an' it's no trouble at all, an' 'tis nice t' have a wee chat." Martha set about filling the kettle.

The kitchen was larger than Lucy expected. There was a round table in the center with four chairs, one of which was occupied by a fat black and white cat, happily curled up and asleep. Above the mantle hung a framed picture of King George and on either side of the picture sat china dogs with white and brown markings. Despite the balmy day, a peat fire burned gently in the grate, and a row of African violets in terracotta pots basked on the windowsill in the early spring sunlight.

This kitchen was the heart of the home, a place where family would gather to eat and talk. As Lucy felt a shard of painful longing for her own shattered family, tears sprang to her eyes. She affected a cough to cover her embarrassment. Brother and sister exchanged sympathetic glances and pretended not to notice. As Martha began setting out cups and saucers for their tea. Bill protested the use of the dainty china cups.

"You girls might like yer tea in yon wee thimbles," he said in his manliest voice, "but I'll be havin' mine in me mug."

Martha laughed and teased him about his lack of refinement.

"Tea tastes better from a china cup, don't ya know that?" Lucy had recovered her composure by now and joined in the good-natured banter.

"I wouldn't know," Bill replied. "I keep away from the prized cups fer fear of breakin' the damn things."

Martha tut-tutted at Bill's choice of language, and then both women giggled as Bill extended his little finger and mimed the sip of the genteel tea drinker.

"Martha," said Lucy after a moment, "the cups are lovely, no matter what yer brother says."

"Thanks'. They were one o' me mother's weddin' presents, an' prized indeed, they are. I understand Bill's feelin' about 'em, but t' me, they're a link to our parents, God rest their souls."

The mood became somber for a moment, as all three reflected on their losses. Martha thought she should offer her condolences for Lucy's recent bereavement, but she didn't know quite how to bring it up tactfully. Searching for the right words, she decided simplest would be best.

"I'm sorry fer yer troubles, Lucy," she said quietly. "Bill's told me about yer losses."

"Thanks' Martha. I still can't believe me mother an' me sister are both gone." Lucy's voice was quiet, but steady. "An' the wee baby never had a chance fer us t' get t' know 'im. I didn't think 'twas possible t' feel such sorrow fer someone ya never met."

Now her voice trailed off, and for a moment there was silence, punctuated by the shrill shouts from the children at play outside. "I was hopin' the wee one would be a boy, an' take after our Richard," she said after a moment. "They say he was baptized and named after him, so at least they are all together in heaven. It's some comfort t' know there is someone t' hold the door open when yer turn comes."

As Bill placed a sympathetic arm around Lucy's shoulders, once again she remembered how kind and compassionate he had been through her family's troubles.

Martha decided to lead the subject away from sad memories. "Will ya be stayin' fer supper?" she asked. "I'm jest about t' make some, an' ye're more than welcome."

"We were goin' t' have fish 'n' chips," said Bill. "Would ya like t' join us?"

"Ah, no, but thanks fer askin'. I'm off to a Bible class with Anne and her husband. The new minister and his wife are havin' a wee get-together afterwards." Now she smiled warmly at the young couple. "The two of you go along an' enjoy yer fish 'n' chips. Lucy, I hope ye'll come again soon so we can have a bit of a yarn."

This brought a sincere smile to Lucy's face. "Thank ya, kindly," she said, "but it'll be a bit further, as I'll be leavin' fer a new job soon. In Bangor. But, yes, I'd love t' come again." She glanced down at Hero, who was sitting under the table and following the conversation as if he understood it. "And thanks for lookin' after the wee dog."

"I'm sure he'll be jest fine," said Martha. She pointed to the hearth, and the dog walked over to it and curled up. "Look at him now, warmin' himself by the fire. Makin' himself at home, he is, though he's keepin' one eye on the cat. She's jest ignorin' him, o' course. 'Tis beneath her dignity t' notice him. She's spoiled rotten, that one is."

"We'll be off then," said Bill. "I'll see ya later. Say a prayer fer us."

"Oh, it's not a prayer meetin'," his sister answered, "but I'll say one anyway."

Good-byes having been said, Lucy went to retrieve her handbag and gloves from the hall table while Bill helped Martha carry the tea things into the scullery.

"Well...what de ya think?" Bill asked his sister as soon as they were out of earshot of Lucy.

"I think she's a lovely girl. Be off with ya, then. An' take good care of her."

"I will, an' I'm glad ya liked her."

As they left, the dog tried to follow them and cried when Martha held him back.

"I feel bad leavin' Martha t' deal with the wee dog," Lucy said as they closed the door behind them. "I wish we could take him with us."

"I know…he must feel abandoned again," said Bill. "But he'll get used t' Martha in no time at all. She loves animals. She'll take good care of him." Giving Lucy's hand a squeeze, he added, "And I'll see him soon enough, anyhow. But in the meantime, who's going t' take care of me?"

Lucy scoffed in mock exasperation. "Right," she said, "Turn right t' the shop for fish 'n' chips. After that, you're on yer own."

Chapter Thirteen

The weeks and months after Mary Alice's death were a nightmare for Feelie. Caring for the three little girls, cooking and cleaning…it was all backbreaking work. She labored from sunup 'til sundown and never seemed to be finished. Keeping up with the washing was her biggest challenge. No sooner had she changed the baby than it was time to change her again. She was constantly doing battle with dirty nappies.

Their father, Brian, came to see them every night, expecting a meal and never lifting a hand to help with his children. Feelie was having a hard time guarding her tongue. She had little sympathy for her brother-in-law and thought he needed a swift kick in the arse. Oh, he was good at kissing and cuddling the wee ones, she admitted, but that was the extent of his fatherly interest. He never offered to help in any practical way.

Although she was of a mind to tell him just what she thought of him, she held back for the sake of the children. They didn't need any more trouble. Right now, for example, her father and Brian were sitting at the table discussing some damn Hurley game. To hear them, you'd think it was the most important topic on their minds. Feeble-minded eejits, that's what they were.

To make matters worse, a night or two ago Brian had actually upbraided her for not being able to keep the baby quiet while he ate. To Tom's credit, he had defended her, telling Brian he was lucky to have a meal made for him, not to mention someone to look after his children. Brian had apologized, but the apology did not sit right with Feelie. Resentment was curdling her stomach. She loved the children, but her position was a bitter pill to swallow.

She had to keep reminding herself that Father Doyle had said this was a trial sent by God. Depending on how she handled it, she would be rewarded, if not in this life then in the next. *Live, old horse, and you'll get grass*, she thought bitterly.

In late summer, she noticed a change in the nightly ritual. Brian still visited the girls, but no longer did he stay for the evening meal, and her father was also absent many nights. She wondered at the change, but was too busy to spend much time thinking about it. At least it cut down on the cooking and cleaning up afterward.

Truth be told, things were a little easier all the way 'round. The two older girls no longer cried every night for their mammy. Feelie felt she had things fairly well under control. She even had a little time at night to listen to the radio or read. Some afternoons, she liked to put the baby in her pram and meet the two older girls coming from school for a walk in the park, stopping on the way home for a quarter pound of dolly mixtures to share or an ice cream. And once in a while her father would stay with the sleeping children, giving her a chance to go to the pictures with her sister Nellie.

Their local cinema was a rough and ready place with wooden benches for seats and floors littered with the debris from the preceding performance. When the lights went down a hush descended on the noisy audience. The sisters liked the romantic, musical Jeanette MacDonald and Nelson Eddy sagas best. For an hour or two and with the payment of three pence, transportation to Canada was provided, courtesy of the silver screen. No longer in a backstreet cinema, the girls smiled when the beautiful maiden took fright in the wilderness, cheered when the handsome Mountie got his man, and sighed happily when he came singing to his woman. The maiden and the Mountie lived in an uncomplicated and thoroughly satisfying world in which evil was vanquished and good prevailed. The men in the cinema identified with the hero, the women with the lovely heroine, and everyone felt lighter and happier when the picture ended. The euphoria lasted for a little while, at least.

On one evening in early August, Feelie and Nellie left the cinema arm in arm and headed for the café for a feast of mince and mashed potatoes. It had rained heavily during the film, and skipping over the puddles made them feel like two schoolgirls. The windows of the little café were fogged up, the result of wet clothing and soggy patrons.

As they entered, they encountered a man and woman about to leave. The man was holding the door open, and the woman was laughing at something he was saying to her. She was young, pretty, and very smartly dressed. A cream-colored raincoat complemented her penny-bright hair, which fell straight to her jaw line in a fashionable bob. Both hair and coat were very becoming and very modern.

If this unexpected apparition startled Feelie and Nellie, it was nothing to their surprise when they recognized the smart lady's companion as none other than their brother-in-law Brian. Gone was the liquor-induced paunch. His hair was gleaming, his navy blue suit precision-pressed.

Feelie couldn't believe her eyes. She hadn't noticed any change in him, but of course she had been too busy with the wee ones to pay much attention to their father. For her part, Nellie was mildly amused and not a little annoyed by Brian's natty appearance. The girl looked out of place in this neck of the woods, she thought. What was her eejit of a brother-in-law thinking about, anyway, to bring her here? She looked as out of place as a nun in a bawdy house. Did he imagine that because Mary Alice was dead, he was a young single fella again? *If he's lookin' t' replace me sister, he's barkin' up the wrong tree with this one,* thought Nellie. Above all else, Brian needed a mother for his children, and this girl didn't look at all like a suitable candidate. She looked as though she belonged on the cover of a magazine, not knee deep in dirty washing.

As Brian closed the door, he almost collided with his sisters-in-law. "Nellie! Feelie! What a surprise. I didn't expect t' see ya here."

"I don't imagine ya did," Feelie said dryly.

"We've jest been t' the pictures. Our da's lookin' after yer wee ones so Feelie can have a night off," Nellie explained, just in case Brian had forgotten he was a father.

"Well, that's grand," he said. "Ya both deserve a break. I hope ya enjoy yer meal." He was trying to guide the stranger past his sisters-in-law, but Nellie would have no part of it. She stood her ground, making it impossible for them to leave without knocking her over. The girl looked confused. Brian felt like a rat in a trap.

"Brian," said Feelie, "where're yer manners? Are ya not goin' t' introduce us t' yer friend?"

"Oh...ah, sure, I'm sorry. Feelie, Nellie, this is Chloe."

"Pleased to make your acquaintance, ah'm sure," the girl drawled as she extended one bejeweled hand in a limp parody of a handshake.

The sisters exchanged a puzzled glance. Who was this woman?

Having made the introductions, Brian was determined to make a fast getaway before any further questions could be asked. He had seen the looks of surprise on the faces of his sisters-in law, and he was not prepared to enlighten them any further at this time.

"Well," he said with an air of finality, "'twas good t' see ya. We have t' run...sorry...we can't stay and yarn."

He pushed past Nellie, grabbed the girl's hand, and was off into the street. Nellie and Feelie were rooted to the spot. They neither spoke nor moved until Brian and the girl were lost from sight. Nellie was the first to recover.

"What de ya make o' that one?" she asked indignantly. "I'm sure I've never seen the likes. He never let on that he was related t' us. What does he think we are? Chopped liver? Where de ya think he picked that one up? I never heard anyone talk like that before. Slow and sweet as treacle and jest about as sticky, I'll bet."

"I...I imagine she's from America," Feelie ventured. "I've heard people talk like that in the pictures."

"Ye're right...ye're right, now that I think of it. Anyway, it makes no sense, him takin' up with a girl like that. He needs a different type altogether. A no-nonsense girl, one who'll be a good mother t' his children."

"Well," Feelie ventured, "ya can't always know jest by lookin' at a body what kind o' person she is. She could be all show on the outside, but strong and steady when the chips are down."

"Aye, I suppose ya could be right," said Nellie, grudgingly, "but I'm not convinced."

"Well, we'll jest have t' wait and see what happens. Right now, though, me stomach thinks me throat's cut, I'm that hungry, so I am. Let's go inside and eat." With that, Feelie turned decisively and led the way into the café.

Inside, it was crowded, but after only a short wait they were seated in a booth. Despite what she had said to her sister, Feelie's thoughts kept returning to Brian and his children. What would happen to them? She had some misgivings. Not many Americans had been known to settle down in Ireland. It was more often the other way around, and had been that way ever since the Famine. Would Brian follow this woman to America and take the children with him?

The thought struck her like a blow. She couldn't bear to think of losing any more of her family. She had given up her own precious dreams to take care of her sister's children, and Brian's nightly visits were becoming shorter and shorter, just a nod in the direction of fatherhood. Now, after having decided to forego nursing school and an independent life to devote her time to raising the motherless children, it was galling to her to think that her brother-in-law could take them away. She realized she had no rights where the children were concerned. If Brian remarried, his new wife would take over, as would be expected.

"Are ya ready?" The waitress's question cut across Feelie's musings.

"I'm sorry; I was lost in me thoughts." She looked at her sister. "Nellie, have ya ordered?"

"Aye. I'm havin' the usual."

"I'll have the same as me sister, thanks." Feelie handed the unread menu to the waitress.

"What were ya thinkin' about?" Nellie asked when the waitress had left. "Ya were miles away, and from the look on yer face, ya were not in a happy place."

"I was jest thinkin' what would happen if Brian married that girl," said Feelie slowly, reluctantly. "If she's American, he might go there and take our wee ones."

"Hold on," said Nellie. "There's a lot of 'ifs' there. Don't go borrowin' trouble. We've enough t' fret over. It's a big jump from takin' a girl out t' marryin' her. Our Mary Alice hasn't been gone a year yet. It'd be indecent fer him t' marry so soon."

Feelie nodded. "Yer right, but I got a real creepy feelin', almost like a premonition, as soon as I saw 'em. Maybe I'm just imaginin' things, but it gave me the collywobbles all the same. I think he's been walkin' out with her fer quite some time. He's spendin' less an' less time at the house with his children. I didn't pay much mind to it 'til now, figurin' it was jest like a man."

Nellie chuckled. "I understand what yer sayin', but I still think yer jumpin' the gun. Try t' put it out o' yer mind now. Let's enjoy the rest o' the night. We don't get t' do this often; it's a rare treat, so it is. Ah, here comes our meal."

Conversation ended while the waitress placed plates of steaming savory mince and mashed potatoes floating in gravy in front of them. "There now," she said. "Kin I get youse anythin' else?"

"No, thanks," said Feelie. "Sure, this is grand fer now. But I'd like a cuppa tea, a slice of rhubarb pie, and custard later. How 'bout you, Nellie?"

Nellie nodded vigorously as she settled in to enjoy her dinner. They both loved rhubarb pie, although, of course, no one made it as well as their mother had. This place was pretty good, though.

~

That was a close one, Brian thought as he guided Chloe away from the café. Things were getting serious between him and Chloe, and he needed more time to sort out his emotions.

For one thing, he was still confused by Lucy's attitude toward him. She had not spoken to him since Mary Alice's death. What had happened to make her treat him like this? He had no idea. Whatever it was, though, it was obvious that there would never be a chance for him with Lucy. Besides, she seemed to be more and more involved with that Protestant bugger.

Brian had been working on repairs to the façade at the Midland Hotel when Chloe had stopped one afternoon to ask directions. He was fascinated by her accent, to say nothing of her looks.

For her part, Chloe had quickly decided that Brian would make the perfect companion during her visit to Ireland. He was authentic, a real, down-to-earth Irishman, and it was this earthiness in him that appealed to her. She'd had quite enough of the counterfeit Anglophiles to whom she had been introduced, and she was also heartily sick of the vapid Southern gentlemen she had left behind in America. So, on impulse, she had invited him for a drink in her hotel suite.

Brian was lonely, and Chloe seemed eager to please him. She was different from any girl he had known. No Irish Catholic girl would have been so generous with her lovemaking, even with benefit of clergy. Chloe was what was termed a "free spirit," but it was more than the spirit that was free. She gave her beautiful body without restraint. Best of all, she enjoyed his and was not afraid to tell him so.

At first his own inhibitions had hindered him, and he wasn't sure what to make of this American girl. Were they all like her? His mother, he knew, would have had a few choice words to describe a girl like Chloe, and some of those words nagged at the back of his mind. Gradually, though, he decided he didn't care, and gave himself up to the sheer pleasure of her.

She sidetracked any discussion of her marital status, however, which made him wonder if this meant she had no intention of any real commitment. Did she think of him as only a good roll in the hay? That'd be a switch, he thought wryly. It would not surprise him, though, given her views on equality.

What did she see in him? She was educated, refined, and well traveled, whereas he was a rough working man with only a basic education and little knowledge of the world. Was he the rich girl's casual plaything?

He had a lot of thinking to do before he would consider introducing this remarkable, confusing woman to his world, even though his day-to-day life had changed dramatically since he met her. He spent less and less time with his children and almost no time with his mates in the pub. Chloe had become the center of his universe, a universe that had shrunk to the size of her bed.

Chapter Fourteen

Bridie and Tom were sitting quietly in the back of the chapel. They had been meeting here for the past seven weeks. There were three weeks left of the novena Tom had promised to make. He was praying for reconciliation with his youngest daughter. He was also hoping that St. Jude would help him to win back the affection of the woman sitting beside him.

Believing that praying together would help mend the rift, Bridie had agreed to accompany him. She loved him, yes, but she was having a hard time coming to terms with how he had treated his wife, now deceased. Tom was trying his best to convince her that he had changed his ways. She wanted to believe him, and she knew that was half the battle. He had promised to be patient until she believed in the new Tom.

The novena ended, the congregation prepared to leave, pausing on the steps of the church to have a few words with the priest and greet friends. Tom and Bridie had chosen to sit in the back of the chapel so that they could make a hasty retreat. They didn't feel like sharing their brief time together with others. After all, decisions still had to be made before tongues started wagging. As a widower, Tom was fair game, and many hopes would be dashed when he and Bridie made their relationship public. They didn't think they were ready for that yet.

The air was soft and balmy. A gentle breeze chased through the leaves, turning them inside out.

"'Tis a beautiful night," said Bridie. "I love the long twilight. Everythin' gets so quiet. Th' light is magic, so it is. I read somewhere there are parts of the world that don't have the twilight we do. That's a shame, so it is. Don't ya think so?"

Tom couldn't help a quiet chuckle to himself. Bridie never ceased to amaze him. Here he was, with the weight of the world on his shoulders, worried sick about his family, about the community, about their future as a couple, and Bridie was concerned about some foreign country not having enough twilight! As much as he loved her, she was a woman, and thus, at times, utterly impossible for him to understand. In Bridie's case, however, he would be grateful for the chance to spend the rest of his life trying.

"Aye, luv," he attempted, gamely, "'tis a shame, sure enough. We're lucky in lots o' ways, though. They say Ireland's the greenest spot on earth. There's beauty t' be found everywhere…in the mountains, the lochs, the rivers, the oceans, and most of all in our people. I think there's a hint o' the poet in every Celtic soul. Sure, there's none like us. We been givin' the English a run fer their money fer centuries!"

"Ye're right," she said. "The English've tried starvin' us t' death, runnin' us out of our homes, forbiddin' the sayin' o' the Mass, even the wearin' o' the green. Bad cess t' the lot of 'em."

"Well, well," said Tom, raising his hands in mock surrender, "how did we get from the twilight t' the English? Let's ferget all the troubles. Like ya said, it's a beautiful night. I'm jest happy t' be here with you. How about a lemonade fer you an' beer fer me?"

"Sure, that'd be grand," she said agreeably. "We could go t' the Harp an' Whistle. It's jest 'round the corner. I like it there. The lounge is quiet."

Falling into a companionable silence, they made their way to the pub. Bridie didn't drink, but she didn't seem to mind if Tom had one. Although she wouldn't tolerate drunkenness, she understood that a man liked his pint. That was one of the things Tom liked about her. She was a companion. He enjoyed the company of men, but given the choice, preferred to be with Bridie.

Suddenly a momentary glimpse of Ellen passed through his mind. Never before had he realized how lonely she must have been. They had been in no way suited. Ellen would never have gone to the pub with him. Then again, had he ever asked her? He pondered the possibility. Was he to blame? Was he so selfish he couldn't see beyond his own pleasure? St. Jude was apparently not going to let Thomas O'Leary off lightly. Not until Tom understood the loneliness he had caused Ellen and had made some attempt to ask his daughter's forgiveness.

"A penny fer yer thoughts," Bridie whispered. "Ya look as though ye're miles away."

"I was jest thinkin' about Ellen," he said in a quiet voice. "I don't think I ever asked her t' come with me t' the pub. Or anywhere else, fer that matter. It never crossed me mind until now how lonely she must've been." He shook his head. "God fergive me."

"I know ya don't hold much with the priests," said Bridie, "but I think doin' the novena is helpin' ya with yer conscience. Until ya set that t' rights, yer never goin' t' be happy."

He looked her in the eyes. "I'm happy when I'm with you."

She smiled, a little. "I know what yer sayin', Tom. I'm happy with you, too. But there's problems that must be dealt with. Anyone our age has a past. We need t' deal with the past an' let it rest. The past is part of us. It'll always be there."

True that, thought Tom.

Bridie continued. "Sometimes we make mistakes that can never be fergiven. Other times, we get a second chance. 'Tis too late fer Ellen; ya can only beg fer her fergiveness. But yer daughter is another thing altogether. Ya must do everythin' ya can t' mend that rift. If we're t' be happy, ya must try t' mend yer broken family."

"Aye. I know what yer sayin' is right." Tom was hasty, also a little defensive. "That's why I'm doin' the novena."

"The novena's a good start, but ya can't leave it t' St. Jude. Ya have t' make the effort yerself."

"I know…I know. I'll do me best." Then, after a deep breath, he dared ask, "The big question is, what about us?"

"I'm still here, am I not? Ya need t' get yer life untangled before ya start t' re-tangle it. We're in no hurry, Tom. We've waited this long fer happiness t' find us. We can wait a wee while longer so we don't lose it again."

But Tom wasn't so sure he could wait much longer. He wanted everything set to rights. His fast-moving personality chafed at uncertainty. He sighed and reminded himself of his promise to wait 'til Bridie was ready. He must learn patience, he told himself, and that would not come easy. Bridie was independent; she had taken care of herself all her adult life. He knew she would not permit herself to be rushed into anything. She would have to be reasonably sure of success before she would make a lasting commitment to him.

"Aye, luv," he said with a sigh, "as usual, ye're right. Please God, we have time t' make sure. It's jest that the waitin' is hard." They smiled at each other. "I want us t' be together. Life is short, an' I feel I've wasted a large part of it."

"I can't see how ya can say that," she said. "Ye have yer children and their wee ones, too. An' Ellen was a good wife t' ya in many ways. She let ya more or less do as ya liked."

Tom felt a rush of anger at these words. He didn't want to hear how noble and hard done to Ellen had been, especially not from Bridie. St. Jude was testing him, he was sure of it.

Well, me boyo, he said silently to the saint, *ya can test away. I'll not be fallin' into that trap. I'll be keepin' me mouth shut an' me temper behind it.* Aloud, he said only, "Aye. I've a lot t' be thankful fer, so I do."

Bridie was happy at Tom's response. She knew she was treading on thin ice. She also knew they had to be honest with each other if they were to grow closer. She could have agreed with him to make him happy, but thinking one thing and saying another was not her style.

Now Tom was wondering what it was about this woman that made him so happy. He wasn't used to a woman who stood up to him. She was honest to a fault, but there wasn't a mean bone in her body, nothing ever said to hurt or demean, just straightforward questions and observations. She was kind, loving, passionate, and nurturing. Not always soothing, but always stimulating. She was a live wire, she was, and Tom felt alive in her company. At that moment, as Bridie slipped her arm through his and gave it a little squeeze, he felt like she was reading his thoughts. The twilight was creeping into darkness, and the breeze now had a bit of a bite in it. Bridie shivered. Her pretty spring coat was no match for the nippy wind.

Rounding the corner, they were glad to see the cheerful yellow light spilling out from the pub's windows. The lounge was fairly quiet, with just a few couples in close conversation. Tom and Bridie selected a round table near the fire and settled into the comfortable red leather chairs.

"This is grand," Bridie said as she took her gloves off and placed her handbag on the floor. "I love a nice bright fire." For once, she almost wished she could have a hot toddy. Cold lemonade was not very appealing at the moment.

"What'll it be, then?" the girl asked as she set two cardboard coasters advertising Guinness stout on the table.

"I'll have a hot chocolate, thanks," said Bridie.

" Sir?"

"I'll have a Guinness, an' thanks," Tom nodded at the coasters.

"Be back in two shakes of a lamb's tail," the girl said. She set off to place their order.

"'Tis nice t' be waited on fer a change," Bridie said.

"When we get married, ye'll be waitin' on nobody but me."

"An' what makes ya think I'll be waitin' on ya?" she teased. "It'll be t'other way 'round, if I have anythin' t' do with it."

Tom was determined not to rise to the bait. It was the woman's place to wait on her husband. That was a given. Bridie would never have to work outside the home again. He would make sure of that. He had always provided for his family. That was his job. Her job would be to keep house and see to his comfort. It was only fair.

"We'll see about that," Tom said darkly. Bridie only smiled and shook her head. Someday she would tell him how she looked forward to spoiling him.

"I don't remember ever agreein' t' marry ye, Tom O'Leary. If and when the time is right, I shall expect a proper proposal on bended knee."

"Now ye're jest toyin' with me." He sounded a bit nervous. "Ya know full well what's on me mind."

"I know right enough," was the answer, "but I've waited a long time t' find someone. I want a proper proposal, followed by a proper weddin' in the chapel."

"Good God, woman, more chapel! Ye'll have me takin' holy orders next!"

"That, I won't!" She smiled and pretended to consider her options. "After the proper weddin', I want a proper honeymoon with a lusty husband. I'm lookin' forward t' losin' me virginity at long last." Tom almost swallowed his teeth, but choked on his beer instead. Birdie giggled at his discomfort. He was actually blushing.

"Is that any way fer a good Catholic girl t' be talkin?" he sputtered.

"Oh, get away with ya! I'm no spring chicken, and neither are you. I've no time fer false modesty."

He shook his head. "Bridie, ye're one in a million, woman."

"I jest hope that when the time comes, ya won't be disappointed," she said, suddenly shy.

"Ah, luv, I have no fear o' that. Ye've shown me more love in our short time together than I ever knew existed. I want ya fer me wife. We'll learn together."

As he spoke, he scraped the chair back and stood, then knelt on one knee. Now it was Bridie's turn to be shocked. Everyone in the room was watching and clapping and cheering. Tom and Bridie laughed to hide their embarrassment.

She reached toward him. "Tom O'Leary, will ya get up off yer knees? Ye're makin' a show of us, so y'are." She was pretending to be cross, but her eyes brimmed with unshed tears.

"Ya wanted a proper proposal," he said. "I'll get up when ya give me a proper answer."

"Tom, get up. We agreed t' wait."

"I'll get up when ya say yes. We'll wait, but I want yer promise that when things are right ye'll be me wife."

"Oh, Tom." Her tears were beginning to fall. "Oh, Tom....Yes."

Tom stood and took the signet ring off his finger. Then he kissed her and slipped the ring on the third finger of her left hand. The lounge erupted in another round of applause. This was a better show than the pictures.

"This'll have t' do 'til I get ya a real one," he said with a catch in his voice, indicating the ring.

She just looked at him, her eyes glistening like the sun on the water. Then she said, "This'll do jest fine. It'll never leave me finger."

Tom laughed. "'Twill fall off, me love, if ya don't get it made smaller" He had never felt happier, and he vowed silently to spend the rest of his life making her happy, too. The barmaid arrived with another round of drinks.

"Yon couple in the corner sent these over with their best wishes," she announced, enjoying the drama of it all. Bridie and Tom smiled their thanks, and the couple across the room raised their drinks in a toast.

Taking a drink, Tom silently thanked St. Jude and once again vowed to do a better job this time around. He prayed that this marriage would turn out to be a blessing for all concerned.

Chapter Fifteen

"Yer sister's a darlin'," Lucy told Bill as they walked arm in arm down the street away from his house.

"Aye, she is that. Ye'll get no argument from me on that score. She thought ya were pretty special as well."

Lucy blushed, turning her head in hopes that Bill would not see. "Oh, Bill, don't be pullin' me leg."

He saw, and smiled to himself. "I'm not," he said. "She said ya were a lovely girl. And that I better take good care of ya."

Lucy wasn't quite sure what to make of this information. She was still trying to sort out her feelings about Bill and the situation with him and hadn't realized that Bill had been talking to his family about her. Their earlier behavior had shaken her quite a bit. She was definitely attracted to Bill, there was no question of that, and she knew he was enamored of her.

Her sisters had told her of his nightly vigil by her bedside in the hospital while she lay unconscious, and now she felt at a disadvantage. Bill had been carrying on some kind of a lopsided courtship, and she wondered how much his imagination had to do with his feelings for her. Was she the damsel in distress being rescued by the white knight?

While she truly felt happy when she was with him, he was not, however, the white knight she was looking for. That white knight would sweep her off her feet and carry her away to a different life. Bill was steady, kind, and considerate, but would he ever want to be anything other than what he was? Not that he was anything wrong with what he was, she told herself. No, not at all. It just didn't fit in with her plans for the future.

She felt that maybe she had better put some distance between them. She didn't trust herself, and she didn't want to hurt Bill. Taking the job in the hotel was a good excuse to back off gracefully. The trouble was, she was not at all sure that she really wanted to back off.

"Here we are then." Bill held the door open to allow Lucy to precede him into the fish and chip shop. They selected a table away from the door and settled themselves in.

"An' what would ya like?" he asked. "I don't know about you, but I'm famished."

"I'd love plaice 'n' chips 'n' mushy peas, if that's alright."

"Sounds good t' me. I think I'll have the same. An' what t' drink?"

"Tea would be grand, thanks."

As Bill went up to the counter to place their order. Lucy decided the little fish and chip shop was very pleasant. The color scheme was bright and cheery. The tables covered with blue and white checked cloths overlaid by clear plastic to guard against stains, and in the center of each table sat a little cobalt blue vase holding a spray of yellow daisies. The seats of the chairs were covered in yellow oilcloth, and blue, yellow, and white linoleum covered the floor. The whole place was spotless. Framed photographs depicting Greek fishing villages and ancient ruins hanging on the walls were silent but unmistakable evidence of the owner's ethnic background. Best of all was the smell. Lucy thought there was nothing that smelled better than a fish and chip shop, especially if you were hungry, which she was. Bill returned and lowered himself into the chair opposite Lucy.

"They'll call when our order's ready," he said.

"If the food is as nice as everythin' else," she said, "it should be just grand. Sure, this is a lovely wee place. Neat as a pin, an' ya could eat off the floor if ya had a mind to."

"Aye, I've been comin' here since I was a wee fella. Nobody makes it better than Theo. He has a very good business in this location."

"Oh? How come? What's so special about this location?"

Bill smiled as he explained. "Well, we are kind of in no man's land here—half way between the Falls Road and the Shankill. But Theo is Greek Orthodox, so neither Catholic nor Protestant has an axe t' grind with him. He's pleasant to everyone, and he an' his family spend their off time with the Greek community. Besides, his food is the best. There's nothin' like satisfyin' a hungry customer t' keep 'em comin' back." His smile faded. "But, ya know, it's strange t' think that if Theo's name was Liam or William, he'd have lost half his customers before they even got t' taste the food."

"That's a soberin' notion," agreed Lucy. "When ya stop t' think about all the troubles, ya get t' wonderin' what the point of it all is. We were taught t' hate Protestants, an' then I get t' know some, an' they turn out t' be like you and yer sister."

Lucy thought again of Martha's kindness towards her and her gentle way with the rescued dog. Neither she nor her brother fit the picture of Protestants as devils she had been brought up with. But there were other Protestants, she remembered, like the Black 'n' Tan boys, who surely were devils. Murderin' bastards, thought Lucy, and she felt the anger rise within her.

She remembered stories told by her mother of the times when no Catholic was safe, not even at home. Military transports would come roaring to a halt at the top of the street disgorging the heavily armed ,booted and undisciplined bullies culled from English slums and regiments, firing shots and ordering the inhabitants out of doors to be searched, questioned, pistol-whipped, and murdered at the whim of the officers. These pseudo military marauding gangs were known as the Black and Tans. The sobriquet was descriptive of their makeshift black and khaki uniforms.

The row houses where the Catholics lived had back yards separated by brick walls, and from each wall enough bricks had been removed so that the resulting hole was large enough to allow room to escape through it. When the lorries arrived, each house would sound the alarm by banging dustbin lids. Doors were not opened willingly, but the brutal bullies who vented their frustration on anyone not fast enough to escape always kicked them open.

Many men, women, and children escaped by climbing and running from one house to the next until they reached the safety of the hills, but some others were not so lucky. They were usually executed on the spot as terrorists. Lucy could remember her mother telling of the time when she was on her knees, praying and pleading for the lives of her father and their neighbors, who had been lined up against a wall at gunpoint. They had been spared only when an officer ordered his drunken louts back on the Crossley tenders, provided by the English government to increase mobility and off to some other sport. As these stories coursed through her mind, Lucy shuddered anew at the injustice of it all, at the sorrow and the loss suffered by so many families, families who were already poor, to whom the loss of the breadwinner would be the final blow. Catholic mothers and children were forced to the ignominy of begging or the poorhouse.

"Lucy…Lucy, where'd ya drift off ta?" Bill's voice snapped her back to the present. "Our food is ready. I'll jest go up an' get it." As she refocused, he went up to the counter and picked up their plates, then returned for their cups of steaming tea. Both were hungry, but they ate quietly, each of them lost in thought.

Bill was trying to decide the best way to bring up the subject of Lucy's new job. While he didn't relish the idea of her being so far away, he considered that it wouldn't be so bad if they had some kind of understanding. He was still embarrassed by his lack of self-control that afternoon. Lucy had said she was as much to fault as he was, but, still, he blamed himself. He had already decided that he wanted to marry her, but he sensed reluctance on her part to make any kind of commitment. Whatever she was thinking about, he felt it did not bode well for his interests.

Taking his hospital visits into account, he had spent a lot more time with her than she had with him. It was a strange thing. He felt he knew more about her than he should have, considering she had been unconscious for much of their time together. He could not explain it, but there it was…he loved her.

"Oh, I'm sorry.... I was jest thinkin' about the Troubles," Lucy suddenly said, as if sensing Bill's confusion. "It's jest too bad that decent people live as enemies. Ye're not a bad man jest because ya were born a Protestant. There are bad men that are Protestant, an' bad men that are Catholic. It's all jest too confusin'. Sometimes I think it's better t' stay with yer own people. Ya don't have t' make any choices then."

Bill nodded and knew then that he had been right to worry about the direction of Lucy's thoughts. "I understand what yer sayin'," he said, "but sometimes life is not that cut 'n' dried. Ya jest said yerself, that there are good an' bad on both sides. I think we each have t' make our own decisions.... I mean, decide what's right and what's wrong, an' follow yer own conscience."

Lucy sat up a little straighter. "I don't mean t' be rude," she said, a little more sharply than she intended, "but it's alright fer ya t' be thinkin' like that. Yer family's never been held at gunpoint just because o' their religion."

"Ye're right," Bill replied after a moment, "but we do have t' worry about retaliation fer things we had nothin' t' do with."

This whole discussion was getting them far off the subject he had wanted to talk about. There would never be an answer to the greater issues that would please both sides. All he wanted, however, was a quiet life with the woman he loved.

That was the subject he really wanted to discuss, but he was thinking better of bringing it up right now. Lucy certainly did not seem in a very receptive state. Romance and marriage seemed to be the farthest things from her mind. He wondered if bringing her to his part of town had been a wise idea, as it had apparently gotten her started thinking about their differences. Still, there could be no going forward unless they were honest with one another.

"Well," he said after a minute, "I think we should jest enjoy this meal before it gets cold. There's nothin' I hate more than cold food when it's supposed t' be hot."

Lucy agreed. This discussion was going nowhere. There did not seem to be any way to resolve it agreeably. It would be better to let it rest. Her prejudice against Protestants was strong, but it was hard to see Bill in a bad light. He was decent. His sister was decent. And sure, she thought, there may be a lot more where they came from. What would she do with her prejudice then?

There was a certain comfort in hating, she thought. You know where you belong. You feel superior to the enemy. They're the bad ones, and God is on your side. It was strange, she realized, that both sides appealed to the same God, but in different ways, of course. Oh, damn. This was giving her a headache. Realizing that she was very hungry, she set aside her confusion and settled down to enjoy the meal and Bill's company.

"When do ya start yer new job?" Bill asked between mouthfuls.

"I have t' go down t 'talk t' the manageress of th' hotel next Monday," she said, "an' if all goes well, I should be startin' the followin' week. I'm a little afraid o' the job, bein' her assistant, t' tell the truth. I've never done anythin' like it before. It's a far cry from the flower shop. But I need a place t' stay and a pay packet, an' this'll jest fit the bill. I'll have me own room, an' meals are included. I have t' pay fer me own uniform, but they said they'd let me pay fer it out o' me first week's wages." Lucy stopped for another bite, then a drink to wash it down.

"At least," she said after a moment, "I have black shoes and stockin's." Her eyes clouded, remembering her lost loved ones, and Bill decided he had better steer clear of that subject as well.

He waited a few minutes, allowing her time to mourn in peace. Then, with a cautious smile, he said, "So…I think ye'll be havin' a grand time at the seaside. Will ya be comin' home on yer days off?"

"I have no home," she said bitterly.

After a promising start, this conversation was turning into a very difficult evening. Bill was beginning to wonder if there was any subject about which they could talk comfortably. He thought about Lucy's situation and decided that she was in a very sad place right now. She needed somewhere to heal and gather some strength, and he thought the ocean might actually be just the place. The cries of the gulls and the fickle weather, with the sun dancing on azure waves one minute and then, quick as a wink, disappearing behind clouds of gunmetal gray as the wind whipped the waves into furious whitecaps. Even when the ocean was at its most turbulent, he loved it. Many times when he was troubled, the ocean had been a calming friend, speechless, but not without its own powerful voice.

Yes, he thought, Lucy would benefit from the brisk, clean air and the soothing sounds of the sea. The fresh salt breeze might help to cleanse her of some of the bitterness she was tasting. The more he thought about it, the more he felt it might be in her best interests. Of course, he wasn't sure whether his absence would make her heart fonder of him, but he knew that he would have to support her in her move.

"Now ye're wool-gatherin'," Lucy said with a smile. "What are ya thinkin' about?"

"Oh…I'm jest thinkin' that yer job might jest be what the doctor ordered," he said. "Salt air. Ocean breezes. A change o' scene could do ya the world o' good." He paused for a moment, took a sip of his tea, and turned to face her. "I'll miss ya, Lucy, an' that's no word of a lie. Would it be all right if I came down t' see ya on yer day off?"

Lucy suddenly realized that she would miss him, too. She had come to lean on him, and the thought of losing his support was bothering her more than she wanted to admit. She didn't know what she wanted…well, maybe what she needed was a swift kick in the arse. But he was a good and gentle man, and he treated her like a queen. What more could she ask for? She didn't know for sure, but she did know that she needed more time to sort herself out. She also knew she would be a fool not to leave an open door. Men like Bill were few and far between.

As Bill watched the changing expressions on Lucy's face, he saw that she was caught up in some kind of inner conflict. How would she answer his question?

Chapter Sixteen

Brian couldn't believe his good fortune. Chloe was going home to America, and she had asked him to go with her! He still didn't understand what she saw in him, and he had no idea what their future might be, but whatever it was, he was grateful. He worshipped her. He would follow her to the ends of the earth.

This American socialite had liberated him from the bonds of inhibition, playing his body like a finely tuned violin, whose, strings threatened to snap with tension before she allowed release. For her, there were no taboos, just experimentation and a joyful union. Night after night, they made love until he felt his body was without form. He was, deliriously happy and totally spent. Chloe had the energy of a lightning bolt and the body of a goddess, and now she had decided that they would go to America. He would experience a new life, a new love, a new country. It was overwhelming. He was so happy, he almost laughed out loud.

But here was not the place and now was not the time. He was sitting opposite Tom by the fire in the kitchen, watching his former father-in-law follow his customary ritual of lighting his pipe with frustratingly slow deliberation. It was driving Brian crazy. To one side, Feelie sat in silence on the sofa, her expression speaking volumes

Brian needed an answer. When he had told them of his plans to go to America just moments ago, she had called him "a selfish good-for-nothin' get" for proposing to take the children from their family. That was before he told them he needed to leave his children with them until he could establish a home.

Now Feelie was speechless. Brian was asking her father to take care of his grandchildren, even though they all knew full well that Tom didn't take care of anyone. SHE DID. This was too much, altogether too much, to ask. Brian was going off to make a life for himself, leaving her to take care of his responsibilities. He was planning to take the children only when and how it suited him.

She had felt this coming ever since the night they had bumped into Brian and the American woman. Apparently her fear had been well founded. She hoped her father would tell Brian to go to hell and decided that if he didn't, she would. They were not going to paint her into another corner. It was indecent, so it was. Her sister and the babe were hardly cold in their grave, and now Brian was proposing to leave his girls without a father as well. She was confused. On one hand, she was angry at the thought of losing the children. On the other hand, she felt used. Brian actually expected her to agree to care for his children while he went off to America.

Tom still had not spoken. This situation had come as a shock. He had never intended that Feelie would take care of the children indefinitely. Brian would surely remarry, and when he did, his new wife would of course take over his family. Feelie would then be free to make a life for herself. But this was not to be the case, at least not for now. It was a dickens of a problem.

Brian was becoming impatient. What the hell was the old man thinking about? He had told them it was only for a while, just until he settled down. He glanced at his former sister-in-law. He had not been prepared for her angry outburst. What did she want from him? They were his children. He could take them—or not take them—wherever and whenever he wanted. He only needed some time to sort things out. Was that too much to ask? Considering what he had been through?

Finally, he could wait no longer. "Well Tom," he said, "what do ya think? Will ya help me out? It'll only be for a wee while 'til I get meself situated."

Tom and Feelie could hear some residual respect in his voice as he addressed his father-in-law, but they could also hear his impatience, despite his efforts to hide it.

Feelie exploded. "What the hell are ya talkin' about? Me da's not the one who'll be takin' care o' yer wee ones. I AM." She seethed and sputtered. "Bad enough, ye're thinkin' t' take 'em far away from their family an' everyone who loves 'em so soon after they're losin' their mammy. But not yet. No, indeed. First, ye're goin' off on yer own an' leavin' 'em without a father. Ya never were anythin' but a bloody selfish lout, and now ye're too busy with yon uppity American hoor t' pay any attention t' yer children. Ya belong in jail fer neglectin' yer family, so ya do, not gallivantin' off to America with yer loose-livin' party girl."

Tom looked from one to the other. "Feelie, watch yer mouth," he said sternly, hiding his smile. "That's no way fer a good Catholic girl t' be talkin'." Although he agreed with his daughter, he still felt required to insist on appropriate behavior. Young unmarried women did not generally talk to men in this manner.

She gave him a hard look. "Never mind me mouth, Da! Think of all the mouths with their tongues waggin' because o' his disgraceful carryin' on before his wife an' babe are cold in their graves." She was nearly beside herself with anger. As Tom shook his head helplessly, Brian misread the situation. Badly.

"Yer right, Tom," he said, smirking a little. "She always did have the mouth of a fishwife. It's little wonder no man would have her."

That did it. In one movement, Feelie sprang from her seat on the sofa, her fist connected with Brian's jaw. She was a small woman, and he a large man, but even so, it was a mighty blow, carrying with it all the weight of her frustration. Unprepared, Brian was rocked hard in the chair and flew over backwards. The back of the chair ended on the floor, and all that could be seen of Brian was his legs milling furiously as he tried to regain his balance, to say nothing of his wounded dignity.

Tom stood up. "Feelie! Feelie! Fer the love o' God, girl, what are ya doin'? Sit yerself down here. Behave like a lady." He was trying to pull her off Brian before she did any more damage.

She raised her fist again. "I'd jest as soon send him to Hell! What in the name o' Christ would I be wantin' a man fer? All ya have t' do is look at me mammy an' me sisters t' see what men can do fer any woman."

Brian was off the floor by now. "Tom, can ya not control yon woman at all?" he asked.

But Tom was too busy tending his own injured pride to reply. Feelie had included him in her denunciation. What were things coming to when a daughter showed no respect for her father? He knew he needed to speak firmly, to exert his authority over the girl, before things got any further out of control, but he required a moment to sort things out.

Brian was not waiting. "I'll not be standin' fer listenin' t' her mouth," he sputtered, gingerly rubbing his jaw. "If she were a man, I'd be makin' mince meat out o' her."

"IF ya were a man," hissed Feelie. "As ye're not, if ya don't like the way ye're treated here, why don't ya jest take yer lazy good fer nothing arse out the front door?" An don't let it hit ya on the way out.

Tom found his voice at last. "Feelie, ye're fergettin' yerself. This is my house, an' ye'll not be tellin' anybody when t' leave it."

She turned her glare back on her father. "Well, Da, it's like this…either that no good piece o' shite goes, or I do. Since yon dunderhead is fixin' t' leave his wains, someone has t' take care of 'em. Lookin' around this room, I don't see anyone offerin', so that leaves *me*."

Neither man knew what to say, and she was beginning to enjoy herself. "I can walk out th' door," she said, "and leave it up t' the two o' youse t' decide what t' do with th' babes. They'll be home soon, an' they'll be needin' their tea. Their dresses'll need t' be ironed and laid out fer chapel in the mornin'. They'll need clean socks, vests, and knickers. D'ye know where their clothes are? Can either of the two of ya make sure they have clean hankies? An' don't ferget their rosary beads an' money fer the plate, besides. The older girls need their shoes polished, an' the wee one has t' have her boots whitened.

Brian's mouth was hanging open in surprise. Tom looked slightly under the weather.

Feelie continued: "Shannon needs cough syrup every four hours. The baby has the runs and a nappy rash. She's teethin' an' very cranky with it, likely t' keep ya up all night, she is. If ye're bringin' her t' chapel, ya have t' make sure ya bring somethin' t' keep her quiet fer the sermon. The father gets a bit rattled when the wains start gurnin'. All three of 'em need a bath and their hair washed, and as Shannon brought lice home from school this week, they'll need t' have their hair gone over with a fine toothcomb t' get rid o' the nits. Don't be fergettin' their teeth, either. They don't think much o' the bakin' soda, though it works fine. Oh, an' the older girls need help with their homework for Monday. D'ye remember *anything* from school?"

As she walked over to the door and took her coat off a hook, Tom held out a hand. "Wait a minute," he said. "Don't be runnin' out the door. Sure, we'd have no notion of how t' do all that." He was panicked at the idea of being left alone with the three little girls.

Feelie turned, keeping one hand on the door knob. "Well, then, tell *him* t' get the hell out of this house before I give him another looter." She was glad to see her brother-in-law rubbing the new lump on his jaw. "He can go to America or t' blazes, fer all I care. If he ever wants t' see his children again, though, he'll have t' come back t' get 'em. Maybe they'll teach him t' be a good father in America. I have me doubts, though."

Tom shook his head sadly. "Brian, de ya hear her? She's speakin' true, so she is. Neither of us has it in us t' take care o' the babies. It wasn't in yer own best interests t' insult the woman who's lookin' after yer wains. Ya owe her yer thanks." He paused. "And an apology. We have no choice but t' see t' the motherless children. Go where ya must. Let it be on yer conscience t' leave yer own flesh an' blood."

Brian had the good grace to hang his head at Tom's words. He knew what the right words should be. "I jest want t' make a better life fer 'em." Then he heard himself say, "I'm sorry, Feelie. I had no right t' say what I did." He wondered if he didn't actually mean it. One thing was certain: he desperately wanted to get out of this house. He didn't want to be there when the children returned, didn't want to listen to their crying when they heard he was leaving. He needed to get back to Chloe, to feel her warmth and forget the past.

It was like Feelie was reading his mind. "Ye best be goin' on yer way," she said, pulling the door open for him. "I don't want the children upset. Shannon is old enough t' understand an' t' be hurt. She's had enough sorrow in her young life. Ye'll not be addin' to it. Not while I have the breath in me ta stop ya."

~

Brian and Chloe sailed from Southampton, bound for New York, a week later. Chloe was thrilled with her "thick Mick," as she called him. He would be a very pleasant antidote to her effete Brahmin husband. Brian was naïve and curiously innocent for a married man, she thought, but that was not a bad thing. She would teach him a few new tricks. He was a fast learner. She could pass him off as a field hand and set him up in one of the renovated slave cottages close to the main house. Life would be good. It was good already, she thought, what with the privileges that went with old wealth and position. All that had been missing was a real man. Not anymore. Now she would have it all.

Chapter Seventeen

Bill was still waiting for Lucy to answer his question. She knew her reply would have far-reaching consequences. If she told him she didn't want him to visit her, she might never see him again. He was a kind and patient man, but he was not a fool, and neither was he the sort who would force his attentions on anyone who was indifferent to them. If, on the other hand, she said yes, she wasn't sure where things would go from there. She was really happy when they were together.

If only he wasn't a Protestant. But that was only one problem. The other was the daydream she still held dear. She had hoped to find an escape from the ordinary.

The answer came suddenly: they could follow the dream together! She was not sure how firm Bill was about his religion and knew they would have to talk about that. And on the heels of that thought came another. He had never asked her to marry him. Was she taking things for granted? Well, she said to herself, that was a thought to reckon with. She had a fine opinion of herself, Miss High-and-Mighty. *Sure*, she scolded herself, *it'd be nice t' wait 'til ye're asked.*

She made up her mind. "Bill, it'd be grand if ye'd come t' see me on me day off. The problem is, though, I'll never be off on the weekends. When would we meet?"

Bill thought that one over. "Well," he said after a minute, "ya must have some time off in the evenin'. I'll jest come down then. It's not so far on the train."

"Oh, aye, that's right enough," she replied. "I think I have Wednesday evenin' off, although I have t 'be back in by ten."

"That's settled, then." Bill smiled as he spoke. All's well that ends well, he thought to himself. Well…it was more of a beginning than an end. As they finished their meal, he asked if she would fancy an ice cream.

"That'd be lovely. I feel like a pig, though, eatin' so much."

"Well, ye'll walk some of it off on the way t' the ice cream shop," he said as he helped her with her coat.

"I think I'll be needin' more walkin' than that," she said, smiling. "The meal was jest as good as I thought it'd be. Hot an' tasty. I enjoyed every bit of it. Thank ya fer bringin' me here. I don't know if I could find me way back, but I'd love t 'bring me sisters fer a treat one day."

"That's no problem," said Bill. "Jest let me know when ya want t' bring 'em, an' I'll show ya the way an' stand everyone to a bang-up meal."

"That'd be grand, indeed," she said, "but I'd not want t' impose on ya."

Bill held the door open as they left the shop. "Ah, don't be a silly girl. Sure, haven't I sat down t' many a meal with yer family? I'd love the chance t' repay their hospitality and enjoy their company."

It was a lovely evening. As the sun was setting, the edges of the clouds turned pink and Biblical rays of golden light broke through piercing them. The air had a fresh dampness to it, but of course that was nothing new in Ireland. Rain is never far away.

Bill and Lucy walked hand in hand, satiated with good food and quietly contented for the moment.

Chapter Eighteen

Tom shrugged himself into his coat, jammed his hat onto his head, and slammed the door behind him. Feelie had been in a towering rage since Brian left. Although she was fine with the children, he was bearing the brunt of her displeasure. It was getting so he hated to go home from work. Meals were dumped on the table in front of him. Tonight it was dried out tripe and onions, kept barely warm in the oven since God knows when. His daughter was trying to poison him, he was sure of it.

He needed to talk to Bridie. Maybe she would know what to do. He stopped in his tracks. That was it. Things had become worse at home since the night he'd told the girls of his plans to marry Bridie. Nellie had taken it in stride, and what Lucy thought he had no idea, but Feelie had been furious.

Well, he had to admit, things were going hard for her. He had hoped Brian and the children would be together, freeing Feelie to go her own way. But now everything was fouled up. Not only was Feelie still to be looking after the wee ones, but she also had to come to grips with the idea of Bridie taking over her role as the woman of the house.

Hell indeed hath no fury like a woman scorned, he thought. And while it was not at all his and Bridie's intention to shut Feelie out, let alone scorn her, he could understand that his daughter must feel she was being manipulated. She had been more or less forced into acting as a substitute mother, and now she faced losing her position in her father's house. But he didn't think the fossilized tripe and onions were entirely deserved, though. He was willing to take his share of the blame, but the whole situation wasn't completely his fault. Not entirely. As he reached the top of the street, there was a loud crack of thunder. Holy Christ! Was Ellen trying to tell him something?

Bridie was just getting home from work when he arrived at her house. She tucked *The Irish News* under her arm and turned the key in the lock. "Tom," she said, "this is a grand surprise. I didn't expect ya t' come tonight."

"Well, I had t' see ya," he mumbled. "Me head's spinnin' with problems, an' I need a dose o' yer common sense." He followed her into her neat kitchen

"That's fine," she said, laying the paper down and taking off her coat, "but first things first. Have ya had any dinner?" She made her way into the scullery.

"If ya want t' honor the pig swill Feelie served me with a name, the answer would have t' be 'yes.'"

Knowing he couldn't see her, Bridie smiled. "Still mad at ya, is she?" She knew the answer.

"Aye, sure, an' I don't know what t' do about anythin', so I don't."

She came out of the scullery. "Sit yerself down and take the weight off yer feet. I'll heat us up some stew, an' after that we'll see what can be done. I've been puttin' a lot o' thought into it. I might have some answers."

Tom followed her suggestion, did as she had suggested, and soon the smell of Bridie's lamb stew was wafting through the tiny house. Noticing that she had laid a fire before she had left for work, Tom rose from his place on the settee and set a match to it. Soon the room was warm and cozy. Warming his hands before the fire, he marveled anew at how different the atmosphere in Bridie's house was from home. Here, everything was soft—soft cushions, soft colors, soft carpet, and soft woman. His house was like an armed camp. Nothing soft there. , and this one was a kindness for the soul.

Bridie had set the little round table by the fireplace, and soon they were tucking into the delicious fragrant stew. Tom hadn't eaten anything as good in a long time. Neither spoke much as they ate, they each had a fair hunger to satisfy. After they had finished eating and the dishes had been done, they both took up their places on the settee again. Tom tamped his pipe and prepared to settle down for a quiet smoke.

"Will ya tell me what's the trouble now?" Bridie asked in a soft voice.

"What's *not* the trouble'd a better question," he replied. "It'd take less time t' tell ya."

"Ya have t' start somewhere. The children…how're they takin' the news o' their father goin' to America? Poor wee mites, it must've been a cruel blow for 'em."

"Feelie won't tell 'em," he answered. "She says they hardly ever ask fer him, she just tells 'em he's at work. They accept that. He never spent much time with 'em, anyway."

"An' how about Feelie? How's she doin? I know she's very angry at Brian, but I think there's more t' it than meets the eye."

"Aye, ye're right about that. And since she can't take it out on Brian anymore, I'm the one who cops it." He considered the nasty food and the unwashed clothes in his bedroom. "She's just downed tools as far as I'm concerned. She's still as good as ever with the wee ones, but I'm convenient to her anger, an' I'm th' one bein' punished fer everyone else's misdoin's. As well as me own."

Bridie nodded. "Well, as I said, I've been givin' it a lot o' thought." Her voice shook ever so slightly as she went on. "Neither of us is gettin' any younger, ya know. I'm gettin' a bit long in the tooth t' be thinkin' about bearin' children, but I'd still love t' have some. I know ye've been through it all before. But this'd be different. I—*we* could take care o' yer grandchildren until their father comes t' fetch 'em. Ye'd get a chance t' put right all the mistakes ya made rearin' yer own, an' we could both enjoy the raisin' o' these wee ones."

She was breathless as she finished, and Tom was unable to speak for a moment. *Is she proposin' what I think she is?* he asked himself.

It took a minute before he was able to speak. "Bridie, are ya out o' yer mind? There's a lot o' work an' little thanks involved in raisin' another woman's children. I never meant it t' be ferever fer Feelie, jest 'til Brian got himself sorted out. And then Brian himself...well, what de ya think he'd have t' say about this?"

"I don't know about Brian," she said briskly, "but from all accounts, he's the least o' the worries. I'm not suggestin' we steal the children away from their father. He's made the decision t' leave 'em with ya. We can offer 'em a decent home until their da comes back. If he ever does. An' we both know there's a chance that he won't."

Tom was still having trouble believing what he was hearing. "Bridie, luv, do ya know what yer sayin? We'd have t' get married sooner than we thought."

"Aye, Tom. I know that. I made me mind up when ya told me ye'd take the children. The fact is, the children need a woman, you need a wife, Feelie needs a life, an' I need you. It's the answer t' everyone's needs. All the way 'round."

"It sounds as though ye've made up yer mind," he said slowly. "It comes as a shock t' me, though. I have t' wonder how Feelie'd react t' ye're takin' over where the babies are concerned. They're her flesh an' blood, ya know, an' she has a right t' have a say in what happens to 'em."

"I've thought about that, too, Tom. Feelie's a young woman. She should have a life of her own. Somehow, we have t' make her see the sense in that." Now Bridie smiled. "We have each other, luv. That takes care of our happiness. And we can pass that along t' the children. We can make a happy home fer 'em."

The more she talked about it, the more it made sense to Tom, even though he was still worried about Feelie's reaction. She was angry enough already. He didn't want to lose her, too. One daughter lost to him was already one too many.

Now Bridie was saying something else. Tom, lost in thought, missed it. "We have t' go t' the chapel t' post the banns," she repeated. "Why don't we ask Father Doyle if he can help us with this situation? He knows Feelie as well as anybody."

Bridie was excited about this idea, Tom, less so, his deep-seated distrust of the clergy putting a damper on his enthusiasm. And another thing was bothering him. Bridie had been dragging her heels for months...but now, all of a sudden, she was bound for the altar at breakneck speed. Was it him or his grandchildren she was in a hurry to marry? To a childless woman, this situation could seem to be the answer to her prayers.

However, almost immediately upon thinking this, Tom scolded himself. This was Bridie, the woman he loved, and in his heart of hearts he knew that she loved him first. She was a kindly woman. It was in her nature to try to fix things. To her, the children might be an added incentive. So what… where was the harm in that?

"Aye," he said out loud, "it might be a good idea t' talk t' the father. We'll go t' see him on Sunday. After Mass. In the meantime, we need t' make some plans fer ourselves. How would you like t' go on a weddin' trip after we take vows? I've been thinkin' about that."

"I've never been outa Belfast," she said, her eyes wide with excitement. "Never further than the end o' the tram line. A trip sounds like a grand idea. But could we afford it? An' where would we go?"

He smiled. "I thought about the seaside. Portrush, maybe. I even thought we could go t' England or Scotland. What do ya think o' that?" By now, he was feeling expansive and adventurous. Why not, indeed? "I can afford it," he said proudly. "Where'd ya like t' go?"

"Oh, Tom…I never thought t' leave Ireland at all in my life. But I'd dearly love t' see Scotland. And can ya imagine bein' on a boat?"

Tom laughed. "I don't have to imagine it. I help build 'em. I'm on one every day."

She blushed. "What an eejit I am. Sure, ya were on the *Titanic*'s trial run, weren't ya? When ya were jest a young man."

"I was that," he said. Then, more soberly, "Who'd have ever thought that mighty ship would founder on an iceberg the way she did?"

It was a sobering thought, and Bridie began to wonder if it might be better to enjoy the ocean at the seaside. The town of Portrush sounded pretty good. She had heard of Bushmills, a little village along the coast of Antrim, and the columns of rocks that were a wonder to see. She wasn't much of a swimmer, but she had always dreamt of walking in the water along the shore.

"I think I'd love t' go t' the seaside at Portrush," she said. "I'm a wee bit scared o' boats. They say there was a time long ago when ya could walk across the land from here ta Scotland. Wouldn't that jest be great?"

"I'm thinkin' it must've have been a long walk," he joked as put his arm around her shoulders and gave her a hug. The fire was dying, so he rose to bank it up with peat.

The next Sunday Tom hailed the priest as he and Bridie were leaving the chapel. "Father, kin we have a word with ya?"

"Surely. Go to the front of the rectory. I'll have Mrs. Duggan open the door for you. I'll be right there after I change out of my vestments."

Mrs. Duggan saw them into the parlor. She was a sparrow of a woman, chirping softly to herself when she wasn't speaking and plucking at the shapeless cardigan she wore over her dress and apron. Everything about her was gray: shoes, stockings, dress, apron, cardigan, and face. The only relief was a frizz of bright red hair, the result of frequent applications of henna. When backlit, it shone like a demonic halo.

"The father'll be here in a minute," she said as she backed out of the room.

Tom and Bridie exchanged nervous smiles. This was it. They were about to make their intentions public. The banns would be read during the announcements at all the Masses for the next three weeks.

Father Doyle entered the parlor wearing his black cassock, a purple stole peeking out of his pocket. He was a tall man, six feet three when he stood up straight, but his shoulders were bowed, no doubt from years of stooping to hear his parishioners. His florid complexion bespoke many a lonely night with a bottle of whiskey as his only companion. White hair escaped from under the black biretta he wore lopsidedly on his head, and the bushy white eyebrows that overshadowed his soft gray-blue eyes had earned him the nickname Beetlebrows, spoken, however, only by the naughtiest boys in the school.

He was a gentle man with a no-nonsense approach to his ministry. He was also a holy man whose own morals were above reproach, and his job, as he saw it, was to see to the welfare of his parishioners and that of their immortal souls. That meant strict adherence to the doctrine mandated by the Church, with as little deviation as possible. Birth control, celibacy for priests, and the regular attention to the sacraments were not open to discussion in his parish. He expected his parishioners to attend Mass on Sunday, perform their Easter duty, and raise the children God sent them to be good Catholics. Helping them to do this made him a happy man, secure in the love of his god and his church. He did not overly concern himself with church politics, nor was he particularly ambitious, for his church was a church of love, albeit strict, and he was content to be the shepherd of his flock. Now he settled himself into his favorite chair and invited the nervous couple to join him.

"We've come t' ask ya t' post the banns," Tom said. "An' we need t' ask yer advice about somethin' else as well." Bridie nodded her head in agreement.

The priest nodded. "So you have decided to get married. I thought that's the way things were shaping up. There should be no problem. You are both free to marry. What else is there that I can help you with?"

"It's our Feelie, Father," said Tom. "I don't know how she's goin' t' take the news. She's been in a nasty mood since Brian left, an' I don't think she's goin' t' take kindly t' the idea of another woman in the house. But…well, Bridie is willin' t' take over the care o' the wee ones, an' we both think Feelie should have a life o' her own."

Father Doyle remembered the lonely figure praying for guidance after Mary Alice's death. Feelie, he knew, had made plans to start nursing school, and it was partially on his advice that she had decided instead to stay at home and take care of her dead sister's children, having come to the conclusion that God would rather she do that than devote her time to study. Now, as Feelie had passed the cut-off age for entering nursing school nine months ago, the priest felt somewhat responsible for the part he had played in this decision. He had hoped Brian would remarry and claim his children sooner.

Still, all was not lost. Father Doyle had devised a plan he hoped would make everyone happy. His sister, Mother Peter, was the administrator of a teaching hospital in Sydney, Australia. He had written to her for advice, and after learning of Feelie's plight, she had been glad to help. Australia, Mother Peter had told him, would welcome a dedicated young woman like Feelie, and so would the Sisters of Mercy. He had written back, both to thank her and to let her know that while Feelie wanted to be a nurse, he was not at all sure that she wanted to be a nun. After some back and forth, it was agreed that Mother Peter would welcome her as a student nurse. If she chose the veil, fine, and if not, so be it. The convent wasn't in the press gang business. Father Doyle had smiled when he read that sentence. So typical of his practical sister.

Now he addressed Tom and Bridie in his most resonant, pastoral voice. "This will all have to be handled in a delicate manner," he said. "Feelie will not be happy if she thinks she is being forced out of her home. But," he raised a finger, "but I have been in touch with my sister in Australia. She is head of a teaching hospital there. She has offered your daughter a place as a student nurse."

Tom was puzzled. "Oh, that was kind of ya, Father," he said, "but I don't think Feelie'd want t' be a nurse."

Father Doyle was taken aback. "Tom, don't you know what her plans were before Mary Alice died?"

"What plans? She never told me anythin' about any plans." He was unsettled to find that the priest knew more about his family than he did.

"The day Mary Alice died," Father Doyle said, "Feelie received a letter telling her that she had been accepted into nursing school. She had to start almost immediately, as she was approaching her twenty-fifth birthday, and twenty-five is the cut-off age for acceptance into the program." He cleared his throat. When he continued, his voice was compassionate but firm. "But after her sister died, you told her she was needed to take care of the children, and she made her decision to do your bidding. As far as she knows, her every chance of doing what she dreamed of doing with her life is gone."

"I never knew any o' this! Feelie never said a word." Tom shook his head. "It's little wonder she's so angry with Brian, an' me, too."

How, he wondered, could they let her go now? She would always feel she had been used and replaced by Bridie. If Brian had taken the children, Feelie would have been upset with him, but she was going to blame everything on him and Bridie now. Above all, Tom did not want Bridie cast in the role of usurper. To have her kind intentions met with hostility would be a tragedy. He knew how the girls could close ranks, ostracizing an adversary, real or imagined.

And was Father Doyle's solution really an answer? Given the chance, would his daughter even want to go to Australia? Tom wasn't sure. It was so far from home and the babies she loved. It would be one thing to study to be a nurse close by, quite another to be on the other side of the world! She was close with her sisters. They would undoubtedly have something to say, too. He would need the wisdom of Solomon to sort this situation out. Thinking aloud, he said, "Father, I don't know how to approach Feelie. I don't want her t' be angry with me. Or t' blame Bridie."

"It is a tricky situation," admitted the priest. "'Tis unlikely that Feelie would enjoy sharing the house with another woman. But," he added, "there are several things you could do."

He rose to stand before the couple, and counted the options off on his fingers. "One. You could postpone your wedding until Brian returns to claim the children, although, of course, no one knows how long that will be. Two. You could get married now and live with Bridie in her home, and, three, have Feelie continue taking care of the children in the family home." Here he frowned. "Though it would be a financial hardship for you to support two houses. Maybe Bridie could continue to work?"

Tom was not happy with any of these choices. He didn't want to live in Bridie's house, and he most certainly didn't want Bridie to work after they were married. He wanted to live in his own house with his own wife and grandchildren.

"Father," he said, "I don't know which way t' go. I'm responsible fer Feelie missin' out on goin' t' nursin' school. That means I have t' take her feelin's into account. But I don't want t' postpone our weddin' or live in Bridie's house. She's had a hard enough life, workin' all these years. She doesn't need t' be workin' t' sort out my—"

"Tom, I'd not mind," Bridie cut in. "It'd only be 'til Brian came back fer the wee ones." Up to this point, she had said little, but now she felt obliged to speak up. This was, after all, her life, too.

"Bridie, the Father's right," said Tom. "We've no idea when Brian'll return. We're fergettin' t' consider what Feelie might want t' do. She's not gettin' any younger, either. If she misses this opportunity, she might not get another. We have t' find a way t' let her make the decision herself. I don't want her t' think she's bein' pushed aside."

The priest raised his finger again. "You know," he said quietly, "I think we are creating a tempest in a tea cup."

"How so, Father?" asked Tom.

"Well, Feelie knows of your intentions to marry. She must have come to terms with the situation, at least somewhat. When all else fails, you know, the truth sometimes is the best way to handle things." He smiled. He loved to nudge members of his flock in the right direction, and this time, he would be helping at least three people. "I will simply tell Feelie the truth. I will tell her that, as I knew you and Bridie would get married someday, I wrote to my sister asking if she would accept her as a student. Of course, at the time I wrote, all of these plans were dependent on Brian taking care of his children…so things have changed somewhat, but not completely. You still want to get married, and I think Feelie would still like to go to nursing school. I will tell her about my sister's offer. She will most likely turn it down because of the children."

The priest smiled again. "And then I will suggest that I ask Bridie if she would take over until Brian returns. This way, Feelie makes the decision without feeling she is being forced out. I will have asked her, so that lets you off the hook. Feelie will be able to resume her life without guilt. And Bridie will then be seen in the best of lights." Pleased with himself, he beamed at his troubled parishioners.

"That sounds like a grand idea, Father. Don't ya think so, Bridie?" The relief was audible in Tom's voice.

"Aye, I do that," she answered. "Jest one thing, though. I think we should not post the banns until Father has settled things with Feelie."

"Smart girl," said Father Doyle.

"Aye, she's that an' more," Tom said proudly.

Just then there was a timid knock on the door. "Come in," the priest called. The door swung open to reveal Mrs. Duggan balancing a tray while pushing the door.

"I jest brought ya all a wee cup o' tea, an' a couple o' wee buns," she said nervously, running her words together.

"Ah sure, that's grand. We thank you. We can use a cup after all the talk. I'm sure we're all parched." The priest took the tray and set it down on the table. Mrs. Duggan hovered, nervously wringing her hands. Finally, she gathered enough courage to speak.

"Ah…Father, would ya be wantin' anythin' else? If not, I'll be off fer the rest o' the afternoon. I'll be back t' see t' yer dinner around five."

"Thank you. No, I won't be wanting anything else. And there's no need for you to be hurrying back. I've been invited out for dinner."

"If yer all settled, then," she said, "I'll jest take a run over t' visit me sister in the hospital."

"Why don't you make a little bouquet of flowers from the altar? Take them to your sister, she'll enjoy them."

"Thank ye, Father. She'll feel like she's been t' Mass, knowin' they came right off the altar, so she will." The housekeeper backed out, bowing slightly.

Tom watched this exchange with wry amusement. He also noted the silver teapot and fine china. *Some vow of poverty*, he thought. And the housekeeper had acted like she was dealing with a king, or maybe even with God Himself. He thought about the vows every priest took. Poverty, chastity, and obedience. The poverty one didn't seem too hard to take, but he wondered about the other two. Priests had women waiting on them hand and foot. Nuns that put the fear of God into their hapless students behaved like twittering nitwits when a priest entered a room. Women washed their clothes, cooked their meals, and kept their houses clean. Not one, but many women hanging on their every word.

The only thing that seemed to be missing was the sex. Well, now…that was something to think about. Did a person miss something he never had? Did a priest's body have the same needs as any other man's? Tom, of course, knew very well that abstinence was not easy. How did a priest deal with his sexual needs? The church forbade pleasuring yourself. That was a great sin. Obedience, he mused, was no big deal. We all had to obey someone, the boss, the law, the government. Although which government was another question. Tom decided chastity would be the hardest of the vows to live with.

All in all, he figured, a priest had the life of Riley. But the clerical life wasn't the life for him, of course. Not for all the tea in China. He could never live the life of a eunuch, surrounded by women he could never touch. Father Doyle, he decided, deserved the silver teapot and anything else he had that made his life worthwhile. It was all cold comfort for having to go without a loving, warm woman in your arms and in your bed.

And then he suddenly realized his marriage to Bridie had been postponed again. He was beginning to feel like a eunuch himself. The priest was doing his best to help; he had to give him that, at least. Hopefully, things would get worked out soon. Bridie was warm, loving, and kind, but she would not squander her virginity. That would be her present to her bridegroom on their wedding night. She had made that promise to herself, and she would not break it, even for Tom. To let her guard down now would be to cheapen the gift. Well, Tom thought, he couldn't care less about the virginity thing. He wanted her in his bed. He thought society's rule was silly at their age. But he would never let her know that he didn't prize her gift as much as she did.

Now he rose, and Bridie with him, saying, "Well, now, Father, we've taken enough o' yer time. Bridie and me best be gettin' along. Thank ya fer all yer trouble."

"It was no trouble at all," said the priest, pleased at the wise counsel he believed he had been able to give the two. "But I think you should keep your thanks until the mission is accomplished."

He then offered a warm smile, and clapping them on the shoulders, bid them good luck and Godspeed. He stood in his doorway for a while, smiling still, as he watched them leave the yard and start back down the road, and only when they had disappeared around the corner did he return to help himself to another bun and finish his now cold tea.

Chapter Nineteen

Lucy was having a hard time adjusting to her new job. Her duties included walking the guests' dogs, waiting on tables, delivering room-service meals, making beds, polishing silver, washing dishes, babysitting, and almost anything else that needed doing. She worked from five every morning until whenever the last guest went to sleep, and when she finally made it to her room, she fell exhausted on her bed. One morning, she had even woken up to find herself still fully dressed in her uniform, with her white cap still on her head. She was terrified of oversleeping and kept having dreams in which she was too late to serve breakfast, once because her feet were covered in syrup. In another dream, she found herself preparing the tea with turpentine, the result being the death of everyone who drank it.

The woman she had thought to be the manageress had in fact turned out to be the owner; a transplant from Dublin named Mrs. Fitzpatrick. This woman, who considered Ulster a step down from what she had been used to, wanted desperately to sell the hotel and return to "the city." The hotel had been her deceased husband's dream, but with him gone, it held no special appeal for her, and she resented every day there. Unfortunately, she had not yet been able to attract a buyer willing to pay enough to make the sale worthwhile.

Over the years, Mrs. Fitzpatrick had eaten her way into considerable curves, and carrying the extra weight made her tired and cranky. The main focus of her life was her Pekingese dog, Ching. She doted on the animal, never realizing that her love was unrequited. The dog couldn't stand the sight of her and vented his frustration on anyone foolish enough to try to pet him. Since the guests were likely to take exception to being bitten, it fell to Lucy to walk him in the morning before the guests were up and about. Mrs. Fitzpatrick didn't like to walk. The exertion left her exhausted and even crankier than usual. In fact, anything that might be construed as work or require effort would bring on a fit of almost terminal crankiness in Lucy's boss. The hotel required a great deal more work than the woman had bargained for, and as she often said to herself and anyone else she thought would listen. Her husband had spent every farthing of their money, even borrowing against his insurance, to buy and renovate the hotel. He then had the bad judgment to get sick and die, leaving his poor wife with a heavily mortgaged hotel and no money.

The more Lucy got to know Mrs. Fitzpatrick, the more she disliked her. The woman was bad-tempered and stingy. Lucy's meals were meager, and her room in the attic was sparsely and uncomfortably furnished. She missed her home and family.

The monotony was broken only by Bill's visits every Wednesday, which quickly became the eagerly anticipated highlight of the week. Early on, Bill had told his sister about

Lucy's stingy meals, and from that moment on, he arrived in Bangor every Wednesday toting a picnic basket. After taking a stroll along the beach, they ate by the water's edge, contentedly listening to the pounding of the surf and the screeching of the gulls.

Lucy was contented at least for the moment, but unasked and unanswered questions lay just beneath the surface. She was becoming increasingly unhappy with her job, and she also wondered why Bill never mentioned the subject of their future together. She also wondered what her reaction would be if he did say something. There were serious drawbacks to such a future, like the difference in religion to consider.

For his part, Bill also wondered where their relationship was going. Apart from that one interlude by the river, the extent of their lovemaking to date had been a recent, furtive goodnight kiss. He loved Lucy, and being near her aroused desire in him that was destined to be frustrated.

Little did either of them know that events about to take place would bring this difficult situation to a rapid end.

Chapter Twenty

Father Doyle was not a man to let the grass grow under his feet. Soon after Bridie and Tom left the rectory, he decided it was time for him to talk to Feelie. The afternoon was more or less free, so he set off on his mission, mentally rehearsing the proposition he would offer for her future.

Approaching the family's home, he heard the children before he could see them. A lively game of hide and seek was in full swing. Feelie sat on the doorstep with the baby on her knee. Rising to greet him, she called Shannon to come and hold the baby. The girl protested the interruption of the game.

"Ye'll be feelin' the back o' me hand if I hear any more lip from ya," Feelie scolded.

"Ah, Auntie, sure and I've only jest finished the dishes. Can I not play a wee bit longer?"

Feelie pointed toward the street. "Can ya not see the father's comin' fer a visit?" she said "I can't be payin' attention t' him with the wee one squirmin' on me knee. Ya can have an extra half hour before bedtime. Now be off with ya, an' take yer sisters fer a walk 'round the block."

Father Doyle, who had arrived in time to hear the last part of this exchange, fished in his pocket and found some change. "Here, Shannon," he said in his kindliest voice, "take this and buy some sweets from Josie's. There's a good girl. I need to talk to your auntie about something important."

As Shannon sent a questioning glance towards her aunt, seeking permission to take the money, Feelie nodded her approval, and the children made off happily with their unexpected windfall.

"Ophelia," the priest said, using her given name, "may we go inside while we talk?"

"T' be sure, Father. How about a cuppa tea? An' I jest made yer favorite treacle farls, too." She knew the priest's fondness for the tasty bread fresh off the griddle.

"Now that's a treat I'd have a hard time refusing," he replied, rubbing his hands together in anticipation.

'Tis nice t' be appreciated, Feelie said to herself as she led her visitor into the house. Cooking for children brought so little in the way of encouragement. Half the time, she had to fight them to get them to eat the meals she prepared.

Having seated the priest comfortably, she busied herself with preparing the tea, accompanied by hot bread slathered with good, fresh butter. She wondered at the reason for the priest's unexpected visit. Quickly making the sign of the cross for protection against bad news, she carried the tea tray into the front room.

"Will ya be helpin' yerself, Father?" She set the tray down on a small table beside the best chair, now occupied by the priest.

"I will indeed," he replied, "but this is a powerful temptation. I could eat the whole plateful."

Feelie smiled. "Ah, Father, sure, an' it's only one farl cut in four. It's nothin' fer a man like yerself. I don't think ye'll be needin' absolution fer gluttony." Smiling, she pushed the plate towards the priest.

"Well, yes, I think I'll be forgiven, considering the penance I go through trying to swallow poor Mrs. Duggan's bread. She's a fine cook, mind you, but treacle bread is her one failure."

Feelie dipped her head. "We'll be keepin' that our secret then. Now, Father, I'm dyin' t' hear what ye've come t' talk t' me about,"

Father Doyle savored the first bite of his farl before answering. "I have great news for you, Feelie. God has seen fit to reward you." *That was good*, he thought to himself. *She can't turn down a gift from God.* He smiled again. "I have in my pocket a letter from my sister, the one who's a nun in Australia. She's the head of a training hospital, you know." As Feelie's eyes widened a little, he went on. "I wrote to tell her about your dream of becoming a nurse and how you had set your own life aside when your family needed you. I told her that you had missed the age deadline to be accepted into training here. The saints be praised, she wrote back and said she would be happy to accept your application."

The priest paused, searching Feelie's face for a reaction. For a moment that seemed like an hour, the young woman was speechless.

Finally, she spoke, almost in a whisper. "Father, I can't be goin' to Australia. What would happen t' the children?"

"Well, I've thought about that," he said. "Remember when we talked about your father getting married again?"

"Yes. But what's that got t' do with anythin'?"

Her question was a sharp one, and Father Doyle knew his next words had better be carefully chosen. "My child,

I told your father and Bridie about my sister's proposal. Bridie offered to take care of the children until their father comes back for them. It's only a matter of time before he comes to claim them, of course, but by then, it might be too late for you."

Here the priest paused as he selected another bite of bread and popped it in his mouth. He chewed and swallowed before he continued. "God has tested you, Ophelia and you passed the test. Now you are free to follow your own dream without guilt. God would not want you to miss the opportunity again. You've done your duty. Bridie is a kind, God-fearing woman. She will look after the children well. You have my word on that."

Feelie could only shake her head. Although Father Doyle began to fear he had failed to convince her, the shaking really signaled her confusion. Her thoughts refused to be caught and studied as they bounced from one unasked question to another. Was this another test? Would Brian really come and take the children away? She had known that could happen since that night when they had seen him at the café with the American woman. Did he even want his girls? How far away was Australia? She knew it was a long way away. And who was this Bridie? What was she like? What would Mary Alice up in heaven think? And how could she, Feelie, leave the children she loved? Of course, they could also be made to leave her at the drop of a hat...and then what? She would be stuck forever in a life she didn't want.

Her brain began to recover its ability to reason. Her decision would be painful, no matter what she chose to do. Either way, she would lose the children. America and Australia would both be too far away for her to ever see her nieces again. When they went with their father, she would lose them and her chance at her own life, too. If she chose to go to Australia, she would lose them, for sure, but she would still have the opportunity to realize her dream of becoming a nurse. What was God's intention? Was he rewarding her? Or was he testing her again?

Maybe, she realized, the answer was sitting across from her. God would not send a priest to do the devil's work. Maybe she was not being tempted. Maybe she was in fact being given a second chance.

"Father," she said at last, "I'll have t' be thinkin' an' prayin' long an' hard on this." He nodded and she went on. "I'm grateful t' ya fer all yer trouble, but I'll be needin' t' meet an' talk with this Bridie woman. She'll have her work cut out fer her, don't ya know, just tryin' t' fill the shoes of a saint like me sister, never mind tryin' t' take care o' three wee ones with no blood connection t' her. The children've had a hard enough time of it, tryin' t' get used t' the idea that their mammy's never comin' back. An' on the heels of that, their good-fer-nothin' father takes off fer America, leavin' 'em behind t' return God knows when." She couldn't hide the anger in her voice.

"I understand what you're saying," the priest replied. "Of course you need to think this over. It's just that I don't know how long my sister's offer will stand. How would it suit you if I made arrangements for you to meet Bridie? I could be present to help you get to know each other."

"I suppose that'd be wise," Feelie said, "since ya know both of us. But don't ya think me da should be there, too?"

"Well, I don't know about that," said the priest. "It might be better if you girls had a chance to get to know each other first. Your father is kind of in the middle. He loves both of you. If there were any problems between you, he would be hard pressed to take sides."

Feelie was having a problem already. The idea that her father loved a woman who wasn't her mother was abhorrent to her. *Men!* Here was her father replacing her sainted mother, and her brother-in-law replacing her sainted dead sister. *They sure as hell didn't mourn for long. Bad cess t' the lot of 'em, good fer nothin', they are.*

Then the line of her thinking turned another corner. If her father married this Bridie, and she *didn't* go to Australia, then she would have to share her home, her father, and the children with a complete stranger. That would be altogether too much.

Father Doyle sat quietly as one expression chased another across Feelie's face. There was no easy choice for her, he knew, but he hoped she would make a good one. He was sure the children would adjust to the situation. After all, they were not being left with strangers. Their grandfather would be present in the house. And he knew Bridie to be a kind, honest, and compassionate woman. The confessional was a great place to get to know a person, he thought wryly. Seeking forgiveness and a clear conscience, people were apt to tell the truth. Bridie had never confessed to anything more than the odd venial sin. He had no reservations about recommending her as a caretaker for the children.

"Father," Feelie said at last, "yes, I'd like t' meet this woman. When would it suit ya t' bring her here?"

"I don't know at the moment," he said, "but I'll arrange it as soon as I can." Now he felt sure that Feelie was coming close to agreeing with the plan. However, Bridie would have to handle the meeting with tact, while Feelie would suffer no such restriction. She would not make it easy for Bridie to take her mother's place. He hoped Bridie's maturity and her desire to marry Tom would help her guard her tongue. *Yes, yes, yes*, he said to himself, he would have to mediate this encounter very carefully.

After some tactful negotiation, he was able to arrange for the meeting to take place the following Sunday, after the last Mass. Tom was thankful that he was not required to attend the encounter between his daughter and his future wife. He'd already had a difficult week. Feelie was making no effort to hide her disapproval of his engagement to Bridie. She had carefully dusted Tom and Ellen's wedding picture and placed it on the mantel, and he knew that it would be more than his life was worth to remove it. The picture was a less than subtle reminder of his dead wife. He imagined Ellen's gaze following him reproachfully as he moved around the room. Moreover, Feelie was also painstakingly replicating her mother's favorite recipes for their evening meals. The tantalizing aromas of steak and onions, apple pie, and fresh bread had filled the house, quite a departure from the warmed-over rubbish his daughter had been serving him lately. When the children were led in prayers for the repose of the souls of their departed mother and grandmother and baby brother, Tom had thought he noticed that the prayers were a little longer and louder than usual.

Feelie had also taken to sitting by the fire in the evening, dutifully mending her father's socks, her mother's sewing basket placed on the table beside her. This was another departure from the norm. Though silent, the message could not be mistaken. This was Ellen's home, and he would not be allowed to forget her. Bridie's reception would be cold to say the least.

Tom had hoped his daughter would be glad to be relieved of the responsibility of caring for the children, but now he realized that this could never be a simple transaction. There were too many mixed emotions afoot.

Although he realized that he was to be made to suffer for his transgressions, he still hoped Feelie would realize that Bridie was in no way to blame for the past, that she only wanted to be a part of his future. He hoped that Bridie's willingness to care for the children would be accepted. He hoped Feelie would feel free to make a life for herself. The children were, after all, only on loan; their father could claim them at any time, and Bridie was prepared to deal with this situation. He hoped Feelie could be made to understand, that she would be able to make the right decision.

Across town, Bridie prepared for her meeting with Tom's daughter. She selected her lemon yellow coat with its matching hat and her white gloves and handbag. Her outfit had been chosen carefully, and she checked the result in the hall mirror a dozen times. Satisfied at last that her appearance was respectable and neat, she offered a silent prayer. Leaving the house, she dipped her fingers into the holy water font and made the sign of the cross. She was nervous, and wished Tom could be with her, even though she fully understood why the priest had advised against Tom's presence. But understanding the situation wasn't taming the butterflies in her stomach.

Feelie had asked Nellie to take the children for a few hours. She wanted this first encounter with Bridie to be quiet, the better to size the woman up. If everything worked out, and she passed muster, Bridie could meet the children later.

The house was spotless. The front step shone, having been freshly treated to an application of Cardinal Woolsey's famous red polish. The doorknocker and letterbox glittered in the sunlight, the result of elbow grease and Brasso. The fire grate had a fresh coat of black lead. Indeed, determined that Bridie would find no fault with her housekeeping, Feelie had polished, dusted, and swept anything that stood still long enough. But she could not bring herself to use her mother's china to entertain the usurper, and so had borrowed cups and saucers from Mrs. Gilvery next door. The tray was properly set for tea, just the way she had learned at the rectory: dainty sandwiches with the crusts cut off, fresh scones, jam, butter, and chocolate biscuits. The wedding picture remained on the mantel. It would stay there as long as she was the woman of the house.

A gentle knock on the door announced the arrival of the priest. "God bless all here," he prayed as he entered.

"Ah, Father, thank ya fer comin'." Feelie indicated a comfortable chair by the fire. "Set yerself down."

"I will that, and glad to," the priest said. "Bridie should be along presently."

He had arranged to arrive first, hoping to make the introductions as comfortable as possible. Feelie's careful preparations and Ellen's silent presence on the mantel were not lost on him, and he wondered for a moment if he should prevail upon Feelie to remove the wedding picture. Deciding that discretion was the better part of valor, however, he opted to avoid a confrontation.

Ten minutes later, Bridie arrived, and Father Doyle introduced her to the first member of Tom's family to meet her. The two women acknowledged each other politely, if coolly, and Feelie took Bridie's coat and offered her a seat.

"Well, ah, aren't we having the grand weather?" Father Doyle began after a long moment of strained silence. Feelie nodded and Bridie managed a timorous, "Ah, grand indeed."

"Well now…grand indeed," the priest repeated.

"Aye, grand it is," said Feelie.

"Grand for this time of year," said the priest, wondering how much longer it would take to beat this subject to death.

"Could I be offerin' ya a wee cuppa tea?" Feelie asked, hoping to give the discussion of the weather a decent burial.

"That would be grand," said the priest. He felt like a needle stuck in the groove.

"Aye, gr…lovely," agreed Bridie. "An' thank ya kindly," she added, mindful of her manners.

"Jest so," said Feelie. "I'll be puttin' on the kettle." She lost no time escaping to the sanctuary of the kitchen.

Bridie took this opportunity to look around the room. As her gaze halted and focused on the wedding picture, a shock of strange emotion rocked her. She finally recognized it as jealousy, and the priest watched helplessly as Bridie wrestled with the strange emotion. Her first reaction was anger. It was cruel of her future daughter-in-law to embarrass her in this way. Feelie must have done this to make her feel as uncomfortable as possible. Then, after the first rush of emotion had subsided, reason returned. Sure, and wasn't this Ellen's home, after all? It was only natural for her wedding picture to be on display. There would undoubtedly be more tangible reminders of Tom's late wife, and while there would be things she could and would adjust, like wallpaper and curtains, some things could never and should never be erased. Yes, she would treat Ellen's memory with respect. She must never underestimate the power of the departed. Ellen would forever be a saint in the eyes of her children. Death had shrouded her faults and illuminated her virtues. Bridie, on the other hand, by virtue of being alive, would have to tread warily.

Now, waiting for the kettle to boil, Feelie returned to her guests. Bridie decided to take the bull by the horns. There was no time like the present.

"I was jest admirin' that lovely picture of yer mother and father," she said. "She looks so young and shy, and he looks so proud."

Smart girl, Father Doyle thought. Now the ball was in Feelie's court. The next few minutes would make or break the tenuous relationship between the two women.

For a moment, nothing was said. Then, just as the silence was becoming oppressive, Feelie found her tongue.

"Thanks' very much," she said. "We treasure that picture."

Was this royal "we" an effort to put Bridie in her place? If it was, Bridie choose to ignore it.

"I'm sure ya all do," she said. "An' rightly so. 'Tis beautiful."

Just then the kettle began to sing and the tension began to unravel. Father Doyle breathed a sigh of relief and settled back to enjoy the tea as Bridie proceeded to praise the house and the lovely china and marvel over the tenderness of the scones and the sweetness of the biscuits.

Feelie couldn't help the spiteful thought that suddenly crossed her mind. *Ye'll be lookin' fer this china fer a long time*, she thought, and almost laughed out loud. Best of all was the idea of being asked to tea next door and finding the china there! Scolding herself for her mean thoughts, Feelie thanked Bridie for her kind words.

"I'm glad ya enjoyed the tea."

"We did indeed," Father Doyle said, wondering how to get around to the reason for the visit. He needn't have worried.

"Well," Feelie offered as an opening gambit, "I think it's about time we talked about the situation."

"Aye, ye're right," Bridie said, relieved to be down to business at last. "As ya know, yer father an' I plan t' get married. I've offered t' take care o' the wee ones. If you agree, that is."

Feelie's expression did not change.

Bridie continued. "I know the children's father'll come back t' claim 'em. My thought was t' make it easy fer ya t' go to Australia t' be a nurse."

"That was thoughtful of ya," Feelie said dryly.

"Oh, there're other reasons, too," said Bridie. I'd not want ya t' be thinkin' I'm tryin' t' be some kind of a martyr. I jest thought we could all benefit. Yer father and I could get married. Yer dream o' bein' a nurse could come true. We'd take good care o' the girls. I've had none of me own, ya know, never havin' been married. I'd love t', mind ya, but I'm gettin' a bit past me childbearin' years."

"Ya understand ye'll have t' give 'em up when their da comes back," Feelie said, thinking of her own complicated feelings regarding the separation. "It won't be as easy as givin' somethin' up fer Lent. Ya grow t' love 'em. 'Twill be hard t' let 'em go."

"But it's harder fer you," Bridie argued. "Sure, you're their flesh and blood. But it'd be even harder if you give up this chance, an' yer brother-in-law comes back fer 'em. Who knows when he'll return to Ireland?"

For a few minutes there was silence again, broken only by the tick of the clock and the crackle of the fire. Finally Feelie agreed, albeit reluctantly. "Aye," she said quietly, "aye, that's right enough."

All three were now lost in their own thoughts. Father Doyle was feeling they were getting somewhere now. The women were doing just fine without his interference, so he decided to sit back, watch, and listen, speaking only when asked for an opinion. Bridie was hoping she was making progress. Feelie was wondering what it would be like in Australia. How she could bear to part from her family? How she could explain this to her nieces? The poor wee things would feel abandoned again. Bad cess t' their miserable father who was bringing this new heartache t' his already troubled family.

Lucy had finally told her what had happened the night Mary Alice died, and Feelie now wished she had known before the miserable piece o'shite left. The fancy American girl would have gotten an earful from her, after which she might have had second thoughts about taking up with a wife-and-baby-killer. On the other hand, if he never returned, the children would actually be better off. This Bridie seemed to have already had a positive influence on her da. His drinking had all but stopped. He was a different man. If he and Bridie had a happy home, wouldn't the children benefit from that?

Bridie had some reservations about taking on the role of mother to three young girls. It would be a lot of work, but what else was new? She had worked hard all her life, and while she had no idea how to handle wee girls, she certainly knew how to make adults happy. That was part of her job. It couldn't be that much different with children, she thought. *Ya keep 'em clean, fed, and warm.*

Just then Father Doyle had an idea, and thought better of his intention to keep quiet. "Well girls," he said, "I think you would both benefit from some time spent together. Perhaps Bridie could stay here for a couple of weeks? Get to know the children, learn their routine, that kind of thing. What do you think? Would that be acceptable to both of you?"

Feelie nodded. "That'd be fine, Father," she said, "but what would me da do? We have no more room."

"I'll take care of that," said the priest. "He can stay at the seminary in one of the guest rooms."

Bridie almost choked trying to stifle a laugh. Tom would have a fit when he heard of this development. She didn't feel too bad for him, though. This had not been the most pleasant afternoon in her life, whereas he had gotten off lightly. Now she would have to agree to stay here. She knew she would have to win the children over, and it was not going to be easy. Feelie would not be too eager to hand over the reins.

Eager to bring the matter to as swift a conclusion as possible, the priest said, "That settles it. I'll make the arrangements for Tom. Just let me know when you girls are ready. I think it would be a good idea for the children to meet Bridie before she moves in. How about next Sunday? Would that suit you both?"

Both women nodded in agreement. Rising from the chair, the priest signaled the end of the visit. Bridie and Father Doyle thanked Feelie for her hospitality and left together.

~

Feelie was thankful for the silence of the house. After making herself another cup of tea, she sat down to collect her thoughts. She was a little disturbed by the speed at which decisions were being made. Her whole life was about to change, and she felt she had little or no control. Still, Bridie appeared to be a kind and respectable woman, and Father

Doyle would surely not have vouched for her if he had any doubts. Nevertheless, the thought of leaving everything and everyone she knew was frightening, to say the least, even though the chance to realize her dream was exciting. She just wished Australia were not so far away. Many families and friends had sailed off, never to be seen again.

The more she thought about it, however, the more she realized she had no choice. Her father was going to remarry. She would lose her place in the family. She would no longer be the woman of the house. She was familiar with the life of the "maiden aunt" who was always just outside the family group, sometimes loved, sometimes not, never really belonging, always dependent on the lives of others to give hers meaning. That was not much of a life. She could, of course, go back to work for the priests. And she knew that some women even worked at the shipyard, though she didn't have the skills necessary to work there. And what kind of a future would that be?

Now that she had been given the chance for a life of her own, she did not feel able to turn it down. She would have to face the future bravely.

Yes, she was going to Australia. Yes.

The decision made, she began to clear away the tea things. She had to wash and return Mrs. Gilvery's china before the children came home, lest something get broken.

~

"Well, Bridie," Father Doyle said as they made their way to the tram stop, "what do you think? Will you be up to the job?"

Bridie nodded. "I think so. Of course, every job looks easier from the outside. I have a lot of experience with adults, but children are another thing altogether. I can only pray to our Holy Mother fer guidance. She's never failed me before." She crossed herself, "The visit with Feelie went fairly well, don't ya think?" she asked, uncertainty evident in her voice.

"I do," said the priest. "She has a lot to think about now, but I'm convinced she will make the decision to accept my sister's offer."

"If it weren't fer yer kindness and yer sister's, Tom and I would never get married, and Feelie would never get the chance t' be a nurse. We all owe ya a debt of thanks."

He made a small, modest bow. "I'm happy for all of you. With God's help everything will work out for the best."

There was an approaching rumble. "Ah, here comes your tram," he said. He waited to help Bridie board, but waved off her suggestion that he come along, saying, "I'll just be walking. I need the exercise."

~

Tom, meanwhile, was waiting nervously for Bridie to return. She had suggested that he make himself comfortable at her house while she was gone. He hoped everything had gone well with the visit, but he knew Feelie's views on his remarriage, and feared that she might have said something to hurt Bridie's feelings. Feelie could be very blunt, and her temper seemed to be on a shorter fuse these days. To be honest, he admitted, that was understandable.

And Bridie had a lot on her plate. Was he asking too much of his bride-to-be? No, he thought. Taking care of the children had been her idea. He smiled, remembering that he had worried that she was more interested in the children than in him.

The cat interrupted his thoughts. Uncurling from her place by the fire, she stretched and made her way to the door. Her mistress was home.

"I'm back, luv," Bridie called cheerfully as she made her way into the room. Taking off her gloves and hat, she laid them carefully on the table.

Tom rose to greet her and helped her remove her coat. "Well how did it go?" he asked anxiously.

"Better than I thought it would, truth be told. Feelie seemed t' take fairly kindly t' the offer. She had her doubts, of course, but she didn't say no. The father is makin' arrangements fer me t' meet with the children next week. He wants me t' stay at yer house fer a couple of weeks t' get t' know 'em."

Tom frowned. "How can ya do that? There isn't enough room."

Bridie knew this question was coming. Her thinking on the tram had centered on the best way to approach Tom with the priest's seminary idea. She had decided that it couldn't be done indirectly.

"Well, the father says he can arrange t' put ya up as a guest at the seminary fer a few weeks," she answered as matter-of-factly as she could. She held her breath as she waited for Tom to digest this piece of news.

Tom exploded. "He'll do WHAT?"

"Don't ya be yellin' at me, Tom O'Leary."

"I'm not yellin' at ya," Tom said, taking a breath. "I'm jest yellin'. Has that priest lost his mind altogether? It'll be a cold day in hell before ye'll get me t' agree t' stay in a seminary.

I was jest jokin' when I said that about Holy Orders! This is too close fer comfort…goin' t' Mass, novenas, Stations of the Cross. Yon priest would have me gelded like them if he could!"

He rose, fuming, and began pacing. "Enough is enough," he said to his fiancée or to God or to both. "I'm not applyin' fer sainthood. I jest want t' have a drink of a Saturday night, go t' the races once in a while, have a seaside holiday, an' kiss an' cuddle me grandchildren. I want t' get married an' bed me wife. I don't want t' be bowin' an' scrapin' an' fastin' an' prayin'. I'm dammed if I'll be forced out o' me own home t' bunk in with a bunch o' pasty-faced eunuchs."

Bridie was flabbergasted. She had expected resistance, but this outburst was more than she had bargained for. But how could she have known the years of frustration Tom had suffered? Although she knew that Tom still laid the miserable failure of his marriage to Ellen at their feet, she could never fully understand Tom's deep-seated distrust of the clergy. The church had interfered with the most private and intimate place, the marital bed. He had felt them forcing him apart from his wife—they were disapproving, frowning, and threatening voyeurs—until their love had shriveled and died in the cold space between them.

Ellen had turned to the church for comfort, and he had turned to another woman. Now he was determined not to allow the church to interfere with his love for Bridie. He had done everything in his power to be the man she wanted him to be. He had kept his word, and now he could not let the Church dictate the terms of this union. He would not let them snatch this last chance at happiness from him. Bridie would have to understand that while he would not interfere with her religious beliefs, he would never allow the Church dominion over their marriage.

The irony was not lost on Tom. They weren't even married, and the priest was giving them orders, separating them by installing Tom in a place where he would be expected to obey church rules. They were both silent. Tom's anger had placed him beyond the reach of reason, and Bridie was too confused to think of a way around this problem. Father Doyle had put himself out to smooth the path towards their marriage, and she could not understand how Tom could be so ungrateful for the help the priest had given them. Listening to Tom, one would think the priest was proposing that he take vows and enter an enclosed order for life.

The silence was becoming more and more difficult to break as Tom began to realize that the very thing he wanted to avoid was happening. If they did not reach for each other soon, the gap would be too wide. But his anger had a stranglehold on him. It wouldn't let him speak.

And now Bridie began to cry softly. The uncertainty of the future and the tension of the day's events had finally caught up with her. Tom's anger withered in the face of her anguish.

"Oh, luv," he said with an awkward tenderness. "Don't be grievin' like that. I'm sorry. I'm sorry I lost me temper."

She melted into his arms, and was comforted for the moment. For the moment, that was all that mattered.

But Tom stood firm in his refusal to enter the seminary, short term or not. Father Doyle was politely told that Tom O'Leary would and could take care of Tom O'Leary. He would avail himself of the accommodations at Mrs. Casey's rooming house, two squares a day and a piece to take with him for noontime. Prayers were limited to grace before meals.

Meanwhile, Bridie had not forgotten Tom's outburst. Would the ring on her finger be accompanied by one through her nose? Tom had a bad temper, she knew that. He had warned her. She also knew he had been abusive towards his wife. He had promised her that he had changed, but she wondered if he would revert to his old ways after the trip to the altar.

She also knew that she would never stand still for any kind of abuse. She loved him, but she had taken care of herself all her life. The only reason she wanted marriage was to be happy in her life. If that couldn't happen, she would walk away. She would never play the martyr for any man, no matter how much she loved him. She didn't expect marriage to be a bed of roses. The reason for marriage, as far as she was concerned, was to be able to help one another deal with the thorns. Then there was that other thing. Sex. She had waited to experience that for a long time. Just kissing Tom made her toes curl, and she was looking forward to the rest. So, she concluded, and not without trepidation, she would take her chances.

~

The arrangement for Bridie to spend time with Feelie and the children worked out surprisingly well. The younger girls, Deirdre and Siobhan, responded easily to Bridie's warm personality. Shannon, being a headstrong lass who didn't like being told what to do by a stranger, was the hardest to deal with. Bridie had enough insight to allow the older girl time to get to know her before she tried to exert any overt control over her. In any case, although Feelie was preoccupied with her plans to emigrate, she was still the woman of the house.

For their part, Tom and Bridie had set a date for the wedding. It would be a small family affair, to take place before Feelie's departure. Bridie had asked her friend Alice to stand up for her, and Tom had asked Bill. The banns had been posted, and a small celebration dinner arranged at the Midland Hotel.

Bridie had chosen a white satin wedding dress with a dropped waist and handkerchief hem. Her veil was held in place by a simple circlet of orange blossoms. She would carry her mother's prayer book covered, for this occasion, in white satin with a single white orchid and long satin streamers.

Lucy, however, was incensed when Feelie called to tell her the news. "I can't believe ye're goin' t' see our da married t' another woman! Have ya no loyalty t' our mammy?"

Feelie had known Lucy would be upset, but she had become quite fond of Bridie. She could see the difference in her father and knew that Bridie made him happy. "Of course I have loyalty t' our ma," she said. "Bridie had nothin' t' do with Ma's death."

"She might not have, but he did. Why should he be happy when Ma lies in her cold grave? Will ya tell me that?"

"I know what ye're sayin' is right," Feelie admitted. "Right to a point. I used t' feel the same way."

"What de ya mean ya *used* t' feel it?" snapped Lucy. "Are ya tellin' me you've fergivin' him fer how he treated our ma?"

Feelie tried to speak calmly. "She was a saint, and unfortunately, our da just couldn't live with a saint. They were mismatched, and it ended in tragedy. He is doin' his best t' be a better man now. He is tryin' t' right the wrongs he did us by bein' a good grandda t' Mary Alice's poor wee ones. Bridie's promised t' help him 'til Brian comes t' get 'em." She paused, but Lucy had nothing to say, so she continued. "Ah, Lucy, I haven't fergiven him fer his part in 'er death, but he didn't murder her. He should never have been with that woman, but he never planned t' kill our ma. He's a changed man now. An' I have t' give credit t' Bridie fer the change. No woman will ever take our ma's place, as far as I'm concerned, but what good will it do fer everyone t' be unhappy? Ma would not want that."

"What do ya know about what she'd want?" Lucy asked. "Ye were never around t' see her poor shoulders heave with sobs, watchin' him take off on a Saturday night t' be with his hoor. Now she's six feet under, and he's found himself another hoor an' is fixin' t' put her in our ma's place."

"Bridie's no hoor," said Feelie. "She's a decent Catholic woman. Father Doyle spoke fer her. He said he's known her since she was a girl. She told me she's goin' t' the altar a virgin, so don't be tarrin' her with the same brush as that other one."

Lucy could only shake her head. "What are ya stickin' up fer that one fer? She's nothin' t' ya."

"I don't think it's right t' call any woman a hoor unless yer sure that's what she is." Feelie felt she was losing this verbal battle with her sister. Lucy's tone was bitter and unyielding, and Feelie could imagine the two bright red spots on her cheeks.

Lucy felt that everyone was deserting her mother's memory. She felt that her father should be alone and miserable for the rest of his life in punishment for what she perceived to be his terrible crime. If Feelie had no backbone, well, she did. She would never forgive her father nor accept his new woman, whore or not.

Chapter Twenty-One

When Bill and Tom met for a pint after work a few days later, they had a lot to discuss. Events at the shipyard were indicating that all was not well. Workman and Clark, a rival facility, had closed its doors. Following the Great War had come the Great Depression, and the level of trade had fallen worldwide, fewer emigrants were seeking passage to America, and the demand for large liners and cargo carriers had plummeted. Tom recognized the signs, having been through hard times before. Bill, on the other hand, had so far been lucky enough to enjoy steady employment.

On a more personal level, Tom wanted to hear about Lucy. He missed his youngest daughter. "Has Lucy's attitude softened any?" he asked his friend.

"She won't say a word about her feelin's fer ya at all." Bill felt sorry for the older man and wished he could have eased his mind, but he felt that he owed him the truth. He knew the rift between Tom and Lucy was a deep one. Lucy had not mentioned her father's name since her move to Bangor, although she had kept in regular touch with her sisters.

Bill felt helpless in the situation. He understood Lucy's anger, but he also hoped time and distance would serve to lessen it. On the few occasions when he had tried to discuss the problem, however, she had always cut him off sharply, so he had decided to back away and hope for the best.

Meanwhile, Tom had been examining his own role in the situation. "I know I deserve a lot o' the sorrow I brought on meself," he said, sadly. "I wish I could take away the sorrow I've caused others. I've made a lot o' mistakes, but I didn't kill Ellen. It was an accident!" He paused, drank deeply, and sighed. "If only Lucy could understand that," he said. "But she was always her mother's girl. I wonder if she'd be as bitter if I had been the one t' die."

Bill was unable to give Tom an answer to this question, but he figured the older man wasn't really expecting one. The tragedy of Ellen's death could possibly, in all fairness, have been avoided. After all, if Tom had not been with the other woman, neither Lucy nor Ellen would have ventured out that night.

On the other hand, Tom could not have foreseen the accident, nor was he to blame for the weather. It was never his intention to kill his wife. He was guilty of adultery and neglect, but not of murder. Bill wondered if Lucy would ever let herself entertain the difference. He had grave doubts on that subject.

Just then two of their mates from the shipyard hailed them.

"Tom, Bill, will ya be joinin' us over here?" they called from across the bar.

Tom raised his hand in greeting. "Ya want t' join the lads then?" Tom asked, glad to end the subject they were discussing. Bill nodded his head.

"Have ya heard the latest?" Mick Hughes asked by way of a greeting.

Mick was a large man in every way. A huge appetite fueled his six-foot six-inch frame, squarely planted in his size-fifteen boots. Flaming red hair fanned out from his head and joined a rough woolly beard below his ears. It would be easy to see him wearing a horned Viking helmet and brandishing a great sword to lay waste to those who would oppose him. His voice boomed when he spoke. His outward presentation was, however, an innocent fraud. Mick had no idea of the impression he made. It was said by some that he had a "heart the size of Ulster." He was a kind and generous giant.

"What's that then?" Tom inquired.

"There's a rumor doin' the rounds," Mick boomed. "They're sayin' there'll be massive layoffs before the end o' the year. The slips are half-empty as it is. Have ya heard anythin'?"

"I've heard plenty," Tom answered "but I don't need t' listen t' gossip t' know what me eyes tell me. I've been through times like this before. Strikes, layoffs, lockouts, and trade union disputes. I've seen it all. I have to admit, though, there seems t' be a feelin' o' doom about the yard and everywhere else these days."

"I hear the orders are not comin' in at all," said Bill. "D'ya think that could be true?"

Seamus, the oldest and the quietest man there, shifted his lean frame to better see the younger man. He foraged for a moment in the deep pockets of his overalls, then lit a Woodbine and inhaled deeply before answering.

"If I was a youngster," he rasped, "I'd be very nervous about keepin' me job. As I see it, things've been goin' downhill since the war. When the war broke out, we had very little work fer the Admiralty. At that time, our slips were full of merchant vessels. We had a hard time launchin' anythin' as all the material t' finish the vessels was bein' diverted t' the war effort."

He paused to take another drag on his cigarette; then continued, squinting through the blue smoke like a bard of old. "Fer a while," he said, "we were at a standstill. But then things picked up. Because of our geography, we were considered a safe area. It was difficult fer th' German U-boats t' reach us, so we were safe from attacks. We were kept busy with repairin' an' overhaulin'. That was our main contribution t' the war effort."

"Construction of new vessels," said Mick. "They continued, o' course. The bosses were findin' it hard t' keep up with the work. Times were good fer the skilled workers, who were much sought after. In 1918, a fitter like Seamus here was takin' home a fat pay packet."

Seamus nodded. "I was makin' three pounds, five shillin's and six pence," he said. He downed a large gulp of beer. The others waited respectfully for him to continue.

"Jerry was sinkin' our merchant ships left an' right," he said after a moment, "an' the losses were great. Since few merchant vessels had been laid down since 1914, we had a big problem. Standardized merchant ships were put at the top o' the construction line. I helped build the first one, the *War Shamrock*. We launched her in 1917."

Tom nodded his head. He, too, clearly remembered those days. His parents had put up the five pounds necessary to insure his good behavior and paid for his tools and he had completed his apprenticeship and signed up for the six years it took to become a skilled tradesman. Like most apprentices, he had aspired to follow in his father's footsteps. Skilled tradesmen were the elite in the workforce in those days

Seamus continued. "I think we've seen the last o' the days when a man'd leave his own business to work in the shipyard because o' the money t' be made. If I were a young man now, well, I'd be lookin' over the water fer a job. Glasgow or Newcastle'd be good choices, I'd be thinkin'."

"Ya give a man a lot t'think about," Tom said. "It'll be a sad day fer Belfast if the shipyard closes." He shook his head as he spoke.

"Oh, I don't think Harland and Wolff is goin' t' close its doors right yet," said Seamus. "I jest think there'll be rough times ahead. Like I said, if I were a young man, I'd start t' look elsewhere for steady work."

The men finished their drinks in thoughtful silence, and then Tom and Bill said their goodnights and left together.

"Well, that was an eye-opener, don't ya think?" said Tom.

"Aye, that it was," the younger man replied. "I was jest thinkin' o' somethin' Lucy said t' me some time ago. She pointed out that as a painter I could get a job anywhere. Ships aren't the only things that need t' be painted."

"She's right. But things are tight all over."

"Well, let's not get too down in the dumps," said Bill. "We still have our jobs. Let's not borrow trouble." He was determined to put the brightest face on things, but Tom was the wiser man.

Age has t' have some advantages, Tom thought as they walked down the street, *and I'm goin' t' prepare fer the worst.*

Still, it came as a shock to both men when they and many others were laid off the next Friday. Men drifted towards the pub in twos and threes and settled into dejected little groups. Their voices never rose above a low murmur. Tom and Bill sat with Mick again. There was no sign of Seamus.

"Well," said Bill, "I never thought this'd happen so quick."

"I had a feelin' things were goin' t' go this way," Tom said. "I jest hoped it would hold off 'til I had more money put by. Wishful thinkin' isn't goin' t' pay the rent, though. I have the children. An' in a few weeks a new wife t' think about."

"After our talk with Seamus, I made some inquiries," Mick offered.

"Well, man, what did ya find out? Will ya be tellin' us? Or is it a big secret?" Tom wasn't in the mood for a guessing game.

"Hold on there, Tom. No need t' get so testy. Gimme a chance t' get me thoughts in the right order," Mick said in his usual booming voice. Every head always turned in Mick's direction when he was speaking.

Bill said nothing. He just played with his drink, making little Olympic rings with the bottom of his wet glass on the bar. Each man had his own worries, he thought. On the face of it, he was the best off. He had no wife and no children to worry about. He also had a little money put by. There was time for him to consider his options.

Mick was continuing. "I made some inquiries after we talked t' Seamus t'other night. Me brother-in-law went t' work in Glasgow a few months ago. I talked t' me sister. She says he had no trouble gettin' a job there. The John Brown Company is still building ships at Clydebank The *RMS Queen Mary* was laid down in 1930, and the *Queen*

Elizabeth has been ordered. Our Kate works in the linen mill here, makin' good money. They decided not t' give up the house or her job. They have a wee neat house here with two bedrooms, a kitchen, an' a parlor. It's hard t' find anythin' the likes of it in Glasgow. It's tough on them, though. He only gets t' come home every three months or so. Still, I'm thinkin' I'll try me luck over there. What d' ya think, lads?"

Bill spoke first. "I'm thinkin' we all have a lot o' decisions t' make, an' not a lot o' time t' make 'em. The more layoffs we have here, the more men'll be lookin' t' find jobs over the water."

Tom nodded. "Aye, that's right enough," he said.

"Ye're right indeed," rumbled Mick. "I never thought of it that way. We'd be smart t' strike while the iron's hot. I'm glad ya thought o' that, Bill. We should be bookin' our passage as soon as we can see our way clear."

The big man slapped his hand on the bar to reinforce his decision and everyone else grabbed his drink to steady it as the bar shook.

Chapter Twenty-Two

After speaking with Lucy, Feelie was troubled. Her heart was heavy, and she was confused as to her own emotions. In just a few weeks, she would be sailing for Australia. She might never see her father or her sisters again, but she had hoped to help mend the rift between her father and Lucy before she left.

She wondered for the umpteenth time if she was being selfish. Was she abandoning the children to fulfill her own dreams? Would this woman, this Bridie, take good care of children not her own? What if she had a baby? She had said she was getting past childbearing years, but there was always the chance. Would she neglect Mary Alice's children in favor of her own child?

Feelie decided to talk to the priest yet again. He had told her what he thought was the right thing to do, but now she needed his help with Lucy. It would break her heart to leave things at odds with her sister. *Father Doyle will surely know what to do*, she thought.

The next Sunday, therefore, she hung back after mass and waited until the priest had said his goodbyes to the faithful. As he walked towards the rectory, she caught up with him, saying, "Father, can I have a wee word with ya?"

The priest had caught sight of Feelie as he talked with the other parishioners. He knew she was waiting for him, but in a weak moment he had hoped to reach the rectory and have a hot meal before being snared. He thought longingly of the contemplative life of a monk…just peace, quiet, prayers, and three meals a day without any interruption, not even from one's brother monks. Right now, having listened to the worries of his flock following the layoffs at the yard, he would be mightily glad of some silence.

None of this showed on his face, however, as he slowed his pace and said in a kindly voice, "Of course you can, Feelie. What can I do for you?"

"Ah, father, sure," said Feelie, suddenly tongue-tied, "it's our Lucy. I was wonderin' if ya can help me with her."

He nodded. "What would you like me to do?"

"Not now, Father. I lived long enough at the rectory t' know it's mealtime now. An' I know how ya hate warmed-over food. Could I come and see ya tomorrow night?"

The priest felt a pang of guilt. He had chosen the life of a parish priest, after all, and interruptions went with the life. They were part of the job. "That's very thoughtful of you," he said. "Tomorrow I have to visit Sister Mary Ita at the convent. She has been very ill. Then I have some hospital visits to make. Could you come to the rectory around eight o'clock?"

"Indeed, I could. That'd be a great time. Everyone except Shannon'll be in bed."

"Good, that's settled then. I'll see you tomorrow night." They each set off, the priest to enjoy his solitary meal, and Feelie to set the family table for Sunday dinner, which Bridie had taken upon herself to prepare this week. *Havin' Bridie around certainly helps*, she thought. She had to admit she was beginning to warm to the older woman. Bridie had held up her side of the bargain under what could not have been the most comfortable of circumstances. *She must love our da very much t' put herself through all this bother an' trouble.*

~

At the same moment, Tom and Bridie were sitting facing each other over the kitchen table. The older children were playing skip rope in the street, and the baby was sleeping. Tom was shaking his head slowly, and speaking softly so as not to wake the child.

"I jest don't know what t' do now," he said. "I have a little money t' tide us over fer a while, but it won't last ferever. It looks as though I'll have t' go t' England or Scotland t' find a job." He raised his head, and there was sadness in his eyes as he continued. "I can't ask ya t' marry me and then go off and leave ya with a bunch o' wee ones an' no help. I'll jest have t' tell Feelie she can't go t' Australia until I find a job and a place t' live."

"How long will we be able t' keep things goin' without yer pay packet comin' in?" Bridie wondered aloud. "I still have me job, o' course...."

"I have enough t' pay the rent and food fer two or three months with a little left over besides," he said. "Yer money is yer own." *I still have me pride*, he thought.

She smiled. "We'll be married, and me money'll be yer money."

"Hold on a minute! Didn't I jest say we can't get married jest now?"

"An' now ya jest listen t' me, Tom O'Leary. We're goin' t' get married, Feelie's goin' t' Australia, an' I'll work the night shift 'til ya get a job."

He had to blink and shake his head. What was she saying? "Jest let me get me mind 'round this proposal o' yers," he told her. "Ya think I'll let ya stay here an' work as well as takin' care o' the children? Who do ya think is goin' t' take care o' the children when ya go t' work? ya must be out o' yer mind. We'll postpone the weddin'. Feelie'll stay here, an' I'll go t' England, find a job an' a house, an' then, an' only then, will we get married."

"Is that so? Well, I have a better idea. I'll be goin' home t' me own house. I'll wait fer ya until our weddin' day. Ya have 'til then t' make up yer mind. If we don't get married on the day we planned, we never will. I'm not waitin' fer the perfect moment t' arrive fer us t' wed. In case ya haven't noticed, the perfect moment never seems t' come. We aren't gettin' any younger. I've waited long enough."

She paused to take a breath, then continued before Tom, startled, could think of anything to say to in response. "Another thing ya need t' think about," she said, "is how ye're treatin' yer daughter. De ya think ya can put her life on the back burner every time ya have a problem? The girl needs t' go about her own business! She can't be doin' as ya bid her fer the rest o' her life. As fer the wee ones being taken care of while I'm at work, I'm sure their cousin could be persuaded. With that said, Tom O'Leary, ya can make up yer own mind. I'll be off now."

As he watched her go out the door, Tom still sat at the table, dumbfounded.

Chapter Twenty-Three

Monday night found Feelie making her way up the rectory steps. As she reached the top step, Father Doyle opened the door himself.

"Well, Feelie," he boomed, "what do you think of this weather? It's raining cats and dogs. Come in before you drown and catch your death of cold."

"Thank ya, Father," she answered, shrugging her wet coat off her shoulders. "'Tis indeed a misery of a night. Sure, it'd not be Ireland without the rain, but I'm thinkin' our emerald isle would not be so green if we saw more o' the sun and less o' the clouds." Feelie shook her umbrella as she spoke.

"Right you are," said the priest. "Come into the parlor. The fire's lit and will take a bit of the chill off you."

Feelie settled herself in a chair by the fireplace. "Ah, this is grand, Father," she said.

"Well, now," he replied, taking his customary chair, "what are we going to do about Lucy? What's troubling you? Tell me all about it, and we'll see if anything can be done."

Feelie was silent just for a moment, then it all came out. "I don't know where t' begin.... Our Lucy vows she'll never fergive our da fer murderin' our ma, as she puts it. She'll have nothin' t' do with him. Or with Bridie. She says Da should be miserable fer the rest of his life, not gettin' married an' bringin' a strange woman into our ma's house. I've tried t' tell her Da didn't kill Ma, that it was an accident, but she'll have none of it. I don't want t' go away with our Lucy mad at me. An' I wish she'd fergive our da."

"Why is she mad at you?"

"She says I'm betrayin' our ma's memory jest by talkin' t' Bridie. But I like Bridie. Sure, she had nothin' t' do with anythin' at all."

Father Doyle nodded. "You are right of course. Your father was guilty of a grievous sin against his marriage. The evil surrounding that sin may have caused your mother's accident, yes, but your father never set out to kill your mother. Tom is truly trying to change his ways. He has never been a man to seek the church's guidance, but I think God may be guiding him despite himself. Bridie is a good woman, perhaps not as saintly as your mother was, but good nonetheless. Let us pray for some help from the Almighty."

Chapter Twenty-Four

The storm lashed the rocks and hurled the spray across the road as Bill made his way to meet Lucy at the café. It was no night for a picnic, he observed, but rather a night for a good hot Irish stew and a slab of homemade soda bread. He wondered how close they would get to that at the little café. More than likely, a bowl of tinned tomato soup and a slice of pan bread courtesy of "Inglis" bakery.

He was not looking forward to this meeting with Lucy. On the one hand, he had never broached the subject of marriage, but he couldn't very well ask her to go to Scotland or England with him if they were not married. On the other hand, they could not get married in Ireland, not without one or the other of them changing his or her religion. He didn't hold much hope of Lucy agreeing to become a Protestant, but even if he were to decide to become a Catholic, that would require months of instruction.

He didn't know if Lucy wanted to marry him, anyway. What he was certain of was that the time had come to resolve the issue, one way or the other. He would have to tell her that he had been laid off, but he had no idea where to go from there. They would have to come to some understanding.

He lifted his head just in time to see Lucy struggling to cross the street against the wind. Bill ran to meet her in the middle and, hugging her close to him, propelled her to safety. They were both drenched by the time they reached the café.

"This is one nasty gale," Bill said as he caught his breath.

She nodded. "Thank God ya were there. I don't know if I'd have made it otherwise. I thought I was goin' t' be swept away t' sea." She was shivering as she took her wet coat off and untied the knot of her kerchief. "I could do with a hot cuppa cocoa now."

Bill wiped his forehead. "I could do with a good strong drink, never mind cocoa," he said. "Brandy or whiskey'd be more like it."

"Would ya rather go down the street t' the pub then? ya can get a nice hot pie t' go with yer drink."

He felt he would need a little fortification to deal with the evening's decisions. "Aye, that'd be a grand idea."

"Come on then," she said. "It's not too far, and we can't get much wetter, can we? They'll have the fire goin' on a night like this, I'm sure."

And so they ran down the street through the pelting rain and the puddles and into the pub. Sure enough, a healthy fire dancing in the grate welcomed them. After shedding their wet raincoats for the second time, they settled themselves into a booth and ordered hot toddies and savory pies.

Not much was said for a few minutes, but Lucy could feel the tension building. Why had Bill called to ask her if she could move their date night from Wednesday to Monday? Why on earth would he venture out on a night like this?

Then their food and drinks arrived, delaying the answers to Lucy's questions and providing Bill with a continued respite. She was so hungry she almost growled as she tucked into the delicious homemade steak and kidney pie. The hotel served the same pies, which she knew they bought from a local woman who made them in her tiny kitchen, but she had never gotten the chance to taste one, of course, as they were served only to the paying guests. Many a night she salivated as the appetizing aroma filled the kitchen at the hotel, only to find that her evening meal would consist of leftovers from lunch. And not necessarily lunch that day; they could be several days old.

Her old biddy of a boss would resuscitate a chicken for days. Day one, it would be roast chicken for dinner. Day two, chicken croquettes for lunch. Day three, what was left of the meat was picked off the bones, doused in white sauce, fancily renamed Chicken à la King, and presented on toast points. Eventually, the chicken would play a final, starring role as the main attraction in Chicken Vegetable Soup. By this time, it was also known as "the resident chicken." Roast lamb got the same treatment, reincarnated as lamb patties, lamb stew, and that exotic dish hailing from India, curried lamb with rice.

"There's nothin' like a good steak 'n' kidney pie t' chase the shivers and the hunger away, don't ya think?" Lucy said as she polished off the last crumbs. "I didn't realize I was eatin' so fast. Ye're not even half way through, an' I feel like a glutton, so I do. But it was so good! Me stomach thought me throat was cut, I was that hungry."

Bill smiled. He was indeed picking at his food. So many thoughts were vying for his attention that food was the least of his worries. "I'm glad it hit the spot," he said eventually.

"I've a lot on me mind at the moment, an' I guess I'm not that hungry." He played with his fork and stared at his plate. Finally he lifted his head to look directly into Lucy's eyes. "I have some bad news t' tell ya," he said in a low voice.

Lucy put down her drink and returned his gaze. "Go on, then. Tell me what's happened," she said quietly, steeling herself for the news to come.

He took a deep breath. "First of all, I got laid off. But that's not all. I have t' make a decision about where I'm goin' from here. Most likely I'll be off t' t'other side t' find work. I'll have t' be goin' soon, or there might not be any jobs left."

Lucy was shocked at her body's reaction to his news. It felt like someone had punched her hard in the stomach. It took her several minutes to find her voice. "An' where de ya think ye'll be goin', then?" she asked softly, not daring to look at him for fear he would see the tears that were gathering at the corners of her eyes.

"I don't know fer sure," he said, "but I'm thinkin' England or Scotland. They say there's work in Glasgow an' Liverpool. An' I'm thinkin' it'd be a mistake t' tarry long. The more men get laid off here, the more will be lookin' fer a job over there." He waited for a reaction, but her head was still bowed. What was she thinking? He needed to know.

Suddenly she raised her head and he saw the tears, which were now coursing down her cheeks. "What about me?" was all she could manage.

Bill couldn't believe his ears. Was she asking to come with him? Would she agree to marry him? He had no job, and the problems they'd had before were worse now. Whatever her answer, he had to find out once and for all how she felt about him.

"Lucy," he said urgently, "I love ya. Ya must know that. I'd have asked ya t' marry me a long time ago, but fer the religion thing. An' now, well, now I need t' know what yer feelin's are."

She couldn't answer. She didn't know. The thought of Bill going away was tearing her apart. The intensity of this emotion, one of bereavement the likes of which she had not felt since her mother's death, came as a shock. She had been happy with things as they were between them. There were times when their goodnight kiss left her with an empty feeling, and she wanted more, but she knew such feelings were sinful. Because Bill had never demanded more of her, she supposed they would go on as they were for an indeterminate time. But now he was going to leave her behind? Or had he just asked her to marry him? She couldn't. He was a Protestant. And so he would go and she would never see him again. The thought brought searing pain. *Oh, God, what am I t' do?*

Her thoughts were as turbulent as the storm outside. Her family would never forgive her if she married a Protestant. She would be excommunicated, sent from the Church in shame, never to receive the sacraments again. Her soul would be damned forever, and she would never be with her mother, sister and the baby in heaven.

Bill watched the tortured expressions chase across her face. More than anything else, he wanted to take her in his arms and hold her. That was the problem. He was always holding back. It was now or never. Rising, he pulled a few bills from his pocket and left them on the table. Then, grabbing their coats, he gently coaxed Lucy off the chair and ushered her out into the wind-swept night. There was nowhere for them to go.

He found a darkened shop doorway, the standard sanctuary for homeless lovers everywhere. Pushing the rain soaked hair away from her face he cupped her chin with his forefinger and thumb and tipped her face towards his. She was trembling with fear and shivering from the cold. Pulling her towards him, he encircled her with his arms and kissed her with all the passion in his soul. As cold as she was, as they both were, her mouth was soft, wet, and yielding. She shuddered as he traced the line between her breasts. His fingers were cold and on fire at the same time, and her body responded as he stroked her through the thin fabric of her blouse. She pulled him closer. There was no more room for doubts.

"Will ya marry me, Lucy? I love ya."

"God fergive me, I will, I will" They kissed again.

Once again the powers that be decided to save them from themselves.

"Now then," the constable said as he shone his torch into the darkened doorway, "now then, ya best be gettin' on home. It's no night t' be abroad."

Lucy was mortified, and she flushed scarlet when she recognized the young policeman. His name was Gabriel, and he had been flirting with her for weeks.

Sensing her embarrassment, Bill hastened to protect her from view by placing his body between her and the policeman. "Thanks, Constable" he muttered. "We'll be goin' along in a minute," he added, mustering as much of his dignity as he could. *T' hell with this*, he declared to himself. *We'll no more be skulkin' around like naughty schoolchildren. I'm goin' t' take me wife t' me bed like a man. An' the sooner the better.*

Gabriel mentally crossed Lucy off his wish list and moved on, whistling softly. As he shone his torch into one darkened doorway after another and tested doorknobs, he thought about his job. Most nights, all he encountered on his beat were lovers like Lucy and her fella…them and stray cats. Once in a while, he would come across an open door, usually the result of the proprietor's absentmindedness. He would mount guard over the premises until the owner could be located to come and lock his or her shop. Yes, that was about the extent of the excitement. Tonight the foul weather would provide him with a new topic of conversation when he stopped for a yarn with the regulars on his rounds.

Lucy and Bill hastily returned to the pub. Wetter and colder than before, they were grateful for the warmth of the fire and another hot toddy.

Bill was the first to speak. "Lucy, we have t' make some decisions about our future. I have t' go across the water t' get a job. I don't see any chance of our gettin' married here." He paused. "So what are we t' do?"

She was still shaken by the reality that she had agreed to marry, and now the facts of the matter were beginning to register, those facts being that no priest would marry them and that she would be in deep trouble with her family. Even though they liked Bill, a mixed marriage would be nothing but further trouble.

"I don't know what t' say," she finally murmured, thinking aloud. "There are so many things standin' in our way. What would yer family say if ya told 'em ye're goin' t' convert?"

That stunned him. Yes, the prospect of converting had crossed his mind more than once, but cross his mind was all it had done. Becoming a Papist would provoke a bitter reaction from his friends and family. He was an Orangeman, for Christ's sake.

"Hold on jest a minute," he protested. "Who said anythin' about me convertin'? An' why do ya assume I'd be the one t' do it?"

His tone was sharper than she had ever heard it. She was confused. It had never entered her mind that Bill would expect her to become a Protestant.

"I'm sorry," she replied, her own tone warier now. "I didn't mean t' take things fer granted. But I could never imagine turnin' me coat an' becomin' a Protestant. Me mother'd turn in her grave, so she would. No…no, I could never do that, never."

Here we are, he thought glumly, *not half an hour after gettin' engaged an' we're already fightin'*. Religion was a powerful force, but whether for good or for bad, he was not certain. *Maybe fer both*, he thought.

They sat in silence, trying to find common ground on which to build their lives.

Lucy was the first to speak. "Bill," she said, "I don't know what the answer is. I want t' marry ya, but I'll never become a traitor t' Ireland, nor t' me religion."

"Well, then…why don't we both stay the way we are?" he asked, not really believing such a thing might work, already predicting her answer.

She gave it. "An' what would our children be then? Where would they belong? With th' orange or th' green? Would they go t' church or t' chapel?"

Having heard what he expected to hear, Bill had no answer. He was still smarting from Lucy's earlier words. *"Traitor to Ireland," indeed*, he fumed. Was he less an Irishman because he was a Protestant? He didn't think so.

But he realized, also, that it wasn't merely a question of religion or politics. His identity was locked into the faith of his fathers. His family had been Protestant for centuries. He liked the quiet simplicity of his beliefs: direct communion with his God with no need for interference from pope or priests, no Roman rituals, no pagan sacrifices at an altar, no plaster saints to kneel before. Yes, he needed time to think things through.

Lucy was just as perplexed. She had no answer to the dilemma. She was pretty sure she loved Bill, but she meant what she said when she vowed she would never give up her religion. She would never betray her country, her faith, or her mother's memory.

They sat without speaking for a while; both realizing it was getting late. Lucy had to get back to the hotel, and Bill needed to catch the last train back to the city. A coolness that had nothing to do with the weather settled around them. Neither had the slightest idea how to bridge the rift that was widening between them. Finally, Bill brought the uneasy silence to a close.

"I think we better be movin' along," he said with exaggerated politeness.

"Ye're right," came the answer, "I'd better be indoors before I get locked out." She was anxious to be alone. She wasn't sure what her situation was. Were they still engaged? Would she ever see him again? She didn't know, but she sure as hell wasn't going to ask. Bill's rebuke had humiliated her. She wasn't going to risk more embarrassment.

Rising from the table in unison, they made for the door, where Bill helped Lucy with her coat, escorted her to the hotel, and wished her good night. Their leave-taking was stiff, formal, and cold, both retreating to nurse their wounds behind shields of long-held prejudice.

Later, on the train back to Belfast, Bill replayed the conversation in his head. What the hell was the matter with him? Could he not have handled things in a better way? What had he gained by being so rough on Lucy? Who was he kidding, anyway? He had always known deep down that she would never convert. *She could've been a little more careful o' my feelin's, though*, he thought. She could at least have discussed the matter. Taking him for granted like that had hurt. It was as though his giving up his religion was of no great importance.

Back in her shabby room at the top of the hotel, Lucy lay flat on her back and stared at the play of light on the ceiling, her thoughts running along the same lines, chastising herself for being insensitive to Bill's feelings. She was still chafing at his rebuke, even as part of her realized she deserved it.

And now he was gone, and she might never see him again. He would leave for England, meet a good Protestant English girl, and forget all about her. Loneliness settled around Lucy's heart as she thought of the lights in her life that had been snuffed out. Her mother, sister, and baby nephew were dead and gone forever. Feelie was going to Australia. And Bill was going to England or Scotland.

She thought bitterly of her father. *Most o' this is his fault. He's the root of all our family's misfortunes.* Sleep was a long time coming, and her dreams were troubled.

CHAPTER TWENTY-FIVE

She woke to the sound of a sharp rapping on her door. *Oh dear*, she thought, *I've overslept. I'm in for it now.* Then she opened her eyes and sat up.

"Lucy, Lucy!" called her boss. "You've a phone call. Come along quickly. It's long distance from Belfast!" Mrs. Fitzpatrick sounded worried and excited.

Lucy checked her alarm clock. It was three in the morning. "Oh, God," she said aloud. "This can't be good." She scrambled into her robe and ran down the stairs to the landing outside her boss's room. The woman handed her the phone and stood waiting to hear what was so important that she had been disturbed in the middle of the night.

"Hello?" said Lucy. "Who is this?"

Her sister's voice replied. "It's me, Feelie. Our da's in the hospital. He's badly hurt."

"What happened?"

"There was a riot at the shipyard. Some o' the fellas were armed with shovels an' pieces o' lead pipe. Da had gone down t' pick up his tools, an' they set about him because he was the only Catholic there." Lucy heard a catch in her sister's voice. "He…he has a fractured skull. An' the doctors don't think he'll come 'round. Ya'll have t' come home now, so ya will."

Lucy's head was spinning. First, Bill, and now this. "When did this happen?" she asked.

"We don't know fer sure. His friend Mick Hughes came lookin' fer him. He was jest checkin' t' make sure he got home. Apparently the boys in the shop were givin' Da a hard time until Mick stepped in an' told 'em t' lay off. Nobody wanted t' take Mick on, but they must've waited an' gone after Da later. When he didn't come home on time, we all went lookin' fer him."

Feelie paused again to calm herself, and Lucy could hear her breathe deeply—or was it a sob?—before she continued. "We found him in a doorway, unconscious an' bleedin' from a wound t' his head. We would never have found him but fer two wee fellas who came yellin' fer help. They'd found Da when they went lookin' fer empty bottles t' sell t' the rag and bone man."

Lucy felt the room spin, and the phone slipped from her hand as she grabbed the banister trying to steady herself. Then the room was out of control, and then there was nothing.

~

Sometime later, as though through a tunnel, she could hear her name being called.

"Lucy, wake up." Someone was slapping her face, something cold was being pressed against her forehead. "Come on now, girl. Pull yerself together. Ya'll be all right. Ya jest had a shock."

It was Gabriel, the constable, trying to prop her up in a sitting position against the wall. He had seen the lights on in the hotel and decided to investigate. When he arrived, Lucy had been passed out on the floor and her boss standing over her in hysterics. Mrs. Fitzpatrick hadn't been able to tell him much, though; only that Lucy had had a phone call with bad news.

Just then the phone began to ring again.

The constable answered. "Hello, who's callin', please?"

"This is Ophelia O'Leary. I was jest speakin' with me sister Lucy, who works there, an' we got cut off. Who am I talkin' t' now, please?"

"Constable Gabriel Sullivan, R.U.C. Yer sister had a faintin' fit, but she's alright, and she's comin' 'round now."

"Oh, God, this is a terrible night! The news must've been too much fer our Lucy."

"What news was that, Miss?" Gabriel asked, trying to get a handle on the situation.

"Our da was beat up," Feelie replied. "He's in a bad way. Our Lucy needs t' get t' the hospital. I'm afraid he'll die an' she'll never get the chance t' make up with him."

"T' make up with him?"

"She hasn't spoken t' him since our ma died. She blames him fer our ma's death. Oh, Da did wrong but he didn't kill our ma."

Gabriel was sorry he'd asked. He prided himself on being a rational man, but this was far more information than he could comfortably process. Feelie's outburst reminded him of the stories on the wireless, especially that part of the program where the announcer brought the listener up to date with the goings on in the last episode.

"Miss," he said, "jest hold on a minute. I need t' get some information." Gabriel took his notebook out of his pocket, licked the tip of his pencil, and prepared to ask his rational questions. "Which hospital is yer father in?"

"The Mater on the Crumlin Road."

"Do ya have a telephone number where I can reach ya?"

"Belfast four five one three five. ya can leave a message with the post mistress."

Gabriel wrote all of this down, and then said, "Lucy is lookin' better now, though she seems a bit dazed." He paused a moment, then added, "Now there is no train or bus t' the city until seven-thirty. But I get off duty at seven, an' I'd be happy t' see Lucy safely t' the hospital. If she wants t' go, that is."

"God bless ya fer yer kindness!" said Feelie. "Now then, can I speak t' my sister?"

Gabriel looked down at Lucy to check. "Sure. Jest hold on 'til I give her the phone."

Lucy looked as if he were handing her a snake.

"Hello, Lucy," came Feelie's breathless voice. "Are ya there?"

"I am."

"Are ya all right?

"Sort of. I don't know what came over me."

"It was the shock, so it was. Ye're in good hands there, with the policeman takin' care o' ya. I have t' get t' the hospital. I'll see ya there."

"Wait a minute," said Lucy, as her sister's words began to penetrate the fuzz surrounding her head. But Feelie was gone.

"Here, Lucy. Take a wee sip o' this water." Gabriel held the glass to Lucy's lips, and she took a couple of sips.

"Lucy," he was saying now, "I told yer sister that I'd see ya safely t' the hospital. That is, if ya want me to, of course. I get off duty at seven an' the train t' the city leaves at seven-thirty. Will ya be wantin'to go then?"

Mrs. Fitzpatrick stepped forward. "She can't be goin' anywhere at that time. We have guests t' be taken care of, so we have."

They had forgotten her. She had recovered from being woken so early and was now fit to be tied. Who did this upstart of a Peeler think he was, anyway? Taking things into his own hands when they didn't concern him at all.

The vehemence of Lucy's response surprised them all, herself included. "What the hell de ya mean I can't be goin' anywhere?" she hissed. "Did ya not hear? Me da's near t' death? I suppose ya think I should stay here t' make sure ya don't have t' exert yerself?"

Truth be told, she had not been sure that she wanted to go. The anger she felt towards her father was still alive, and she had not had time to think through the issues with Bill. And now this latest trouble.... Now Lucy would go to the hospital, even if only to confound her boss.

"Ye better not be thinkin' ye'll have a job if ya leave me in the lurch," the older woman sputtered. "If ya go, ya better not show yer face here again."

"Mrs. Fitzpatrick, can ya not see Lucy's upset?" asked Gabriel, his voice calm and reasonable.

"Can ya not see this is none o' yer damn business? The girl has responsibilities. She can't be gallopin' off every time her family gets into some backstreet brawl."

That did it.

"*Brawl*, is it? Responsibility, is it? Gallopin' off, is it? Well, Mrs. High an' Mighty, ya can take yer job an' shove it up yer fat arse. Me first responsibility is t' meself, and then comes me family. It'll be a cold day in hell when I put yer God-damned flea bitten hotel anywhere near the top o' *that* list."

The anger Lucy felt towards the fates and her father found a worthy target in the person of the hotel owner. She had been dying to tell the harridan off for some time.

Gabriel affected a cough to hide the chuckle that was threatening to erupt. Mrs. Fitzpatrick was a sight to behold. For once, she was speechless, her mouth wide open, her face beet red.

She gathered herself into a self-righteous ball of indignation. "Ye're nothin' but a common cheeky trollop," she shouted. "Oh, yes, I've seen ya hangin' 'round outside the hotel, kissin' that fella. An' ya should be ashamed o' yerself, speakin' disrespectfully to a decent wida woman."

"A queer idea o' decent ya have!" Lucy's eyes spat fire. "Ya overcharge yer guests an' overwork yer staff, that bein' me, o' course. Ye're lazy an' tightfisted an' fer yer information, though it's none o' yer damn business, that fella happens t' be me fiancé."

Lucy turned to Gabriel. "I'll be goin' t' the hospital t' see me da," she said, "an' I'm much obliged t' ye, sir, fer offerin' t' escort me t' Belfast. Would ya mind helpin' me with me things? I'll not be comin' back here, so I won't."

"Ah, Lucy." The constable sighed and turned to the owner. "Mrs. Fitzpatrick, are ya not actin' too rashly?"

The hotelkeeper sniffed as she reconsidered the situation. If Lucy left, she would have a hard time dealing with all the work by herself. "Well…if Lucy apologizes, I might reconsider."

But Lucy was having none of it. "I told ya what ya could do with yer job. If ya didn't hear me, I can tell ya again."

Gabriel again urged caution, advising Lucy to think before she spoke, as she'd had a shock and knowing as he did so that his words were of no use.

"I've done all the thinkin' I'm about t' do," she said. "I've been thinkin' while I've been tryin' t' sleep in a hard bed, thinkin' while I've been near starvin' t' death from the miserly food rations an' I've been thinkin' while I've been workin' me fingers t' the bone. I am all done thinkin', an' I've no intention t' be after apologizin' t' that lazy old harpy with the face like a monkey's miscarriage."

That was it. Mrs. Fitzpatrick informed her in no uncertain terms that she was to get her things and get out of the hotel. And she shouldn't be thinking she'd be able to get her job back, either.

"Well," said Gabriel, "I suppose it doesn't look as though there's any chance of an agreement between you. I'll jest finish me beat an' be back at seven t' help ya with yer things, Lucy." His last few words spoken to Lucy's retreating back, as she made her way up the stairs.

But Mrs. Fitzpatrick was determined to have the last word. "Ya can jest wait outside fer her when ya come back," she said. "I'll not be havin' that foul mouthed tinker under me roof or any more interference from those who should know their place."

As Gabriel left the hotel, he was thankful for the quiet of the street, the storms inside and out having subsided at last.

Chapter Twenty-Six

News of the attack on Tom had spread at lightning speed. Before breakfast, his injuries were the topic of conversation throughout the Catholic community.

Bridie heard about the beating while shopping at the butcher's. Horrified, she rushed to Tom's side.

Mick told Bill about it when they met at the pub, warning him to be very careful. An incident like this could cause tempers to rise, and he was afraid there might be some reprisals against Protestants, for there would not be much care taken to weed out the guilty from the innocent. Men were scared. Their livelihoods were now in jeopardy and they had no clear focus for their anger and fear. It had happened in the past, both Mick and Bill knew. Men had turned on each other, to the extent that those who had been friends became enemies overnight. Belfast had seen it all before and once again Belfast was troubled.

Bill left the pub and went straight to the hospital. He wanted to see his friend for himself, as each time the story was told, the extent of Tom's injuries became more extensive. He hoped the rumors were exaggerated.

Arriving at the hospital, he found the family in conference with Sister Domingo, who was explaining that she "would keep an eye on Tom." She was not officially on duty in the male wards, but she felt the need to help.

Feelie was the first to spot Bill, who had paused in the doorway, reluctant to intrude. "Oh Bill," she called, "thanks fer comin'. Our da's in a bad way, so he is. Those rotten cowards could've killed him."

"What're the doctors sayin'?" Bill addressed his question to Feelie, but Nellie answered.

"He's unconscious," she said, "an' badly bruised. One arm is broken. They thought at first he had a fractured skull."

"He doesn't then?"

"No," said Nellie, "they say it's a bad concussion."

Bill tried to smile. "Well, that's good news at least."

"Aye," said Feelie, "but our da's no youngster. God knows what the damage is. We won't know 'til he wakes up." She shook her head to try to clear it. "I jest can't believe we're goin' through this again. First Mammy, then our Lucy, then Mary Alice, and the babe—"

"Have ya heard from Lucy?"

"I rang the hotel this mornin'. Early. She had a turn when I told her about our da, she did. The constable was there, an' he said he'd bring her here."

"Did she say she was comin', then?"

"She didn't say much atall. The Peeler did most o' the talkin'."

The memory of the previous evening's events came back. How quickly things can change, he thought. He had left Lucy in anger, but his main feeling now was one of regret. And what was the policeman's interest in all of this?

This thought had no sooner crossed his mind than Lucy and the constable walked in. Lucy's face was pale and her eyes were red-rimmed, and the policeman had a steadying arm around her waist. Bill had a strong urge to punch him.

"How is he?" Lucy asked softly.

"He's still unconscious," Feelie replied. "We've jest been talkin' with Sister Domingo. Bridie is stayin' with him in case he wakes up."

Feelie thought the sooner she told her sister of Bridie's presence, the better. Sister Domingo knew this revelation was likely to set Lucy off, so she decided to stay and offer any assistance she could.

When Father Doyle had been there earlier to give Tom the last rites, he had also discussed the situation with the nun, reminding her of Lucy's anger towards her father. He had also told her of Lucy's refusal to approve Tom's forthcoming marriage. The priest hoped that in the light of Tom's condition, Lucy's ire would soften. Administering the last sacrament had been a precautionary measure, for at that time Tom was in a sorry state. He was not quite ready to depart this life, however, although his soul was grateful for the priest's concern.

For her part, Lucy was already having a bad time with her conscience. An argument had been raging within her since she'd heard the news. Her father could die and she would never see him again!

Of course, she had chosen not to see much of him of late. The possibility of never seeing him again had not bothered her overmuch, as long as she was in control. Deep in her subconscious, she knew she could change her mind, but now she was realizing that if he died she would no longer have the power to make any decision with regard to her relationship with her father. She knew she had to make up her mind before it was made up for her. She would never forget his neglect of her mother, and she would always hold him accountable for Ellen's death. She needed help to sort out her feelings. She decided to ask for it.

Approaching the nun, she asked quietly, "Sister Domingo, would ya come with me t' the chapel?"

The response was warm and immediate. "Of course, dear. Father Doyle should be leading the rosary now, and we can say a few decades for your father's recovery."

Lucy rose from the chair Gabriel had fetched for her, and on her way out, she quietly reached for Bill's hand and squeezed it. The gesture was not lost on Gabriel, who once again sighed softly. His mission was accomplished. It was time for him to go.

Bill stopped him before he reached the door. "Constable," he said, reaching out to shake his hand, "thank ya fer takin' such good care o' me fiancée. I'm much obliged t' ya." He escorted Gabriel out the door.

Feelie and Nelly exchanged questioning glances.

"Did ya hear what he said?" Feelie whispered.

"I did indeed. What de ya make of it?"

"Our Lucy's lost her mind. She can't marry a Protestant."

"Hush! Bill's comin' back. I'd not want t' hurt his feelin's."

"Well, he's on his way," Bill said as he reentered the room. He felt a great deal more relaxed.

"'Twas kind of him t' take care of our Lucy like that," said Feelie.

"Aye, it was," said Bill, "but I'll be takin' care of her from now on."

There was a long moment of awkward silence, and then, after a deep breath, Feelie took the bull by the horns.

"Bill," she said kindly, "d'ye understand ya can't be marryin' our Lucy?"

Bill seemed unsurprised by the question. "An' why is that?" he asked.

"Oh, Bill," said Nellie, sympathetically, "it's nothin' against ya, but she can't be marryin' a Protestant. Her immortal soul would be in peril."

"An' why is that?" he repeated.

The sisters could see a determined set to his jaw. They weren't quite sure how to answer his question. Bill certainly didn't seem to be a representative of the devil. Finally, Feelie spoke.

"Well," she began, "the priest says we can't be goin' into Protestant churches or singin' Protestant hymns. An' so it follows that we definitely can't be *marryin'* Protestants. That's all there is to it."

"We'll see about that." Bill's expression was grim.

Chapter Twenty-Seven

Lucy sat with the nun at the back of the chapel until Father Doyle finished the prayers and approached them.

"Lucy, how are you?" he asked. "I'm sorry about your father. This is a terrible thing." As Lucy began to cry, he was quick to add, "There, there now. You must have faith. The doctors are saying that things are not as bad as they appeared to be. He has a fighting chance for recovery."

Lucy shook her head. "Oh, Father," she said through her tears, "I don't know what t' do. I'm so confused. I never wanted t' see him again. I can't fergive him—"

Sister Domingo rose from the pew, patted Lucy on the arm, and left her with the priest.

"—Lucy," the priest said, "you say you can't forgive him? What do you think our Lord Jesus would think of that? He died on the cross so that all sinners could be forgiven. By refusing to forgive your father, you are disobeying God."

"But he killed me mother!"

Father Doyle shook his head. "No, he did not kill your mother. He committed a sin, and it was that sin that indirectly caused her death. Your father is a sinner, but he is not a murderer. As are we all sinners, I would remind you."

Here the priest sighed and shook his head. "Your mother was a saintly woman," he said. "She would not be happy to know that you were using her death as a pretext for bitterness toward your father. Honor, not bitterness, is due your parents. It's in the Commandments, after all."

Father Doyle had been standing over her. Now he lowered himself into the pew next to her. "Your father has asked for and been granted absolution for his sins. You have no right to withhold what God has already allowed. The devil works to cause conflict in the world, in countries and also in each family. Do not be his handmaiden." He pulled his stole from his pocket and placed it around his neck. "I will hear your confession," he said with quiet authority.

After making her confession, Lucy stood up, made the sign of the cross, and left the chapel.

Sister Domingo was waiting in the hall for her. "Would you like to see your father now, Lucy? I'll go with you if you like."

Lucy thanked her and fell into step next to her. She felt like a great weight had been lifted off her shoulders. She had been carrying a burden of bitterness, and now she had been given permission to let it drop away. She would pray for the grace to fight the devil, and she would hold her mother's memory in her heart forever, but she no longer felt that it was her job to punish her father. Maybe it never had been.

As they entered the ward, she scanned the beds, looking for Tom. She hated the smell of the place. It reminded her of her time there, and the memory touched off a resurgence of anger and hostility towards her father. But that was nothing to the white-hot anger that rocked her when she saw the woman bending over Tom, whispering in his ear.

Tom's head was swathed in bandages, as was his right arm. He lay still and pale, and did not respond to the woman.

As Lucy stopped in her tracks, trying to catch her breath, Sister Domingo put a comforting arm around her shoulders. Tom's daughter's face was flushed and her back was rigid, and she was having a hard time feeling the mercy and forgiveness that God, through Father Doyle, was demanding of her.

Seeing the strange woman at her father's side where her mother should have been was too much. God was asking too much. The devil was curling round her heart and squeezing hard. She began to turn away. She was not going to do this. She could not forgive her father.

Just then a soft breeze touched her cheek, and the priest's words echoed in her mind. *Your mother was a saintly woman*, he had said. *She'd not be happy*. Remembering this, Lucy seemed to feel the devil uncurl and slither away, taking her anger with him. Lucy just would not, could not, cause her mother any further unhappiness. She could not deny her emotions, but she would work towards overcoming them.

As they approached the bed, Bridie turned. Her worried frown dissolved into a soft smile when she saw the nun.

"How is he doing?" asked Sister Domingo.

"I'm not sure, Sister," Bridie said. "I talk t' him, but I don't know if he can hear me."

Not saying anything to Bridie, Lucy walked around the bed and lifted her father's good hand.

"Da," she said, "it's me. It's Lucy." Her voice was hoarse and unsteady to her own ears. "Can ya hear me? Da,

I know ya just want t' stay where it's quiet an' nothin' hurts. But ya have t' come back. Ya have a lot t' live fer. I had t' come back, an' it wasn't easy. Can ya squeeze me hand? Can ya hear me?"

Tom was indeed in a place where nothing hurt, and he had no intention of coming back. He had found peace at last. He felt himself floating up towards the ceiling and looking down at the scene below.

And there was Lucy was holding his hand and whispering in his ear. What was she saying? He would have to get closer. He had to know what she was saying. It had been a long time since he had heard her voice.

As he began to descend, he felt a strong force pulling him towards his body. All at once, he could hear the voices and feel the blinding pain in his head and a slightly less vicious pain in his arm. He opened his eyes and quickly closed them again. The light was too bright.

"Did ya see that, Sister?" Bridie whispered excitedly. "He opened his eyes!"

"Yes, Bridie, I saw it. I did. He heard your voices. Now, with God's help, he will begin to recover." The nun took a step back from the two women, saying, "I understand you have not met. Bridie, this is Tom's youngest daughter, Lucy. Lucy, this is Bridie, your father's fiancée."

"I am happy t' meet ya, Lucy." Bridie's voice was warm. "Yer father's told me a lot about ya. I'm sure it was the sound o' yer voice that brought him back."

Lucy was dumbfounded by Bridie's generous remark. Seeing this, Sister Domingo smiled. She knew that Bridie's tact would go a long way in bringing about a reconciliation between father and daughter. She had just taken the first step in winning Lucy's confidence.

"Thank ya fer yer kind words." Lucy could think of nothing else to say.

She was saved from embarrassment by the arrival of her sisters and Bill. Sister Domingo excused herself, saying she would return later and reminding them that there could only be two visitors at a time. Bill respectfully offered to wait until Nellie and Feelie had visited with their father, and so he, Lucy, and Bridie withdrew to the hallway. Bridie politely and immediately took her leave of them, saying she wished to visit the chapel.

Bill turned to Lucy. "A little fresh air seems like a good idea about now. Would ya like t' take a wee stroll outside?"

Glad of a break from the hospital's oppressive atmosphere, Lucy nodded. They had a lot to discuss, but neither of them knew how to start. As they walked along the path outside, Bill kicked an imaginary stone and Lucy wound the ribbon from her blouse round her finger.

He finally found the courage to start the conversation they had to have. "Lucy," he said, "I'm sorry."

"Thanks." She was quiet for a moment. "'Twas an awful shock, ya know. I thought me da was goin' t' die."

"I am sorry about Tom, but I meant about last night."

"I'm sorry, too. I shouldn't have taken things fer granted. I should never have spoken t' ya the way I did. We can try again, but, oh, Bill...the problem's still there. What are we t' do about it?"

"Well, I've been thinkin' long an' hard about everythin'," he said. Ya said ye'd marry me. Is religion the only thing standin' in our way?"

"What are ya talkin' about?"

"That policeman seems t' have taken a great interest in ya. He's a Catholic an' has a good steady job. It seems t' me he'd make a good husband fer any girl."

"Aye, fer *any* girl." She finally smiled. "Jest not fer *me*."

"Why is that then?"

"Sure, he'd bore me t' death. Oh, he's a nice enough fella, but there's no wit about him. He's as slow as an arthritic turtle, an' I hear he has fishhooks in his pockets. If there's one thing I can't abide in a man, it's stinginess. Besides, I don't feel anythin' fer him."

Now Bill smiled with her. "Well, I think that answers that question," he said. Lucy certainly wasn't one to mince words.

"Anythin' else ye'd like t' know?" In spite of the smile, Lucy was getting more than a little annoyed.

"Yes. D'ye still want t' marry me?"

"Did we not jest go over that? Have ya gone a wee bit deaf? Yes, I want t' marry ya, but I can't change me religion."

"I'll change mine, then," he said bravely. "I have only me sister here, an' she's off t' Australia soon. If we go t' England, there's no one we know. I won't have t' worry about the lodge. ya still have family. It'd be harder fer ya…t' change."

Bill was doing a good job rationalizing his decision. The bottom line was, of course, that he had little choice. He loved Lucy and knew she was not going to budge on the religion issue.

Lucy was still thinking. "We have one other small problem," she said. "We can't go t' England together if we're not married. It wouldn't be right. People'd talk."

Now Bill was getting annoyed. "Well, luv," he said as patiently as he could, "that has crossed me mind more than once. This is the way of it. We can't get married here. I'm willin' t' change me religion t' marry ya. That means ye'll have t' trust me with yer reputation. It doesn't matter if people talk! Ye'll be a decent married woman before they know it. Married t' the man ya ran away with."

"What de ya mean 'ran away with'?" she sputtered. "I'm not *runnin'* anywhere."

"Ye are if ya want t' marry me. Yer family's already told me we can't get married. I'm goin' t' England as soon as I can get things arranged. I want ya with me. It's up t' you now. There'll be no more talk about it."

His tone was decisive. For once Lucy was at a loss for words.

"We'd best be gettin' back," he added. "I want t' see yer father."

Chapter Twenty-Eight

Tom was released from the hospital three weeks later. His arm would take more time to heal, but other than that, he declared himself to be "fit as a fiddle." Meanwhile, the original date for his wedding to Bridie had been put off. It was now scheduled for the following week.

He and Bridie sat in her kitchen discussing their plans. There had been some mention of delaying the wedding until the following year, but Bridie would have no part of that.

"I'm sorry about our weddin' trip," said Tom. "I did have a wee bit put aside, but this injury set me back. I can't be goin' t' find a job 'til me arm is better."

"Me luv," replied his bride-to-be, "a trip's the smallest of our worries. At least we have somethin' t' fall back on. I'm glad I still have me job. There's been so many laid off at the yard it affects everyone."

"I never wanted ya t' work once we got married," he said, "but there's nowt I can do about it now." He sounded rueful, but she was determined to be patient.

"Tom," she said, "I've told ya time an' time again, I've always worked. I'm used to it."

He nodded. "Well, at least I'll be able t' take care o' the wee ones 'til I'm fit t' go back t' work. Our Feelie's all set t' sail three weeks after the weddin'. Lucy's up t' somethin', but I don't know what. At least she's talkin' t' me now. But not much." He paused, and took a swallow of his tea. "There's a strain between us, y' know. I can feel it still. She still blames me fer her mother's death." Now he scowled a little. "I think that she should take some o' the blame herself, y' know. She should never have been pokin' her nose in things that had nothin' t' do with her. If she'd stayed home where she belonged, neither of 'em would've been hurt."

"Now, Tom, I don't want t' get into this argument. I see both sides o' the coin. Nothin' is goin' t' change what happened. We can only take care o' the things that haven't happened yet an' try t' avoid things that'll hurt us or those we love."

Tom had a feeling he had just been chastised, but he wasn't sure. He merely nodded his head and decided it was time to give that subject a rest. "Bill's off t' Liverpool after the weddin'," he said. "I wonder what our Lucy thinks about that?"

"I'd be the last t' know what she thinks about anythin'," Bridie replied. "She avoids me like the plague. But I can't see her an' Bill being happy about a separation. They're together every minute they can be."

"Aye," he said, "that's what I mean. I have a feelin' she's up t' somethin'. She'd never agree t' stay at home after we get married."

Now Bridie nodded. "I'm sure o' that, I am, an' ya can't blame her. It'd be like rubbin' salt in a wound, so it would. Wonder what she's plannin' t' do?"

"I don't know. But I know Bill has a level head on his shoulders. The girls've told me Bill an' Lucy are engaged, though Bill hasn't said anythin' t' me." He paused. "Apparently, Feelie an' Nellie told him he couldn't marry our Lucy because o' the religion problem."

"Oh? What de you think about Lucy marryin' a Protestant?"

"If the Protestant is Bill," he said, loyal to his friend, "she could do a lot worse."

"Are ya tellin' me ye'd not be worried about Lucy's soul?"

"Darlin' girl," he said, "we'll surely never agree on this subject. I don't believe Lucy's soul would be in jeopardy. Do ya really think God gives a hoot about all this religion nonsense, anyway?"

"Tom, that's blasphemy!

He nodded amicably. "We could discuss this all night or to the end o' time. The fact is that I have no problem with Lucy an' Bill gettin' married. I'll tell ya this, though," he added soberly. "Lucy herself would have a real problem. She's her mother's daughter. She'll not marry outside the faith."

"Are ya sayin' they won't get married then?"

"No, that's not what I'm sayin' at all. I think if Bill's in love with our Lucy, he's the one who'll have t' change. Like I said, Lucy's up t' somethin'. I find it very strange that Bill hasn't asked me fer me blessin'. I have a feelin' they're plannin' to elope."

"Oh surely not! Lucy's reputation'd be ruined."

"Jest think about it fer a minute," he replied. "They can't get married in a Catholic church here. It'd take months of instruction before Bill could become a Catholic, an' Bill can't wait fer months. He has t' find a job overseas right away. Besides, he'd have a hard time of it on both sides if he converted. In fact, it'd be downright dangerous fer both of 'em. It'd not be the first time a woman's been tarred 'n' feathered fer consortin' with the enemy."

Bridie shook her head. "Bill can hardly be called the enemy! He's been good t' yer family an' a friend t' you."

"Try tellin' that t' a bunch o' no good louts out fer a night's sport." Tom touched his bandaged arm. "That kind o' situation is just what those hooligans thrive on. They get t' molest someone an' feel self-righteous about it. They're rarely caught, an' if they are caught, nowt is done about it. He scowled. "In fact, there's been more cruelty in the name o' religion than fer any other reason I can think of. Human bein's have been tortured and maimed, murdered and burned at the stake, all in the name o' religion. Wars've been fought and whole countries laid waste, and all in the name o' religion. It never ends. Of course, sometimes the real cause isn't religion at all but greed. One man has a bigger piece o' bread than the other does. He'll be killed fer his bread, but they'll say it was t' save his soul. Other times, the reason t' kill a man is because he prays in a different way. Not even t' a different God! Jest a different way. Protestants, Catholics, Jews—every man worships the same God, but in different ways." He seemed to be running down, but then he added, "Why can't people jest live and let live? That's all I'd like t' know. If our Lucy an' Bill have t' run away t' get married, I say it's a shame. It's a shame that they can't share their happiness with the family. I fer one won't be judgin' 'em—"

"Well," Bridie interrupted, "ya certainly got goin' on that hobby horse. I understand what ye're sayin', o' course, but I can't agree with all of it. The Jews might be prayin' t' the same God, but do ya think He's listenin' to 'em? After all, they killed His Son."

He had to correct her. "The Romans killed Jesus. It was a Roman who condemned him to death. It was Roman soldiers who nailed him to the Cross."

"But the Jews said 'crucify him'."

"No, a mob said that—the same kind o' mob that waits outside a jail when there's a hangin'. I often wonder what Jesus meant when he said, 'Father, fergive 'em fer they know not what they do.' Was he askin' fer fergiveness fer the soldiers, the mob, or all mankind? If he could ask fer fergiveness as he was dyin', why should we still be blamin' the Jews?"

These opinions were new to Bridie. "Tom," she slowly asked, "do ya believe in yer religion?"

"I was born a Catholic an' I'll die a Catholic. It's not jest the religion. It's part o' who I am." Taking her hand in his, he continued. "But I can't agree with a lot o' the rules. Fer example, I think priests should pay attention t' our souls an' leave our bodies t' ourselves. They do more harm than good, drivin' married folks apart. I've lived through that once, an' I'll not live through it again. I'll go t' Mass an' t' confession. I'll try t' keep the Ten Commandments. I'll pray fer me soul and the souls of the departed. I'll try not t' harm anyone. That's the religion I believe in."

"I expect that's as good an answer as any," she replied. "Now let's talk about less serious things. I'm gettin' a headache tryin' t' figure it all out. I can see ye've spent a lot o' time tryin' t' fathom these questions."

"Aye, that I have," he said, "an' I'm no nearer the answers then I ever was. I jest have t' think me own thoughts an' live me own life as best I can. I have t' make up fer a lot o' past mistakes, so I do. Ye're right, though. That's enough o' that talk." He gave her a lascivious grin. "Let's think about our weddin' instead."

And she smiled. "I have a surprise fer ya," she said. "I wasn't goin' t' tell ya 'til next week, but I think ya need a wee lift now."

"What is it then? I'm holdin' me breath."

"Well, ya said we couldn't take a trip fer our honeymoon? It won't be t' the seaside, but how about a wee trip inta the country?"

"An' how d'ye propose t' manage that?"

"Well, ya see, me uncle owns apple orchards in Glenavey. He an' his wife rattle around in a big farmhouse. They never had a family. Why, sure an' we'd be welcome there. How does a few days o' good food, fresh air, an' a soft featherbed sound?"

Tom was delighted. "But ya fergot the best part."

"What's that?"

"Ye'll be beside me in that featherbed. Sure, the whole thing sounds grand."

She blushed. "Aye. I must admit the thought that we can finally lie together gives me th' goose bumps."

"It gives me more than goose bumps, me girl. But we won't go into that jest now."

"Tom! What a thing t' say t' a decent woman," The rebuke was a gentle one accompanied by a giggle.

"Ah, woman, decent or not, come over here. I need t' put me one good arm 'round ya an' feel ya near me."

Still blushing, she rose to sit beside her man. Her thoughts were far from pure, and she suddenly wondered if she would have to confess them. The idea of talking to Father Doyle about such matters was disturbing until she realized she had to distance herself from this temptation. She had saved herself for her wedding night, and she could not spoil it now.

Yes, she would be with Tom as his wife and not before. When he put his arm around her shoulders and pulled her close, she allowed no more than a careful kiss, and then she gently pulled away.

"Ah luv, what's the matter?" He looked bewildered and a little hurt. What was he doing wrong? "Why're ya turnin' away from me? Sure, we haven't been together fer an age."

She folded her hands between her breasts before she spoke. "I want t' be with ya as much as ya want t' be with me, luv. An' we'll be together fer the rest of our lives. But I want it to be *right.* I want t' wear me white weddin' dress an' know I have a right to. We can wait another two weeks. We've waited this long."

He knew there was no point in arguing. She had waited so long, and she had a right to experience her wedding night without guilt, a right to walk proudly down the aisle with her head held high. This was her gift to him. His gift to her would be patience and understanding.

The passion waned and drifted off like a bubble in the wind and they held each other in comfortable silence as lovers often do.

Chapter Twenty-Nine

Sitting on a bench in the zoo at the bottom of the Cavehill, Lucy and Bill hardly saw the tufts of white clouds with gray bellies scudding across the sky towards an unknown destination or felt the playful breeze chasing its tail through a field of dancing bluebells. The decisions they were making weighed heavily on them both.

"Lucy," Bill was saying, "I feel bad about yer father, sure I do. I hate deceivin' him. I promised t' stand up fer him an' Bridie, an' I don't like the idea o' skulkin' off t' England without gettin' his approval fer our marriage. It's a bad way t' start, with the family mad at us. Yer father'll be me father-in-law, an' our children's grandfather. Like it or not, Bridie'll be a part of our lives as long as she's with yer father."

"More's the pity," Lucy whispered almost to herself. She and Bill were still having a hard time seeing eye-to-eye on this issue. She didn't see any way to avoid waiting to marry Bill until after her father's wedding.

"Ye'll be expected t' go t' the weddin'," Bill unnecessarily reminded her.

"I know. That's what's worryin' me. I know he's goin' t' do it. I jest can't bear the thought of that woman tryin' t' take me mother's place."

"Do ya want yer da t' be on his own fer the rest of his life?"

"I think that's what he deserves, so I do. Me ma's gone. She had her life taken from her. An' now he's puttin' a woman in her place. Father Doyle says I should fergive him, an' I've tried, so I have. He says God gave His Son so sinners could be fergiven. He said me ma'd not want me t' be so bitter. He said me ma'd not want me t' disobey God's will. It's just so hard t' do God's will sometimes! I miss me ma." She began to cry again. "Me ma will never see me married or hold me babies."

"There now." He wanted to take her in his arms and comfort her, but this was neither the time nor the place. "Don't be cryin'. Ye'll be makin' those pretty eyes all red."

"I'm sorry. I can't help the way I feel."

"I know it's hard fer ya, luv. Try t' heed the priest. He knows what's the right thing t' do. He said yer mother'd fergive, and God wants ya t' fergive, too. Ye're jest hurtin' yerself. The anger is eatin' ya up an' spoilin' yer life. Yer mother'd want ya t' be happy, so she would." He produced a clean handkerchief from his pocket and dabbed at Lucy's face, "Ya have me now, an' I'll try t' make ya content. Try t' put the past behind ya. Yer mother will always be in yer heart. Come on now, dry yer tears. We'll go an' have a wee cuppa tea an' one o' them wee cream buns ya like so much."

"Oh, Bill," Lucy was still sniffling, "what would I do without ya? I'm sorry t' be bringin' ya into all this trouble."

He managed to smile at her. "Well, I kinda brought meself into it. I could've left a long time ago. But I love ya, an' the decision t' stay was me own. Ye've no need t' be sorry about that. Yer father has been me friend fer a long time. I have t' stand up fer him at his weddin', like I promised. Sure, an' I'd not even know ya if it wasn't fer him. If ya can't find it in yer heart t' forgive him now, jest make a motion of it. Allow yerself time, an' maybe someday it'll all come right."

"I jest thought o' somethin'." She had stopped crying, and suddenly was all business. "Ya can't stand up fer him. Ye're a Protestant! I wonder if me da told the father that."

"By God, ye're right! I never thought of that. I don't know what I was thinkin', or what Tom was thinkin', either. I took a vow never t' enter a Catholic chapel. It's more than me life's worth t' be seen goin' into one. If the boys from the lodge found out, I'd never be able t' show me face on the Shankill Road again."

Lucy, who had had heard tales of the Orange Order, shivered. "Bill," she said, "what's goin' t' happen if they find out ya married a Catholic an' turned yer coat?"

"We're goin' over the water," was the reply. "It won't matter there."

"But a lot o' the lads from the yard are goin' over t' find jobs. Ye're bound t' meet up with some of 'em."

He nodded emphatically. "An' I've decided we'll not be goin' t' Clydebank fer that very reason. We'll go t' England, as not many o' the boys're goin' there. Most o' the lads are headed up north to Scotland, so I feel we'd do better in England. It's too bad. The Scots are more like us, an' we'd fit in better in Scotland. Most of our ancestors came across the water from Scotland."

"Yers, maybe," said Lucy. "Mine were all Irish, far back as we know."

"Well that mixture will make fer bonnie babies," Bill said with a wink, "an' smart ones, too, I'm thinkin'."

"Go on with ye! Ye're embarrassin' me." She was blushing and smiling at the same time.

"There's nowt embarrassin' about it. Sure, it's nature's way. I fer one can't wait. Ya jest mentioned babies yerself."

"Aye. But that's different."

"Oh, I see. It's alright fer ya t' talk about havin' babies, but I'm not t' mention th' subject. Would ya mind explainin' that particular bit o' cockeyed thinkin'? The last I knew, it took two, an' as far as I know, that hasn't changed. At least I hope not. I was lookin' forward t' that pursuit."

Lucy was still trying to hide her smile. "Ya know what I mean! I get embarrassed when ya talk about things like that."

"Well, we'll jest have t' help ya over that nonsense. We're goin' t' be married, an' there's no room fer false modesty between married folk."

"When we're married, it's different, don't ya see. It's necessary t' talk about havin' a family."

"I think it's necessary t' talk before ya get married," said Bill. "Ya need t' be sure ya both want the same thing. Ya have t' decide what size family ya want. No good findin' ya have different ideas about that after the fact."

"What on earth de ya mean by that?" She sounded genuinely puzzled. "Ya have whatever size family God sends ya."

Realizing that he was on shaky ground again, Bill fell silent for a moment. He had forgotten, or had never paid much attention to, the Catholic views on birth control. No matter, he thought. He would be happy with a large family or a small one. Basically, all he wanted was to marry Lucy.

Today, the size of his future family was of no importance to him. He knew they both wanted children, and that was all that mattered.

He decided to change the subject. "We had better go over t' see Tom," he said. "If I can't be his best man, he'll have t' find someone else. But I'd like t' tell him the truth about our plans."

"What if he refuses t' give us his blessin'?"

"We'll jest have t' cross that bridge when we come to it. I know fer a fact that yer sisters are against us gettin' married. There is nothin' we can do about that. But if I've been honest with yer father, th' man that's my friend, why then I'll feel better."

"Me sisters will jest have t' get over it," said Lucy. "It's our lives, not theirs. But I suppose ye're right about me da. It's one thing not to tell me sisters, but it would be another thing altogether not t' ask me da fer his blessin'."

"Ye're right at that. Come on. Let's go find that cuppa I promised ya." He stood up and pulled her to her feet.

"Sounds good t' me. I'm feelin' the cold." The sun had ducked behind a cloud and the breeze now had a bit of a bite to it.

"I can see where ya would. That dress looks pretty, but I don't think it keeps the wind out." He took off his jacket and draped it around her shoulders.

"Thanks, luv," she said, "but now ye'll be feelin' the cold."

Cold though he was, Bill dismissed her concern with a wave of his hand, taking care not to shiver.

Lucy felt protected and loved, a feeling that was rare in her life. She had been so angry about everything—her mother's death, her illness, her father's involvement with not one but two other women, the loss of her sister and the babe her thankless job and stingy boss—that the past year had seemed like a nightmare. She had not allowed herself to feel much of anything but anger, and the small happiness she had experienced had been only with Bill. Feeling a surge of gratitude for his kindness, she kissed him on the cheek.

"What was that fer?"

"Jest because."

"Jest because what?"

"Quit yer fishin'. Ya must know ye're a grand man."

"Well, I never thought about it." He smiled. "But if ya say so, why then, it must be true"

"Go on with ya! Don't be gettin' a big head."

"Ye're jest an Indian giver, givin' a compliment with one hand an' takin' it away with the other."

They both began to laugh and, linking arms, they set off in search of hot tea and sweet cream buns.

Chapter Thirty

It was a few days later when Tom and Bill made their way to the Hole in the Wall for drinks and conversation. Tom had a good idea what Bill wanted to talk to him about. Entering the bar, they greeted friends but made it clear they wanted to be alone. After ordering and settling into their chairs, Bill came right to the point

"Tom," he said, "there's a few things I need t' talk t' ya about."

Tom nodded. "I kinda got that idea. Go on then, lad. Spit it out."

Bill took a moment to frame his reply. "Well, first of all," he said, "I can't be standin' up fer ya."

"Why not?"

"Neither of us, nor the priest, fer that matter, were thinkin' right. I can't stand up fer ya because I'm a Protestant."

All Tom could do was shake his head. "That never even crossed me mind."

"Mine neither. Not 'til Lucy pointed it out."

"So I'll have to look fer someone else. I'm right sorry, lad. I really wanted ya t' do it."

"I'm disappointed too," said Bill, and he meant it. "But it's too dangerous. An' the priest's bound t' catch on before long."

Each took a swallow of his beer, and Tom finally broke the silence.

"Ya said ya had other things needin' t' be off yer mind."

"Aye." Bill hoped he didn't sound as nervous as he felt. "I'm wantin' t' tell ya that Lucy an' I want t' get married."

All Tom did was nod. "I guessed as much," he said calmly, "but ya have the same problem there. What do ya intend t' do about that?"

"We're goin' t' go t' England an' get married there."

"Ya still won't be able to get married in a Catholic church," said Tom, "an' Lucy won't be agreein' t' a civil marriage."

"Tom, I'm goin' t' turn." As Tom raised his eyebrows, Bill continued. "Lucy means more t' me than which church I pray in," he said. "I've always loved the idea that I can talk direct t' God. T' me, that's the beauty o' me religion. But I realize now that I can still talk t' God in me own way. If it pleases Lucy fer me t' take instructions an' become a Catholic, well then, so be it. I'll make an' keep whatever promises I have to, but I'll pray t' God in the manner I was brought up t' do."

Bill paused, but Tom said nothing.

"Tom, we're friends. I'm askin' fer yer blessin' an' yer trust. Lucy an' I will have t' go t' England unwed. We were goin' to elope, but that's no way t' start a marriage. I promise t' take care o' yer daughter an' marry her as soon as the church will let me."

Bill stopped there, but Tom said nothing and only sipped on his beer. Finally, the older man set his beer down, took off his glasses, and rubbed his eyes.

"Bill, ya most certainly have me blessin'. But th' question of takin' Lucy across th' water without bein' wed is a little tougher. I have yer word on it, but passion can overcome the best intentions. Ya get me meanin'? Ye're young an' in love, an' it'll be hard fer ya t' keep yer distance. Jest fer a moment, lad, consider what'd happen if Lucy was in a family way, unmarried, an' somethin' happened t' ya. Where would that leave our Lucy and her child?"

"I thought about that," said Bill, coloring a little. "I could promise that I'd not touch Lucy until we were wed. In fact, I *will* promise that. But t' set yer mind at rest, I'll ask Lucy if she'll agree t' a civil marriage until we can get married in the church."

Tom chuckled. "I think ya might have an easier time sellin' snow t' the Eskimos," he said.

Bill could only nod. "I know she won't think much o' the idea," he admitted, "but it makes sense t' me. She'd be me wife in the eyes o' the law. If anythin' were t' happen t' me before the church weddin', well, she could come home as a married woman. No one need know that there was no clergy involved. I promise ya we'll live as brother and sister until we're wed in the church."

Tom smiled at this declaration, thinking, *Ye're a better man than I am, Bill Nicholson.* Though if Lucy was as determined as Bridie, he might be in for a long siege. As long as a valid marriage certificate protected his daughter, however, he would be satisfied.

"Me boy," he said, "I'll advise ya t' talk things over with Lucy. If she agrees t' a civil marriage, fine. Ye'll have both me blessin' and me trust. Ya can get married as soon as ya get t' Liverpool or better still, get married in the town hall here."

Bill's relief was evident on his face, and the two men raised their glasses quietly to the arrangement and drank to settle it.

"Well, now that that problem's resolved fer now," said Bill, "how're things goin' fer yer big day?"

"Things were goin' fine," Tom grinned, "but now I have t' find another best man. I think I'll ask Nellie's husband Séan."

"That sounds like a grand idea. He'd have been goin' t' the weddin' anyway. His best suit'd already be out o' mothballs." Smiling at his own joke, Bill hailed the bartender and ordered another round, whiskey this time, a drop o' the hard stuff to celebrate. If all went well, they would soon be family.

~

Bridie woke to a bright sun streaming through the lace curtains in her bedroom. It was a beautiful day, but she would have been equally happy if it had been raining cats and dogs. Today was her wedding day, and nothing was going to spoil her mood.

Her beautiful white dress and veil hung from the curtain rod like a friendly ghost, swaying gently in the breeze. Her white shoes sat primly side by side, and her white underclothes were neatly folded on the dresser. Gazing at all this white finery, she smiled triumphantly.

The rest of the morning was a blur, and it seemed as if she had only just finished dressing when, at twelve noon, she heard the chapel bells peal for the Angelus. As she walked down the aisle, only Tom was in focus, waiting nervously at the altar. Everything else was still a blur.

When she reached the altar, he held out his hand and grasped hers firmly. Half an hour later, Tom O'Leary and Bridie McGuiness were pronounced man and wife.

Lucy was still sitting alone in the chapel after the bridal party and guests left. She would meet Bill at the reception, but for now she just wanted to sit quietly and think. She was startled, therefore, when the side door opened and Bridie came back into the chapel. Not seeming to see Lucy sitting in the shadows, she strode purposefully to the statue of the Blessed Virgin. Lucy remained silent as she watched her new stepmother kneel before the statue, remove the white orchid from her prayer book, and place it at the Virgin's feet.

"Holy Mother, I never knew Ellen," the new bride whispered, "but you know I pray fer her soul every night. Everyone says she was a saint, so she must be with you. I know I can never take her place, but I would like t' be friends with her girls. Please ask Ellen to fergive Tom, bless our marriage, and help him an' Lucy to make peace. Amen. Oh, by the way, the orchid's fer both o' ye."

Lucy wasn't sure if she should announce her presence, so she was relieved to see Bridie hurry out again. Then she rose, walked to the statue to which Bridie had just prayed so earnestly, and knelt before it herself.

"Holy Mother," she said, her tone contrite and self-conscious at the same time, "I'm sorry fer bein' so thran. I'll try t' make me peace with me da. I'm even beginnin' t' like that woman in spite o' meself. If ya don't mind, I'd like t' take the flower. I promise t' bring one fer each o' ya next week."

After crossing herself and picking up the orchid, Lucy made her way out of the chapel and into the bright sunlight.

She felt lighter than she had for months. Bill was waiting for her at the entrance of the hotel.

"There y'are," he said. "I was beginnin' t' get a bit worried. Everyone's gone in already. What kept ya? Is everythin' right with ya?"

"Aye. It's righter than it's been fer a long time."

He was surprised to see her smile. "I'm glad ye're feelin' that way," he said cautiously, "but what exactly changed yer mind?"

"I was sittin' inside the chapel when Bridie came back in t' speak to th' Blessed Virgin. She called me ma a saint, and asked her fer forgiveness. Bill, she asked nothin' fer herself except a blessin'. She didn't know I was there. It feel like me ma wanted me t' hear her prayer."

"An' what are ya doin' with the flower?"

"I'm goin' t' put it back int' Bridie's prayer book," she said with a sly grin. "Then she'll know her prayer's been heard."

"But she might not be too happy with ya fer eavesdroppin'—"

"Oh, I don't intend t' let on how the flower got back on her book! I'll jest let her think 'tis a sign from God. I mean, in a way her prayer *was* heard. Maybe I was meant t' be in the chapel t' hear it. In any case, I intend t' try t' make up with me da."

"Well, if ya think it's right," he said, "who am I t' argue?" He would have chalked the whole business up to superstition, but if it made Lucy happy, then it was all right by him.

Chapter Thirty-One

They entered the reception hall just as Nellie's husband Séan, the best man, was reading the telegrams. There was a flutter of excitement as he held one from America up and waved it.

"'Congratulations,'" he read, "'and best wishes fer yer happiness. Brian.'"

Feelie nudged Nellie in the ribs. "Here, girl, what de ya think o' that?"

"What?"

"There's no mention of his fancy American woman. His letters've been few an' far between, an' with little or no mention o' the woman at all. Don't ya think that's a bit odd?"

Nellie gave her sister a tight smile. "Sure, an' I think everythin' about him is odd. He's a disgrace, so he is. That American must've been up t' no good. Jest because ye're posh, it doesn't mean ya can't be fast."

"Ye're right about that! I heard the posh ones are worse than regular folk when it comes t' bein' fast."

Overhearing this self-righteous conversation, Bill and Lucy claimed their seats at Tom's family table and Lucy held her finger to her lips to signal her sisters to be quiet. The best man soon finished the reading of all the greetings and resumed his seat during a round of polite applause.

"Lucy, what kept ya so late?" Feelie asked her after the applause died down.

"Oh, I had a wee errand t' do."

"Well, ya missed the best telegram, so ya did."

"Who was it from then?"

"It was from America, from Brian. But there was no mention o' the woman. Don't ya think that's a wee bit strange?"

Nellie broke in. "Everything about the whole thing is strange. I think the woman was fast. No better than a hoor…posh or not, still a hoor."

Lucy turned to her sister. "Oh, Nellie, don't ya think ye're bein' a bit harsh? Sure, we don't know anythin' about the American. She might be the nicest woman ya ever met, fer all ya know."

Nellie was having none of that. "Have ya been drinkin' holy water or somethin? I know what I saw. So does Feelie. That woman was far too uppity fer that Brian. She was only after one thing. 'Twas as plain as the nose on yer face!"

Bill almost choked on his beer. He doubted that Nellie or her sisters had any idea how unfortunate Nellie's choice of words was, or how funny.

His wife-to-be looked at him. "An' what's tickled yer funny bone?"

"Oh, just somethin' Nellie said."

"An' what was that? Come on, let us all in on the joke."

"I don't think it's a proper thing t' be talkin' about with girls." His face was getting redder by the second. He had no idea how he was going to get himself out of the situation he had gotten himself into.

Feelie leaned forward. "How can it be unsuitable if our Nellie said it? Can ya tell me that?"

Séan came to Bill's rescue. "I don' think what the American woman was after was the *nose* on anyone's face. If ya get me meanin'."

"Billy Nicholson! Ya should be ashamed o' yerself."

They all burst out laughing. It was the first time Lucy had called him Billy, and she would use that form of his name to signal her displeasure, feigned or not, for the rest of their lives.

Everyone was having a grand time by now, and the grand time continued late into the night. They danced the sixteen-hand reel, accompanied by John Dobbin, who played the accordion with great gusto. Not to be outdone, Jim Shirley led the guests in a hilarious rendition of "Paddy Mc Ginty's Goat" and serenaded the bride with his own version of "The Belle of Belfast City." Eventually, traditional jigs and reels led by the pipes gave way to modern dances, as the younger guests kicked up their heels to the Lambeth Walk and the Lindy and the Jitterbug. The more whiskey flowed, the more riotous the dances became. The atmosphere changed again when the bride and groom cut the cake and Margaret, Birdie's matron of honor, sang "Believe Me if All Those Endearing Young Charms" in her beautiful clear soprano. The bride was then presented with the traditional rolling pin (to keep the groom in line) and a horseshoe for luck (presented upside down so the luck could not run out).

When the time came for Bridie to throw her bouquet, she became a little flustered as she remembered she didn't have a bouquet to throw. "What'll I do?" she asked her matron of honor.

"Sure, ya can jest throw the orchid ya have on yer prayer book," someone called out.

Bridie was confused. "But I can't. I don't have it anymore. I left it fer the Blessed Mother."

"Don't be daft," said Margaret. "I jest saw it."

She went to retrieve the orchid, only to be intercepted by Lucy.

"I'd like t' take this over t' Bridie meself, if ya don't mind," Lucy said. "There's somethin' I want t' say t' her."

Hoping Lucy wasn't about to make a scene, Margaret nodded cautiously, and so Lucy took the flower and made her way through the guests to where her father and his bride were standing. She kissed her father and handed the orchid to Bridie, saying, "Congratulations, an' welcome t' our family."

Bridie wasn't quite sure how the orchid had arrived at the reception, but she smiled and hugged her new stepdaughter. She'd seen Lucy in the chapel out of the corner of her eye and knew that she must have overheard her prayer.

God helps those who help themselves, she said to herself as she watched father and daughter exchange another hug. Margaret breathed a sigh of relief. Bill smiled proudly and nodded his head. Nellie and Feelie just stared in open-mouthed disbelief.

"Ah, will youse two shut yer mouths," Lucy said cheerfully as she returned to the family table. "Ye'll be catchin' flies, so ya will."

Nellie was the first to speak, "Shut our mouths, is it? What I'd like t' know is what the hell was that all about? Jest the other day, ya were vowin' never t' fergive him or have anythin' t' do with her. Would ya mind lettin' us in on the reason fer yer change o' heart?"

"Let's jest say the Blessed Mother made me see the folly o' me ways."

Feelie was still astonished. "Well, it took ya long enough to get the message," she muttered.

"Ah, well then, all's well that ends well," Lucy answered.

Bill observed this interchange with some amusement, wondering how Lucy's sisters would react when they heard Lucy and he were to be married. Would all indeed end well? He was still reflecting on this question when Lucy dropped her bombshell.

"Bill an' me are t' be married."

Nellie and Feelie gasped. "YE'RE WHAT?"

"Ya can't be marryin' a Protestant," added Nellie, with real sympathy in her voice. "Sorry, Bill, it's nothin' against ya."

"She's right," said Feelie. "No priest will marry ya, an' I doubt any Prod minister will, either. All ye'll be doin' will be bringin' a heap o' trouble down on us all."

"We'll be bringin' no trouble down on anybody," said Bill. "We'll be goin' over the water t' be married. I've already spoken with yer father. He trusts me t' do the honorable thing. I've promised Lucy and yer father that I'll take instruction and become a Catholic. Yer father trusts me. Will ya not, too?"

There was a stunned silence around the table.

"Ah, sure," Lucy finally said, "we're supposed t' be here enjoyin' this weddin'. I shouldn't have said anythin' about Bill an' me. We'll talk about it later." She felt a little guilty now and wished she had picked a more appropriate time and place to tell her family of her intentions.

Bill agreed. "That's a grand idea," he said firmly. He also thought the day belonged to Tom and Bridie and that there would be time soon enough to discuss the plans he was making for Lucy and him. He had Tom's approval, and that was enough. The rest of Lucy's family would feel as they chose about it, but they would have to accept Lucy's decision.

In any case, he still needed to talk to Lucy about a civil ceremony, and that was not a conversation he intended to share with an audience, especially not this audience.

Tom and his new wife were now making the rounds and greeting and thanking their guests. When they reached the family table, Tom asked Lucy to dance with him. She smiled and stood up and they made their way to the tiny dance floor.

"Lucy luv," said Tom, "I jest wanted t' thank ya fer makin' this day so much happier fer me. I know how hard it's been fer ya. I've missed ya, so I have."

"Thanks, Da."

She could say no more. Her offhand attitude with her sisters belied her true feelings. Yes, she felt better about Bridie, and she had promised to forgive her father, but deep down, a hard knot of bitterness persisted. She remembered Bill telling her that even if she could not forgive and forget the past, she should pretend to. This was the best she could do for the time being.

She had made a promise to the Holy Mother and had kept it, at least this far, and she had to admit that she felt lighter and happier having done so. Her mother was dead, but life would go on. Her father had a new wife. Mary Alice and her baby were dead. Feelie was going to Australia. She would be going to England with Bill.

The life she had lived until recently was gone forever. Her family had changed, shrinking and growing in unexpected ways, with some members now alive only in her memories. She had to leave her beloved ghosts behind, but she would never forget them. She would be happy to put distance between herself and the sorrow evoked by familiar surroundings.

A voice interrupted her thoughts. "Can I cut in?"

With a smile, Tom released Lucy into Bill's arms and rejoined his bride at the head table.

"Now, where were ya?" Bill asked Lucy. "Ya were miles away. Ya looked as though ye'd jest lost yer best friend."

The smile Lucy had worn while dancing with her father was gone, replaced by a wrinkled brow. "I was thinkin'," she replied, "about our family as it used t' be."

"Ah, that's never good t' dwell on," he murmured. "I have t' tell ya that I'm proud o' ya fer what ya did today. I know it took a lot o' courage."

Lucy was not sure she deserved the compliment. "I jest did what I promised t' do," she said. "Yer advice had a lot t' do with it, ya know."

"How so?"

"Well…ya told me if I couldn't fergive me da that I should jest pretend. An' I took yer advice. There's nothin' I can do that'll change what's happened. Nothin' will bring me ma back. Everyone's been tellin' me t' let the anger go. I can't do that yet, but I can pretend. Maybe," she added, "maybe if I pretend long enough the anger will go away. Like not stokin' a fire an lettin' it go out."

"That's a good way t' think about it," he said, giving her a whirl. "Come on, then. Let's enjoy the rest o' this grand day."

Chapter Thirty-Two

After the reception, the bride and groom left for their honeymoon amid showers of rice, good wishes, and ribald jokes. Bridie's aunt and uncle, Kathleen and Seamus Mallon, had offered to give them a lift to the farm in their pony and trap. The bridal party had been busy, and the little carriage was bedecked with ribbons and trailed a noisy collection of tin cans. A large cardboard sign proclaimed the occupants *Just Married.*

Tears spilled down Bridie's cheeks as she waved to the disappearing crowd of well-wishers.

"What ails ya, luv?" Tom asked anxiously.

"I'm jest so happy. I can't believe we're finally married."

"Well, Mrs. O'Leary, ye'd better believe it."

This triggered fresh tears. "Oh Tom," said Bridie, crying and laughing at once, "I am. I'm Mrs. Thomas O'Leary. Can ya believe it? I feel like a silly schoolgirl."

"Jest make sure ya don't act like one," he replied with a smile. "I'm lookin' forward t' lyin' with the woman I love, not with a schoolgirl."

She blushed prettily and said, "I feel giddy, fer sure, but I've waited a long time fer this day and the night that follows. I don't have any experience, 'tis true, but I'm a fast learner."

"I told ya before I'm no great expert," said her husband. "We'll learn together."

As they left the city behind, the shadows lengthened and the warm breeze turned cool. Tom draped a plaid blanket around their shoulders, then pulled Bridie close and kissed her softly and tenderly, mindful that they were not alone and not wanting to cause her any embarrassment or offend her relatives.

Darkness had fallen by the time they reached the farmhouse. Someone had lit the paraffin lamps, bathing the house in a cozy warm glow. While Aunt Kathleen ushered them into the kitchen, her husband unhitched the horse.

Accustomed to the small rooms in his own home, Tom was amazed at the size of the farmhouse kitchen. A large table dominated the room, set with places for four people. In the middle of the table stood a round basket displaying shiny red and green apples. On both sides of the stone fireplace sat wooden rocking chairs with checked gingham cushions. A large black pot hung suspended over the banked fire. Something savory was cooking in the pot, reminding Tom that he had not eaten all day. With all the excitement of the wedding and greeting their guests, he had only picked at the wedding supper, and now he was starving.

As he rose to investigate, a large black shape detached itself from the shadowy corner, and suddenly Tom felt his wrist firmly clamped in the jaws of an enormous dog of indeterminate lineage. But the pressure from the dog's jaws was gentle, and so he thought it wiser not to try to remove his arm. By the time Kathleen realized what was going on, the animal had herded Tom to the door.

"Jacko," she ordered the dog, "will ya leave the man alone! Go lie down now." She turned to Tom. "I'm sorry. Yon beast is harmless, but he scares the wits out of a body if they don't know him. He's jest askin' ya t' let him out."

"So I'll let him out;" was Tom's good-natured reply. "He must need t' go." He examined his arm. "He's a bit of a fright, but gentle with it."

As Tom opened the door to let the dog out, Seamus appeared with the newlyweds' suitcases and set them down at the bottom of the stairs.

"I'll be after takin' these up an' showin' ya yer room after we eat," he offered. He was as solid as a tree trunk, seeming almost to be a part of the earth he farmed. His complexion was ruddy, his hair stood out in unruly spikes from his large head, and his dark eyes peered out from under bushy eyebrows. He had a barrel chest and thick neck. He was a man of the soil, tough and bereft of a formal education.

Bridie's aunt Kathleen, by contrast, was tall and spare and carried her slight frame with an economy of movement and perfect posture. She wore her silver hair in a soft chignon, her features were angular, a pair of wire-rimmed glasses sat perched on the bridge of her aquiline nose, and her voice was soft and melodious. She was dressed for the occasion in her "Sunday-go-to-meetin'" dress, a severe gray frock that was softened at the neckline by a pretty lace collar on which was pinned a gold brooch with a single tiny diamond. The brooch had belonged to her mother, and apart from her wedding ring, was her only piece of jewelry. At first meeting, her appearance was severe and forbidding, but that impression was quickly dispelled by a radiant smile that transformed her face.

"Here, Bridie," she said, "come an' take the weight off yer feet. Sit here by the fire. I'll give it a poke an' bring it back t' life. Tom, make yerself comfortable. I'll be gettin' us somethin' t' eat. Sure, an' ya must be starved."

She donned her apron and bustled around making preparations for their meal.

At the same time, Seamus excused himself to take care of the evening chores that are part of a farmer's life, though he promised to be back in time to eat with them. With Jacko at his heels, he set off on his rounds. The wind had freshened and a full harvest moon had risen, silhouetting the apple trees in a manic dance. Seamus particularly loved the trees. He looked, spoke, and behaved like a farmer, but in his heart he was an artist. The attic in the farmhouse held hundreds of his canvases—apple trees in spring, lovingly captured with abstract abandon, shades of red and tints of pink with glorious springtime green splashed across a cerulean sky. There were also summertime's warm greens and swelling fruits, autumn's harvest hues of yellow and orange, woven through the shiny reds and greens of mature fruit. Winter provided studies in black and white, twisted limbs set against angry winter skies streaked in red and purple, trees standing naked in a shroud of snow. Seamus loved his trees, and his farm, and his love showed in every impassioned stroke of this secret artist's brush.

"Can I give ya a hand?" Bridie asked her aunt back in the kitchen.

"No, thanks luv. I set the meal t' cookin' before we left fer the weddin'. I knew we'd all be tired an' hungry when we got back." She gave the pot over the fire a stir. "Seamus'll be back in a tick. Jest take it easy by the hearth 'til he gets here. Ah, speak o' the devil, here he is now."

Seamus and the dog entered the room, followed by a sharp gust of wind and a few dry leaves. He made his way over to the sink and pumped some water to wash his hands and splash his face. Jacko melted back into the shadows by the wall.

"Here we are then," said Kathleen beaming. "Everythin' is ready. Will ya be comin' t' the table before it gets cold? There's nothin' worse than cold food that's supposed to be hot, or hot food that's supposed to be cold."

She pointed to the seat opposite Seamus for Tom and sat Bridie opposite herself. Her famous mutton stew had been transferred to a soup tureen that had belonged to her mother. Large glasses of buttermilk now sat at each place on the table, and slabs of homemade wheat bread and fresh churned butter completed the main meal. Four dishes of home-canned plums smothered in custard sat on the sideboard for dessert.

After Seamus led the little party in the prayer of thanks, Tom dug into his stew.

"Aunt Kathleen," said Bridie, sniffing appreciatively, "if that stew tastes anywhere near as good as it smells, it must be a blue ribbon winner."

"Ye're not far off," said her uncle. "Kathleen's cookin' has taken many a prize at the chapel's bring and buy sale. People come fer miles t' buy her apple pies. O' course," he added with justifiable pride, "she starts off with the best apples."

"Seamus!" Kathleen's scolding had a smile in it, "it's not seemly t' be pattin' yer own back. Or mine fer that matter."

Tom broke in. "Mrs. Mallon, this stew is the best I've ever tasted. Mutton's usually tough, but this almost melts in yer mouth. What's yer secret?"

"Thank ya kindly, Tom. But first, ya must call me Aunt Kathleen or just plain Kathleen, if yer more comfortable with that. Ye're part o' the family now, an' t' answer yer question, the meat's been simmerin' over that fire all day. The flavor is helped by addin' a tiny pinch o' cinnamon."

"I'd never have thought o' that," said Bridie.

"A cook that worked fer a big hotel in Belfast told me t' try it," said her aunt. "Ya have t' be careful, though… too much an' yer stew ends up tastin' like Christmas puddin'," Kathleen said with a quiet little laugh.

The conversation faded as they enjoyed the meal. Truth be told, Tom would have preferred a pint to the buttermilk, but the food was delicious, and he wasn't about to look a gift horse in the mouth.

"That was grand, Aunt Kathleen," Bridie said as she scraped her bowl with her last bite of bread. "Thanks again. I'll help ya rid up."

"Indeed, ya won't," was the reply. "Ye've had a long day an' ye'll be needin' yer rest." This last was said with a tactful smile, almost but not entirely without a twinkle in her aunt's eye.

"Come on then, I'll show ya to yer room," Seamus said, rising from the table with the newlyweds.

As they were ushered upstairs, Bridie realized that she was feeling embarrassed, even self-conscious, despite her aunt and uncle being kindness itself. She wished she and Tom could have spent their first night as man and wife alone. She also imagined the farmhands' knowing smiles that would greet them in the morning.

Unaware of his niece's anxiety, Seamus bade the couple goodnight and closed the door.

~

The room was large and frigid, and very little attention had ever been paid to the décor. The walls were whitewashed and rough, the floors painted brown, and curtains that had been flour bags in a previous incarnation hung on the windows. A beautiful cherry, four-poster bed sulked against one wall, and its companion in misery, a cherry dresser, was pushed in the corner. Accustomed to finer things, the furniture had never adapted to this ugly room. Kathleen always intended to make a more fitting setting for the pieces she inherited from her parents, but she just never got around to it. The bed had a fine feather mattress and a lofty down comforter, however, and completing the room's appointments were a chamber pot with an ornate rose pattern, a washbasin and jug to match, a Windsor chair, and an oil lamp on the night table.

Bridie felt a sudden shyness. She had looked forward to this night for so long, and now she didn't know what to do. Tom opened his suitcase and carefully placed his clothes in a dresser drawer. She did the same. Neither said a word. The silence stretched out and settled over them. Bridie had never undressed before a man in her life. She was beginning to panic.

Her body was no longer young. The taut muscles and smooth skin had long since been replaced by what her mother had called "the lumpy bumps." What if her middle-aged body repulsed Tom? Modesty and fear got the better of her, and she retreated into a curtained alcove that served as a wardrobe.

Tom was confused. Sparks had flown with their very

first kiss, and now Bridie was acting as cold as the room they were in. He had so wanted this night to be perfect for her, for both of them, and now he realized that he would have to be very careful if he were to help his bride overcome her obvious anxiety.

He undressed quickly and got into the big bed, which was warm as toast. Investigating, he discovered that two large stones had been warmed, wrapped in flannel, and placed in the bed. He bestowed a benediction on the head of the person who had been so thoughtful and turned on his side so he wasn't facing the alcove.

At last, Bridie emerged from behind the curtain, turned down the lamp, and padded towards the bed. She slipped under the covers. This was her wedding night. She would not let her fears spoil it. But when she snuggled up to Tom, he didn't respond. *Oh, my God!* She thought. *What a way to start our marriage. He'll think I'm cold and frigid.*

For his part, Tom lay quietly, giving her time to relax. He had no idea what she was thinking, but just wanted to give her time to get used to being in bed with him. Then he felt her body shaking and realized that she was crying. She must think he didn't want her. *A fine way to let a woman know how much ya love her*, he thought. He turned and pulled her close.

"There there, then, don't cry," he murmured, gently stroking her hair.

"I'm sorry," said his bride through her tears. "I didn't mean t' spoil our night."

"Ya haven't spoiled anythin', me luv. The night is still with us."

He kissed her neck and traced the line of her shoulder with butterfly strokes, sending little electric darts of delight and arousal all the way to her toes. She felt giddy, elated, and scared all at the same time. Tom turned her face to his, wiped away her tears, and kissed her with exquisite tenderness. The kiss deepened and for them the outside world ceased to exist.

Chapter Thirty-Three

While Tom and Bridie were enjoying their honeymoon, Feelie was sitting by the fire, watching her three nieces playing on the floor beside her. Bridie and her father were due back in a day, and she had yet to tell the children that she would be going away. She could no longer put it off. Shannon, the eldest, already knew something was about to happen, as she had seen her aunt washing and ironing everything she owned. Even the two little ones were unusually still, as though they also sensed a wind of change.

"Auntie, what do ya want t' tell us?" Siobhan asked finally, giving voice to their mutual curiosity.

Feelie had thought long and hard about how to answer that question. The children had already suffered mighty losses, and she did not want them to think that their aunt, who had cared for them for so long, was deserting them, too. She must try to make them understand why she had to leave, but she had no way of knowing how they would accept the news. *Ya just can't put an old head on young shoulders*, she thought.

"Well me luvs," she said aloud, "Auntie is goin' t' go away fer a while. Ye'll be fine, though, fer Bridie will be comin' t' live with ya fer good. She's yer grandmother now, an' that means ye're related t' her. She loves ya already an' says she'll be happy t' take care of ya 'til yer da comes back fer ya."

"I don't want t' go with him," Shannon cried almost immediately, and the two younger girls nodded vigorously. "I don't care if he never comes back. I want ya t' stay! Ya can't be goin' away an' leavin' us. Ya can't."

She was becoming hysterical, her words punctuated by great sobs. Siobhan and the baby began to cry in sympathy with their sister. *Jaysus, Mary, and Holy Saint Joseph*, Feelie implored, *help me*. "Oh, darlin'," she said aloud, "don't take on so. Ye'll be makin' yerself sick."

As Feelie gathered the grieving child in her arms, Shannon buried her head in her aunt's chest and threw her arms around her in a fierce hug.

"Please…oh, please, don't be leavin' us. I promise we'll be good, so we will."

"Ah, sure." Feelie stroked the girl's hair. "Sure, ye're always a good child. All o' ya. The best children in the whole world."

"Then why did our Mammy leave? An' our da, too?"

"Yer Mammy went t' heaven. God called her, an' she had to go. Yer da went to see if he could make a better life fer ya in America. He'll be comin' back t' take ya with him." *An' may God fergive me fer telling them such a load of codswallop* she thought.

"Me mammy did NOT go t' heaven," Shannon corrected her bitterly. "They put her in a box in the ground, an' everybody knows the devil lives in the ground. Why did me mammy go to live with the devil an' take our baby brother with her? Why did she take him an' leave us?"

And now Siobhan chimed in ignoring her aunt's explanation "Why did our da leave us? Is he in the ground, too? Where are ya goin'? Are they goin' t' put ya in a box in the ground?" A fierce light burned in the little girl's eyes. "I won't let 'em!"

"Oh, child, what have ya been thinkin' all this time?" Feelie gathered the second little girl to her, then the third. "Ye poor wee things. Let me get a wet flannel an' wipe yer faces, an' then I'll try t' explain things fer ya. Jest sit here by the fire fer a minute."

She disengaged herself from her nieces and went into the scullery. She needed time to think. How in God's name does one explain life and death to a child? She hadn't even figured it all out herself yet.

Returning with the wet flannel, she tried a more matter-of-fact tone. "Here now, let me wash those faces. Well, first of all, ya must believe that yer mammy's in Heaven. When God calls us home, that's where we go."

"But why would God want our mammy, when He has one of His own?" Siobhan asked.

They all looked expectantly at their aunt. She tried again. "Everyone has a body an' a soul, an' when good people die, their soul flies up to Heaven. Ya don't need yer body anymore, so it stays down here."

The younger two still looked confused, but she felt she was getting somewhere with Shannon. She went on. "Without our soul, our bodies don't work, so we bury 'em." She saw Shannon nodding thoughtfully. "Now, yer mammy was a good woman, so her soul went right up to God. An' God must've needed another angel, so he called fer yer wee brother, too."

"An' me da?" asked Shannon.

Careful, Feelie said to herself as, with scarcely a pause, she answered. "Yer da went t' America. They say it's a grand place, an' he wants t' try t' make a good life fer ya there. He'll be back fer ya as soon as he can. Until he comes, ye'll have a great time with Bridie and yer grandda."

They had stopped crying, but Siobhan was both curious and persistent. "An' where are YOU goin'?" she asked.

"I'm goin' t' a place called Australia," said Feelie. "I'm goin' t' be a nurse. I'll be sad to leave, but grown-up people have t' work t' make a livin', an' so that's what I'll be doin'. I'll write every week an' send ya pictures of all the strange animals they have over there." The girls perked up their ears. Strange animals were interesting. "Won't that be grand?" Feelie continued. "When ya get a wee bit older, ye'll come t' see me. An' I'll save up so I can come home."

"But why can't ya stay here with us?" asked Shannon, who was still skeptical.

"I jest told ya, luv. Grown up people have t' make a livin'." She could see that adult logic was confusing them. She tried again. "I have t' make me own way in the world. I need fer ya t' try t' understand that. I know it's hard. When ya grow up ye'll leave too."

This idea was strange to the children, so Feelie tried to put it in terms they would understand. "If ya get married," she said, "yer husband will want ya t' live with him. If ya don't get married, ye'll have t' work t' support yerself."

"So why don't ya get married an' make yer husband live here with ya?" Shannon asked stubbornly.

"Well," said Feelie. Wondering how to answer that, she paused to think, then said, "That'd not work, because this is yer grandda's house, and he has a wife, an' she'll live here with him soon."

"Why did he need t' get a wife? He has you t' take care of us an' the house."

"Ah, luv, ye're full of questions that are hard t' answer. A wife is special, an' a daughter can't take the place of a wife. Grandda was sad and lonely when yer grandma went t' Heaven. Then he found someone who loves him. An' he wants t' be with her. Jest like what I told ya. When ya find someone an' get married, ye'll go t' live with him. That's the way things are."

Fer them as want that life, she thought. *It's jest not fer me.*

Shannon was still not satisfied with the projected changes in her life. "I don't like the way things are," she said. "God is greedy. He took our grandma and our mammy and our wee brother. It's not fair!"

"Shannon! Ya can't be sayin' that about God. Sure, it's a sin t' be talkin' like that. Ye'll have t' be tellin' the Father about it when ya make yer first confession."

And even as she said this, Feelie realized with a shock that she would miss Shannon's upcoming First Communion. In fact, she would miss all the special days in the children's lives and those of the rest of her family. A wave of grief, sorrow, and loss suddenly rocked her, and she wondered, not for the first time, how she would ever have the courage to say goodbye to everyone and everything she loved and knew. She would be trading the affection and comfort of her family for the rigors of training to be a nurse, trading the soft green glens and silver rains of Ireland for the harsh, red-hot climate of Australia.

Everything would be foreign to her. She had read of the relentless heat of summer, months of drought that left the land brown and dry. She had seen pictures of the strange and dangerous animals and reptiles. She hated snakes and spiders. There were no snakes in Ireland, and the spiders were harmless, unlike those in Australia. An involuntary shudder left her cold and comfortless.

"Auntie, what's the matter? Ya look scared."

"Aye, me luv, even grown up aunties get scared sometimes. But it's not fer ya t' worry, though. I think we've all had our fill o' sad things." She stood up and gathered her nieces into another hug. "Let's go t' the park have a wee swing, feed the ducks, an' go t' Angelo's ice cream parlor fer a slider."

The children's mood changed instantly. This was a rare treat altogether, a three-in-one jackpot. Their sorrow was tucked away for future review. These children had a large reservoir of grief from which to draw for the rest of their lives, their aunt told herself. But for now, swings, ducks, and ice cream belonged in the realm of childhood.

The little group set off for the park, bundled up against a raw wind that sent the clouds hurrying across a mauve and ultramarine sky. It was fairly late in the afternoon for such an excursion, but it was much needed and, besides, darkness would be a long time in coming.

Although the weather was unseasonably cold, the children decided that they still wanted ice cream. Feeling the chill, their aunt had suggested that hot chocolate might be more suitable, but she was vetoed on the grounds that they were quite warm from their exertions in the park. She gave in gracefully, aware that this would be her last outing with them. Had she been able to, she would have given them the sun, moon, and stars.

~

Bridie and Tom had returned from their honeymoon while Feelie and the children were out. There was a happy reunion that evening, followed by a hearty dinner prepared by Bridie. Feelie had resolved to defer to her as the new woman of the house. In her soul, she had already begun the process of separation. With less than a week to go, she knew it would be better for the children if the transition were made as smooth as possible. To this end, she behaved like a well-mannered guest in her father's house. She offered help when there was an obvious need, and made herself scarce when there was none. She slept in the back room, the one her mother had been laid out in.

Tom and Bridie, of course, occupied the room in which Tom and Ellen had slept. Their bed had been replaced by one of Bridie's choice, which gave both her and Feelie some comfort.

On the last night before she was to leave, Feelie listened to the sounds of the house as she lay in bed. The mantel clock chimed the hours and ticked away the minutes. The fire sighed as it settled, and outside a gentle rain pattered against the windows. Two cats were having one hell of a fight outside, sounding, Feelie thought, like banshees gone berserk. She smiled at the thought, never having actually heard a banshee, though the older women she knew swore to their existence. But Feelie had her doubts.

Her bags already stood in readiness at the front door. She would be gone before the children awoke, and so had tucked them in and bade them a tearful goodbye.

Her father was to accompany her to the boat. Birdie had offered to stay with the children. Lucy, Bill, and Nellie would be at the dock to wish her Godspeed.

Sometime during the night, she fell into a fitful sleep and dreamed that her mother had come to comfort her. She looked the same in the dream as she had when Feelie and her sisters were young. And her sisters were there, too, although she could not make out their faces.

Then there was a gentle tap on the door, and she was suddenly awake. It was time.

Bridie's voice: "I've brought ya a wee cup o' tea. Can I come in?" Not waiting for an answer, she poked her head into the room.

"Aye," said Feelie, blinking the fog from her eyes. "I'm awake an' dyin' fer a cuppa, thank ya."

"Yer father's been up an' around fer a while," said Bridie, handing the cup to her. "I'll have breakfast ready in a few minutes."

Feelie drank the strong sweet brew greedily and felt it revive her. The smell of bacon set her stomach to growling, and she felt a new gratitude for Bridie's thoughtfulness. "I'll be out in a jiff," she said, "Jest need t' pull meself together. Thanks again fer the tea, it's grand."

"I'll get ya some warm water t' wash up with," said Bridie over her shoulder as she returned to the kitchen. "I put the kettle on, won't be a sec."

Warm water. *What a luxury*, thought Feelie, who was used to washing up with the cold water in the basin. Bridie returned with the steaming kettle, and Feelie washed and dressed. Then, taking a moment to glance around the room and commit it to memory, she quietly closed the door.

~

Four hours later, standing on the deck of the ship, Feelie watched as her waving family became smaller and smaller. She stood bareheaded and motionless at the rail, oblivious of the gentle rain, until the coast melted into the mist and was gone from view. A lump the size of Ulster wedged in her throat, preventing her cry of wrenching isolation from escaping into the night.

And the family stood on the dock until the ship became a dot on the horizon. Bill tried to comfort a distraught Lucy, Tom's blue eyes glistened with unshed tears, and Nellie twisted her sodden handkerchief into a knot. At last there was nothing left to see and the little group turned its back on the ocean.

Tom invited the somber gathering to his house for a drink and a meal. Everyone knew that they would be back to see Bill and Lucy off in a few weeks' time, but going across the Irish Sea to England was not like going across whole wide oceans to Australia. Many families crossed the water to find work. Those who went to Scotland and England often returned, some crossing back and forth frequently. Those who went to America and Australia, however, almost never came home. Only generations later, would well-heeled descendents with names like Erin and Tara make the obligatory pilgrimage to "the auld sod," the desperation of their barefoot, hungry and homeless ancestry clouded in romantic myth. They would lay claim to ancient family crests, marvel at the castles and narrow cobblestone streets of the towns, and descend on gift shops to buy fishermen's sweaters, Belleek china, Waterford crystal, and Celtic jewelry, all of them treasures the likes of which their forefathers would not even have known to dream about.

Chapter Thirty-Four

When Bill had first broached the subject of a civil marriage, he thought Lucy would have a heart attack. It had taken several hours of careful and patient persuasion to get her to even entertain the idea. Now, as the time drew near, Bill sensed something was still amiss.

They had already taken care of all the paperwork necessary to obtain a license, and he was on his way to meet Lucy so that they could make the final arrangements for the wedding and their trip to England. He had decided to ask her right out what she was bothered about. He knew it would not bode well for their marriage to leave this particular stone unturned.

As she sat by the fire waiting for Bill to arrive, Lucy kept thinking about the situation in which she found herself. Having made peace with her father, at least on the surface, she had returned to the family home while awaiting her marriage. But she couldn't wait to leave her father's house. The strain of trying to remain pleasant while hiding the residual anger she still felt was making her miserable. Her feelings toward Bridie were complex—the two women were closer since the wedding, but some tension remained—and her feelings about her own upcoming wedding were confused. Recalling her sisters' weddings and Bridie's small but beautiful event, she realized that she was feeling like she was being robbed of the day she had dreamed about all her life. Her mother and two of her sisters would not be there. She would be wearing a serviceable green suit instead of a beautiful white gown.

And there would be no priest to bless the union, no familiar chapel with its soft candlelight and smell of incense. Instead, they would make their promises to each other in the town hall. They would pass through a door marked *Births, Deaths, and Marriages*, and a servant of the King of England would record their marriage. It would be legal. In the eyes of the state they would be man and wife.

But she hated it. She wanted God's blessing, not the king's. She wanted to be Bill's wife in the eyes of her church, her family, and her neighbors. She couldn't give a tinker's curse about the law of the land. The hell with them, she thought. She didn't recognize the English landlords or their idea of civil marriage. All she wanted was to be married in her own chapel, with her family, friends, and clergy in attendance.

Bill's sense of foreboding was thus well founded, and so he was determined to clear the air and find out what was wrong. He approached Tom's house. Lucy had been watching for him and opened the door before he could knock. She set her finger to her lips, signaling silence.

"Come on in, luv," she whispered. "We'd best be quiet. The girls are asleep." She led him into the front room and closed the door.

"Are ya ready t' go?" he asked after kissing her lightly.

"Aye," she said. "Jest let me get me coat an' hat."

He looked around the quiet room. "Where is everybody?"

"Bridie an' me da are in the back room. They decided t' fix it up as a bedroom fer Shannon after I go. They're jest doin' some money figurin' now."

With that, she turned and opened the door to the back room that had served as her bedroom since Feelie left and gave Tom and Bridie a quiet call. They were sitting on the bed, deep in discussion.

"Bill an' me are off now," she told them, gathering her coat, hat, and handbag. "We won't be back 'til late, so don't worry about us fer supper."

Tom looked up first. "Take care, an' enjoy yerselves," he said.

"Aye," said Bridie. "'Tis a beautiful day, so try t' make the best of it."

As he and Lucy made their way into town, Bill finally summoned up the nerve to broach the topic on his mind. "Lucy," he said, "I've a feelin' we need t' have a talk. Ye're behavin' like someone goin' t' a funeral, not a weddin'."

Lucy flushed, but her voice remained level. "Is that so?"

"Yes, 'tis so. Let's go t' the park an' talk things over. I hate t' see ya sad. You should be happy."

After buying two bottles of lemonade, they found themselves a comfortable bench by the water. For a while, they were content to watch the activity on the lake. Ducks were landing and taking off amid sparkling sprays of water, and they both smiled when the ducks went bottoms-up to forage for food under the surface. Two graceful swans also sailed by, and a pair of geese honked a warning at a daring squirrel. The sound of children's voices at play carried across the lake.

"They mate fer life ya know," Bill said in a low voice, almost to himself.

"Who do? What on earth are ya talkin' about?"

"The swans."

"Oh, yes, I know." She was wondering what he was getting at. "Me ma told me that a long time ago. She said it was like marriage. Forever."

"That's what I think we should talk about," said Bill. He had been looking out at the swans, but now he turned to face her. "I want t' know what is makin' ya unhappy." He took her hand in his. "Have I done somethin' t' hurt or upset ya?"

"Oh, no. It's not that."

"What is it, then?"

There was a long silence while Lucy considered her answer.

"Come on, luv," he said. "Ya can't be holdin' things back from me. In a few days we'll be man an' wife together fer the rest of our lives. What kind of a marriage will we have if ya can't trust me with yer worries?"

"Aye, ye're right," she said, "but it's hard t' explain t' a man."

She flushed, and he smiled gently. "Well, at least give me a chance to understand."

Lucy was silent for a moment, visibly collecting her thoughts. Finally, she spoke. "All me life, I've looked forward t' me weddin' day." She had yet to face him squarely. "But our weddin' will be nothin' like I dreamed of. I feel cheated, so I do. I don't want to get married in a cold office. I want t' get married in me own chapel. I want t' have what's left o' me family there."

As he slowly nodded that he understood, she spoke more heatedly. "I know me ma's soul would've been there.

But she'd never bless a civil service. I feel trapped. We have t' go t' England, an' I know that. An' I want t' get out o' me da's house. I can't stand bein' there with his new wife in me ma's place."

Words tumbled as she threw caution to the wind. "I understand Bridie's a good woman, but she's not me ma, an' God damn it, it makes me mad jest t' see her touch me ma's things. God help me, I want t' crown her with me ma's fryin' pan every time I see her usin' it."

Bill valiantly suppressed a smile at the mental image of Lucy clocking Bridie over the head with a frying pan. It was more than his life was worth to treat Lucy's outbreak with anything less than total seriousness and undivided attention. Lucy had wound herself up, and now hot tears spilled down her cheeks.

He put both his arms around her and pulled her close. "Ah, me luv," he whispered in her ear, "don't be takin' on so. Let's see if we can make some things better, if not perfect. First of all, I promise ya a church weddin'. We're jest havin' a civil service t' protect ya if anythin' should happen t' me. It was the only way yer father'd give his blessin', ya know. That was important t' me an' fer our future wee ones."

Now he pulled back a bit to look her in the eye. "An' I'll take instruction in England," he said, "an' then, when we can, we'll slip back across the water an' get married in yer chapel. Till then, we'll not lie together as man an' wife. I give ya me word."

A radiant smile broke through Lucy's tears. "Oh Bill, I do love ya. I do, I do. I'm sorry t' be such a misery." And she kissed him with such unbridled passion that he wondered how on earth he would keep his promises.

A few hours later, after all the arrangements had been made, they were walking briskly toward the home of Bill's sister Martha, who was due to sail for Australia in a few days. She had invited Bill and Lucy over for supper so that she could congratulate the pair in person.

As Lucy became engrossed in planning and replanning their wedding and future together out loud, Bill did not say much. He and his sister had never discussed the subject of his possibly converting to Catholicism, and he had decided to keep it quiet for as long as possible. He didn't want to create any tension between himself and his sister, especially now. He felt he had better warn Lucy off the subject before their arrival so that she would not inadvertently begin a conversation he was not yet prepared to have.

"Lucy luv," he said, not sure how to begin this conversation, "I have t' tell ya somethin'. I haven't told Martha that I intend t' become a Catholic. I don't want t' do anythin' t' cause her any hurt. She is goin' far away from her home. I don't want t' have any hard feelin's between us."

"I understand," said Lucy, and she really did. "She won't be hearin' it from me. Ye'll be missin' yer sister, an' I know how that feels. I still miss our Mary Alice, and I can't get me mind 'round Feelie bein' gone fer good, either. I keep expectin' her t' come walkin' through the door."

"Aye," said Bill soberly, "it's a hard thing t' get used to."

They walked on, and in an effort to distract herself, Lucy looked around. Over the months, she had become a little more comfortable in Bill's part of town, although she still disliked the huge murals on gable walls, portraying King William astride a white horse crossing the Boyne. She wished she could knock King Billy off his white horse and run his sword through his black heart.

But she kept these murderous thoughts to herself. She had to admit that the present king looked harmless enough. He was slight of build and handsome in an inoffensive sort of way, although there was apparently some big scandal surrounding his relationship with an American woman.

These American women must have some powerful attraction for men, she said to herself. Even the King of England couldn't resist them! She thought of Brian and the woman he left his home and family for. Both that woman and the king's, while stylish and smart, had a hard and brittle look about them. She reluctantly felt a little pity for the men caught in their clutches. It was understandable why the king would appeal to any woman. Apart from his obvious rank, it was said that he possessed an engaging charm. Brian, on the other hand, possessed no kingly attributes at all. What on earth did that American woman see in him? What did they—

"Lucy, luv, what on earth are ya thinkin' about?"

She blinked. "Oh, I was jest thinkin' about the English king an' our Brian an' those American women."

Bill was totally mystified. He knew he would probably regret asking, but curiosity got the better of him. "An' why would ya be thinkin' about the king, of all people, an' what has he to do with yer brother-in-law?"

"Well, yon picture on the wall put me in mind of the present king, an' then I thought of our Brian."

"I still don't understand." He was having a hard time following her train of thought.

Lucy sighed. Men could be so thick! "Yer king an' our Brian have both been caught in the clutches of the Americans."

"They have?" Bill was more puzzled than ever.

Lucy nodded her head vigorously. "Aye, they have indeed."

"How so?"

"It's as plain as plain can be! Yon two women are as hard as nails. The men were no match fer 'em."

Ah me, he thought, *I don't think I get the comparison…King Billy, King Edward and Brian.* He decided, however, that he had better treat the whole subject with a great deal of tact, given the mood Lucy had been in recently.

Her explanation wasn't very plain at all, and so at the risk of becoming more confused, he made a last attempt at understanding the relationship between the King of England, Lucy's brother-in-law, and a pair of tough American women.

"Will ya explain this whole thing one more time?"

Lucy sighed deeply.

"The king an' our Brian have somethin' in common," she said with exaggerated patience. "They've both been lured away from their responsibilities by fancy women from America." Scowling, she continued, saying, "The king I can understand, but I don't know what the other one wants with our Brian. He's a spineless get, leavin' his poor wee wains t' go chasin' after a woman he hardly knew. One look at her, an' you could tell she wasn't our kind."

"What kind would that be?"

"The honest, workin', decent kind." The words were no sooner out of her mouth than Lucy realized the irony of what she had just said. Not too long ago, she had promised herself that she would find a way to leave the ranks of "the honest, working, decent kind" and find a way to a better life. Now she was ridiculing the class she had hoped to join.

Life was rearranging her plans. She loved Bill. She hated living in her father's house. Both she and Bill were out of work. She would marry Bill and go with him to England because that was the way it had to be.

This did not mean, of course, that she was giving up her dream of a better way of life, What it meant was that she and Bill would find that new life together. She might never go to university, but someday she would wear silk underwear, stylish frocks, fur coats, and live in a house that had a room with running water and a gleaming white bathtub. Her children would go to university and become whatever they wanted to be and speak with upper-class accents. No, indeed, she was not giving up her dream; she was merely bestowing part of it on a future generation.

"Well," said Bill, interrupting her thoughts once more, "no offence t' the king or t' Brian, but we had better be gettin' a move on. I want t' stop an' get a wee bunch o' daffodils fer Martha, if ya don't mind. She loves flowers an' they're her favorites."

Lucy was agreeable. "That's a grand idea," she said. "It'll be a treat fer me, as well. I've missed the smell o' the flower shop."

She had indeed missed working in the florist's, and she had learned that the hotel business was not for her. Perhaps someday she would own a flower shop herself.

"That'd be grand, t' have me own flower shop," she said out loud.

How her mind does work, thought Bill. "Would that not take a lot of money t' get started?" he asked.

"Aye, that it would, but there's no charge fer dreamin', an' I do believe that if ya work hard enough, ya can do anythin'."

Bill nodded his head in agreement. He was a firm believer in the rewards of hard work. Unfortunately, it wasn't always possible to find the work to do. Their present situation attested to that.

Chapter Thirty-Five

Hero the dog saw them first and made a great show of welcoming them. He had grown into a handsome animal, looking more like a collie than a terrier, as they had first thought. Hearing the barking, Martha was soon at the door to greet them.

"Ah, there ya are," she said. "I was beginnin' t' think I had the wrong night."

"I'm sorry we're a bit late," said Bill, producing the flowers. "We stopped at the florist's t' get ya these."

"Oh, they're lovely. Thanks a bunch." Martha said, laughing at her own joke.

"It's mostly my fault we're late," said Lucy. "I got t' talkin' t' the woman at the shop an' lost track o' the time."

"Don't be worryin' yerself about it," Martha said, dismissing the need for apology. "I jest thought I'd misunderstood."

They entered and followed Martha to the dining room.

"Supper's all ready," she said. "Ye'll never guess what we're havin', Bill. I'll give ya a hint: Mr. Stevenson was by this mornin'."

"Fresh salmon?" guessed Bill.

"Aye. He came over t' make arrangements t' pick Hero up. He's goin' t' be takin' him in at his farm, an' the fish was a goin' away present fer me. He said it'd be a long time before I'd get a taste o' the likes of Irish salmon again."

"Well, I don't know what they have in the way of fish in Australia," her brother replied, "but they'd be hard pressed t' out-do our salmon."

"Aye, ye're right about that," Martha agreed.

Lucy had nothing to say on the subject. The only fish she was familiar with was plaice and haddock. She had never tasted salmon.

"Come on, then," Martha said. "Let's tuck in before everythin' gets cold."

She guided them to the table and served the meal that consisted of new potatoes, salad, and salmon with a hollandaise sauce. Lucy was impressed by the ease with which she appeared to have put everything together. The table was set with a snow-white tablecloth, their mother's china, and the sunny yellow daffodils had been arranged in a pretty glass vase. And the food was simple and delicious. Lucy was unfamiliar with the sauce on the fish, but soon decided it was perfect and that she would ask Martha for the recipe.

The evening progressed pleasantly until at last it was time for Lucy to say goodbye to her soon-to-be sister-in-law.

"Martha, thank ya fer the grand meal," she said. "I'm sad t' be sayin' goodbye. Have a safe journey an' a happy reunion with yer family. I hope we'll meet again sometime. Our Feelie's in Australia, ya know. I wrote her address down fer ya." She handed Martha a slip of paper. "Ya might want t' get in touch with her."

Martha was touched. "Thank ya, Lucy," she said, tucking the address in her purse. "I'm sorry t' be missin' yer weddin'. I hope you will both be happy together. Take good care o' each other. I'll be askin ya t' write an' tell me all the news, because our Bill's a hopeless letter writer. An' o' course I'll get in touch with yer sister as soon as I get me bearin's. I hope we can be friends. We're both single, an' it'll be nice t' have someone me own age t' talk to."

"Ah, that'd be grand. Thanks again fer everythin'," Lucy said, and she meant it. Without Martha, she would never have ventured "across the tracks," and she now felt that she would have been the poorer for not having done so. She guessed that Martha would wonder what understanding had been made between herself and Bill with regard to religion and was grateful for Martha's good manners in not bringing the matter up at this time. She also hoped the difference in religion would not prevent a friendship developing between her sister and her future sister-in–law.

Martha took Lucy's hand and said, just as sincerely, "It's been jest grand t' meet ya. An' ya can pay me back by keepin' this one in line." She winked at Bill, who blushed and muttered something. Both women laughed.

Lucy gathered her belongings and Bill helped her on with her coat.

"Well," he said, ushering Lucy to the door, "we best be gettin' along. Thanks fer the tasty supper ye're a grand cook, to be sure.

"Get away with ya so. Flattery will get ya everywhere," Martha said making light of the moment of farewell. Bill would be at the dock to see her off, off course, but she would not be seeing Lucy again.

Chapter Thirty-Six

Well, I'm as ready as I'll ever be, Lucy said to herself as she sat waiting for her father. Tom had taken the children next door to their good neighbor, who had offered to take care of them while the adults went to the wedding. Sitting in the back room alone with her thoughts, she brought her mother, laid out in this room, to mind, and then she thought about Feelie, and about how she must have felt on her last night with her family.

This was a last time for her also. After today, she would no longer be the daughter of the house, but a married woman. The problem was that she didn't feel as though she was *really* getting married.

She examined her reflection in the mirror. She was smartly dressed in a pale green suit, and on her head she wore a saucy little hat that perched atop her curls and tipped over one eye. A whisper of a veil accented her eyes. Shoes, gloves, and handbag in a darker shade of green completed her bridal outfit.

It wasn't at all what she had dreamed about when she imagined her wedding day. Oh well, as she was learning, life is full of compromises.

Her bags were packed, and she and Bill were leaving for England the following night. Tom had arranged a small reception for the family after the ceremony and booked a room at the Midland for the newlyweds.

"Come on, luv, or we'll be late." Tom lifted the suitcases and joined Bridie at the front door. "I have a wee surprise fer the bride. We'll be travelin' in style."

Lucy gasped when she caught sight of the shiny black motorcar waiting at the curb. "Da, where on earth did ya get that?'

"Would ya believe, McNulty?" said her father. "He rents the fancy car out fer weddin's. He's not goin' t' be doin' funerals anymore, though. Says his nephew can take over that part o' the business as he breaks in, just as he had to."

Just then McNulty presented himself to help with the bags. Gone was the sepulchral undertaker, and in his place a cheerful driver, resplendent and sartorially correct in the uniform of a professional chauffeur.

"Good mornin' t' ya, Miss, Sir," McNulty said formally as he opened the doors. He behaved as though he had never met Tom or Lucy before, which they both found amusing. They decided to go along with the charade.

"Good mornin'." Tom's voice was equally formal. "We'll be goin' t' the city hall," he announced, as if McNulty didn't already know their destination.

"Yes, sir. Right ya be."

McNulty helped Lucy to step up to the running board and into the car. She had never been in an automobile before, and immediately began examining the interior with great interest. The car, she decided, smelled like a new pair of shoes. The seats were upholstered in gray leather, and the floor was covered with plush gray carpet. There was even a little vase of flowers attached to the window. The passenger seats were separated from the driver by a glass window.

"Well, isn't this grand!" said Tom.

"Aye, it's the grandest thing I've ever been in," Lucy answered, settling into the comfortable seat beside her father.

The car was creating quite a stir in the neighborhood, and curtains were discreetly pulled aside to give the housewives a better view of the vehicle and its passengers.

Because Lucy's family had kept her marriage as quiet as possible, as an interfaith union was frowned upon, and the family sought to avoid any trouble, the neighbors, with the exception of Mrs. Gilvery (who had been sworn to secrecy), were left to wonder what occasion would warrant such an extravagant mode of transportation. Tongues would be wagging for weeks. Eventually, the secret would be out, of course, but by that time Lucy and Bill would be in England and out of harm's way.

"Sure, and this is the life," said Tom in his grandest voice. "I feel like a king, so I do."

"Da, this is a great surprise," said Lucy, surprised by and grateful for her father's thoughtfulness. "It was kind o' Bridie t' let us have this t' ourselves. Many's the wife would've insisted on goin' with us."

"Ah, sure," said Tom. "Bridie's not like that at all. In fact, she insisted we go alone, even though the car is big enough t' seat six, never mind three."

"She's a kind and generous woman, that's fer sure," Lucy admitted out loud, nevertheless thinking, *She's just not me ma, and me ma should be sittin' with us now.*

Bill was waiting in front of the town hall when the car pulled up. After McNulty made a grand production of helping Lucy and Tom out of the vehicle, Bill presented his bride with a huge bouquet of pale pink roses and lilies-of-the-valley.

"Oh, Bill… these are gorgeous, thank ya! Now I feel like a real bride."

"No bride ever looked lovelier."

Tom was impatient. "Come on, then," he warned, "we best be goin' upstairs, or we'll be late."

Within minutes, the clerk made it official. "I now pronounce you man and wife"

~

"Mom! Mom, wake up!"

Lucy was confused and disoriented for a moment.

"You fell asleep! You almost missed the whole wedding!" Her daughter's tone was slightly accusatory.

And now she remembered everything in a flash. She was at her granddaughter's wedding. Reluctantly, she returned to the present. "I did not fall asleep," she protested. "I was jest restin' me eyes."

She would never admit that her memory tended to wander. They would say she was senile. Sure, her trips into the past were more frequent now, but she felt comfortable there. It seemed that the older she got, the further back she remembered. Although she sometimes forgot what she had done yesterday, she could recall an event that took place sixty years ago.

Now she studied her granddaughters as they walked up the aisle past the congregation. The smiling bride, arm in arm with her new husband, was followed by her sisters. The bride had never known her grandfather, who had died before Lucy immigrated to America to join her grown family already there, but Bill had bequeathed to this grandchild his height, the same soft green-gray eyes, and elegantly tapered fingers. The other girls had inherited their grandmother's fair skin, dark eyes, and hair, they had all been endowed with her purposeful personality and their own sense of duty. The grandsons also carried Bill's height and between them his sense of humor, artistic creativity and generosity.

Surrounded as she was by her family, Lucy marveled at what she and Bill had wrought. She was content and well pleased. Echoes of her beloved ghosts would forever live on in their children and their children's children.

Life will always have its ups and downs, Lucy thought, *but they are the descendants of generations of survivors, and their lives are blessed with opportunity. Success depends on their ambition and their own interpretation of success, not their religion or political persuasions. Their goals are tethered only to their own industry. They are Celts, and so humor and laughter are never far away. They are as mercurial as the wind, loyal to a fault, and as hard to contain as smoke in a bottle.*

Recipes

Feelie's Irish Treacle Farl

Treacle is similar to molasses which may be substituted. Treacle may be found at a British import site or shop. Farl is an old celtic term denoting one forth of a round. The term may also be used for soda bread and potato bread cooked the same way on a griddle. This recipe substitutes a baking sheet for the griddle (better still, a dutch oven may also be used without the lid.)

4 cups plain flour
1/4 cup sugar
1 teaspoon baking soda
1/4 teaspoon salt
1/4 unsalted butter, diced
1 and 3/4 cups buttermilk (a little more or less at the cooks discretion)
2 tablespoons dark molasses
(1/2 fresh ground ginger may also be included though I doubt they used it in medieval times which this bread can be traced back to.)

Preheat oven to 425. Combine first five ingredients in a large bowl. Add butter and cut in until mixture looks like small lumps. Whisk molasses (treacle) into one cup buttermilk. Mix into dry ingredients. Gradually add enough of the remaining buttermilk to form soft dough. Turn out onto a lightly floured surface, turn and knead a few times (do not over work,) pat into an 8 inch round. Cut into four wedges set slightly apart. Place on baking sheet or in dutch oven and bake until a rich golden brown. About 30 minutes. Serve hot or cold with good creamery butter (lots) yummie.

More free recipes for the Irish dishes prepared by the women of "Celtic Knots" and adapted for today's busy cooks by Chef Lisa Carelli may be found at authors website.

CelticKnots2012@gmail.com

www.audreynicholson.com

Made in the USA
Middletown, DE
08 May 2022